Postmark Vietnam

A Novel

I0648358

by

James August

ISBN 978-0615920658

First Edition

Published by
Badgley Publishing Company
Canal Winchester, Ohio
www.BadgleyPublishingCompany.com

Dedicated

To the Boys of
Hotel Company
2nd Battalion
26th Marine Division

And to the girls they left behind

Also

To Tracey
A father, husband, and a Marine.
One of the best of the best to slog that red mud,
He was my friend, comrade, and hero.
I will miss him, and that smile.

R.I.P.
19 January 2002

~ v ~

POSTMARK VIETNAM

CHAPTER ONE
The Patrol

The bead of perspiration had gained enough volume and mass to finally push its way out from under the sweatband of the bush cover. It began its descent of the forehead, leaving a pale path through the red dust and occasional olive-drab grease paint. The droplet gained a little momentum as it progressed down the forehead, to the brow, where it slowed in the thin taffy colored hair of the eyebrow. It fell until it reached the corner of the eye, where it was helped along on its way by a single blink. Its path downward continued over the high cheekbones, to the hollow below, leaving a trail through the dust and camo paint until it crossed the prominent jaw line and fell toward the open neck of the jungle shirt.

During the entire duration of the droplet's journey, the only movement had been the blink of the eye. Corporal Mick Holtzman's face and entire body, seemed to be carved of stone. There was and had been no movement for the last three minutes. No movement, that was, except for the eyes. They moved constantly, peering through the thin fringe of jungle vegetation that separated Mick from the clearing before him. The jungle clearing was half again as large as a football field. Squad Leader Holtzman had been watching the clearing for three...now four minutes. His objective, a long abandoned rail bed that had been constructed by the French fifty years previously. It lay only a few hundred meters beyond. His patrol's mission was to determine if the Communists were using the rail bed as a roadway for troop and supply movements.

Mick had several options. The first was to directly cross the clearing which would make his patrol vulnerable to ambush while in the open, but they could reach the objective quickly and thus allow them to return to the company perimeter and safety soon. The second was to skirt the clearing, which would take hours and they would not get back to the perimeter till after nightfall. The second alternative would expose the patrol to enemy ambush while traveling at night, and friendly fire danger on re-entering their own perimeter after dark. Holtzman continued to stare without making a motion. Slowly his left hand started to rise. Ski, the First Fire Team Leader watched, tensing slightly, anticipating the signal to move up even with the Squad Leader. Directly behind Mick, Tracy O'Meara, First Squad's grenadier, could see the hand move too. Tracy was ready. He was always ready to place the 40 millimeter grenade rounds where they were needed most.

Suddenly the hand froze an inch or so above the jungle floor, then it pushed down ever so slightly twice. Tension ran like electricity between the men. No words were spoken. The men of the First Fire Team on the left pressed themselves further into the dirt and vegetation, as did those of the Second and Third Fire Teams positioned slightly behind and to the right of Squad Leader Mick Holtzman. O'Meara wished like hell he could see, so he would know where to put that first round. Next to O'Meara, Radioman Joe Kuhl turned the volume control down to zero and stared hard at the insects crawling on the leaves less than an inch from his face.

Holtzman's body and face remained immobile, but the eyes had picked up the tempo. What had caught his attention? The clearing was still vacant. *There!* Toward the right, a slight movement. His eyes focused on the bush, then moved left, then right, then back left. Now he saw it. He could just make out a boot at the bottom of a clump of saw grass. Mick continued to let his eyes move left, right, up and down. The Corporal could now distinguish the form of a man behind the bush observing the clearing just as he was, but from the opposite side.

Mick's opposite number remained motionless for several minutes. The enemy officer then moved slightly away from his concealment, gave a hand signal, and four North Vietnamese Army regulars rushed into the clearing to Mick's right. The team of four stopped on a small mound in the clearing and set up a light machine gun, thereby gaining cover and elevation.

Mick remained frozen in place, wishing to flatten himself into the jungle but knowing that any movement could give away his position. *How many were they?* That machine gun was positioned to cover the clearing and could rip up Mick and his men from its present placement. If the North Vietnamese Army gun team picked up and moved down the clearing, Mick's squad was in position to take them out. *Patience, patience, patience*, Holtzman reminded himself.

The NVA officer opposite Mick moved his hand again and four more men rushed down the clearing to Mick's left setting up another defensive position. More hand signals and a steady stream of enemy soldiers started moving down the clearing from right to left in front of the squad of Marines. Ten, fifteen, twenty, infantry soldiers…now sappers with explosives…then a heavy machine gun team, the gun mounted on bicycle wheels. This was at least a company-sized unit. An ambush by a squad was out of the question, in fact it would be suicidal.

Corporal Mick Holtzman's heart felt as though it was beating a thousand times a minute. Imperceptibly, a millimeter a minute, Mick lowered himself into the jungle floor. By now close to a hundred enemy troops had moved down the clearing and more were coming. Holtzman started inching back ever so slowly. If they were seen now there would be little chance of survival. Finally he was back even with the rest of his men. The Corporal's eyes moved left and made contact with Ski, his First Fire Team Leader. No words were spoken. He gave an almost imperceptible nod. Mick then eyeballed the Second and Third Team on his right. Together almost in unison the squad inched back ever so carefully. When the Marines had moved back twenty feet, the Corporal looked to his left then right, gave the hand signal for single file and moved out on his knees. After traveling fifty feet further he arose. The Squad Leader signaled the First Fire Team to lead off, Third to walk tail end Charlie supported by O'Meara and his grenade launcher, leaving Mick, Second Fire Team and Kuhl in the vanguard. They moved in this fashion silently for a hundred and fifty yards, then the Squad Leader signaled a halt. He gave the sign for a tight 360. The men of First Squad formed a closed circle, each man lying on his belly with his weapon pointing outward with Mick, Kuhl, and the radio in the middle.

For the first time for what seemed hours Squad Leader Holtzman spoke in a strangled whisper, "Kuhl, get me Hotel six." Hotel six is the radio monitored by their Company Commander's Radioman.

Seconds later Kuhl handed Mick the handset whispering, "Hotel six, I think you got the CO."

Mick picked up the handset, "Hotel six, Hotel six, this is Rover one…over." The earpiece crackled as the reply came back.

"Rover one go ahead, this is Hotel six, read you loud and clear…over,"

"Roger Hotel six, we have visual contact…over,"

"Rover, Rover what is your position and strength of contact? Over."

"Hotel six…enemy strength is company to battalion size, November Victor Alpha at position from rose, down two clicks, left three clicks, moving west. We have more to follow and are comin' in…over," the Corporal informed his Commanding Officer.

"Rover, this is Hotel six, bring your patrol in and report to company Command Post ASAP!"

"Roger that, Hotel six, this is Rover one out." The Squad Leader finished.

"Was that the CO?" asked Kuhl,

"Yeah, that was the Captain…he knows the score." Mick replied.

Quickly, Squad Leader Holtzman outlined his plans for their return to his men. He kept the same order of travel with the M-79 grenade launcher covering their retreat. The squad started moving carefully, slowly, so that their own comrades didn't blow them away as they approached the company perimeter. Mick Holtzman had a lot to tell the Commander. Over the radio, he had given only the most critical information such as the number of enemy troops, position, and direction of travel. Radio transmissions were open, and the enemy could change plans if they realized that the Marines knew where they were and what they were up to.

"It's a good thing the Captain is a smart son-of-a-bitch," Mick thought to himself.

Captain Fred Weller hadn't asked about a fire mission, air strike, or possible attack. He quickly surmised that if Corporal Holtzman wasn't calling in a fire mission, it was not warranted. Weller had quickly plotted the enemy position and their direction of movement. He realized that neither the company nor battalion were in immediate jeopardy. Holtzman had said he had "more to follow." Weller wondered what it was.

Fred Weller had come to trust the judgment of the young Squad Leader in the four months since he had joined the Company. Weller, then a First Lieutenant, had been an aviator prior to joining this infantry company. He developed night blindness and was grounded, he volunteered to go infantry. He was assigned as Platoon Commander, 2nd Platoon, Hotel Company. Second Platoon consisted of three rifle squads of 14 men each, a CP group, and attachments. The Command Post group consisted of the Platoon Commander, Platoon Sergeant, Guide, Radioman, Corpsman, and Runner. Attachments came from Weapons Platoon and included machine gun teams, rocket teams, and sixty-millimeter mortars.

First Lieutenant Weller joined Hotel Company during Operation Bold Mariner as a replacement for the previous Platoon Commander who had been wounded in a prior engagement. On the day that he arrived in the field to take command of Second Platoon, the company had been in combat the previous night. That night First Platoon had sent out a squad-sized ambush which was in turn ambushed in an enemy village and the relief unit had taken casualties as well. On his arrival, Weller had been advised that First Squad, of his new command, was now out on patrol at the site of the ambush and moving on into the enemy ville. Weller decided that he should get a first-hand view. The Lieutenant, accompanied by a Radioman and a couple of riflemen, crossed through the waist high saw grass toward the tree line beyond which First Squad was searching the enemy village.

Weller moved cautiously across the open grassy area, trying to remember everything they had taught him in Officers' Candidate School about the enemy.

"Here comes First Squad." said one of the riflemen. Out of the tree line appeared 12 men spaced about 20 feet apart, led by a tall lean Marine wearing a bush cover. As the two groups approached, the point man for First Squad signaled a halt and gave his undivided attention to Lt. Weller's group.

After a moment of observation the point man yelled out, "Hey!! Don't fuckin' move!" Weller froze, the voice of authority was obvious. Instinctively he knew he must outrank this man but training made him respond to the command. The point man signaled the squad to stay put, and walked toward Weller. When within twenty feet he stopped, then moving slowly came within five feet of the Lieutenant, halted and motioned Weller toward him.

"See this?!" The point man said, putting his thumb and forefinger together forming a circle.

Weller could see nothing.

"It's a trip wire! Another step and you'd have killed yourself and everyone with you!" the point man exclaimed.

At that instant the sunlight flashed along the thin wire stretched across the path that Weller had been walking down. The Squad Leader motioned his patrol up and when they were within earshot he hollered.

"Call up engineers. This rear echelon commando found a booby trap. We'll have them blow it in place."

Lt. Weller looked at the young man and realized that he was probably not yet twenty. "Who are you, Marine?" The

Lieutenant asked.

The point man turned and gave Weller a cool appraising look and then said in formal tone of voice, "Corporal Holtzman, First Squad Leader, Second Platoon, and you?"

Weller smiled and said, "Lieutenant Weller, your new Platoon Commander."

Holtzman stood a little straighter and with a half smile said, "Sir, it's a pleasure to make your acquaintance, Sir."

Captain Weller, now Company Commander smiled as he remembered his first meeting with Holtzman. He wondered what information the Squad Leader had and if Battalion Command had monitored the radio transmission. The PRC-25 radio crackled back to life and he heard his Radioman talking to the Battalion Command Post. The radio operator said, "It's Battalion sir…they want to know when the patrol will get in and the Colonel wants to be there for the debriefing."

CHAPTER TWO
The Debriefing

Squad Leader Holtzman called a halt when he estimated that the patrol was approximately fifty meters from the company's perimeter. On his signal the men went into a tight three sixty defensive position once more.

Mick motioned Kuhl for the handset, "Hotel two, hotel two, this is Rover one…over."

The handset crackled back "Rover one, rover one this is Hotel two, where y'all been?" came the mellow Texas drawl through the radio static.

Mick smiled as he recognized the voice of Corporal G. W. Lincoln, Squad Leader of Second Squad, who, next to O'Meara, was Mick's closest friend. "Hey, Mr. Prez." G. W. stood for George Washington Lincoln, hence the nick name "Prez", or "Mr. President". "I'm sitting out here in the weeds fifty meters in front of Tex and Willey's position…would you drop by and ask those two crazies not to blow my ass up when I come in," transmitted Holtzman.

Over the handset one could almost hear the smile in Lincoln's drawl, "Roger, Charlie copy, rover Dover, y'all give me two minutes, then send up a star cluster and I'll keep them crazies quiet Bro…Two out."

Exactly four minutes later Squad Leader Holtzman fired a white star cluster pop up flare as a signal. Mick then counted to 30 slowly. He stood up, motioned his squad to stay where they were, and stepped out in front of the jungle canopy. He was facing the business end of Tex Schultz and Willey Jordon's M-60 machine gun.

Tex smiled and said, "Howdy boss…did ya have a nice walk?"

"You bet, Tex!"

The Squad Leader then motioned the rest of the squad in. Mick spoke to each Team Leader as he passed, telling them to go back to the positions they'd left before they went on patrol.

Mick looked around and saw Lincoln grinning at him

from a few yards away.

"So…boo-coo gooks?" Prez questioned.

"Hey, you been readin' my mail!"

"They comin' for a visit tonight?"

"I don't think so, but be ready."

"You a popular dude," commented the Prez, "The Captain's wantin' you ASAP."

"Yeah…now I know what it's like to be famous!" Grumbled Holtzman. Mick stood and looked toward the Company Command Post.

"Re-supply choppers came in while you were gone. They got C-rations, ammo, SP's, and mail at the landing zone," spoke up Lincoln.

"Thanks, Prez, I'll send a workin' party."

Corporal Holtzman looked around and saw O'Meara sitting on the edge of Tex and Willey's machine gun position joking with the two gunners. "Hey, Trace!" called Mick motioning the grenadier over, "pick one man from each position and go to the LZ for re-supply; food, ammo, water, whatever. I'll get the mail at company."

"Man, how come I always get the shitty end of the stick?" groused O'Meara.

Mick smiled and said, "You're just one lucky guy! Would you like to go over to the CP and be debriefed?"

"No way!" grimaced Tracy, "I get nervous around all those brass hats. I'll do the working party!"

Captain Weller saw the twenty foot tall, whip antennae moving through the brush in his direction. That would be Colonel Smith and his radio man Webb. The other Radiomen preferred the short, two and a half foot tape antenna, as it was not as cumbersome and less likely to give away your position. Weller didn't know if it was the Radioman or the Colonels' idea, but if you saw the whip you knew the Colonel was close by. *"Maybe that's a good thing,"* the Captain thought to himself.

Lieutenant Colonel Smith had started his career as a sixteen-year-old enlistee at the end of World War Two. He had become an officer in Korea and was now on his second tour in Vietnam. Smith was a no nonsense officer who had served as an enlisted man, non-com, and officer. He moved with the gait of one long familiar with foot travel. With the Colonel were Lance Corporal Webb the Radioman, his Aide, Second Lieutenant Bob Gregory and leading the small column was Gunnery Sergeant Joe Riker. Riker had been a friend and confidant of the Colonel's since the bad old days in Korea. Gregory was fresh out of Officer's Candidate School and the States, arriving at Smith's Command just three days previously. Smith was curious as to why the young junior officer had been selected as his Aide, such jobs were often given to officers who had served previously in the field. The Colonel wondered if this young Lieutenant was politically connected.

As the Colonel's group approached Hotel Company's Command Post, Gunny Riker stepped to one side and motioned the others into what was an old bomb crater that now doubled as the company CP. The men seemed to break into groups according to rank and position. Riker smiled and nodded to Gunnery Sergeant Shaw who was the Company's acting First Sergeant. Webb teamed up with Hotel Radioman, Boston Jones. Captain Weller stood up, came to the position of attention in front of Lt. Colonel Smith. He refrained from saluting his superior as snipers identified officers in this manner.

"Good afternoon Sir!" Weller said.

"Good afternoon Fred...as you were," replied Smith, "Meet Lieutenant Bob Gregory, my new Aide."

Fred Weller then shook hands with the Lt. Colonel and his Aide in that order.

"It sounds as if your patrol encountered a sizable enemy unit from the radio traffic I monitored," Smith said. "First Squad? Is that the young Corporal that I have walk point for battalion when we're in Indian country?" asked the Colonel.

"Yes...Corporal Holtzman." Answered Weller, "He made his bones at point. He was Recon before he came to the infantry."

The Colonel's eyebrows rose slightly; "Well, that explains some of it. An independent sort isn't he?"

Reconnaissance Marines were the commandos of the Corps, working in small four to twelve man units behind enemy lines where independent and decisive thought patterns determined whether you lived or died.

"Yes Sir, he is very bright. I wish I had ten more just like him." said the Captain.

"When do you expect him in?" queried Smith.

"He's back Sir. I expect him momentarily. He's probably dispersing his men."

Lieutenant Gregory frowned at this, wondering what a lowly Corporal was doing making a Colonel and other officers wait.

Almost as soon as the thought crossed Gregory's mind, a long lean infantryman appeared with a bandoleer of magazines tied around his waist, another diagonally across his chest, and wearing a camouflage bush hat that had never been issued by the U.S. Military.

Corporal Mick Holtzman nodded at the two Gunnery Sergeants as he took two long steps forward, placing himself squarely in front of the officers. He then came to the position of attention and said in a calm voice, "Corporal Holtzman…reporting as ordered, sir."

Captain Weller started to respond but was interrupted by Colonel Smith.

"Good to see you again Corporal. Apparently you ran into a sizable detachment of enemy soldiers. Tell us about it."

"Yes Sir!"

Mick reached into his jungle shirt and produced a topographic map, damp with perspiration. He unfolded it carefully and placed it before the three officers. As he did so, the two Gunnery Sergeants moved in for a closer look.

"My patrol's objective was to traverse from our lines to this old rail bed. There, to determine whether the enemy is, has, or is likely to use the abandoned rail bed as a route for troop or supply movements." Holtzman said, pointing to the map as he spoke, pausing just for a moment to survey the three officers in front of him. He knew them all except the young pale Lieutenant whose appearance told the infantryman that he had just arrived from the rear.

"Here, we came upon a large clearing." The young Corporal stated pointing to the map with his finger. "While observing the clearing to determine whether to cross it or skirt it, we observed a large number of North Vietnamese Army regulars moving west with sappers and heavy, as well as light, machine-guns." Holtzman paused glancing from the Captain to the Colonel to see if there were any questions.

"Exactly how many enemy troops did you see Corporal?" asked the Colonel.

"A hundred fifty to two hundred." Mick answered.

"Do you think that was the entire enemy unit?" queried Captain Weller.

"No Sir, I believe there were more troops moving parallel with these beyond our scope of vision." answered the Corporal.

"What do you think, Fred?" Colonel Smith asked Weller.

The Captain replied, "I'm not sure sir. I knew from the direction of travel that they didn't intend to engage us immediately."

"Why didn't you engage the enemy or call in an artillery or airstrike?" broke in Lt. Gregory.

There was silence in the Command Post. Holtzman's gaze settled on the Lieutenant without wavering. "I did not engage, call in artillery, or an air strike while the enemy was within my vision because if I had even lifted the radio mike, both my squad and I would have been blown to bits and pieces. If I had called in a strike after the enemy had passed, it would have done little damage and they would then know that we knew their position, numbers, armaments, and potential plans. "Such," Mick paused for a second, "ill advised action would allow the enemy to change their plans and suffer little damage." The Corporal did not add a "Sir" at the end of his statement.

Gregory's face turned scarlet. He started to sputter but was interrupted by Lt. Colonel Smith,

"Good point, Corporal. At present we know their numbers, direction of travel, and strength. Now we simply need to know what they are up to. What's your guess?"

Gregory's face darkened even more. Holtzman stood quietly pensive for a full minute. He then looked up, met the Colonels gaze and stated, "I think they mean to ambush us, or part of the battalion, just like they did at Meade River when they wiped out Echo Company Sir."

"That was a bad day for the battalion, Corporal. What makes you think they're planning the same sort of tactic?"

The loss of Echo Company lay heavy on the Colonel's mind, as he had been in charge that day as Mick Holtzman knew.

"I think it's the same outfit." declared Mick, "When Echo was ambushed I was a Fire Team Leader. Our platoon crossed the river with the relief element to try to break Echo loose. We were engaged by a heavy machine gun position, that kept us pinned down for an hour. When we finally gained fire superiority, they withdrew, taking the gun with them. I saw that it was a modified anti-aircraft weapon. During their withdrawal our M-79 man hit that gun team and one of the carriage struts was damaged. The gun I saw today had a bent strut, same side...same place."

"What's your opinion Fred? If you were the enemy, where, and how, would you ambush us?" Smith asked.

Capt. Weller thought a moment then said, "We've been moving north by northwest for three days...and the patrol saw this large unit about six clicks to the north of us, moving west across our path. They might try to use the Song Lai River to our northwest in their ambush. Corporal Holtzman, however, seems to be able to think like the enemy. What's your opinion, Corporal?"

The stone-faced Corporal was silent a moment then responded, "The North Vietnamese Army seems to like to use the topography to their advantage, as the Captain indicated. And they, unlike the U.S. Military, are not tied into L shaped ambushes which are safer for our own troops. To quote Vo Nguyen Giap," (Holtzman pronounced the name Vo Gwinn Yap in the sing-song Vietnamese dialect) "the life or death of a hundred, a thousand, or tens of thousands of human beings, even if our own compatriots, represents really very little." You see sir, the NVA don't care how many of their own they lose as long as they inflict significant casualties on us. I think they will hit us when we cross the Song Lai here." Holtzman pointed again to the map and continued, "There's a fordable spot for us to cross and they will have a ridge to the east where they could have heavy weapons dug in part way up. They could have the majority of their force forming a V here, in the valley below. They'd let as many of our troops as they felt they could handle ford the river…then spring their ambush. A very small number of dedicated NVA could keep relief and reinforcements from crossin' the river while they annihilate our troops caught on their side." After the long dissertation Mick felt embarrassed, his face flushed, he came back to the position of attention and stared into space.

After a few moments of silence, Colonel Smith spoke, "Thank you Corporal…just like Meade River." Sensing the young man's discomfort, he added, "You are dismissed and may return to your duties."

Mick did a parade ground about face and was out of the CP shell crater in two strides.

Lt. Gregory, still angered by the Corporal's rebuff sputtered, "And who the hell is this Yap guy he's quoting?"

The Colonel looked at Gregory and with a half smile commented, "None other than the Commander of the North Vietnamese Army, the general who defeated the French at Dien Bien Phu." Smith paused a moment then looked at Captain Weller and said, "Fred, where did you find this young man, we could use him in the Officer Corps."

Weller smiled, "Wish I could take credit for finding him Sir, but he was a Squad Leader when I arrived. My third day with the company I found him reading a translation of

Mao Tse-Tungs writings on guerrilla warfare. He also has books by Giap and Ho Chi Minh. I've borrowed them from time to time but Holtzman's memorized them. As for making him an officer? He just turned nineteen last month."

"So what?" queried Smith.

"You have to be 21 on or about the time you graduate from Officers' Candidate School. Marine regulations wouldn't even let him into OCS for two years, sir." replied the Captain.

"Shit! Regulations!" exclaimed the Colonel, "And no battlefield commissions anymore! This is a sorry state of affairs." Colonel Smith shrugged, "Well…let's try to formulate a plan now that we have insight into the enemy's mind." Smith gave a wry smile and continued, "Perhaps after we have devised a plan we can have the Corporal critique it for us." he said with a chuckle.

Fred Weller smiled back at the Colonel. He said nothing, but thought to himself that he would get Holtzman's opinion one way or the other.

As Mick rapidly left the company CP, Gunny Shaw, Hotel Company's acting first Sergeant moved to intercept him.

"Hey Corporal, wait up a minute, your legs are too damn long. A fat old man like me can't keep up!" Hollered the Gunnery Sergeant.

Mick slowed, waiting for Shaw to catch up. It was high praise for a senior Non Commissioned Officer to joke in this way with a junior NCO.

"What can I do for you Sir?" Holtzman asked when Shaw came within a stride. It wasn't necessary to call a senior NCO Sir but Mick generally did so as a sign of respect for their age, seniority, and experience.

"Good work back there," Gunnery Sergeant Shaw said, "You knocked that struttin' second lewie down a peg or two."

"Oh, I didn't realize he was an officer." said Mick with a tug on the right corner of his mouth.

"Yeah...likely story Corporal...by the way, I gave all of Second Platoon's mail to your Platoon Sergeant so when you see Morrillo, that's where your squad's mail is."

This being the second war that the Shaw had served his country in, he was well aware of how important mail was to these young Marines. In fact he thought of the three letters in his pocket, one from his wife, another from his daughter, and one from his son who was just finishing Marine Corps Boot Camp.

"Thanks Gunny" Mick said, "I'll look for the Sarge, but he may have the mail all passed out by the time I get there. I think he wants to be Company Mail Clerk."

After this exchange the Corporal headed back to the section of the perimeter that was his squad's responsibility.

CHAPTER THREE
Recon to Infantry

Marine infantry regiments are composed of three battalions. Each infantry battalion is further broken down into five companies. Four infantry companies designated by the letters of the phonetic alphabet and one weapons company. In the first battalion of a regiment, the companies are Alpha, Baker, Charlie, and Delta. In the second battalion it is Echo, Foxtrot, Golf and Hotel. Infantry companies are further broken down into platoons of approximately 50 men. Each company contains three platoons, First, Second, and Third. A platoon consists of three squads of fourteen men and a command element. A squad consists of three four-man fire teams, a Squad Leader and a Grenadier. The fire team is the smallest integral unit in the infantry and is composed of four Marines. A fire-team leader, an automatic rifleman and two riflemen.

Weapons Company consists of men and teams that are specially trained with light and heavy weapons. These weapons include, machine guns, mortars, rockets, and flame throwers, to name a few. Most weapons teams travel with an infantry company with which they associate and from which they receive their orders and supplies.

Every battalion has a reconnaissance unit assigned which are their eyes and ears. These Recon units are split into teams of four to twelve men. These teams are inserted via helicopter, parachute, rubber boat or by foot, behind the enemy lines to determine the enemies strength, assets, activities and armaments. When possible, these Recon units use supporting arms such as air power, artillery, or naval gunfire to inflict damage on the enemy units under their observation. Because these teams are so effective and inflict so many casualties on the army of the north, the Vietnamese Communists particularly hate Recon Marines. Some reconnaissance Marines are attached to Force Recon units which operate with Special Operations Groups well behind enemy lines, often in North Vietnam, Laos and

Cambodia. It was from SOG that Holtzman came to Hotel Company six months previously as a rather salty Lance Corporal.

The Grenadier carries the 40mm grenade launcher. This weapon looks like a short, fat, pregnant, single barreled shotgun and is called a blooper or blooker. The weapon fires a 40 mm projectile that explodes on impact spraying shrapnel in a killing radius of 10 meters, or thirty feet. This makes the grenade launcher the most effective weapon at the Squad Leader's disposal.

In general, a Marine knows every member of his fire team and squad intimately. He knows every man in his platoon and most people in the company. These are the men they see, speak to, work with and fight shoulder to shoulder with each day and night.

Corporal Mick Holtzman is Squad Leader of First Squad, Second Platoon, H Company of the Second Battalion of the 26th Marine Regiment, which is further assigned to the 9th Marine Amphibious Brigade. This is an infantry Marine's extended family as well as his mailing address.

The Second Battalion, 26th Marine Regiment is also the "Float" battalion or the BLT (Battalion Landing Team). What this means is the Second Battalion has no fixed rear area. They are assigned to ships afloat in the South China Sea from which they are deployed to whatever spot is hottest in the Marine's primary area of operation…that most northern sector of The Republic of South Vietnam known as "I Corps".

When the siege of Khe Sahn ended, the defenders, including the 26th Marines, were relieved and replaced by other Marine and Army units. Several months later the Special Operations Group with which Holtzman was working was disbanded and he and the other Recon Marines of the group were given new orders. Mick steamed when he read his orders. He was being sent to an infantry outfit.

When Holtzman reported to Hotel Company as his orders indicated, his first action was to find the Company

First Sergeant. After being transported by helicopter to the USS Duluth, Holtzman found the 10'x12' compartment which is Hotel Company's office aboard ship. The Corporal banged his fist three times on the open hatch cover. Gunnery Sergeant Shaw looked up to see a six-foot two, lean, blue eyed Marine in camouflaged jungle utilities with bush cover in hand, standing at attention in front of his office.

Shaw grunted, "Enter!" He watched as the young man stepped directly in front of his desk and handed him his orders and Service Record Book.

"What can I do for you?" asked Shaw.

"Sir, I'm a Recon Marine! I've been assigned to this infantry unit. I request a transfer to another Recon unit within my Military Occupational Specialty." Holtzman stated.

Shaw was quiet for a moment. He stared at the copy of the orders that had been handed to him without seeing them. Shaw had noted the stubborn set to the young man's jaw when he entered and it reminded him of his own attitude as a young Marine. He opened the Service Record Book and glanced at the entries from the soldier's last duty station. All entries were written in superlatives, not common in such reports. Hotel Company could use this man, thought Shaw.

"Lance Corporal," began Shaw in a stern voice, "as I'm sure you are aware, Recon is a secondary Military Occupational Specialty. All Recon Marines are grunts, infantry Marines first, and Recon Marines second." There was no change to the stubborn set of the jaw, "It may surprise you to know that I have an Infantry MOS, Recoilless Rifle MOS, as well as a Recon MOS. I don't know if you have a death wish or what, but humor me. I've been in this Marine Corps for nineteen years! This is the second war I've fought…and my second tour here! Right now, we need Marines with combat experience right here in this company. We took a hell of a beating at Khe Sahn, Con Thien, and LZ Margo." The Gunnery Sergeant took a breath and continued, "Stay here for thirty days…if you still want a transfer after that, I'll go to bat for you." Shaw bartered.

Mick continued staring straight ahead, his mind working fast. He read between the lines...*if I stayed a month and asked for a transfer, the Gunny said he'd go to bat for me...what that meant was that if I insisted on the transfer now the Gunny would bury it and it wouldn't see the light of day for six months.*

"All right Sir, you've got a deal." the Lance Corporal paused looked at the name plate on the desk and finished, "Thank you, Gunny Shaw."

That afternoon Holtzman was assigned as a Fire-Team Leader in First Squad. The next day the battalion was helo-lifted out to participate in Operation Meade River. Meade River turned out to be a rather long operation and lasted over a month. Much happened and when the operation was over Mick was Squad Leader of First Squad. Holtzman wore the coat of responsibility as if it were a garment tailored just for him. He realized he was responsible for the lives and actions of these fourteen men both in and out of combat, and in return he felt needed. When Operation Meade River ended and his thirty days were up, Mick didn't go looking for Gunnery Sergeant Shaw. The Gunny had played his cards just right, and scored a new leader for the company. Of course that was the job of the acting First Sergeant.

CHAPTER FOUR
Mail Call

Holtzman walked back through the patchwork of jungle, swamp, and grassland that was inside the Company's perimeter. His thoughts were on the debriefing just completed, his eyes however were busy as usual. As he walked along thinking of the debriefing and its implications, his eyes and brain logged each defensive position he passed and who manned it. Occasionally, as he moved by a fighting hole, someone would call out, comment, or "hello" him in passing.

Mick came to a location higher than the surrounding terrain. He stopped there and sat on his heels, gook style. Holtzman had taught himself to sit silently in this position for hours as a boy hunting whitetails in the river bottoms of Wisconsin. From this high point Mick could observe his area of operation. He surveyed the positions and his men for a few minutes, noting his connection with Lincoln's Second Squad on his left and the connection to Third Platoon on his right. After surveying the layout for several moments, Holtzman moved off to check with his Third Fire Team which linked up with the adjoining Third Platoon and to make sure everybody was on the same page.

Boone Riley was First Squad's Third Fire Team Leader, a fourth generation Tennessee Hillbilly and proud of it! Boone was six foot five and weighed around one hundred and forty pounds, making him one long, tall drink of water.

"Hey Boone," Mick called as he approached the team leaders position.

"What's goin' on Mick?" queried the team leader, "We goin' after them gooks?"

"Not right away." answered the Squad Leader, he noted the other men in the position were tuned in to the conversation. "Who's on your right with Third Platoon?" asked Mick.

"Nielson's team, and yes I've been over there and talked with Nielson and will recheck with him just before dark."

Reported Riley with a grin.

Mick kept his lips tightly pressed together. "Boone, you need to send out a listening post tonight...about a hundred yards in front of the lines between your position and Second Teams pos. That clump of grass next to the grave mound would be good." Holtzman said nodding in the direction he indicated.

"Man...how come we gotta send out a LP tonight, my dudes are tired man!" complained the team leader.

"We gotta send out an LP because I told you to...because the Platoon Sergeant told me to...because the Lieutenant told him to...because the Captain told him to. You know Boone...shit rolls downhill and you're at the bottom." Mick said with a disarming grin.

"Hey, here comes the Platoon Sergeant. He's supposed to have our mail," commented the Corporal as he watched the silhouette of the stocky Hispanic Sergeant approach.

"Sergeant M, I hear a rumor that you're trying out for Company Mail Clerk. Any truth to that?" Mick asked, as he intercepted the Sarge.

"Very funny Corporal!" Sergeant Hector Morrillo replied. "Here's your squads mail." The Platoon Sergeant passed a large bundle of letters, bound with a rubber band, to Mick.

As Mick took the letters Morrillo, watching carefully continued, "And a letter from the Commander." He pulled a letter from his pocket handing it to Holtzman. Morrillo always needled Mick about his Dad who was a retired Naval Officer. "And one from Mrs. Holtzman," Sarge handed him a second letter, "And what's this?" Morrillo said with obvious delight, "It looks like a Chickie letter!"

Mick took the three letters and stuffed them into the chest pocket of his jungle shirt, hoping that Sergeant Morrillo couldn't hear his heart pounding.

"Thanks Sarge." was all Mick said, and turned to walk away.

"Hey! Ain't ya gonna read the Chickie letter?" Morrillo asked grinning ear to ear.

"Eat shit and choke on it" said Mick "I can understand why women don't write your homely ass." With that the Corporal walked away.

"My! Aren't we touchy today!" declared Morrillo, unable to keep the laugh out of his voice.

Holtzman moved on down his lines, first passing out the mail to Boone and his team, then to the second and finally to Ski's First Team. None of the men of First Squad were married but three were engaged and several had steady girlfriends. Mick tried to keep track of the mail these men received so if there was a sudden halt, he could observe them to see if they became emotionally unstable and if this would affect their performance. As a Squad Leader, Mick did not have the authority to remove men from combat duty. However, through contacts at Company and Battalion headquarters, he could usually temporarily find other duties for a Marine who wasn't in the proper frame of mind for combat.

When Holtzman passed out the mail to First Team he noted that Team Leader Joe Sokouski seemed anxious until Mick handed him a letter from his fiancée. *"This guy's got it bad."* thought Mick. The whole time he was passing out squad mail, the letter in his shirt pocket felt like it was burning a hole into his chest. The last two letters remaining were for O'Meara, one from his mother and one from his buddy, a former Marine who had lost his foot to a anti-personnel mine.

Squad Leader Holtzman walked back to the position he and his Grenadier shared. Tracey was sitting in the shallow fighting hole, smoking a cigarette.

"Hey Trace, here's the mail." said Mick tossing the two remaining letters to O'Meara.

"Thanks Mick" replied the Grenadier, "I picked up Ammo, C-rats, water, and SPs. Yours are by your gear."

"Good work. How much ammo, frags, and claymores did we score." Holtzman questioned.

"Two hundred rounds M-16 ammo per man, five frags each, and a claymore per team. They're all screamin' about the three cans of gun ammo we inherited along with what we got." Explained Tracey.

"Yeah, they'll bitch about that machine gun ammo until those M-60s start tuning up, then we'll be damn glad we have it." Said Mick, "And thanks again. You even got me my favorite meal, chicken and noodles."

CHAPTER FIVE
The Letter

Mick pulled out a Lucky Strike, lit it with his Zippo, then pulled out the letter. He stared at the return address for a second. He had recognized Lori's handwriting when Morrillo handed him the letter, but the return address was from California not Wisconsin. Holtzman's heart was pounding in his ears and he was having a hard time swallowing as he slit the top of the envelope with the razor-like double edge of his K-Bar combat knife. It had been eight months since he had seen Lori and he would just as soon forget that day.

The Squad Leader quickly read through the letter, a page and a half. The fear drained out of him, and although he remained excited, his emotions were mixed with disappointment. It was a friendly, personable letter. She had gotten his address from Don Forest, she told him. Don had joined the Corps a year or so before Mick and had been Lori's next door neighbor. Mick had started reading the letter over again in an attempt to find some meanings between the lines when he heard O'Meara swear.

Holtzman looked at his friend. O'Meara was about five foot ten, medium build, with brown hair, a clear tanned complexion and brown eyes that usually had a twinkle. He had a rather dapper mustache of which he was very proud. Just now Tracey's eyes weren't twinkling but staring into the horizon.

"Hey, what's the deal?" Mick asked his friend.

Tracey looked at Mick and spat out, "My buddy from back in the world says my old lady is fuckin' everybody in town."

"What?" responded Holtzman.

"Well not exactly," went on O'Meara "MacDrumond, my buddy, he got a new prosthetic foot and decided to go to some of the bars we used to hang out at. He said he ran into Gina at two of them. I know if she's out hittin' the bars, she ain't goin' home alone."

Tracey looked over at Mick and could read the concern in his Squad Leader. Suddenly the twinkle returned to O'Meara's eyes, "Hey...why should I be surprised?" he bantered. "It was easy for me to get in her pants...why should that make it hard for Jody or the next guy?" Tracey grinned at Mick and invoked the grunt slang often saved for when a buddy was lost in combat, "It don't mean nothin!"

"There it is Brother! There it is!" Mick replied as he reached across the space between them and they signed, brother style, with closed fists. Each fist coming down on the others then side to side, then knuckles to knuckles.

They stared at each other for a second and repeated, "It don't mean nothin!"

O'Meara broke the silence that followed, "So what did the Chickie letter say? Good news?"

Mick's jaw dropped.

Tracey, laughing out loud now said, "You should see yourself buddy. You got the best poker face in the battalion and you just got ambushed big time. Hey, before you got back with the mail Sarge came by and asked if you'd read the chickie letter yet."

"Why that son-of-a-bitch! I ought to put a frag in his pocket! Where does he get off tellin' everybody my business?"

"He didn't tell everybody your business...just me." remarked Tracey.

This seemed to calm Mick down.

"Seriously" said Tracey "Tell me about your letter."

Squad Leader Holtzman smiled to his friend O'Meara and said, "Really not much to tell...just a friendly letter from a girl I dated in high school."

"Ya, Ya, Come on...come clean." replied O'Meara.

Holtzman looked away, gave a sad smile and said, "OK."

Mick Holtzman stood six-foot two, weighed one hundred seventy-five pounds. He had broad shoulders tacked on to a lean build. His hair was brown but bleached to a sandy color by the weather. His complexion was ruddy but the weather couldn't hide the sprinkle of freckles across the bridge of his nose. His features would be boyish if not for the steel blue eyes, the serious mouth, and the stubborn set to his jaw.

"I took her to the senior prom," Mick stated, "The only date I had in high school. We dated on and off but she was goin' out with this football hero jock who was a couple years older than me.

"So what happened? Did ya kick the jock's ass or what?" asked Tracy.

"Don't I wish!" smiled Holtzman, "I just kept callin'…askin' her out and by the end of the summer after I'd graduated, we were goin' out every Saturday night. Man…I was in heaven! Then one night I called and she told me she had a previous engagement. She kept tryin' to explain but I cut her off. I was sure it was the jock…I was so jealous I couldn't see straight. I hit the bars, got in a lot of fights and about two weeks later I went down and enlisted. I was gonna enlist anyway. I was just waitin' to turn eighteen, but they were happy to take me at seventeen. Lori tried to talk to me before I left but I was still so eaten up with jealousy I wouldn't listen. Guess I kind cut off my nose to spite my face."

"So when did you see her last?"

"When I went home on leave, before Recon School. I was gonna try to straighten things out." Holtzman paused, "Turned out she was goin' with one of my friends."

"Why…that Jody motherfucker! Did ya pound his ass?" O'Meara responded. Jody was a term for anyone who stayed back home in the World and went out with a soldier's girl, or drank his beer.

"Naw, it wasn't his fault." Mick declared.

"So that's it? Now out of the blue you hear from her?" O'Meara asked.

"Yeah, sorta…there's more to the story but that's it in a nutshell." Mick concluded.

"What did she say in the letter? Did she tell you she loved you…wanted your body or what?"

"No, just a friendly letter."

"What's she look like? Does she have big tits? Is she good in bed?" O'Meara asked, smiling.

"Eat shit you fuckin' pervert! Make up your own wet dream!"

Mick was glad to see his friend had regained his normal ribald sense of humor. "Here I thought I was goin to have to send you on RR to Taipei, and have some Chinese babe fuck you till you came back to your senses. But I can see you're the same old pervert you always were." Mick observed grinning.

O'Meara, now drooling and looking cross-eyed moaned, "I'm crazy! Send me, send me!"

"Go see the Chaplin. Your personal problems are out of my area of operation. Hey…do you want to check lines on first watch or start your check on second?" Mick asked.

Mick and Tracey manned a position and monitored the radio each night. Their main duty was to make sure that the positions First Squad manned, were able and alert. Nights were broken up into watches at each position on the perimeter. Generally three or four watches, depending on how many men were available to split them. During each watch, Mick or Tracey would move from one position to the next, making sure that the men were alert and awake. Also, if action threatened, both men went down the lines alerting the men of the squad as to what was happening and from where they might expect trouble.

At 0300 Tracey woke Mick to check lines on the fourth and final watch from three till sunup, around 0530. Tracey informed Mick that he had found Jones in Second Team asleep on watch.

"What did you do, wake him?" questioned Holtzman.

"Not right away." responded Tracey, "I sat down next to him and moved his weapon to my off side, then I cleared my throat."

"What happened then?" the Squad Leader queried.

"Well…he jumped about ten feet in the air, and reached for his piece, which I had." Continued Tracey, "Man, the look on his face. I don't think we'll ever have to wake him again…he was scared shitless. I did ask him to think about what would have happened to his buddies sleeping behind him if I had been the enemy."

"Good move, Trace. You probably made a good Marine tonight."

O'Meara then rolled up in his poncho liner and was asleep in less than a minute, leaving Mick Holtzman alone with his thoughts. Mick pulled out the letter and in the starlight, occasionally interrupted by artillery illumination flares, he read the letter again.

CHAPTER SIX
The Alamo

At 0515 hours Corporal Holtzman returned from his last check of the lines. All was well. Mick almost always took this watch. The hour just before dawn is when the sentinels are least likely to be alert. That makes it the most likely time for an attack. The Squad Leader also liked to watch the sun come up. Perhaps because not too many months before, he and O'Meara thought they had seen their last sunrise. During Operation Valiant Hunt, Mick's squad was sent out for a night ambush. A patrol earlier that day had noted signs of enemy activity near what had once been an old French plantation. All that was left were the ruins of a few buildings and overgrown fields.

O'Meara had just joined First Squad two days before. Prior to that he had been Second Squad Leader. Some sort of political fight developed between Tracey and some clerk-typist Staff Sergeant. Tracey's promotion to Corporal was lost in the office clutter. Feeling cheated, O'Meara gave up the leadership of Second Squad, and asked Mick if he could be his Grenadier. Mick was more than happy to have someone with Tracey's experience.

That night as First Squad, reinforced by a machine-gun team, moved out, they traveled through double canopy jungle. In a double canopy jungle at night, it was so dark that the men had to put a hand on each other so as not to become separated. In general, during night actions, soldiers moved with an interval between themselves and the next man that just allowed visual contact. In a double canopy jungle you couldn't see your hand in front of your face.

The jungle had a different, foreign smell to it. It was dank and musky. There was an alien feel to it. It made the hair on the back of Mick's head prickle.

On a night ambush the men left their flak jackets, helmets, canteens, and rucksacks behind, carrying only essential combat gear. Mick's squad carried 185 rounds of ammo per man, that were contained in the ten M-16 magazines each man carried. Most Marines only load eighteen or nineteen rounds into the 20 round magazines. A full load, carried for a long time, could stress the spring fed mechanism and cause a jam when firing. Each squad member carried three to five fragmentation grenades, and each team also had a Claymore antipersonnel mine. The M-60 machine gun team consisted of three men, who also traveled light. They carried the M-60 with an assault pouch (300-400 rounds) and one can of machine gun ammunition. This amount of ammunition, fired at full auto, would only last several minutes. The idea was to surprise the enemy in a well designed ambush, blow them to shreds with the claymores, open up with the automatic weapons, check the dead for documents and weapons and get the hell out of there.

On this occasion things did not go as planned. After passing through the jungle they emerged into what had once been the fields surrounding the French Indochina era plantation buildings. Here, the visibility was better due to the moon and stars that showed themselves occasionally through the monsoonal clouds. The intent was to move just beyond the ruins of the plantation and set up an L shaped ambush.

As soon as the squad moved out into the long, fallow plantation fields, they began hearing voices. As they neared the ruins they could hear voices all around them and could see movement in all directions. Mick, using hand signals, directed the men to take cover in the nearest ruin, probably the masonry remains of a storage building. While the squad was taking cover in the building, there were loud exclamations in Vietnamese and then First Squad was taking fire.

When Holtzman saw his last man make it into the ruin, he dived over the waist-high wall, landing in the center of the ten foot by ten foot building. The back wall was standing and solid eight feet high. The sides kind of sloped down to the waist-high front and there were gaps in the sides and the front. Some of these gaps may have once been openings for doors or may have just appeared as the building fell into ruin.

Mick quickly positioned his men to defend the building. All the while, an occasional bullet would whiz by or ricochet off the stone walls. There was a lot of shouting and confusion outside, all in Vietnamese…and there were many voices. First Squad was in a bad spot. The squad was equipped for a hit and run ambush, not for a prolonged defensive battle against a numerically superior enemy force. Mick looked over at Kuhl, his Radioman, and said in normal voice,

"Get me Hotel two."

Hotel Two Actual was their Platoon Commander Lieutenant Baker. When the Lieutenant came up on the Radio, Corporal Holtzman reported that he had encountered a large number of enemy troops, that they were taking fire, and had taken cover. He gave his grid coordinates of his location. Mick also requested support from 80 millimeter mortars. Baker came back quickly and said that the eighty mike-mikes were on the way and for Mick to adjust fire. The 80 millimeter mortars were a part of Weapon's Company and were usually located near the Battalion Command Post.

Baker was Recon trained and Stanford educated. A black First Lieutenant for whom Holtzman and the men had great respect. He had shown his courage in combat on many occasions. Mick new that the Lieutenant would leave no stone unturned in his attempts to get First Squad out of their predicament.

By now the ruins were taking regular small arms fire. Bullets zinging and ricocheting off the walls of the ruins as the enemy probed, trying to determine just how many Marines they had encountered and how they were dispersed.

O'Meara tapped Mick on the arm and asked, "Where do you want the gun?" and pointed to the machine gun team.

Mick looked around and answered, "Put 'em in the back corner and have 'em build a wall out of the rocks and rubble about six foot in front of them. If worst comes to worst we can all fall back there with both flanks covered and dance the last dance."

"Shit!" replied Tracey, "If worst comes to that, we're fucked...totally fucked!"

Holtzman did not reply. From the radio handset he heard Bakers voice say "Shot out!" This was the signal that the mortar had fired and the round was in the air.

Mick got to his knees and seconds later heard, "Splash" which indicates the mortar round should be landing. The flash from the exploding mortar round was pretty far to the front.

The Corporal spoke into the handset, "Drop two-zero-zero and right five-zero."

The building was taking more fire. One of Mick's men tossed a fragmentation grenade back at a muzzle flash. The Marines heard the dull thud of the frag's explosion and in the flash could see the body of an enemy soldier flying through the air. Third Team leader Boone looked at Mick and said, "That should back them up a bit."

"Yeah," commented Holtzman, "that was good work, but try to save those frags. Have the men pair up and throw a rock at anything suspicious...then the other can shoot when you see them move away from what they think is a hand grenade."

"Shot out!" Mick heard Lt. Bakers voice say in the handset. Then "Splash!"

This time the single 80-millimeter mortar round armed with white phosphorus, which was used as a marking and anti-personnel shell, landed about 80 meters in front of the Marine's position.

The Squad Leader hollered, "Fire for effect!" into the handset. This was the signal that the mortars were on target and to fire all of the mortar battery tubes with high explosive antipersonnel rounds.

The Squad Leader yelled to get the men's attention over the continuous small arms fire punctuated by the occasional explosion of a grenade.

"Be ready to hit the dirt when I holler! We got incoming mortars on the way!"

Seconds later Mick heard Bakers voice, "Shot out!"

Mick shouted, "Take cover!"

The barrage of 80 millimeter mortar rounds hit about 70 yards in front of the squad's position. The blast was deafening and for ten or fifteen seconds after the shells impacted, you could hear the hot metal shrapnel fragments whizzing through the air and clanging into the stonework. Occasionally a piece that had arched high in the air would fall down on the men behind the stone walls. These pieces of shrapnel had lost their force in the upward flight but were still searing hot when they landed.

"Drop twenty-five, fire for effect" Mick spoke into the radio. "Let's see if that don't back 'em off some." he said to O'Meara as he approached.

"Yeah...let's just hope they don't fire any short rounds and blow our asses to hell!" Pronounced Tracey as he readied another 40mm grenade round in his launcher.

"Try to save your ammo...no tellin how long we're gonna be here." Mick ordered.

"Just trying to make sure they don't get close enough to read our mail." The Irishman explained with a grin.

The next volley of mortar rounds landed about 50 meters in front of the ruin, spraying the walls with lethal hot shrapnel. However, the enemy was still out there in front of them probing...moving in...looking for the weak spot, trying to figure how many Marines they had encountered.

Mick told Lt. Baker to keep up the mortar fire at that range and give them the "shot outs" so they could take cover. He ordered the radio back into the corner with the gun team where Kuhl could monitor it, while he moved around the position taking stock. As Mick started to move past one of the openings, he quickly stepped back. He had seen movement in the brush just five feet in front of him. Boone, on the other side of the gap, looked at Mick, and without a word smiled and picked up a rock. Mick nodded and Boone tossed it. Mick stepped quickly into the opening when the rock struck the ground and saw the soldier move. Mick put a six round burst into him and then fired a short burst to either side. As he stepped back he was suddenly propelled to the rear into and through the crumbling masonry. He landed on his back inside the ruin. While flying backwards through the air Mick had felt a hot fiery pain in his thigh. He knew he was hit before he landed.

O'Meara was immediately at his side, "Where ya hit Mick?" asked the grenadier.

"Left thigh." Holtzman replied as his hand found the wet spot in the middle of his leg.

Tracey ripped the trouser leg open revealing a small pencil sized hole oozing blood. O'Meara then lifted the leg and examined the exit wound, eliciting a groan from the Squad Leader.

"Sorry buddy!" was Tracey's response, "the exit is only about an inch wide so I guess it didn't hit the bone…got a battle dressing?"

"Yeah, I wasn't planning on using it on myself!" Mick commented as he pulled the prepackaged battle dressing out of one of the pockets of the bandoleer across his chest. After O'Meara applied the dressing along with some sulfa powder, Mick tested the leg gingerly. He was able to bear weight but he would not be able to move much faster than a hobble.

A few minutes later the enemy voices arose in all directions around them. Then the voices stopped and there was silence for a moment that was followed by laughter. It was really quite unnerving to hear hundreds of enemy voices laughing at you so close by. The laughter was followed by a few seconds of dead silence. An amplified Vietnamese voice spoke through a loudspeaker in very precise English, "Marines of the 26th Regiment…you are too young to die. Think of your wives and sweethearts back home. You have so much to live for." The amplified voice went on and on.

"Stay cool," Mick said with a voice that was steadier than he felt. "They're trying to psych us out."

Mick motioned to Kuhl to bring the radio and when he got the handset he called Lieutenant Baker and told him to drop the Mortars 25 meters and fire for effect.

"Let's see how funny that is!" Mick said to no one in particular.

When Baker called the shot out, Mick ordered everybody back into the corner behind the barricade. The mortar barrage landed fifteen to twenty meters in front of their position. The explosions deafened them and bounced the Marines along the ground like basketballs. Searing shrapnel filled the air everywhere. It was worse for the NVA soldiers in the brush. They had no rock walls to protect them from the hot metal fragments that could tear a man in half. As the smoke cleared away and the Marines jumped back to their positions on the wall, they could hear the moans of the wounded Communists.

"How Goddamned funny is it now, You sons-a-bitches!" Mick hollered. Most of the men chuckled nervously. The men knew they couldn't keep calling the mortars in on themselves without eventually getting hit. How long would this tactic back the enemy off?

Holtzman got on the radio and reported the distance the last volley had landed. He asked them to number that target and be ready if they needed it again. Lieutenant Baker came back and told Mick that he had permission to lead the remainder of the platoon out to First Squad's present position as a reaction force, and that they were saddled up now and would move out within three minutes.

"Hey guys," Mick spoke loud and clear, "Lieutenant Baker is on his way out here with the rest of the platoon to save our young asses. So keep your heads down. All we gotta do is survive till the platoon gets close, then make a run for it."

The small arms fire had begun again, along with the probing. It wouldn't take long before they had the squad in as tight a fix as they were in before Mick called the mortars in on them.

"Mr. Baker must have had the platoon saddled up long

before he got permission to come to our aid." Tracey commented. "What's the plan till they get here?"

"Try to keep them from getting in so close. Get a couple of guys to work on the barricade by the gun. If they get too close we will fall back to the corner and call the mortars in on top of us again. Then when the smoke clears jump back out to what's left of the walls." said Mick.

"We won't get away with that often!" said O'Meara seriously.

"I know." replied Holtzman.

CHAPTER SEVEN
Puff the Magic Dragon

Mick's leg ached and was stiffening up. He moved but could find no position comfortable. *"When it comes time to make a run for it, I guess I won't be included."* he thought sardonically. Checking the battle dressing, he discovered that it hadn't bled through and concluded that the wound probably wasn't serious. The men were back to returning small arms fire. Mick wondered why the enemy didn't just rush them. With the Communists superior numbers, they could overrun the Marines position in seconds. He guessed that the enemy wasn't sure what they had. They might be thinking they had hit the battalion's perimeter. Surely if they knew there were only fifteen Marines with only a few hundred rounds of ammo, they'd have ended the standoff.

Earlier Mick had placed two of his three claymore mines in front of the wall on either side of their position. These mines are slightly curved and can be aimed by placing the curve facing away from your position like an upside down U. When fired, the shape charge inside blows hundreds of ball bearings at a 45 degree angle, creating a fifteen to twenty meter kill zone. These devices are devastating. If the enemy did try to overrun them, Mick would blow the two outer claymores and drop back to the gun position, where he now sent Tracey to set up the third and final claymore. Once behind the barricade Mick would call the mortars in on their position. After that, things would really get interesting.

"The way you got this set up Bro, it's going to cost them plenty to get us." asserted O'Meara on his return.

Mick said nothing as at that moment automatic weapon fire erupted in the distance. The weapons fire came from the south, the direction from which they had come.

"What the fuck?" choked Tracey.

"The Lieutenant and the platoon." responded the Squad Leader still listening intently to the distant gunfire.

Joe Kuhl, the Radioman scuttled over, "They ambushed

the Lieutenant and the platoon! They've taken casualties. They are stuck and diggin' in on the other side of that bridge we crossed in the jungle!"

"Damn!" Thought Mick, *"If only the Lieutenant had gotten closer, we could make a run for them and join up. At least there would be forty-five of us rather than fifteen and thirty separated by a thousand yards!"* Holtzman knew that if his squad tried to make a run for it they would be picked off one or two at a time and none would make it to the platoon's position.

Without consciously thinking, Mick reached down and pulled his bayonet from its scabbard and fixed it on the end of his M-16. Looking up, he saw Boone staring hard at him, then Boone smiled a big smile, pulled his bayonet and fixed it. One by one the men fixed their bayonets. This was the exclamation point on the finality of their situation. Now only time and the enemy would have any say in what happened. Their way had been chosen.

Time passed slowly for the men of First Squad. Each man had his own thoughts. Each went to his own private world for a little while. The enemy continued the small arms fire and probed the lines. Twice more Mick called in the eighty millimeter mortars at the fifty meter distance to back off the NVA soldiers. It was midnight when Radioman Kuhl plopped down beside the Squad Leader. He gave him the handset and said, "It's the Lieutenant, he wants a word with you."

"Hotel two, this is Alpha two." Mick said over the radio's static.

"Roger Alpha two. I can't get to you, but we have "Puff" coming on station. Do you have any way to mark your position? Over."

Holtzman thought a moment and replied, "That's affirmative, we can mark our position."

"Roger Alpha two, we copy. Hotel two will mark our position and Alpha two will mark its position then puff will take out everything in between. If that works, can you make a run for our position with your casualties?" Inquired the

Platoon Commander.

Mick pondered a moment and replied, "That's affirmative…can do!"

"Puff will contact you directly when he comes on station. Be ready to mark your position then. Hotel two out." finished the Lieutenant.

Puff is short for Puff the Magic Dragon. The name is slang for an old, slow, W.W.II AC-47. This propeller driven antique was converted to a flare ship that has been armed with mini-guns. Mini-guns are actually Gatling guns that fire over 6,000 rounds per minute. This rate is so fast that the sound is a constant brrrrrr. It is said Puff can put a round into every square foot of a football field in seconds. The Communists fear Puff and with good reason. When Puff appears, there is no place to hide. He just rains death down on all that is below him.

As the Squad Leader handed the radio handset back to Kuhl, O'Meara said, "So…what do we use to mark our positions with, I didn't bring any illumination flares."

"Got any heat tabs?" queried Mick. Heat tabs are the tablets, about the size of a silver dollar that the Marines use to heat their C-Rations. They are made of trioxone and they create a lot of heat. They burn with a blue light. Holtzman reached into the pocket of his utility trousers and dug out two of the tabs, Boone had one, O'Meara three. Soon there was a small heap of the chemical tablets on the ground.

"Mick," called O'Meara "Looky here!" Tracey had scrounged around the rubble and found two tin cans which he was now brandishing in the air.

"Great work!" called out Holtzman "Now if we can find two more we can drop a heat tab into each and put one on each corner of the building. Only Puff will be able to see them from above."

The Marines continued to trade small arms fire with the enemy, but now First Squad had a way out. The four tin cans were placed by each corner with several heat tabs close by to use as target markers.

As promised, about fifteen minutes later the Marines

heard the drone of a propeller. The plane came from the south and on its approach dropped illumination flares supported by parachutes that turned night into day. The slow moving craft's advance decreased to a snail's pace. As it came even with Lieutenant Baker and Second Platoon's position, a smile crept onto the Corporal's face as he monitored the radio. Holtzman heard the pilot talking with Baker and saying that he could see their position markers and that he and his craft were on their way to find the others.

Minutes later the PRC-25 Radio crackled and a voice with a strong southern accent came on, "Alpha 2, this is Puff, do y'all copy? Ovah."

"You bet Puff, Alpha two copies you Lima Charlie!" Mick replied. He nodded at O'Meara and Boone to light the heat tabs and set them in the cans on each corner of the ruin.

"OK alpha two, I hear y'all loud and clear. Now I just gotta figure where y'all are." Came the drawled response from the pilot.

"Look to bearing zero-three-zero, you should see four little blue lights in a square. That's us inside the square." responded Holtzman.

"My my...how very professional y'all are! Now I got you and your friend's positions marked. How much pressure y'all under boys?" drawled the Puff pilot.

"They're starting to get up close and personal again, they can probably read the label in my BVD's!" replied the Squad Leader.

"OK, tell your boys to lay down flat, cause I'm goin' to give ya some relief. Say...any of you boys down there from Louisiana?" asked the pilot.

"Yeah, we got a guy from Baton Rouge here. He's a Cajun...can't understand a thing he says" said Mick smiling into the handset.

"Well now...Baton Rouge y'all say. You tell him to tell his momma that Lieutenant Beauregard J. Forrest sends her his regards and I'll make damn sure y'all get back safe tonight. Get them boys down now cause I'm fixin' to cut the grass on your lawn." came the reply from the southerner.

"Get down, stay down low, Puff's gonna work now!" Holtzman commanded.

Many of the Marines had seen Puff work before but always at a distance.

Seconds later there was a deafening roar from the ship above and fingers of light resembling laser beams went to the ground in front of the Marines position. One could not hear individual reports just a roar as the mini-guns fired. The red beams of light were really the tracer round trails of every fifth round from the mini-guns. There were just so many tracers coming so fast that it appeared as single beam.

The ground, jungle and foliage to the squad's front was ripped to shreds as the twenty millimeter canon rounds tore through it and whatever enemy might be hidden there. First to their front, then either flank, then to their rear. The mini-guns laid waste to all that was there. Puff then flew south and did the same for Lieutenant Baker and the rest of Second Platoon.

Twenty minutes later the now familiar southern drawl crackled over the handset, "Well, y'all should be breathin' a might easier now. I'm gonna work on the ground between your positions. When I start runnin' low on ammo, I'll head back your way, Alpha 2, and give ya a once-over. Then y'all can make your run for it. Ovah."

"Roger that Bro, that's a-firm-a-titty Puff. We all love ya down here!" Mick smiled as he replied.

"Now don't y'all get all soft and slobbery on me." came the jocular reply from the flying officer. "Good luck boys, Puff out."

Holtzman organized his men with Boone leading off and Third Team being followed by Wright's Second Team, then finally Ski with First Team.

"I'll be tail-end Charlie on this trip," announced Mick, "O'Meara, you stay with Kuhl and the radio."

"Like hell I will," replied Tracey "I'm with you and I'll carry your skinny ass all the way back if I have to! You can't move fast with that leg."

I'm with O'Meara." spoke up Sokouski , "My teams goin'

last so I'll help Tracey with Mick."

"Like hell you will!" Holtzman roared, "Trace and I will get along just fine. We'll run it like a three legged race at the county fair."

O'Meara looked at Ski and they nodded to each other. The deal was done without a word being spoken. If Mick and Tracey lagged behind, Ski would drop back to help and slow the leaders.

"Is this some sort of fuckin' mutiny?" snarled the Squad Leader.

Tracey and Ski just smiled. Then O'Meara said, "If you get a fuckin' medal it won't be a posthumous presentation Mr. Corporal Fuckin' Holtzman!"

With that, the discussion ended. The Marines watched Puff finish up his work, waiting for the word to move. It wasn't long in coming. Off they went with long, tall Boone Riley leading the way. Mick and Tracey were last, watched closely by Ski. Holtzman put his arm over the shorter O'Meara's shoulder and Tracey put his spare arm around the Squad Leader's waist. In this manner they were able to keep up with Riley's pace and handle their weapons.

Fortunately Puff had done good work and no enemy soldiers were encountered. When they crossed the single plank that passed for a bridge, Mick called a halt and radioed the Lieutenant that they were close by. He then fired a green star cluster pop-up flare to signal they were friendly. The squad moved into the defensive positions that the platoon had taken when they were attacked. Here, amongst their comrades, First Squad waited for morning and every man rejoiced at the sight of that first gray light of dawn.

CHAPTER EIGHT
Bird is the Word

Holtzman recalled the engagement at the ruins that had occurred months earlier, which was now referred to as the Alamo. His eyes could now make out the bamboo grove about 50 feet in front of the position he and Trace occupied. He couldn't yet see the individual trees…they were more of an amorphous mass. Another morning was coming to Vietnam. Soon, the sun's rays would warm his flesh and remind him that he was alive.

Mick's eyes moved continuously during his watch. Moving from one object to the next, letting the subconscious sort out movements, or irregularities. His were the eyes of a hunter and this was a society of hunters…a warrior's society.

Damn, he wanted a cigarette! He knew he could wait till the sun was up, rather than risk the flare of the Zippo illuminating him for a enemy sniper. He thought of the phrase, *"I'm dyin' for a cigarette!"* and wondered how many had died for…or because of a cigarette in Nam.

His thoughts returned to Lori and the letter. He had read and re-read the letter. Trying to find some deeper meaning, looking for something, some special message hidden between the lines. In the end he knew it was just a friendly letter, but it was a letter.

"You got it bad, dippy!" he chided himself, *"You're as bad as Ski! That poor son-of-a-bitch sweats a gallon at every mail call, waitin' for a letter from his fiancée. You get a little letter from a girl you dated in high school and your trying to make a federal case out of it!"*

But it was a letter and he had started his reply that night while on watch, adding a word here…changing one there. It was all in his mind for now, but soon he'd put it on paper. It would be a masterpiece, *"Hemingway would be proud!"*

"Words,
they're only words,
And words are all I have,
To take your heart away."

These lines of a popular song by the Bee Gee's came to mind.

Static from the radio disrupted his thoughts. The Marines refer to their standard radio as the prick-25. The PRC-25 is rectangular in shape, about fourteen inches by twenty-four inches and four inches thick. It weighs twenty-five pounds and is mounted to a pack frame and of course, is olive drab in color. The platoon Radioman does a security check of each radio in the platoon every thirty minutes to make sure all those on radio watch are awake. During this radio security check, he also contacts the listening posts to be sure that they have not detected an enemy presence. When the Radioman had completed the security check he announced, "All sierra limas, which is code for Squad Leader, report to the Platoon CP at 0630."

O'Meara sat up. He, like Mick, was a master at the art of sleeping with his ears on. They could be dead asleep but wake up and recite the conversation that just took place.

Tracey looked at Mick while stretching and said with his northeastern accent, "I guess the bird is going to give you the word." Then continued, "Bird, bird, bird...bird is the word." mimicking the sixties surfing song.

The grenadier was referring to Second Lieutenant Byrd who had replaced First Lieutenant Baker as Platoon Commander. Officers generally spent about half their tour as a line officer and the other half in the hierarchy of battalion command. Baker was now the Battalion Intelligence officer or S-2. The respect and admiration that the men of Second Platoon had given Lieutenant Baker and Captain Weller had not been accorded to Lieutenant Byrd. Respect and admiration are earned by individuals and given freely to that individual by the men he commands. It doesn't come as the accouterment of rank or position.

"Yeah…now we get the word." said the Squad Leader as he flipped open the Zippo and lit the Lucky Strike he had been craving for the last two hours. "Have the men pack up and be ready to move out. They'll bitch but this way they'll get more time to eat if we are packed up before everybody else." Mick drew deeply on the Lucky, inhaling the smoke, feeling the bite as it went deep into his lungs. The Corporal looked at his watch. It read 06:20, he took another drag on his smoke, shrugged on his flak jacket, picked up his weapon and headed for the Platoon Command Post.

The platoon CP is no more than the area where the Platoon Commander, Platoon Sergeant, Guide, Corpsmen, and Radioman bedded down. As the Squad Leader approached, he saw Boston Jones on radio watch. He and Boston had known each other since boot camp and infantry training. Later they had gone on liberty together once or twice but lost contact when Mick volunteered for Recon School. It had come as a pleasant surprise to both when Holtzman ran into Boston after being reassigned to the rifle company. Boston was a black man who had grown up in Massachusetts. When he spoke he sounded like one of the Kennedy brothers. He was a natural as a Radioman.

"Hey Boston!...what's happening Brother?" asked Mick as he approached.

Boston smiled and did an exact impersonation of Walter Cronkite, "So far, I can report that very little is happening on this day, April the sixth, nineteen hundred and sixty nine."

Boston smiled and nodded to his left, "The Papa Sierra is waiting for you over there." he lowered his voice to a stage whisper with a British accent, "The Lieutenant will be along as soon as he's finished with his tea."

The Corporal sauntered over and plopped down opposite Sergeant Hector Morrillo, Second Platoon's Platoon Sergeant. "Hey, Sarge, What's Up?"

Morrillo looked over each shoulder in a conspiratorial fashion and grinning said, "What did the Chickie letter say Mick?"

"Why you motherfucker! What the hell are you doin' pryin' into my personal matters, I'm gonna report your ass to the Chaplin." Mick proclaimed with a smirk. Both Holtzman and Morrillo had been wounded the night of the Alamo. Mick at the ruins themselves and Morrillo with the relief unit led by Lieutenant Baker. They had been medevaced out together and spent a couple of weeks recovering at the Battalion Aid Station aboard the WWII aircraft carrier the USS Valley Forge which was acting as the Battalion Rear Area for the 26th Marines.

"What are you two cookin' up?" came the deep Texas drawl as Lincoln walked over.

"Hey, what's happenin' Prez!" said Mick as they signed with their fists.

"Where be the Lieutenant and Schmidt?" asked the Second Squad Leader.

"The Lieutenant will be here shortly…I can see Schmidt coming now." confirmed Sergeant Morrillo who was now getting serious.

Schmidt, Third Squad Leader, was from California, about the same age as the rest. Lincoln was cool towards him because he felt that Schmidt was prejudiced, although there was no outward expression of racism. It was just a gut feeling. O'Meara really had a case against Schmidt. It went back to an action at Con Thien. Apparently, during a patrol into an enemy area, they found a bunker with gooks in it. They were unarmed, mostly women and old men. According to Tracey, Schmidt opened up on them, O'Meara grabbed his weapon, disarming Schmidt and things got real ugly between the two for a few moments until cooler heads prevailed. Mick sensed his friend Lincoln's reservations, and knew what O'Meara thought, so no friendship had developed between him and Schmidt. All this said, Schmidt did seem to perform his job as Squad Leader well, so Mick held back any judgment on the man.

As Schmidt arrived, Lieutenant Byrd emerged from his poncho hooch and joined the group.

Byrd informed the men that they would be moving out

in the direction of the river at 0800 hours. He ordered them to get the area policed, their men fed, packed up and ready to move out by 0745. As the meeting adjourned Lieutenant Byrd said, "Holtzman…you're wanted at the Company CP, ASAP!" With that the Lieutenant went back into his poncho hooch.

Morrillo walked over to Mick and whispered, "He seems a bit pissed that you're invited to the company CP but not him! I'll go pass the word to your squad, get 'em packed up and fed."

"Thanks Sarge, Tracey's already got 'em packin', and they should be eatin', but tell O'Meara the time schedule." replied the Squad Leader.

"What are you some kind of a fuckin' mind reader, Holtzman?" asked the Sergeant "Are you buckin' for my job or what?"

Mick just smiled a mysterious smile as he headed off for the Company Command Post.

CHAPTER NINE
Ambush the Ambush

"I wonder what's goin' on now?" Mick thought. Holtzman felt the sweat starting to saturate his jungle shirt under his flak jacket. *"Jesus,"* he thought, *"it ain't even 0700 and it must be a hundred degrees and 90 percent humidity."* As he approached the Command Post he could see the long whip radio antennae indicating the presence of the Battalion CO or at least his Radioman Webb. When Mick stepped into the shell crater serving as CP, the cast was the same as the debriefing, with Colonel Smith, Gregory the aide, Captain Weller, and Gunnery Sergeants Shaw and Riker. In addition today was Lieutenant Baker, now the Intelligence Officer, as well as the Company Commanders of Golf, Echo, and Fox Companies. Once again the young Corporal stepped into the CP, came to the position of attention and proclaimed, "Corporal Holtzman reporting as ordered, Sir!"

"Well, Holtzman," remarked Lieutenant Colonel Smith, "we meet once again." The Battalion Commander paused for a second then continued, "As it was you who discovered this enemy unit, I felt you should have a prominent role in their demise. We have devised a plan to ambush the ambush that you predicted. Our Intelligence Officer, Lieutenant Baker, has had a Recon Team move over to that valley across the river and sure enough, they detected a heavy enemy presence there. Lieutenant Baker take over."

Lieutenant Baker stepped forward.

"Following up on the report that Corporal Holtzman provided, along with his suspicions of an impending ambush after we cross the Song Lai River. Our reconnaissance units detected a large enemy concentration in the valley just across the river. They appear to have heavy weapons emplacements being prepared partway up the ridge here and along a large paddy dike here. This will form a V shaped ambush of the type we have seen before. They could allow a company or more to cross the river then spring their ambush. For us to retreat back across the river would be suicide as the enemy would have us in a devastating crossfire. Our troops would be trapped and there would be nowhere for them to go."

"Now," interjected the Colonel, "what we plan is to approach the river crossing as if we have no idea of their activity…a decoy if you will. We will move out this morning and follow the general direction we have been going and halt this afternoon about 1500 hours here." The Colonel pointed to the map that Baker had been using, "We will set up a normal battalion perimeter within 500 meters of the river crossing. Tonight at 0200 hours Echo Company will move out and cross the river downstream to our east and begin moving up the backside of the ridge. That's where the enemy has placed their heavy weapons. At the same time, Golf and Fox Company will night march to these positions behind the paddy dike on the other side of the enemy ambush. This will place Echo on the east side of the enemy's V and Fox and Golf on the longer, flatter west side. Hotel Company will be the blocking force here along the river, as well as the bait." The Colonel stopped and looked at Holtzman, "That's where you come in. In the morning I want Hotel Company to break camp as if they were an entire battalion and move to the river crossing. There I want you and your squad to buy time by setting a rope across the river to help us pitiful Marines ford the mighty Song Lai." Smith said smiling. "While you are buying us time with the rope, we will make sure we have all our ducks in a row. Then we'll spring our own ambush. When we initiate our attack, Echo Company will assault over the ridge gaining the high ground on the enemy dug in below. Echo will be reinforced by elements of Weapons Company including 60 millimeter mortars who will set up on top of the ridge and begin finding targets of opportunity below. I am giving this assignment to Echo Company as payback for what happened to them at Meade River. Your platoon, Corporal, will be held in reserve, so after you get done playing the part of bait, you'll have to get your men out of the river and behind the positions dug by First and Third Platoon quickly. Can you handle that?"

"Yes Sir." Holtzman agreed.

"My guess," Smith continued, "is that the enemy will try to fade away to the west when Echo comes over the ridge. Here they will run into Golf and Fox Companies behind the paddy dikes…they will bounce back and forth like a steel ball in a pinball machine looking for weak spots where they can break out." The Colonel finished with, "Company Commanders will meet at the Battalion CP this evening at 1800 to discuss individual assignments. Any other questions?"

There was silence in the crater.

The Colonel turned to Mick and said, "Corporal? Comments?"

The Squad Leader turned red in the face as he said, "Well Sir, if I were the enemy, I'd have a sentinel or two on top of that ridge. If we have a Recon Team in that area, it might be wise to have them eliminate the sentinels so as not to spoil our surprise."

"Good point!" replied Smith, "And what else?" he prodded.

"It might be a good idea not to close the point of the V off completely. A rat with his tail in a corner can get pretty vicious."

"So you're saying that we should let them escape from our ambush!" interrupted Lieutenant Gregory. "That's not very smart."

"No, don't let them escape. Let them start funneling out into this draw. It has steep sides. In there, we can blow their ass to doll rags with supporting arms, artillery, and air strikes. Some will escape but they will no longer be an effective fighting force…and we will take fewer casualties, Sir!" responded Mick to the verbal attack.

"Interesting…very interesting idea Corporal. Thank you for your insight. You are dismissed to your normal duties." Colonel Smith ordered.

"Aye, Aye, Sir" responded the Corporal as he turned to

go.

"Lieutenant Baker...can that Recon Team clear that ridge in the morning?" asked the Colonel.

"They are in position to do so...one of them knows the Corporal." commented Baker.

"Hey Mick" called Baker as the Squad Leader was leaving, "do you know a recon Marine called Buzzard?"

Holtzman stopped, turned and surveyed the group, "If you send Buzzard and his team up there you'll have the element of surprise on your side. There will be no sentinels and no noise." he finished with a cold smile and walked off.

"What makes him so damn sure?" muttered Gregory.

Gunny Shaw, standing next to the Colonel's Aide, replied in a whisper, "Because they were Recon teammates up on the Z. Those two are bad dudes" the Gunny belatedly added, "Sir."

CHAPTER TEN
Mother Hen

Mick Holtzman returned to the position he shared with O'Meara. Upon his arrival he asked Tracey if the men were packed and ready to go. Tracey informed him that they were packed, fed and ready to rock and roll...just sipping their coffee.

"I got a cup brewin' for you." said O'Meara

"Thanks man, you're a lifesaver." replied Mick, as he lit another Lucky and took the proffered cup.

The coffee that the Marines drink is instant. It comes with the C-Ration meals. They brew it with heat tabs, boiling it in a tin can with the top cut off and bent over to make a handle. The stuff tastes awful by itself, so they always add a couple of packs of instant creamer and as many sugars as they can find. The resultant brew is thick, kind of tan in color, and doesn't taste much like coffee. The brew does however cut the taste of the halazone pills they use to purify the swamp water they have to drink.

Holtzman sipped his coffee and smoked the Lucky Strike, glancing at his watch it was 0735and they would be moving out in ten minutes.

"You gonna eat?" queried Tracey.

"Naw, I'll just have another smoke and sip the java." answered Mick. "Remember the time that Tex was puttin' that Red Rooster Hot sauce in his coffee?"

"Yeah...I remember!" laughed O'Meara, "You tried some and spent the rest of the day diggin' cat holes and scroungin' for shit paper."

"Man...that's the last time I'll have any of Tex's coffee! That stuff really burned my ass! I still ain't got even with him for that one." smiled Holtzman.

Joe Kuhl appeared and took the radio, attaching his haversack to the pack board that came with the prick-25. The squad Radioman stood watch with his team at night and humped the radio during the day, trying to keep close to the Squad Leader. As Kuhl was adjusting his gear the word came over the radio that they would be moving out in five minutes.

"What's the scoop, Mick?" asked Kuhl.

"We'll be moving' about 4 clicks to within about 500 meters of the river. There, we'll set up a battalion perimeter again." responded the Squad Leader.

Holtzman had already outlined the entire plan to Tracey. This abbreviated plan was all that the men needed to know till this evening. Then they would be briefed as to their individual assignments for the night and morning.

The Squad Leader stood and stretched, then swung his rucksack onto his shoulders. He picked up his weapon, while Kuhl and O'Meara followed suit.

"Trace…you go to the rear and saddle up Boone and his team. I'll head up front and get the rest of 'em on the road. We'll meet in the middle after we're movin'." ordered Mick as he walked off with Kuhl on his heels.

"Saddle Up!" the Corporal shouted as he approached Leroy Wright's Second Fire Team. Wright, the Second Team Leader, carried an M-14. Leroy had fired Expert when he qualified in boot camp and was proud of his marksmanship. Mick considered him his token sniper and wondered if his marksmanship had been honed to a razor edge in the black gangs he'd belonged to in Chicago, before he was drafted.

It was stifling hot, the battalion moved slowly with many starts and stops. There was no contact with the enemy. By 1400 hours Holtzman could see the heavy tree line that indicated that the river was close…about five hundred meters away. First Squad was on point so Mick called a halt, estimating that they had covered the four thousand meters. He had Kuhl radio the Captain that they were approaching the objective. The word came back as the Squad Leader had expected, to find a place to set up for the night.

Mick found an elevated spot that appeared large enough to hold the battalion. Here Holtzman halted the squad letting the company and the battalion loop in behind, forming a somewhat oval perimeter.

After the lines were established, Mick moved among his squad, showing each team where to dig in and pointing out their fields of fire. During this period he also checked to see that the men were moving OK. He examined them visually for signs of sickness or disease. He asked if they had spare socks and if they'd changed them lately. The last question often brought a response such as "Yes Mommy".

Holtzman smiled his tight little smile, *"Yes,"* he thought, *"I am the mother hen of First Squad and these twelve men are my brood."*

The Squad Leader worried incessantly about his men. Yes, it was true that they came and went, some wounded, others sick with malaria, some KIA, but their life, health, and conduct were his responsibility both in and out of combat. It was this responsibility that filled some sort of paternal need, some empty space within.

The young Corporal remembered an incident several months previous. They had only been out three days when, during a rest stop, Boone had come up to Mick and told him he had better look at Dago's feet. Dago was a lovable, tall, ungainly Italian from the Bronx and had been in country about six months. He was six feet four inches tall and about 140 pounds. He'd been losing weight since his arrival. When the Corporal had Dago take off his boot, some of the toes were purple, his big toe was ulcerated and oozing. The bone was visible and the jungle rot was evident up both legs.

"Damn it, Dago!" Mick cursed, "Why didn't you tell me you were all fucked up."

"Honest Mick, it wasn't that bad yesterday! They were just gook sores, ya know." came the reply.

Dago was put on a medevac chopper, never to be seen again. Holtzman cursed himself, *"If Dago walks with a limp the rest of his life, the blame is on me."* he thought.

The Squad Leader was now a fanatic about hygiene, socks and foot powder. Some of the men thought he was a fanatic about everything but they looked up to and respected him for it. The men knew that their Squad Leader was looking after their welfare when they were too tired to care, too mentally and emotionally drained to give a shit. Their mother hen was always looking after the brood.

At 1600 hours Mick heard the radio order an officer's call to the Battalion CP, *"Now the bird can get the word,"* he thought *"then the bird can give me the word."* Holtzman had a hard time taking his new Platoon Commander seriously. The first time that Lieutenant Byrd went to the bush, they had set up for the night in a position similar to the one this evening. They were receiving sporadic inaccurate sniper fire which most of the Marines were ignoring. Lincoln decided to come chat with Mick and Tracey and as he walked past the new Lieutenant's position, he found him buried in the bottom of his fighting hole, under his Helmet and flak jacket. The Prez stopped and then commented,

"Did y'all drop your watch down there, Lieutenant?"

Byrd did not answer him but the story was told and retold. In a warrior's society this wasn't the kind of story that would add to an officer's reputation or boost his leadership skills.

At 1725 hours the radio called all Squad Leaders to the Platoon CP. There, Lieutenant Byrd briefed them on the plans that Mick had heard that morning. It was as Lt. Colonel Smith had explained. In the middle of the night Echo, Fox, and Golf Companies would move out to occupy their positions in preparation for tomorrow's attack. Hotel Company would spread out occupying many of the positions left by the other Marines, giving the impression that the entire battalion was still there. In the morning they would pull out, making enough noise to simulate an entire battalion. They would move slowly to the river where 1st Squad would work on setting up a rope to help with the ford. While Mick was doing his rope trick, First and Third Platoons would be digging in along the river bank out of sight in the tree line. When Echo Company gained the top of the ridge, First Squad would get out of the river "post haste" and join the rest of Second Platoon behind First and

Third Platoon and be a reserve and reaction force.

After the Squad Leader's briefing, Corporal Holtzman returned to his squad and briefed, in turn, each fire team. Mick didn't just tell them their part of the attack but gave them the whole plan. He felt they would operate much more effectively if they understood why they were doing what they did. He demonstrated on the map where the enemy was…where they were…how the assault by Echo Company would go until he was sure each man had a complete grasp of what was about to happen.

"Better get some Chow." O'Meara told Mick when he returned from briefing the men."You ain't had nothin' but cigs and coffee all day."

"Yeah…Yeah, I know. I'm a bad boy Daddy O'Meara." Holtzman replied, as he rummaged around in his rucksack looking for rations.

"Better try to get some Z's Trace, at 0200 we'll be movin'…spreadin' out into two man positions for the rest of the night."

With a can of beans and franks heating over the heat tab, Mick leaned back against his rucksack smoking. He pulled out some bug dope and put it on his ears. He didn't really care if the mosquitoes bit him, but he didn't want them keeping him awake buzzing around his ears all night.

"Hey Trace, did ya ever notice the bugs here. I think they're union," mused Holtzman.

"Say what?"

"You know…the mosquitoes, ants and the flies…they got a union deal." the Squad Leader continued, "The mosquitoes got the night to themselves…the ants and the flies, they share the days but stay on their own turf, it's a union deal sure as shit!"

"Hey Mick…how much more time you got left on your tour?" O'Meara asked seriously.

"I'm over half way…maybe five months left."

"You don't count?"

"Hell no…bad luck!"

"What are ya gonna do when you get back to the world?"

"Drink beer and screw babes!" Holtzman added glibly.

"Yeah...yeah, aren't we all...no, I mean you gonna stay in the Corps? Be a lifer or what?" O'Meara pumped his buddy still serious.

Mick looked over at his friend, smiled that characteristic tight smile and in a serious vein said, "I don't really know Trace. This is the only thing I've ever done really well. I didn't do so good in high school. It wasn't that I didn't have the G2...I just was in a lot of trouble...fightin' you know...stupid shit. Since I joined the corps it seems to be a fit. I don't know man, I guess I gotta finish the tour first."

Of the laws of physics, all remain in place except for time. In Vietnam time was no longer a physical constant. Back in the World a day was twenty four hours long. In the Nam a day could be a week, a year or a lifetime and it could pass in a second. Time seemed to stand still and travel at mach one...all in the same moment.

"Time,
Is on my side,
Oh yes it is.
Time,
Is on my side."

The words of the popular Rolling Stone's song proclaimed, but for the grunts in Vietnam time was your enemy until you stepped aboard that Freedom Bird back to the World. A world that would be as strange and foreign to them as Vietnam had been on their arrival.

A firefight might age a youthful Marine a week in ten minutes. A night action, like the Alamo, could add ten years to a man's age. Holding your buddy while he breathes his last, staring into his eyes and telling him he'll be OK, ages a boy a lifetime. "It don't mean nothin!" was what a grunt said when his buddy died. Perhaps the number of times this phrase had passed his lips signified his age rather than the number of days since his birth.

CHAPTER ELEVEN
The Song Lai River

At 0200 Fox, Golf, and Echo moved off quietly on their individual assignments under the cover of a light rain. This left Hotel Company, part of Weapons Company and the Battalion CP group behind. The remaining soldiers split into two man teams and spread out to take over most of the positions vacated by the three infantry companies.

Corporal Holtzman and Grenadier O'Meara made sure that First Squad accomplished their moves quietly and efficiently. As Mick moved along his section of perimeter he stopped at each position to give each pair a little pep talk. Team Leader, Joe Sokouski, had teamed up with PFC Clarence who had arrived in Vietnam only a week earlier.

"Hey, Ski, Clarence, how goes it?" Mick asked as he sat down by the edge of the fighting hole the two would share till morning.

"Were getting situated." said Joe, "I was just tellin' Clarence here, that after a while you can recognize most enemy weapons by their sound."

Corporal Holtzman realized that his Team Leader was trying to make conversation to calm the new mans tensions.

"That's affirmative," replied the Squad Leader, "The AK-47 has a very distinctive cracking sound when fired at you. After you hear it once you'll never forget it. The SKS has a softer sound. Their 61 or 82mm mortars sound different or the same dependin' on whether they're usin' their ammo or ours. All 50 Caliber machine guns sound the same to me and once you hear that thump, thump, thump, staccato beat you'll know it. Our forces don't carry heavy machine guns in the bush, so if you hear one out here you'll know who it belongs to."

"What do you mean about the gooks using our ammo or theirs?" inquired Clarence.

"Well, sometimes grunts get tired and shit-can the mortar round they're carryin'. Or an ARVN unit gets over run and the NVA gets their mortar ammo. Because their mortar tubes are 61mm and 82mm, our ammo will work in their tubes with only a little loss of accuracy. Whereas we can't use 82mm rounds in our 80mm tube…won't fit. Pretty smart eh?" explained Mick, "Never underestimate the enemy…these people have been at war for over 50 years…they know how to play the game."

Holtzman continued to move from one position to the next until he was sure that the men were settled in for the remainder of the night. In the morning the "shit was going to hit the fan".

The steady drizzle was slowing as the cinder-black of night muted into the dull grays and browns of early morning. As usual, the Squad Leader was on watch at this time.

O'Meara sat up for no apparent reason and without a yawn said, "How bad do you think this one's goin to be?"

"Shit!...I ain't got no crystal ball!" replied Mick, then thoughtfully added, "It's set up pretty good. Echo will be assaulting from the east downhill and blow into and through those heavy weapons positions near the bottom of that ridge. I think Golf and Fox are gonna get hit hard when the gooks try runnin' to the west where they're dug in."

"Should we chow down?" asked Tracey changing the subject.

"Yeah…eat drink and be merry." the Squad Leader didn't finish the saying. "Remember we are supposed to make as much noise as a battalion."

Mick put on his flak jacket, picked up his M-16 and headed off to get everybody eating and making noise. The idea was to buy more time for Echo to go up the backside of the ridge. During the night radio watch, Mick had monitored the progress of the operation. Golf and Fox had reached their objectives and were digging in. Just moments before dawn, Echo reported that they were in position on the backside of the ridge. It would take them an hour and a half to two hours to climb to the top.

The word was passed that in thirty minutes they would saddle up and move out. They would travel slowly and make a lot of noise. Corporal Holtzman guessed it would take about forty minutes to get to the river so that was an hour and ten minutes of the two hours needed by Echo Company.

"I guess I get to go play in the water for twenty or forty minutes." he thought to himself. He had decided earlier that he and Sokouski would do the rope trick in the river. On an earlier operation, he had noted that Joe was a strong swimmer. When he told Joe of his plans, he just smiled and said.

"Well, hell's bells...I need a bath anyhow!"

As the column approached the river they were right on schedule, still needing to buy twenty to fifty minutes for Echo's climb. Mick pushed his way through the tree line and stood looking at the Song Lai River. The river was about eighty feet across...dark brown in color, with a slow and powerful current.

"Do ya suppose there's leaches in there?" asked Boone.

"Shit!...Tell me a river in Nam that don't have leaches." contended O'Meara. "I'm going over there with you." the grenadier said to Mick.

"Like hell! You're staying over here to cover me and Ski with that blooper so we can get back. Now, get these men moving around in the cover of this tree line. Make it look like there's a whole shitload of us millin' around here," ordered the Squad Leader as he coiled the rope given him by the combat engineer last evening.

Mick found a stout tree on his side of the river and tied the rope to it using a bowline. He then put the coiled rope cross ways over his shoulder like a bandoleer. He and Ski moved into the fast moving coffee colored water.

"Nice and slow Ski...keep an interval of about 25 feet and a little upstream of me," Holtzman said with a steady voice. "I may step in a hole and you'll have to come rescue my ass," indicating a ploy that the Corporal might use to eat up more time.

Ski looked over at Mick with a grin...his blonde, almost white hair showing under his helmet. Sokouski was powerfully built, with strong shoulders and thick muscular legs. He had an easy going disposition and was very popular with the men. It was Holtzman's guess that when he and Tracey were gone, Ski would get First Squad.

"We've eaten up twenty out of the fifty minutes and we're only half way across." thought Mick. He looked back over his shoulder every few minutes. When Echo Company was in position, O'Meara was to whistle and hold a closed fist up in the air. The Corporal decided not to fall in the hole on the way across. He estimated that by the time he reached the far side of the river and had secured the rope there, they'd have used up thirty or forty minutes. He could always fall in the hole on the way back…besides with the rope attached on both sides they could really haul ass on their retreat out of the river.

Mick could feel the leeches attaching themselves to his body as he waded shoulder deep through the current. He played out the rope with one hand while holding his weapon above his head with the other. He was in no position to defend himself…a sitting duck for anyone on the other side of the river. Time seemed to creep by. The water was now up to his neck, the current pulling him downstream. Escape, defense, any rapid movement would be impossible.

"I wonder how many gooks got a bead on me right now?" Holtzman thought. This caused the hair to stand up on the back of his neck as he waded out onto the far bank of the river. Ski remained in the water about waist deep, slightly upstream covering Mick. The Squad Leader found his tree and secured the rope. He looked back across the river hoping to see the signal, but to no avail.

"OK Ski…you lead off going back…when you see that hand signal, pick up the pace. I've enjoyed about as much of this as I can stand."

Ski nodded back, his clean handsome features set in a serious expression. Only eighty feet to their side of the river…eighty feet to relative safety, but eighty feet could be ten miles in the Song Lai River.

They moved off through the river, each with a hand on

the rope and their rifle in the other. When they reached the halfway point Mick heard a piercing whistle and saw Tracey standing in full view with his fist straight up in the air. Both he and Joe picked up the pace, pulling on the rope with their free arm and driving with their legs.

"God, I hope were out of this damn river before Echo starts firin'!" thought Holtzman.

The two Marines pushed hard, their breaths coming in ragged gasps. Speed was impossible in the shoulder deep water. It was like a bad dream…running in deep sand, your legs moving in slow motion…a nightmare. Finally they picked up speed as the water became shallower. Now the bank was only fifteen feet away.

They made their way up the friendly bank and past O'Meara to the positions in the tree line manned by First and Third Platoons. The three Marines then bolted behind the tree line to where Second Platoon was dug in as reaction and reinforcement element.

Both men immediately pulled their shirts off, lit a smoke, and started burning the leaches off each other's backs and body.

CHAPTER TWELVE
Echo Assaults

The point man for Echo Company stopped…frozen, unmoving for several minutes. He could see the gook sandal cut from the tread of a tire fifteen feet in front of him on the crest of the ridge. There appeared to be a foot with a leg attached, but the position was odd. He inched forward. Peering through the saw grass, he could make out the Communist soldier lying where he had died, his throat cut ear to ear. They would find another a half a mile to the south. The two North Vietnamese sentinels had died without uttering a sound, just at dawn's first light.

Echo Company regrouped when they reached the top of the ridge, moving from single file to a long skirmish line. The one hundred fifty men of Echo Company were spread out five to ten feet apart all along the ridge with their weapons pointed downhill.

Slowly and as quietly as possible, the company moved downhill on line. Occasionally, through the saw grass and brush, they would catch glimpses of the enemy below…dug in…waiting for the Marines to walk into the ambush they had set up.

As soon as the infantry began moving, the 60 millimeter mortar section began setting up on the top of the ridge. Several forward air artillery observers found positions along the ridge. From these observation points they could spot targets of opportunity in the valley below.

When Echo was about two hundred meters from the enemy's heavy weapon positions, a Vietnamese voice started yelling hysterically and the dance began.

Almost at the same instant, every man in Echo opened up. The cacophony of noise was incredible. Even more incredible was that the Marines didn't hear the deafening roar of the one hundred and fifty assault rifles and machine guns going off at the same instant. Somehow, adrenaline blocked the din from their conscious mind. After fifteen seconds or so there was a sudden break in the fire. Only the

M-60 machine guns and a few M-16s were heard. Then again, the din crescendoed. Each infantry Marine had opened fire on full automatic and all their magazines had emptied at the same instant, causing the two second long let-up as each man changed magazines. Then the firing began again.

The North Vietnamese troops were caught completely off guard. They had expected the Marines to walk into their ambush below, so their weapons were pointed in the wrong direction as the crushing attack from the rear swept closer. Many of the Communists just picked up and ran, leaving their crew-served weapons, machine guns and mortars behind. Others tried to get their weapons turned around to fight back, while some attempted a retreat to the west.

It was too late for the NVA. The men of Echo Company were now only fifty meters away...a solid wall of fire, orange tracer rounds turned the air around the Communist positions the color of flame. No man could stand against that onslaught. Those that didn't run...died. Echo assaulted through the enemy positions. The grunts had fixed their bayonets on the ridgeline and now used them to ensure that all the Communists were dead as they passed them by. Echo had the element of surprise and now, the North Vietnamese were down in the valley, caught in their own ambush kill zone.

CHAPTER THIRTEEN
Get Some!

When Ski and Mick crawled out of the river and back to Second Platoons position, Holtzman glanced around as Ski burned the leeches off his body. Morrillo had come over and was getting the leeches off Ski.

"Hey, Sarge, where's Prez and Second Squad?" asked Mick.

"Captain sent them over to reinforce Golf Company on the right flank, just across the river. Golf ran short of men there." answered the Platoon Sergeant.

Just then came Echo Company's opening volley.

"Well, shit damn! We're goin' to have a hot time in the old town tonight!" mumbled Holtzman.

"You ain't just a shittin'!" countered Hector Morrillo.

"Get some Echo!" yelled Ski.

"Get some motherfuckers!" yelled Boone.

The Vietnam grunts battle cry was picked up all along the blocking force's lines. The cry "Get Some Echo!" arose as the Marines of Hotel Company watched Echo assault through the enemy's ambush positions. To the grunts it meant, kill the enemy...kick ass and take names...go for it! Marines would holler, "Get some!" as they began a bar fight in a saloon or as they walked into a whore house. It was their mantra for any kind of action.

After Echo had assaulted through the enemies east flank, the company stopped and regrouped, staying on line and now occupying the high ground of the Communists old position. The automatic weapons and small arms fire had virtually ceased, making the silence that followed almost unbearable. The quiet quickly ended as 60mm mortars on the hill began hitting Communist targets easily visible below. The mortar explosions pounding the NVA were soon accompanied by 105 howitzer shells called in by the forward air artillery observers.

To his right Mick heard small arms fire beginning to crescendo, then the steady, staccato, thump, thump, thump, of a fifty caliber machine gun.

"That fuckin' fifty!" Mick thought.

The fifty caliber machine gun is an awesome agent of destruction. Fifty caliber bullets are one half inch in diameter and an inch and a half long. This is fired by the powder charge contained in the shell casing that is about four inches long. So the entire assembled round is approximately five to six inches long. The weapon is accurate to over a mile. One round can bring down a jet or go through both sides of an Amtrak. What the weapon does to a man is hideous. If it hits you in the hand, it will take off your arm. If it hits you in the body you are dust. This perhaps is the reason the NVA carry the weapon in the field. Marines fear the fifty cal and with good reason.

"Fox and Golf are in the shit now," commented Holtzman as a few rounds cracked over their heads.

"Yeah…be ready," instructed the Platoon Sergeant, "They're gonna try to break through over there."

"Where's the Lieutenant?" asked Mick.

Sergeant Morrillo smiled and pointed with his nose to the Lieutenant's position. If you looked real hard, you could just see the top of a helmet above the edge of the fighting hole. Under this helmet, one would assume you'd find Lieutenant Byrd.

Mick shook his head. Just then Kuhl's radio crackled and the voice of Second Squad's Radioman came on, "Hotel two, hotel two, this is two Baker…over. We're being hit hard, taking casualties. The Squad Leader is down…over."

Mick was already moving, *"Not the Prez!"* he thought, *"Shit man, it can't be the Prez."* Platoon Sergeant Morrillo gave Holtzman the hand signal to go as he talked back into the handset to Second Squad's Radioman.

"First Squad, follow me!" the Corporal bellowed as he took off on a dead run to the right in the direction of the increasing automatic weapons fire. Joe Sokouski was right on Mick's tail followed by his team. Boone with Third Team and Leroy Wright with Second Team were in the rear, trying to round up Kuhl who had to wrestle the handset from Morrillo.

Mick raced to his right, upstream past Hotel's position as a blocking force. At the last fighting hole, he could see the trampled grass where Lincoln's squad had crossed the river to reinforce Golf Company. Mick raced down the bank and back into the river. No thoughts of leeches crossed his mind, his friend Lincoln was hit and his squad was in trouble. He waded strongly into the current with Ski and the rest of the squad following. Holtzman was soon on the opposite bank. He climbed the brush covered bank and peered through the tree line, while the peculiar cracks of the Communist AK-47 assault rifle filled the air around him. Just in front of the tree line, only 20 meters away, was Second Squad where they had joined Golf Company, now under heavy attack. Most of Lincoln's squad was hunkered down behind what was probably an overgrown paddy dike. In the center, there was a mound where Mick could see several men, one was obviously the Prez...identifiable by his size. The NVA had a fifty caliber heavy machine gun about 100 meters in front of Second Squad. The big gun, well placed behind an even larger burial mound. The fifty cal. along with a company of NVA infantry, were blasting away at what remained of Lincoln's squad.

The rest of Mick's squad caught up and gathered to either side of him, behind the relative safety of the river bank. Squad Leader Holtzman quickly explained the situation to his men and described his rapidly formulated plan.

"Leroy...you and your team move up into the tree line to our left and give us coverin' fire. O'Meara, Kuhl, Tex, Wiley and the M-60 are with me. Were headin' for the burial mound where the Prez is. Ski...you take your team to the paddy dike just to the left of the mound. Boone...take your team to the paddy dike just to the right of the mound. When we get up there, Leroy, try to find cover on that rise behind Second Squad and us. You might be able to put that M-14 to use up there." Instructed Mick.

Leroy Wright led his three teammates into the trees.

Turning the selector of his M-14 to full auto and extending the bipods. Fired in this manner, the enemy would believe it was an M-60 machine gun. He found an earthen bank in the tree line that gave him cover and spread his men out behind it. On his order, he and Second Fire Team opened up on the enemy positions one hundred and fifty meters away.

Ten seconds after Wright's fire team began their covering fire, Corporal Holtzman, the gun team, O'Meara and Kuhl raced the twenty meters to the burial mound. Seconds later Joe Sokouski launched his team to the left of the mound and Boone Riley led his team to the right. The air was filled with tracer rounds both green and red. It could have been some crazy Christmas fireworks display if not for the continuous clamor of the automatic weapons and the periodic explosion of a grenade.

Mick dove…landing at the base of the burial mound followed by the others. They each crawled…curling around any depression, trying to make themselves small…looking for cover from the withering fire now being laid down at them. The gook fifty cal was tearing up the mound and the paddy dike beside it.

"Shit man! I don't need all this here attention! Things was nice and quiet here till y'all come!" drawled Lincoln.

"Hell!...they must have seen the M-60…they're concentrating all their fire on us!" grunted Holtzman, "Prez, Where you hit?"

"I took one in the right leg…don't think it broke the bone. Check Lopez first…he's hit hard." said Lincoln indicating the soldier lying to his right just below him.

The Corporal crawled over and examined Lopez then crawled back to his friend. He pulled out a battle dressing and applied it to the wound.

"Lopez is dead. Tex…you and your team dig a gun pit on the backside of this mound. We've got to gain fire superiority or we're all dead."

The fifty-caliber gun was still blasting away at them along with many AK-47s. Mick peered around the mound for a split second.

"There's a couple more burial mounds out in front to the left and right about 40 meters. If we could get coverin' fire from there, we might be able to get our machine gun goin." Mick yelled over the din to no one in particular.

Team Leader Sokouski had seen the twin burial mounds as he made the dash to his present position behind the paddy dike to Holtzman's left. As the heavy machine gun tore away at the burial mound, Ski bolted into the open. He had been a half back in high school, all-conference, all-state. Broken field running was his game. Joe ran left then cut back right. The big fifty followed him with the green tracer rounds clipping at his heels.

Behind the paddy dike on the right, Boone Riley exclaimed, "Ski! You crazy fucker, damn you!" Boone and Ski were tight. They had been friends since boot camp. Riley jumped to his feet, streaking for the second burial mound to the right of the one Ski was headed for.

The NVA gunner had been getting the range on Ski when long, tall, slower moving Riley appeared. The green tracers swung away from Sokouski towards Boone. Tex Jordon's gun team had their pit dug and the tripod set. Tex plunked the M-60 down into the ball and socket housing in the tripod, slammed the belted ammo in the machine guns receiver and began firing. The Communist gunner immediately realized his error and swung his big fifty back to the burial mound which was now raining deadly fire on his own position.

From his cover behind the Prez's mound, O'Meara set out a steady stream of fire from his grenade launcher. Boone and Ski, from their new positions were now able to get a cross fire on the enemy. The amount and accuracy of the enemy's AK-47 fire seemed to diminish. However if this was to be a machine gun dual the fifty would win. The three remaining men of Sokouski's team made a rush for Joe's mound. Only two made it...one man going down half way. Boone's team mates took off at the same time and arrived intact at the other mound. The cross fire against the enemy position was stronger now. The NVA 50 Cal. was still concentrating on Tex and his M-60.

Mick looked to his rear to see if Leroy and his fire team had made it to the small hill behind his present position. To his surprise he saw Platoon Sergeant Morrillo leading Rocketeer "Sleepy" Sommers and his B gunner onto the side of the hill. It was well known that "Sleepy" wasn't one for heroics...perhaps that was why the Platoon Sergeant had him by the collar. From the elevation of the hill, the three point five inch rocket launcher, a relative of the WW II bazooka could take out the enemy machine gun. They would have to get them with the first shot because Morrillo and rocket team are in the open.

"Sleepy" quickly assembled his launching tube. His B gunner loaded the three point five inch round, tapped "Sleepy" on the helmet and moved to the side to avoid the back blast. The Rocketeer took careful aim and fired. There was a "Whoosh" as fire belched from the rear of the launcher and the high explosive round soared...landing seemingly within inches of where the green tracer rounds had been emanating from. Just as the B gunner began to reload the tube a "whoosh" came from the opposite direction and an explosion knocked all three men flat. The Communists had fired a rocket-propelled grenade at the Platoon Sergeant's exposed position. "Sleepy" rolled over and retrieved his launcher. He looked at his B gunner who lay in an awkward position like a broken rag doll. Hector Morrillo had been blown ten feet up the hill. He dragged himself back down, his left leg covered with blood and useless behind him. Morrillo took the rockets from the lifeless man's pack and crawled to the launcher where he loaded the tube and patted Sleepy's helmet, signaling that the rocket launcher was loaded and once again ready to fire.

"Get Ready!" Mick called to the gun team. O'Meara and Kuhl...when that rocket fires again, were going to assault! I think they got the big gun."

Tex kept the M-60 roaring with ten to fifteen round bursts. O'Meara's M-79 sounded semi automatic. The grenade launcher made a steady bloop...bloop,...bloop, with the resounding explosions as the projectiles landed.

Then the rocket fired again. As the projectile exploded, the gun team, Mick, O'Meara, and Kuhl moved out on line shoulder to shoulder, firing into the enemy positions in front of them. As they came even with the other two fire teams, they left the cover of the twin burial mounds, moving on line with the rest. The eleven Marines were producing a devastating rate of fire. There was no response from the fifty…only AK's. The rocket fired from the hill a third time landing 30 meters to their front. They continued forward. Mick saw the fifty caliber machine gun then 15 feet in front of him. It lay on its side, a twisted hulk of scrap metal, the gun crew dead around it. "Sleepy" had made a direct hit with his first shot and damn close with the second. Tex Schultz made sure the gun team was dead with a few well directed bursts of M-60 fire. The remaining NVA now broke, heading south, away from the advancing Marines. Their attempt to break through the lines had been thwarted. As the enemy retreated the men stopped their assault, switched from full auto to semi automatic fire and were now taking aim at the retreating enemy soldiers…firing for accuracy.

"Hotel two, Hotel two, this two Alpha. We need a Corpsman. Two Alpha and two Baker have multiple casualties. Do you copy? Over." Mick yelled into the handset.

"Roger two Alpha, two Baker called for a Corpsman while you were busy taking out that fifty. Doc VD is over there now. The six wants you to bring your men back onto the defensive line as air strikes are on their way…over." Replied Boston.

"Roger Hotel two. We'll be back on the lines in five mikes. Alpha two out."

While Mick and his men headed back to Lincoln's original position, he wondered where Leroy Wright and his team were. The crack of that M-14 told him they were still in the tree line where he had originally sent them. He heard the fourteen crack again and a retreating enemy fell in his tracks 500 meters away. *"Shit!...ol' Leroy can shoot!"* the Squad Leader mused.

CHAPTER FOURTEEN
Valley of Death

Mick and the eleven Marines with him, moved rapidly back toward the original defensive lines that had been set up with Golf Company and Lincoln's Second Squad. Mick moved to his right and came up next to Ski," I saw one of your guys go down on the way to the mound." the Squad Leader said worriedly.

"Yeah, it was Clarence, the new guy. I'm going to check him out now...don't know if Doc found him." replied Ski.

"I'm with you!" said Holtzman as they walked through the waist high saw grass near where the young PFC had been hit.

They both spotted Clarence at the same instant. It was obvious that the Corpsman had found him as there was a medevac tag attached to his boot. Clarence was dead, with two AK-47 rounds through the chest. He had died instantly. The Corpsman had tagged him as a "Regular Routine" which is the lowest priority medevac. A Regular Routine means one more dead Marine.

"Shit!" was all Sokouski could manage.

"How many days had he been in country?" asked the Corporal in a quiet voice.

"I think ten days." Joe answered.

"Last night, I guess I forgot to tell him you won't hear the round that kills you." Mick responded softly.

"There it is...damn it...there it is!" Muttered Ski, using the colloquialism unique to the infantryman. "There it is" was used whenever a basic truism, or a profound statement, was voiced.

"Collect his personal gear and bring it over to my position after this is over. In the mean time, move his body over by Lopez's." Ordered Holtzman as he bent over and took one of the dog tags off the chain around Clarence's neck. Clarence hadn't been in country long enough to learn to lace his dog tags into his boots. The Marines wear their dog tags in their boots for several reasons. The shine of a metal tag around ones neck makes a nice bull's eye for an enemy sniper. The tags make no noise when separated and laced into the boots and they are unlikely to get lost when attached in this fashion. If a blood transfusion is necessary the Corpsman knows where to find them. If both legs are blown off you probably aren't in need of medical attention anyway.

The Squad Leader moved rapidly away from Clarence leaving Ski and the remainder of his team to tend to the move. He headed for the rise where he could see Corpsman Vince Dogherty, also known as Doc VD, working on his friend, Platoon Sergeant Hector Morrillo.

"Hey Boone," Mick yelled as he passed, "Everybody in your team OK?"

"Yeah, we're all right. Johnson's got a scratch, but he's OK." came the reply.

"Make sure Doc looks at it when things are quieter." The Corporal ordered, his long legs rapidly taking him to the small group on the knoll.

"Sleepy" Sommers, the rocket man, had set down his rocket launcher and was now holding a plasma bottle from which a long thin plastic tube ran to the needle in Morrillo's arm. Doc was bent over working on the multiple wounds that the Platoon Sergeant had sustained from the RPG.

"Hey, Sarge, looks like you got some R&R coming!" said Holtzman forcing a smile for his old friend. "When you're in Subic Bay, with a couple of those Filipino chicks sittin' on your lap and a bottle of San Miguel Beer in front of you, think of your old buddy Mick, stuck back in this hell hole."

The Squad Leader had observed the Corpsman giving Morrillo a morphine injection as he approached. As the Sergeant responded he noted that particular, far away, "morphine high" look in his friends eyes.

"Yeah...I was lookin' forward to catchin' some R&R, but I wasn't figurin' to get it this way. How bad am I Mick?" Morrillo asked, suddenly serious. Doc VD had finished his work a few seconds earlier. He had looked at Mick and tapped the field expedient tourniquet he had applied to the Sergeant's injured leg. He had nodded to the Corporal and moved on to treat the next wounded Marine.

"Oh, you're gonna be fine buddy. Doc's got you wrapped up like a Christmas present. You'll be drinkin' beer and chasin' nurses in no time." Mick lied. Holtzman had seen enough to know that if Morrillo's leg could be saved it would be a long time before he was walking. The Squad Leader checked his watch. He would need to loosen the tourniquet in a few minutes.

"Yeah, chickies and beer...hey, Mick, come visit me, we'll have a few brews together." Insisted the chunky Hispanic through the morphine haze that was settling over him.

"Hell, you bet, buddy! We'll punch down a shitload of brew and chase them girlies till they're ready to be caught." The Corporal continued while motioning to the litter bearers coming to take the wounded Sergeant to the LZ for evacuation.

With Hector suspended on a poncho between them, the four litter bearers lifted the wounded Sergeant. Mick reached down and touched his friend's hand, Their eyes met. Morrillo was grinning through the morphine. Mick looked away quickly hoping that his comrade couldn't read his thoughts. He watched for a few moments as the group moved toward the landing zone, wondering if he would ever see his friend again.

Squad Leader Holtzman assessed his casualties and situation. Clarence was dead. Johnson had a shrapnel wound to the arm that had been dressed. Wright's team had taken no casualties in their position in the tree line. Leroy had explained to Mick that when he was about to change positions, the Platoon Sergeant had come by with the rocket team and ordered him to remain where he was and provide a base of fire.

Holtzman had his men reinforce Lincoln's positions, and dig two new ones. The Prez's Second Squad had two KIA, and three wounded in action. Mick moved to the mound where Lincoln was.

"Prez, how's it hangin' bud?" he asked the big Texan. "Must a been a big day for the Lone Star State…you and the Sarge gettin R&R the same day."

"I don't think I'll get no R&R out of this!" responded Lincoln pointing at his leg. "That round just cut a big ol' groove and hole in the meat. They'll probably have me back here in a month. How's the Sarge?"

Mick shrugged noncommittally.

"Will he lose the leg?" asked the Prez.

Mick shrugged again.

"That bad huh." concluded Lincoln, reading between the lines of his friends silence, "That sucks, the Sarge probably saved all our asses with that rocket team."

"Yeah," said Mick "I'll come looking' for you when we get back aboard ship. If they send you any further than that you bring some liquor back with you." The conversation ended as the litter bearers picked up Lincoln and started for the LZ.

During this period there had been occasional small arms fire from Echo Company's position up on the ridge and the positions of Fox and Golf companies. The valley's center was being pounded by Marine artillery and mortar fire, which now suddenly ended.

The silence caused the men to look up from whatever tasks they were working on and look at each other.

"Them Phantoms will be swoopin' in most rickie-tic." Proclaimed Boone, as the Squad Leader approached.

"Yeah, I wouldn't want to be the bad guys, cause it's going to get ugly out there. Have your men dig in deeper and reinforce their positions. They may try to come back this way to break out when those jets start poundin' 'em."

Just then two Phantom jets careened out of the sun, diving for the center of the valley. When the jets were about two hundred feet above the ground they pulled up at the same time and each released a pair of two hundred-fifty pound bombs. Seconds after the bullet shaped bombs were released the spring loaded fins appeared, carrying the bombs on a straight trajectory to the intended target. The jets had climbed several hundred feet and traveled a thousand meters forward when the four bombs exploded, shaking the earth and sending shrapnel flying in all directions. The first pair of jets was followed moments later by a second brace that deposited their bombs a few hundred meters south of the first strike.

Minutes later, the first pair of Phantoms were back over the target but not diving. Just coming over the target slow and low. The Phantoms were so slow and low that Mick could see the pilots white helmet with black visor as the plane roared by him, only 75 feet off the deck. As they approached the target, each jet loosed a cigar shaped projectile which traveled earthward end over end. When the twin projectiles landed, red flame and black smoked belched out, splashing over a one hundred foot area and burning everything within it. Napalm! Once again the Marines on the lines began yelling "Get Some! Get Some Phantom!"

The jets continued their attack with bombs, napalm, and their twenty-millimeter automatic cannons, moving a little further south with each strike. The enemy was on the run and taking a horrible beating as they ran south to get away from the artillery and air strikes that were funneling them into the steep-sided canyon that led out of the valley.

As suddenly as they had appeared, the Phantoms were gone. There was silence in the valley. Black, ugly, oily, smoke arose from where the napalm had landed. Most of the trees were blown down or stood at cockeyed angles from the impact of the bombs. The stench of the napalm and death prevailed over the scene. The silence lasted perhaps five minutes, finally broken by the sound of large shells passing overhead and the tremendous roar and blast as the naval gunfire pounded the canyon where the North Vietnamese were now concentrated. The Recon Team that had eliminated the two Communist sentinels on the ridge prior to Echo Companies assault, had moved to a position from which they could observe the canyon to the south.

After the artillery and jets had herded the remaining NVA soldiers into the canyon, the Recon Team called in the naval gunfire they had arranged four hours earlier. Now the canyon truly became the valley of death for the Communist forces.

CHAPTER FIFTEEN
Mr. Lonely

The roar of the high explosive shells exploding in the canyon at the end of the valley had ended before dusk. The eight inch shells from the ships on the South China Sea had pulverized the canyon for hours. Now, as the sun began to set, the scene in front of Mick and Tracey's position looked like something from prehistoric times. Smoke, rank and black, drifted over what had been the battlefield. Flames burned and glowed eerily in the growing dark where the napalm had started fires. Most of the trees and taller vegetation were blown down, broken, or stood at crazy angles due to the rain of destruction from the artillery and air strikes.

Mick sat in the fighting hole, propped up by his rucksack, sipping C-ration coffee, smoking a Lucky Strike and surveying the view to the south. O'Meara was laying flat, trying to read a well-worn western novel. He sat up and said, "I sure hope nobody ripped a chapter out of this book to use for shit paper!" Then on a more serious note, "What ya thinkin' about Mick?"

"Oh, just thinkin'. There ain't much glory in this. Perhaps some honor…but not much glory." answered the Corporal, " Just thinkin'…you know."

"Yeah, but we sure kicked ass today!" Tracey added.

"That's affirmative…couldn't have gone much better. Hotel took three KIA, Clarence, Lopez and one other. Golf and Fox had seven KIA and Echo a few wounded. I'll bet that not more than fifty of the four to five hundred enemy survived." mused Holtzman. "Tomorrow we'll sweep the valley, count the dead, take some wounded prisoners. Hopefully in a few days we'll be back aboard ship."

"If all operations went this way, we'd be goin' home mo-scoshy." O'Meara suggested.

"I don't think the politicians want us to finish this. Look what happened after Tet 68." Mick stated, "Sure, we took casualties, but the NVA were a damn professional and tough bunch before Tet. Afterwards, there wasn't anything but little boys and old men. We coulda finished it then. They were hurtin'! But…instead we back off for four or five months. They get a chance to lick their wounds and regroup. With all the troops we got here now, we coulda lined 'em up shoulder to shoulder across this narrow-ass little country, faced north and marched to Hanoi, blasting everything in our path."

The two soldiers heard music coming from the position to their immediate left.

Mick grinned and said, "Sounds like Boone got that transistor of his workin', should we go over and join the party?"

The nonsensical words to the popular tune filtered through the evening air.

> "Electrical banana,
> Is gonna be a sudden craze.
> Electrical banana,
> Is bound to be the very next phase.
> They call it mellow yellow….."

When Holtzman and O'Meara arrived at the adjacent position the music had stopped and the AFRVN announcer had moved into the news. As the Marines were exchanging greetings, the announcer said, "And today at the University of Wisconsin, students and police rioted with many protesters arrested and several police officers hospitalized."

"Hey Mick, ain't that where you're from?" Boone questioned.

"You related to them beat-nick protesters?" teased another.

"Hell…my brother was probably one of them!" Mick said, with a knowing grin.

The men didn't want to let their Squad Leader off the hook and kept up the ribbing about him being from "Hippie Heaven".

Corporal Holtzman was taking the ribbing with good

nature, but finally answered back. "Well...isn't that why we're here? So that someday the South Vietnamese could have the freedom to protest the actions of their government? It's a cinch the Communists won't allow it."

This seemed to put the topic to rest, and the men enjoyed the music, smokes, coffee, company and just having lived through another day.

"I'm a soul man!" screamed James Brown, and Wilson Picket "Boogaloo'ed down Broadway!" while each man's thoughts drifted to home...to the music, and to the loved ones still there.

"Lonely,
I'm Mr. Lonely,
I have nobody,
To call my own,
Lonely,
Yes, I'm Mr. Lonely...

This sixty's tune is probably an accurate description of how these men, not much more than boys, actually feel. When wounded in battle they don't cry out to the president, congress, the flag, or apple pie. While hurt or dying, the name that passes their lips is usually a woman's... a sweetheart or their mother. Few of these Marines are old enough to grow a beard or even need to shave, but they all love someone.

CHAPTER SIXTEEN
Back to the Ship

The next morning the Marines got on line and swept through the valley. As they found dead soldiers and weapons they stacked them like cordwood into different piles. As Mick had suspected, they would occasionally hear the cry "Chieu Hoi!"...Vietnamese for "I surrender." The prisoner was usually a seriously wounded North Vietnamese soldier. Although there were some with minimal wounds. There were others, uninjured, who had just seen enough. By the time they had swept through the valley, the Marines had tallied one-hundred eighty dead enemy troops, thirty five prisoners and many hundreds of weapons.

Next they swept into the canyon. There was a whitish haze still hanging in the air. The smell of cordite from the high explosive shells, and the stench of death was everywhere. The Marines had a hard time counting the dead here, as few whole bodies were left. Limbs and body parts were scattered all over the devastated terrain, mixed in with parts of trees, rocks and vegetation. Much of the debris was unrecognizable as to having ever been human. Just yesterday, the blood, goo, and grisly remains were living, breathing men. The Marines made their way through the canyon of death, grim faced, finding no joy in this victory. Each man simply wanted to get away from this ghastly place as soon as possible. Thankfully orders came over the radio to move back into the valley to set up a perimeter and flag an LZ. They would be helo-lifted back to ship tomorrow.

In the morning the Marines packed their gear. At 10:00 hours the word came over the radio to move, the choppers were in the air and to throw red smoke when the choppers appeared. These would mark the landing zone as well as give the helicopter pilots the wind direction. Five minutes later the CH-46 helicopters came into view looking like a small swarm of giant green locusts. Their ungainly, double rotor shape was a welcome site to the tired Marines below. The steady slap, slap, slap of the rotor blades was music to the grunt's collective ears. Each infantry company loaded by fire team, squad, and platoon. The Marines were whisked away by the helicopters to the ship, aboard which each unit was billeted. The USS Valley Forge, a remodeled WW II aircraft carrier is home to Fox, Golf, and Weapons Company as well as the Battalion Headquarters Group. The USS Duluth is home to Echo, and Hotel Companies. It had been a heavy cruiser in its previous life now the stern sported a flight deck. It also has modifications to allow amphibious vehicles to load and unload from the water line at the stern.

When the choppers landed, the Marines scuttled off the flight deck in a half crouch to avoid the helicopter's rotor blades. Then they climbed down ladderways to below decks, carrying their standard issue 782 combat gear with them. Mick and First Squad headed for the compartment that they called home while afloat. Each compartment is thirty feet long by fifteen feet wide. There are sleeping berths, similar to a cot, six feet long by thirty inches wide, stacked vertically, bunk bed style, six high. There's about eighteen or twenty inches of personal space between. The Marines threw their combat gear and weapons on the rack of their choice, keeping a semblance of squad and fire-team integrity. This compartment houses the enlisted and noncoms of Second Platoon. The officers and staff NCO's are billeted elsewhere.

As soon as the gear was stowed, the tired Marines headed for the showers. What a luxury for them! It was their first shower since leaving the ship weeks earlier. They reveled in the warm water with two to three Marines using each showerhead. One Marine stood in the main flow, another in the spray and perhaps a third standing clear, lathering his body with a bar of soap. The shower floor ran red with the brick colored dirt that had buried itself deep into every crack, seam, orifice and pore of the infantrymen's bodies. It would take many showers, over several days, to finally be rid of the red dust that permeated everything in the bush. Even when finally clean, if the grunts spit it would have a red tinge as the fine dust collected in their lungs during the dry season. During the monsoon the brick red dust was replaced with mud of the same color.

Squad Leader Holtzman usually took his shower in the last shift, as he had extra duties to perform while aboard ship. He had already made sure that each squad member threw his dirty jungle shirt, trousers, and olive-drab T-shirt into a labeled, squad laundry bag. Few infantrymen wore underwear as they chaffed and rotted in the field. Mick also realized that he would have to search out the company mail clerk and retrieve what mail was waiting for First Squad. As yet there was no replacement for the good-natured Platoon Sergeant Morrillo.

As the men returned from showering, they found clean clothing from their last visit aboard. It was stacked on the community table in the center of the compartment. Mick saw his chance and headed for the showers. He knew he wouldn't have long as the men would become anxious about their mail as soon as the showers were over. The Corporal showered quickly, while the others languished in the luxury of hot water, bull-shitting and joking in the sauna-like steam that had been created in the shower compartment.

On completion of his short, but sweet, shower, the Corporal headed back to the compartment and dressed in clean jungle shirt, trousers, olive drab T-shirt, and headed for the compartment that served as the company office. When Mick arrived he stepped in, looking around for the mail clerk. Not seeing him, he asked another enlisted man as to his where-a-bouts. He was informed that the mail clerk was running an errand. As Holtzman turned to leave, Gunnery Sergeant Shaw called out to him from the office he was sharing with the CO. "Corporal, step in here for a minute."

The Squad Leader stepped into the office and came to attention without thinking.

"At ease, Corporal." Gunny Shaw said, with a smile.

"Looking for your squad's mail?"

"Yes Top." Holtzman replied.

Acting First Sergeant Shaw threw a large bundle of letters bound with four thick brown rubber bands onto the desk.

"That's all of Second Platoon's mail. With Sergeant Morrillo gone, you are now acting Platoon Sergeant of Second Platoon."

"Affirmative," answered Mick, "and still First Squad Leader to boot I take it?"

"You've got the picture. Can you handle it?" asked the Company First Sergeant.

"You bet, Top."

"Good," replied Shaw "One other thing…rumor has it that you're on the Sergeant's list Holtzman. A nineteen year old Sergeant!" he said shaking his head. "Shee-it! I can't believe what this Corps is comin' to."

After a moment the Gunnery Sergeant went on, "What's your schedule tomorrow morning?"

"Well, Sir, if I am to assume all of Morrillo's duties, after chow, I'll have to lead the platoon in physical training on the flight deck at 0900." Mick asserted.

"Well make it a short PT. These men need rest more than anything. After the noon-meal today, take this chit down to supply. They'll issue you brand new jungle utilities, boots and an issue cover. Tomorrow at 10:30 hours be on the flight deck. You will catch a chopper ride over to the Valley Forge where you will report to First Sergeant Riker. He has some papers for you to fill out."

The Squad Leader looked confused.

"Don't worry about it, Corporal…just do it! Riker will explain everything to you when you arrive. Just be there on time and squared away. Gig lines straight, shave, haircut etc. Do you understand?" Shaw demanded.

"Yes Sir!"

"Now return to your duties, Platoon Sergeant." The Gunny finished.

Mick left the company office in a daze trying to absorb

everything that had just happened. As he walked along the passageway sorting the platoon's mail by squad, he wondered what the new shiny uniform and trip to the Valley Forge was all about. The Corporal had been planning to try to catch a ride over to the carrier in the next few days to visit Lincoln in the Battalion Aid Station and see what he could find out about Morrillo as well. This way he wouldn't have to beg or bribe somebody to get there and he was guaranteed a ride back.

When the Corporal, now acting Platoon Sergeant, got back to his compartment, he passed the mail out to each squad. He gave First Squad's to O'Meara, and he explained about his additional duties. Second Squad's he gave to A. J. Vasquez who was Lincoln's First Fire Team Leader and now acting Squad Leader. Mick had checked the mail to see if there was a letter from Lori but it was too soon. He had managed to get his reply out only two days ago.

CHAPTER SEVENTEEN
When a Man Loves A Woman

Joe Sokouski grew up at his family home just outside of Bessemer, Michigan, far north in that state's Upper Peninsula. Joe's dad, Tom, started the boy hunting at eight years of age and Joey took to it like a duck to water. Joe hunted everything. The deep forests, ponds, lakes and streams surrounding his home gave him ample opportunity to fine tune his skills. Most of all, Joe loved bird hunting. The native ruffed grouse and bobwhite quail were often found on the Sokouski's table. But it was the waterfowl that he hunted most. With Lake Superior to the north and Lake Michigan to the east, the Upper Peninsula was a magnet for ducks and geese.

Joe's father was a mechanic for one of the big timber companies that had fallen on hard times. He was trying to make ends meet by working at home on automobiles during the layoffs that the company was enduring. The family was grateful that young Joe was supplying much of the meat for their table.

In October 1964, Joe's fourteenth year, he brought home a brace of Canada Geese, and went to the garage to clean them. His dad, working on a neighbors car, stopped and helped Joe with the bird cleaning.

"Your pretty late tonight, Joey." Tom Sokouski observed.

"Yeah...I know. I'm sorry Dad but one of the geese I shot fell in the middle of Blue Lake. I had to wait an hour before the wind and waves pushed it close enough to shore for me to get it," young Joe responded.

"Hmmm, sounds like you need a dog." the older Sokouski commented. "You know Henry Ferguson? I fixed his pickup last week. He's got one of those big brown curly haired retrievers, what do ya call 'em?"

"Chesapeake." replied Joe.

"Yeah Chesapeake's, that's it. Well, the bitch whelped a couple of months ago. They think she was bred by the neighbor's lab. Maybe we should go over there after dinner and see if we can get a pup for you. What do you think?" asked Tom.

"Wow! Really? A dog for me! Boy, oh boy, that'd be great Dad!" Joey burst out.

After dinner Tom drove Joe over to Fergusons where they were met by Henry and his daughter Audrey. Audrey led them into the garage where, in a large cardboard box, the mother and her pups were nested. There were eight pups, ranging in color from black to light brown. Joe went to his knees at the box's edge staring at the pups. After a few minutes he carefully reached in and started petting a large brown, curly haired pup, which immediately licked his hand.

"I think he likes me Dad!" Joe squealed.

"He's my favorite." said Audrey. Audrey Ferguson was twelve, thin as a stick, with long auburn hair that she wore in pigtails.

"Well, I guess I better pick another." Joe said, sadly.

"No!" cried Audrey, "We can't keep any of the pups. If you take him, I can come and visit him now and then," she said with a smile.

"OK, I'll call him Curley…is that OK, Dad?" Joe asked looking to his father who was standing with Henry. The two men smiled as they watched their respective children.

"That will be fine son, and a good name for a hunting dog." the elder Sokouski responded.

Father and son took the pup and returned home. All that fall Joey continued his hunting but spent a great deal of time with Curley…the two were soon inseparable. True to her word Audrey came to the Sokouski home as often as she could to visit. She liked Curley but the dog was really an excuse to see and be with Joey, to whom she had lost her twelve year old heart.

Joe Sokouski liked Audrey and enjoyed the time they spent together in the woods with the dog, but he thought of her only as a skinny little girl. Two years in age made a lot of difference when you were fourteen.

That year Joe was playing freshman football at Bessemer High. He played so well that the coach told him he would probably start on varsity next year when he was a sophomore. Joey hurried home each night after football practice to go hunting with Curley. Despite his tight schedule, with Curley's help, he kept the table full.

In his sophomore year, true to the coach's predictions, Joe made the varsity team and started as halfback. His thick muscular build and powerful legs made him a natural. Despite the time spent on football and the popularity that his play had gained him, Joe continued to hunt almost every evening with Curley, occasionally accompanied by Audrey.

The great North Woods that surrounded Bessemer was a playground for Joe and Curley. The boy and dog hunted when the seasons allowed, or fished and did odd jobs to help with family finances. Life for Joe Sokouski was simple, and he was enjoying the things he loved to do.

When Joe started his junior year in high school, life became more complicated. Bessemer High played Ironwood in their first preseason game. Ironwood was just thirty miles west of Bessemer but a much larger town. Their football team was in a different league. Bessemer wasn't expected to do well. The first half of the game went as predicted with Ironwood scoring three touchdowns. Joe had managed to break loose and score once, but as the second half began the score was twenty-one to seven in favor of Ironwood.

Bessemer received on the kickoff and Joe managed to get the ball out to the thirty-yard line. In the huddle the play was called, a hand off to Sokouski up the right sideline.

"Give me some blocking you guys and maybe we can keep from getting creamed!" begged the young halfback.

Joe got the ball and punched through a hole created by the right guard. Following his fullback, who threw a cross body block on a defender, Joe was on his way. Sokouski crossed the thirty-five to the forty, then the fifty! It looked like he was going all the way. But then a defender streaked in, catching Joe from behind. They went down in a pile in front of Ironwood's bench.

When Joe was tackled he held the football tight to his midsection when he hit the ground. With the defender on his back, the ball was pushed up into his solar plexus and it was lights out. Instinctively, although unconscious, Sokouski held tightly onto the ball.

When Joe regained consciousness, he was looking at an angel. Looking down at him, only inches away was an oval face framed with blonde hair that set off the emerald green eyes. The face belonged to one of Ironwood's cheerleaders, Roseanne Antoni. She seemed genuinely worried.

"Are you all right!" Roseanne asked with some concern. She had not seen a person knocked unconscious before.

Joe tried to respond, but all that came out was a croaking noise.

"What?" asked Roseanne.

"You're beautiful!" the halfback managed to gasp.

"What?" urged Roseanne, confused.

"You're beautiful!" repeated Joe as the trainer for Bessemer arrived and started examining the injured halfback. This ended the interlude between the two.

The game ended with Ironwood winning by a score of twenty-eight to fourteen. Joe had scored a touchdown three plays after the incident near Ironwood's bench. After he had showered, Joe rushed out to find the bus that would take Ironwood's team back to their high school. He waited here and intercepted Roseanne as she came out.

"Hi, I'm Joe Sokouski, what's yours?" he stammered.

"Roseanne Antoni, is mine." she said with a smile that turned the halfback's knees weak.

"Can I call you?" Joe asked.

"Sure if you have my number," Roseanne responded confidently. She gave him the phone number which he quickly wrote down. Roseanne got on the bus and chose a seat on the side near Joe. The two's eyes stayed riveted till Sokouski, feeling self conscious, tore himself away.

Joe called her that week and they had their first date the next Saturday. By the end of football season they were officially going with each other. Roseanne loved to wear Joe's letter jacket to school. It was covered with awards for football as well as letters for wrestling and swimming. She was a sophomore and liked having a football hero boyfriend from another school.

Joe Sokouski's simple existence had come to an end. He had never had a girl friend before, nor been in love. Joe fell head over heels now, totally consumed, infatuated with Roseanne.

The following summer saw the couple together three or four days a week. Curley languished, left alone often to guard the house and chase the cats while his master was off with his girlfriend. Joe lived for the hot, steamy, humid nights when after a movie, the pair would park in a secluded spot and neck. Roseanne had a great body with ample breasts and a heart shaped derriere. Joe was crazy for her and loved everything about her, but as of yet they had not gone all the way.

When Joe began his senior year, the pair were still an item. Ski was voted "All Conference" for the second year in a row and received "All State" recognition as well. This could have propelled him into an athletic scholarship, but Sokouski wasn't really interested in college. He was an average student generally receiving C's and B's. Joe had decided to follow his father's steps and join the Marines after high school. Tom Sokouski had served in Korea where he had been awarded the Purple Heart for wounds received in combat.

With graduation approaching, Joe had some decisions to make. He knew he was going to enlist, but what about Roseanne? Ski decided to put off joining up until winter. That wasn't a problem as he wouldn't turn eighteen till December anyway. If he followed this time schedule he would get his leave about the time of Roseanne's senior prom. Joe Sokouski had a plan.

The war in Vietnam was heating up in mid January as Joe got ready for his last Saturday night date with Roseanne. On Sunday, both families would have dinner together after church. On Monday, Joe was to report to the induction center and from there to the Marine Corps Recruit Depot at Parris Island. Earlier that month the Communists had launched their Tet Offensive. One could sense a different attitude towards the conflict among the members of the press.

Joe picked up Roseanne in his dad's car and told her family that they were going to dinner at Francie's, then to a movie. Francie's was an Italian-American restaurant run by a friend of the Antonis. When they arrived, the owner led them to a booth by itself in the back of the restaurant and returned in a few minutes to take their order. Roseanne ordered linguini and clam sauce. Ski smiled at the owner and said,

"You have the best steaks in town...I'd like the filet mignon and a bottle of chardonnay."

The owners head rose. He knew very well that neither of the young people in front of him were of legal age. He also knew the situation and without a word, took the order and left.

"Do you think he'll really serve us?" whispered Roseanne.

Joe moved closer and said into her ear, "Nothing ventured, nothing gained."

Their appetizers appeared in a few moments and shortly after that the owner brought them a bottle of chardonnay which he opened and setting the cork near Joey, he poured a small quantity into his glass. Ski sampled it and said, "That will be fine."

When the owner had gone Roseanne could barely control herself. Laughing, she mimicked, "That will be fine." Still laughing, she continued, "Do you even know what chardonnay is supposed to taste like?"

Joe, laughing along with her replied, "No, but after tonight I will."

The couple enjoyed their meal laughing and giggling like the school kids they were...with the help of the unfamiliar chardonnay. When they finished, Ski paid the bill leaving a generous tip. The only movie playing in town that night was *Dr. Zhivago* and the pair had seen it several months before so they drove around for a while and not too surprisingly, ended up at one of their secret spots.

It was cold outside but warm and cozy in the Sokouski's family car, a 1957 Chevy. When Joe set the parking brake, he slid out from behind the wheel and Roseanne moved down the seat in his direction. They had done this many times over the last year. Soon their arms were wrapped around each other. They began kissing with their tongues darting in and out of each other's mouth, searching, probing. Their passion mounted, the tongues were now writhing like snakes doing some kind of ritualistic dance. They breathed in rapid little gasps. Ski moved his hand up and fondled Roseanne's breast, squeezing gently. Roseanne let out a gasp of pleasure. Joe's hand moved under her sweater, cupping the breast now covered only by her bra. Their tongues were still lashing in each other's mouth. Joey embraced her passionately, letting his hand travel behind her back where, with a minimum of difficulty, he undid the bra's fastener. Now he caressed her bare breast…his hand feeling her nipple harden and become erect under his fingers. Roseanne moaned.

Usually this was where Roseanne said no. Ski knew she really didn't mean it but it was normally where the end began. It was up to him to see how much further they could push it. Tonight there was not a no, but a moan of delight. Perhaps tonight was the night.

Joe pushed the sweater up exposing both of Roseanne's breasts. They were large, well shaped, with nipples that were the pinkest of pink. His lips caressed them. She cried out in pleasure. Roseanne pulled the sweater over her head, and they again embraced, kissing tongues dancing in each other's mouth…breathing as if they had both run a marathon. Joe's lips were quickly back nibbling on Roseanne's breasts…her nipples hard. Then he began kissing her hard, flat stomach while his hand roamed under her skirt, stroking her inner thigh.

Ski slipped his hand inside Roseanne's panties, feeling the damp warmth there. Massaging gently, his lips moved back to her breasts. Still she hadn't tried to stop him or say no. With a sudden chill of fear and excitement he realized they were going to go all the way.

What if he bungled it? He pushed the thought away and his hand continued its exploration.

Joe was caught off guard as Roseanne's hand rubbed against his crotch. Her hand found him and massaged his erect organ. Ski new that he couldn't take much of this and that things were going to have to move along quickly. He pulled the panties downward. As the panties slid downward Roseanne stepped one foot out of them as she undid Joey's zipper. His jeans slid to the car floor to join her panties.

Joe moved awkwardly over Roseanne. Fear gripped him because he was unsure what to do. Roseanne took charge of the situation. She gripped him and guided him into her. He felt her sensuous warmth, the slick wetness. He pushed tentatively and she responded…sobbing in ecstasy. Instantly a euphoric rhythm was established. Ski managed about five strokes before he exploded but he did not lose his erection and they kept up the tortuous thrashing until Roseanne's sobbing crescendoed into a wail and she went limp.

"*So this is what it's like,*" Ski thought, "*It's even better than I imagined.*" They lay together on the car seat virtually naked. Her skirt was pushed up and wrapped around her waist and his underpants hanging from one ankle. The warmth of their bodies and the recent activities steamed the Chevy's windows beyond visibility. They lay that way, gently stroking and kissing each other, for twenty minutes, then they quickly dressed.

Joe turned the Chevy's engine on to keep the car warm. They cuddled as they listened to the radio. Ski kept trying to push away an unwelcome thought about their love making. He quickly banished the errant thought, believing that women just instinctively knew about such things. They held each other and Percy Sledge crooned,

"When a man loves a woman,
Can't keep his mind on nothin else,
He'll trade the world for the good thing he's found.
If she's bad he can't see it,
She can do no wrong,
Turn his back on his best friend if he put her down
When a man loves a woman."

CHAPTER EIGHTEEN
Enlisted Candidates Program

Mick took the platoon to lunch at 12:00 hours. The sailors aboard the USS Duluth are always amazed at how the infantry Marines eat. They consumed the food at a rate and quantity that was incredible, often returning to the chow line for seconds within five minutes. The Navy food is good. There's often fresh fruit and vegetables and there's always meat and potatoes with every meal. The Marines wolf down this fresh food after weeks of eating canned C-rations.

Holtzman ate quickly then headed to the ship's barber shop. As he entered the Navy barber asked, "What can I do for you?"

The Squad Leader sat in the chair and announced, "I need a high and tight." That was the description of the regulation Marine Corps haircut, where the sides were clipped almost to the skin and the top was left about a quarter of an inch long.

"You really want side walls?" the sailor asked, using another slang description. Most combat Marines grow their hair out, maybe an inch long, as there aren't many opportunities for haircuts and the officers and NCOs didn't enforce the regulation haircut in the bush.

"That's affirmative," Mick answered. And the barber went to work.

Ten minutes later Holtzman arrived at Supply and handed the chit that Gunny Shaw had given him to the Sergeant at the window. The Supply Sergeant nodded, left, and returned a few moments later with a new jungle utility jacket and trousers, each starched and pressed. On top of the jungle utilities the Sergeant placed a regulation Marine cover that had been starched, blocked and shaped. Mick stared in amazement, "What's the deal?" he asked incredulous.

"The Gunny guessed your size and had me starch and fit your cover." the Supply Sergeant divulged. "He made it worth my time."

The Corporal walked away with his new uniform issue, shaking his head. *"What the hell are they planning on doing to me tomorrow aboard the carrier?"* he thought.

When acting Platoon Sergeant Holtzman returned to the ship's compartment, Tracey, Boone, and Leroy Wright were playing Back Alley Bridge at the community table. Willie Parker, machine guns Squad Leader, had a huge transistor tape player blaring out soul music. The Corporal stopped and watched the card game for a while.

"Did ya hear the scuttlebutt, Mick?" O'Meara asked.

"No, what's up?"

"Lieutenants Byrd and Gregory are writing each other up for the Silver Star for the battle in the valley." Tracey went on.

"Ya gotta be shittin' me! Morrillo's the one who should be getting' a medal if anyone should! He probably saved all our asses takin' out that gook fifty." the Corporal spat.

"I didn't know they give the Silver Star for hidin' in your fightin' hole." Leroy commented.

"You just don't understand brother," responded Willie, who was thumbing through a Leatherneck Magazine published by the Marine Corps, "Now looka here!" Willie pointed to the list of Silver Star Medals awarded in the past month. Willie began reading the ranks on the list. "Captain, Lieutenant, Colonel, Captain, PFC, Major, Sergeant, Lieutenant, Major, Lance Corporal, Captain. Ya know there's a little asterisk thing next to the PFC and Sergeant's name. That means that those medals was awarded posthumously. The way I see it, you got to die to get a Silver Star unless you're an officer."

"Well…you can bet that neither of those two risked a hair on their head for anything," added Boone.

The next morning at 10:00 hours Corporal Holtzman climbed up to the flight deck to board the UH-34 helicopter that would carry him and four others from the USS Duluth to the USS Valley Forge. On the flight deck, Gunnery Sergeant Shaw was waiting. He nodded his approval of the junior non-com's appearance.

"Now you look the part," Shaw commented.

"What's goin' on Gunny?" asked Mick

"First Sergeant Riker will fill you in when you get to Battalion HQ," the Gunny retorted.

Corporal Holtzman stepped aboard the Korean War vintage UH-34 helicopter and away it went for the short trip over the South China Sea to the carrier. Mick surveyed the other passengers on board. Captain Weller was across from him. They nodded to each other over the rotor wash. Captain Engleton, the Commanding Officer of Echo Company and two Corpsmen were the other occupants.

"Must be an Officers gathering, or briefing." the acting Platoon Sergeant thought, *"The Corpsmen are probably going to the battalion aid station to pull duty there."* Navy Field Hospital Corpsmen did a twelve month tour of duty, generally doing six months in the bush with the Marines and the other six in the BAS working on the wounded Marines that would be medevacked in. During their "six in the sticks" their life expectancy in a fire fight was measured in seconds. NVA and VC were always on the lookout for the "Bac Si" or medic. They made an easy target while moving to treat the wounded.

The helicopter landed on the flight deck of the USS Valley Forge and the occupants disembarked, each heading for their respective destinations. Mick wasn't quite sure where the Battalion HQ was located so he stopped to ask directions. Upon arriving at headquarters compartment, he entered and told one of the enlisted clerks who he was and that he was to see First Sergeant Riker. *"Riker must have got promoted,"* The Corporal thought, *"last time I saw him he was wearing Gunny chevrons…must a got another rocker."*

A door in the back of the Headquarters Office compartment opened and First Sergeant Riker's grizzled features appeared. "Corporal Holtzman…step right in here."

Mick stepped into the small office. There was another

door that connected to Colonel Smith's office. To get to the Colonel, you had to get past the First Sergeant.

"Stand at ease Corporal." Riker said, "Are you interested in becoming an officer?"

Holtzman was caught totally off guard, "I hadn't really thought about it sir."

"Well, your Company Commander and the Colonel have. They've found a program called the Enlisted Candidates Program. If your selected, you will be sent to the Preparatory School for The Naval Academy," explained the first Sergeant.

"The Naval Academy! Sir, I uh, didn't have very good grades in high school," Mick blurted out.

"You scored high on all your Marine Corps Testing, you have the highest GCT score in the battalion." Riker said, peering down at the corporals service record book.

"I didn't know that sir." Mick replied still confused.

"We can probably get around your poor high school records, by using your decorations as camouflage." The grizzled top Sergeant went on, "Well! Do you want to be an officer or not?

"Yes, sir!"

"Well then, start signing and filling out all these damn forms. You and the Colonel are going to have me buried in paperwork up to my ass!" Riker growled.

As Mick sat in First Sergeant Riker's office filling out the many forms and requests for the Enlisted Candidates Program, the first Sergeant made small talk. "Well what's the latest scuttlebutt? Any good rumors floating around?"

Holtzman smiled and said, "Just heard a good one, Top. They say that Lieutenants Byrd and Gregory are writing each other up for the Silver Star from our last action."

The first Sergeants face darkened, "It's not a rumor, but I'm gonna do my best to make sure it don't happen." He declared, looking meaningfully at the door to the Colonel's office.

"I thought Morrillo should get something for taking out that fifty." Mick told the Top.

"There it is, Marine...there it is." grunted Riker.

With the paperwork finished, acting Platoon Sergeant Holtzman headed for the Battalion Aid Station where he found his friend Lincoln.

"Hey, Prez, how they hangin'?" Mick inquired.

"They be hangin' high, cuz you talkin' to one hung dude."

"How long will you be laid up?"

"I can't see more than a couple of weeks, but they be talkin' a month!"

"Hey brother, don't you be goin AWOL from this hospital...you earned your skate time." Holtzman added. "Can I bring you anything?"

"Yeah, get me some Kool's man. I know all you got are those chest buster Lucky's...I need a Kool to smoke."

"I'll run up to the PX and get you a carton." Mick replied, as he headed for the ships Commissary.

Mick encountered Corpsman Hanson, who had served with him in the bush. He questioned him as to what had happened to Sergeant Hector Morrillo. Doc Hanson told him that Morrillo was critical and had been sent to Guam, from where he would go to a hospital in Japan or the states when he was stable.

When the Corporal arrived at the tiny but well-supplied ships Commissary, he picked up his friend's cigarettes. Then found three magazines he thought the Prez would enjoy. Knowing Lincoln's vociferous appetite, he picked out a variety of goodies and sodas then headed back to the BAS ward. Holtzman spent the next two hours chatting with his friend, talking of old times both good and bad. When it was time for the chopper ride back to the Duluth, Mick promised Lincoln he would try to get back before the battalion took off on another operation.

As Holtzman turned to go, Lincoln spoke up, "Thanks Bro! I mean it, your numba one. Things have sure changed since we met, huh?"

"Yeah, I didn't know anything about black people but what I saw on TV, read in a book or heard from some know-it-all. All you knew about white people was the prejudice you had to endure most of your life. Maybe it takes an ugly little war for us to learn we all bleed the same. We fight to keep each other alive…not for the glory of the flag. Strip away our jungle shirt and our skin and were all brothers in the blood," replied Mick.

"There it is Bro…there it is!"

They signed with their fists, and Mick walked off.

On the flight back to the Duluth, Mick's head was spinning. The Enlisted Candidates Program, the Sergeant's list, the U.S. Naval Academy…all this opportunity so suddenly. Holtzman had not ever been sure what to do with himself. He hadn't performed well in high school as he just wasn't interested, nor was he disciplined. The Corps had given him discipline…perhaps he could use it to advance himself. He realized intuitively that this was what he had been created for. He didn't glory in the killing and violence of war, but when under pressure, he was at his best. In combat he excelled as he never had before. When this was over, where could he go? What could he do to equal the excitement and sense of fulfillment that he received here? *"Perhaps I've found my home."* Holtzman thought.

CHAPTER NINETEEN
Frenchy

On his return to the ship, Mick headed to Second Platoon's compartment where he changed out of the starched utilities into his older uniform. At the community table, a bunch of the men were having a rap session which they referred to as trippin'. They each told a story or experience from home trying to take each other back to the world they had left...and which now seemed so far away.

After carefully folding and stowing the starched uniform he had been issued the day before, Squad Leader Holtzman joined the group by the central table. Willie Parker and Leroy Wright had the tape player blaring Wilson Pickett, and they were dancing the bugaloo, the shing-a-ling, and the fly. Twisting and floating across the deck like enraptured cobras to their keepers flute. When the song was over they cut the music and it was someone else's turn to entertain.

O'Meara cleared his throat, "Gentleman...I have here a letter I would like to share with you. It is from my beloved Gina who, it appears, has been sleeping with every Jody in New Jersey and Southern New York." He pulled the letter out of the chest pocket of his jungle shirt with a flourish. "It begins:

Dear John...I mean Dear Tracey," he said, in a falsetto voice, "It has been so long since I saw you last and it seems so unfair that it will be so much longer until you come home. It must be so hard for you to keep the promises we made each other with all those attractive Oriental girls around." O'Meara looks up arching his eyebrows and the giggles and laughter fill the room. "I guess she thinks Suzy Wong is behind every bamboo shoot over here." Then back to the falsetto reading voice, "I want to be fair." he looks around the room to get everyone's attention, "and set you free of our agreement that must be so hard for you to keep." Cat calls arise from the room,

"Yeah Tracey...pretty hard to be unfaithful when there

ain't no women around." hollered Boone. "She's being so kind to set you free!"

O'Meara continued on, switching from his rich baritone narration to the squeaky falsetto Gina imitation. He quickly had all of the listeners laughing at the letter that should have brought him down. O'Meara had turned what might have been a personal tragedy into a platoon joke and frolic. He would read the letter out loud over and over for the next several weeks.

When O'Meara had finished his letter and the laughter died, Leroy looked over at Mick and asked, "Hey bro…what you got?"

Holtzman, normally shy and retiring in such situations, thought quickly, then stepped in front of the table facing away from the men toward the bulkhead. He turned back to the men and in a very polite proper voice said, "The Lion…from the Wizard of Oz." He then turned back towards the bulkhead. He dramatically shook his head as if he had a huge mane of hair and leap across the deck landing in a crouch facing the men.

"If I were a Hippopotamus!
I'd tear ya from top to bottumus
Cause I'd have c-c-courage!!!"

He leaped into the air, spinning landing in a crouch and finished,

" Why does a muskrat guard its musk?
C-C-COURAGE !!"

Mick then straightened and gave a little bow, followed by applause from the peanut gallery.

In the world back home, Holtzman would have never done this charade for fear of ridicule. But he did not fear the ridicule of these men, at least not for some foolishness like this. These men were warriors and bound by the blood they had shed and let together. It was a bond so strong that to hear their laughter for whatever the reason, was music to his ears.

As Mick rejoined the gallery, he saw a stranger standing in the compartment hatch. He was dark, broad of shoulder, not tall, with a huge bushy black handle bar mustache. The Corporal approached the stranger and raised his eyebrows questioningly.

"You must be Corporal Holtzman," the stranger said. "Gunny Shaw sent me down here to see you. I'm Frenchy DeBeque...I'll be the new Platoon Sergeant. Can we take a walk?"

Holtzman answered in the affirmative and the two stepped out of the compartment into the passageway. Frenchy stopped smiled and said, "Nice Lion, Corporal." after which his smile widened seeing Mick's face color.

The two NCO's walked up several ladderways till they were on the flight deck.

"Gunny Shaw said you were acting Platoon Sergeant and to see you to get the scoop. Now, that tells me one of two things...either the Lieutenant doesn't know what's going on...or you and the former Platoon Sergeant have been running this outfit."

Mick just looked Frenchy in the eye.

"So tell me about the platoon." DeBeque said when he got no response.

The Corporal went into detail describing the platoon, it's squads, the leaders, each man's capabilities. He told of the Corpsmen, and the Weapons Company attachments such as machine gun, and rocket teams that traveled with the platoon, giving an accurate and detailed account of the internal workings of this combat unit.

"Very good, Corporal, by the way I knew Sergeant Morrillo stateside. He's a good man. I understand you two were friends." observed the Sergeant.

"Yeah, we were friends, if you're the Frenchy DeBeque that Morrillo knew then this is your second tour?" Holtzman asked.

Frenchy nodded, this explained a lot, as the story was

well known. Frenchy DeBeque had won the Navy Cross, the second highest medal a Marine could be awarded. He had taken out a quad fifty caliber ensconced in a fortified bunker. That was a year and a half ago. Frenchy had suffered wounds and been shipped back to the states where he was promoted to Staff Sergeant and given a job in an infantry training battalion. After having been there awhile, he got into a dispute with a Second Lieutenant and had told him where to stick his rank insignia. Frenchy was busted in rank back to Private First Class. He had since regained his rank up to Sergeant and was back in the bush.

This story would sweep the platoon the next day and Frenchy would be accorded a warrior's place of honor among them for his courage and particularly for telling off a stateside non-combat officer without fear of retribution.

"OK, Holtzman, now what's the deal with the Lieutenant?" DeBeque asked again, watching the Corporal carefully. "Is he stupid?" Frenchy paused. "Gutless?" Another pause, "Thank you Corporal, I guessed it was something like that. So, it's up to us to make this platoon function, we'll get it done."

CHAPTER TWENTY
The Cabin

Ski's plan worked just as he'd hoped. He completed boot camp at Parris Island. He then attended Infantry Training Regiment and Battalion Infantry Training at Camp Lejune, North Carolina. When his infantry training was over he was given sixteen days leave before reporting to Staging Battalion and the flight to Nam.

Joe watched the trees go by as he rode the bus towards Bessemer. He really loved these woods. He wondered if Curley would go crazy when he saw him, but what he thought about most was Roseanne. He had thought about her every day since leaving. He had replayed that last night in the car over and over in his mind.

The bus stopped in Bessemer. Joe got off and walked the half mile to home carrying only his AWOL bag and a spare uniform in a plastic suit bag. He rounded the corner to the house and came into the yard expecting Curley to come bounding out. There was no sign of the dog, so Joe went in through the back door. His mother turned around from the stove, startled at first, then ran and hugged him.

"You almost scared me to death!" Mrs. Sokouski exclaimed.

"I thought Curley would give you plenty of warning." Joe replied. "Where is he?"

"Oh, Audrey stopped by to take him for a romp in the woods about an hour or so ago." Joe's mother replied. "She comes by a couple a times a week since you've been gone."

Joe looked out the window and saw Curley come out of the woods on the other side of the field by his home. Curley ran into the field and turned to look back at the woods from which appeared the figure of a woman.

Joe stepped outside and walked to the gate at the edge of the yard near the field. Curley, seeing someone in the yard alerted, then walked forward testing the air. The scent came to him and he started for Joe at full speed, baying like a hound as he ran. Joe had to drop to his knees to keep from being bowled over by the pell-mell charge of the big dog. Then Curley was all over him, jumping, licking, whining, barking, all at once in his excitement. Joe fondled his ears, then hugged and patted him.

"Guess he remembers you." a soft voice said.

Joe looked up, and there was Audrey. He stood quickly, confused, for this wasn't the Audrey he remembered. Audrey had been tall, skinny, and pigtailed. This Audrey had an hourglass figure with curves that were unbelievable. The pigtails had been brushed out and her wavy auburn hair hung to her waist.

"Hi, Audrey." Joe said, his voice cracking. "Thanks for being so good to Curley."

"You look really good in your uniform Joey." Audrey said in her soft melodic voice.

"Th-thanks." Ski stammered, "You've really grown up."

"Oh…really, in what way?" she parried.

The PFC turned scarlet. He quickly reached down and picked up a stick and threw it yelling, "Fetch!" Curley went after it like it was a cat.

"Well…I guess he hasn't forgotten how to fetch," Joe said, hoping that the subject was changed.

Joe and Audrey made small talk about Curley and asked him about his Marine training. She eventually excused herself and Joe watched her walk down the road towards her house.

Ski could barely control himself as the afternoon crept on. His dad came home and they chatted about their experiences in boot camp, but Ski's mind was on Roseanne. Even though it was a school night, her parents had said they could go out to dinner as long as she was home by ten. At least he'd get to see her and hold her. This weekend would be Roseanne's senior prom.

Joe picked up Roseanne at home and took her to dinner at Francie's. They rushed through dinner without bothering to try for the wine. Afterwards they quickly headed for the Chevy and their secret spot. They kissed and fondled each other for an hour when Joe pulled out the little velvet box and handed it to Roseanne.

"What's this!" cried out Roseanne her eyes lighting up with excitement.

"I bought it for you in North Carolina. Go ahead, open it up." Ski urged.

Roseanne opened the box and gasped at the diamond engagement ring inside. Ski had spent all that he had on it and would be paying on the installment plan for over a year.

"It's beautiful!" she whispered, "For me?"

"Who else?" responded the youthful Marine. "Put it on."

The ring fit perfectly, Roseanne was simply glowing with pleasure and pride. "Oh, let's go somewhere." she cried.

The couple went to Johnny's, a popular young people's night spot where they didn't check IDs too closely. Roseanne went around visiting everybody she knew, flashing the engagement ring at every opportunity, dragging Joe happily in her wake. Joe was proud to have her on his arm, wearing his engagement ring. She really was his girl now.

That Saturday Joe took Roseanne to her senior prom. She looked devastating in her prom dress and showed the engagement ring to everybody whether they had noticed it or not. The next day her sorority was to go to a friend's family summer home for an overnight. Roseanne told Joey that she had told her parents she was going and because it was supervised they had said OK. She, however, had other plans. She had a girlfriend to cover for her while she and Joe rented a cabin nearby.

The next day Joe picked up Roseanne at her friend's house and they drove up toward Lake Superior in the Chevy. They found a cabin rental just a few miles from the summer home of her sorority friend. Joe went to the office to rent the room. He told the proprietor he needed a room and felt the sweat drip down his brow and could feel the dampness in his shirt. The proprietor looked him over carefully, looked out at the Chevy and Roseanne and quoted a price that was ten bucks higher than that on the sign out front. Joe paid in cash without a complaint at the sudden inflation.

Ski took the key and drove the Chevy over to the cabin. With Roseanne in tow they went inside. It smelled musty and close in the cabin so Ski opened several windows, while Roseanne quickly grabbed the telephone and called her girlfriends at the summer home several miles away. Ski lit a Marlborough and took a deep drag, enjoying the feel of the smoke in his lungs. He looked around the room as Roseanne gabbed excitedly with her sorority sisters. He noted that there was a radio, a stove, a kitchen sink and a bathroom with a shower…all the comforts of home for a Marine.

It was still early so when Roseanne got off the phone to her girl friends, Joe suggested that they drive over and visit. He knew the drill. The sorority girls would be at the summer home and their boyfriends camped close by. Roseanne shook her head adamantly at his suggestion. She was uncharacteristically quiet for a few seconds, then stood up, gave Ski a devilish smile and grabbed him by his shirt. She sat down on the bed and pulled him down on top of her.

Things progressed rapidly from there. With the exception of a horrible struggle getting Roseanne's skin tight jeans off, followed by a similar battle with his own. The lovemaking was much less clumsy this time. Two hours later Ski lay staring at the ceiling, a Marlborough in hand. Roseanne was back on the phone to her girlfriends but still didn't want to go visit. An unwelcome thought crossed Joe's mind again. Roseanne had again taken charge during the love session and seemed to know what to do. Joe once again banished the thought. Women were just instinctive that way. Ski drew on the smoke in satiated bliss as the radio played.

> When a man loves a woman,
> Down deep in his soul,
> She can bring him such misery.
> If she plays him for a fool,

He's the last one to know,
Lovin' eyes can never see,
When a man loves a woman.....

CHAPTER TWENTY-ONE
Boxing

The Marines really enjoyed the relaxation aboard ship. They chowed down and started to pick up some of the weight they had lost on the previous jungle operations. The Corpsman examined each of the Marines and classified them as to body weight, physical problems and diseases. The ulcerous jungle rot was treated and began to regress with the many fresh water showers. Although the men took anti-malaria medication, many of them had night sweats and chills. Dysentery among the grunts is not uncommon as the water they drank in the field was foul, purified by the use of halazone pills which tasted awful and lost their potency quickly in the humid climate. These disease processes' take their toll on the young men. And for most Marines, their top weight in Vietnam was the day of their arrival.

Corporal Holtzman and Sergeant DeBeque began a series of inspections. First, weapons were inspected and damaged or worn parts were replaced. A few days later the 782 gear, the Marines combat equipment, was inspected and inadequate or inoperable gear was repaired or replaced. The Marines were experts at making broken or less than operable equipment do. They seldom had the luxury of new and efficient gear. They stole or "liberated" much of what they had from other army or navy units.

Five days after Mick's trip to the Valley Forge, a helicopter brought Lincoln back to the Duluth. He was still on sick call but no longer needed to be at the Battalion Aid Station. When the Prez limped into the platoon compartment grinning ear-to-ear, he received a rousing chorus of cheers from the platoon.

Squabbles were beginning to break out among the men. These healthy, strong, vital, young men were in the habit of moving about freely, with lots of space. And now, they lived on top of each other. Frenchy stopped Mick and said,

"You havin' any trouble with your men?"

"A few fights here and there," Mick responded.

"What do ya think?"

"How about you requisition us three or four pairs of boxing gloves. We could have some matches on the lower hanger deck at about 1400 hours and let them take out their frustration on each other," the Corporal suggested.

"Why 1400 hours?" DeBeque questioned.

"It'll be about 120 degrees down there at that time, so that way they'll pass out from heat exhaustion before they kill each other."

"Good thinking Holtzman. No wonder they want to make you an officer." laughed Frenchy.

"So you know."

"Yeah, it's all over the ship. You can't keep any secrets in the Corps. Besides, we'd dig havin' one of our brother enlisted grunts become an officer. At least you'd know what you were doin' from day one," finished the Sergeant.

The next day, after noon chow, they had a company formation on the hanger deck, just below the flight deck. This is where the helicopters are stored and repaired. The company was informed that boxing would be allowed for recreational purposes under the supervision of Sergeant DeBeque and Corporal Holtzman.

They had four pairs of gloves so they divided the hanger deck into two even square rings marked with chalk. DeBeque then called the names of two of the Marines that had been in a scuffle below decks. Mick called two others. The men stripped to the waist and on went the gloves. Referees were chosen and the two bouts started simultaneously. The action initially was fast and furious, using up some of the adrenaline and anger from the days before. As Mick had suspected, in the 100 plus degree heat, the tempers cooled quickly. Frenchy and Mick moved quickly through the list of trouble makers and matched a few Marines they suspected would be wanting to buckle in the near future. Soon the crowd, which had swelled with large eyed sailors and laughing Marines, began to call out matches they wished to see. The boxing improved as these Marines had nothing against each other but were matched for size and athletic ability.

The crowd started calling for Ski and Mick. The Corporal looked at Joe and arched his eyebrows questioningly. The Team Leader shrugged his shoulders in reply and a cheer ensued. The two stripped to the waist and put on the gloves. Mick was six feet two inches, Ski, five ten. But what Joe gave up to the Corporal in height he made up in bulk. Sokouski was heavily muscled on an athletic frame, his abdominals sculpted like railroad ties, arms thick with bands of muscle. Holtzman was lean with broad powerful shoulders. His waist was thin…only 30 inches, and he was long of leg.

Mick had boxed as boy. He had lots of fistfights as a teenager and possessed tremendous hand speed. He had discovered a knockout punch in his left when he was a senior in high school. He knew this would be no day at the beach. Ski was a natural athlete and could excel at any physical endeavor.

The match in the other ring was put on hold and all attention was on the two men from First Squad. The two stepped out smiling. They nodded to each other and touched gloves, returned to their corners and Frenchy dropped his hat to begin the match. They moved out dancing around each other warily, exploring potential opportunity. Mick began flicking a left jab in Ski's face. It seemed to be working because the Team Leader seemed perplexed. Holtzman kept the jab going then followed it with an overhand right to the cheers of the crowd. Circling, Mick kept the jab kept flicking away. Suddenly Joe ducked, lunged in low and connected with a tremendous body shot to Mick's abdomen. Holtzman immediately clinched, pinioning Ski's arms with his own and holding on for dear life. His wind had been stolen by the blow. Mick immobilized Ski in this manner until Frenchy broke the clinch. Then Mick backpedaled, circling away from his friend. Sokouski followed remorselessly sensing his advantage and a possible victory.

Holtzman danced away, gasping for air and trying to keep his distance from the relentless pursuit of Sokouski. In a minute Mick had regained his breath, but kept dancing away from Joe. A change in plan was needed. The Corporal now moved off defense and came in with the left jab firing incessantly. He followed with the overhand right again, scoring. Then he switched his stance to that of a south paw. Mick had learned to fight in the conventional right hand style. He was however naturally left-handed and that's where his power was.

Joe Sokouski was immediately muddled by the style change. He was facing the mirror image of the fighter in front of him just an instant before. Every time he moved in, the right jab was now in his face. Often followed by a wicked left hook to the body that he couldn't seem to escape. In frustration he tried his previous tactic of ducking low with a rush inside. His rush was met with a left uppercut to the chin. He did a slow loop and landed upon his back on the hanger deck. The crowd was cheering as Frenchy started the count. Ski was on his feet at seven and they went at it again.

Ski could not fathom the left handed style and kept getting his wind stolen by the wicked left hooks thrown as combinations following a right jab or overhand right.

Mick jabbed and clinched, throwing the left hook to the body over and over. It was taking its toll. Ski moved slower and slower. Holtzman moved in for the finish, and hooked again, but Sokouski had been waiting for this and he unleashed a straight right at the same instant. The Corporal never saw it coming. In an instant he wondered what he was doing on the deck. Quickly he struggled to his feet. DeBeque had counted to eight when he shook Holtzman's gloves and allowed the fight to continue. Mick tried to backpedal but his legs didn't seem to want to do as his mind commanded. Ski threw a body punch and Holtzman went down on one knee. As he struggled to regain his feet, Joe moved up to him, touched his glove, and went to one knee.

The blonde haired Team Leader then helped his Squad Leader to his feet. The crowd roared. Ski smiled and raised his Squad Leaders hand in the sign of victory.

As Sergeant DeBeque helped Mick take off his gloves he whispered, "Jesus Christ! I thought you two stubborn bastards were really going to hurt each other."

"Believe me!" Mick replied breathlessly, "We're both gonna be hurtin' puppies tomorrow.

CHAPTER TWENTY-TWO
Dodge City

Three days after the boxing matches the battalion again moved out. This time to the area known as Dodge City. The Marines named it that because every day there, is like the shootout at the OK Corral.

The plan was for the Marines to make company-sized sweeps and engage the heavy concentration of Communist forces located there. When contact was made the rest of the battalion could sweep, block or envelope the enemy. Holtzman had his doubts about these tactics.

The day of debarkation came and at 04:00 hours the Marines lined up in the passageways and flight decks, carrying full combat gear. The heavy elevators had been running all night, moving the first wave of choppers to the flight deck of the USS Duluth from the hanger decks below. Echo Company from the Duluth and Fox Company from the Valley Forge would be in the first wave. While Echo was loading into the choppers, the Marines of Hotel Company moved out onto the gangways on either side of the flight deck to wait their turn. They watched the helicopters take off, then circle the ship, waiting for the contingent from the Valley Forge. When the two groups of Chinooks from each ship reconnoitered in the air, they headed inland, about a twenty-minute flight each way. Mick looked at his watch for a time check, 06:03 hours. He'd start looking for the birds to return at 06:40.

Holtzman sat down on the gangway and leaned his rucksack up against the bulkhead. He pulled out a Lucky and lit it. Inhaling deeply the Corporal looked back at the rest of his squad. Kuhl was behind him with the radio. O'Meara was behind Kuhl, then Ski and First Team, followed by Leroy and Second Team, and finally Boone and Third Fire Team.

"Hurry up and wait!" Mick said to Trace and Ski with a smile.

"Yeah...it's the Marine Corps way," The blond Fire

Team Leader replied.

The Marines smoked and engaged in desultory conversation for the next forty minutes, trying to hide the nervousness they felt. The waiting was the worst. You didn't know for forty minutes if the first wave hit a hot LZ or not. They would know when the choppers returned. Every eye would be counting. If there were Chinooks missing they had been shot down at the LZ.

Hot LZs are an infantry Marine's nightmare. In each Chinook there would be twelve to fourteen Marines in full combat gear. The skin of the choppers is paper thin, and in fact, flammable. The Chinook has dual rotors. If hit, they go out of sync and beat each other to pieces. When hit, these big powerful helicopters go down like a ton of bricks. If hit, the older UH-34 helicopter goes down in what is called helo rotation, giving it and the Huey a much softer landing. If the Marines survive being shot down at the LZ, the enemy usually has it zeroed in for mortar barrages. As the Marines drag their dead and wounded from the wreckage, the mortars will be blowing them to pieces. The safest bet is to get as far from the LZ as quickly as you can. Marines, however, never leave behind their dead or wounded.

Mick ground out another cigarette into the metal deck, field stripping it to shreds of paper and tobacco. His mouth was dry, the smoke leaving a stale taste, not giving him the satisfaction he desired. He looked at his watch...06:42. Holtzman's gaze went to the western horizon, *"They should be coming in sight any minute,"* he thought. He noted Boone craning his neck in the same direction.

Ten minutes dragged by, slower than cold molasses. Now all the men had their eyes on the horizon. "Shit, what if it's a hot LZ?" someone said. Another nervous Marine down the line misheard and said, "They say the LZ is hot!" the general commotion started to gain volume.

"Hold it down, we don't know shit!" Corporal Holtzman yelled as he got to his feet to survey the nervous Marines in waiting. Then the slap, slap, slap, of the chopper blades turned the Corporal around. All eyes looked to see the birds coming toward them and everyone was counting. The Chinook contingent from the carrier split off and were easily counted. All present. The helicopters coming straight toward the Duluth were harder to count. Over and over the Marines counted, coming up one short each time. Then in the distance the errant chopper was spotted...struggling. *"Was it hit or is it having engine problems?"* Mick wondered.

The Klaxon horn blared as the elevator from the hanger deck ground into motion. It arrived on the flight deck with a replacement Chinook that was rolled off and forward. The crippled chopper would come in first and be taken immediately below for repair. Then, the other birds would land and reload, along with the replacement just brought up.

Platoon Sergeant DeBeque called to Holtzman, "I got the word from S2 that the chopper has engine problems. The LZ is not hot...I repeat... the LZ is not hot!"

A general sigh of relief passed through the waiting group of infantrymen. Going into Dodge City was bad enough...hitting a hot LZ there was double trouble. Seconds later the injured Chinook began maneuvering to land on the flight deck with its engine sputtering and missing. The big ungainly bird was having a hard time. The Marines now had a new worry. They were stuck on the gangways to the port and starboard sides of the flight deck with a huge helicopter trying to position itself to land on the rolling deck of the cruiser. The Marines felt their vulnerability while the big bird hovered clumsily for position with the rotors beating and tearing the air above them. Mick turned and looked out to sea, trying to take his mind off the scene above him.

Finally the pilot managed to bring the chopper down to a not-so-soft landing. Quickly the deck crew rolled it onto the elevator. The Klaxon horns sounded and the big bird disappeared into the bowels of the ship. The rest of the flight began coming in, one by one, landing and being pushed into formation. The flight deck became chaotic with the noise from the rotor wash of numerous helicopters. Somehow, over the noise, Squad Leader Holtzman heard the order to begin loading. He looked back to see Frenchy signaling him to go. He started forward, moving in a crouch to avoid being decapitated by the many rotor blades beating the air around him. He looked back to be sure his men were following. The deck crew indicated which Chinook to load first. When the Corporal arrived, he stepped to the side of the rear-facing loading ramp and assisted his men aboard. He was always the last man on and the first off. In seconds all the men loaded into the bird and they sat waiting as the other choppers were loaded. The men looked at each other then away. There wasn't a hell of a lot to look at on the inside of a CH-46 Chinook. There is the thin metal skin, hydraulic hoses everywhere, the door gunners with M-60 machine-guns mounted on either side of the bird wearing their bullet proof flak jackets that appear like an oversized double thick catcher's chest protector. The Crew Chief was at the front of the compartment in radio communication with the two pilots in the flight cabin. The Marines have seen it all before. All they want is to get this ride over with and back into the bush that they hate, yet understand.

One by one the big birds take off, climbing and circling while waiting for the flight from the Valley Forge to join them. Then the two flights converge and head west, moving powerfully through the air towards Dodge City. The Marines aboard begin to enjoy their ride…they are up high and have a good view of the vista below. The countryside down there looks like the surface of the moon. It seems that anywhere you looked there was a shell crater. The pockmarked terrain looks diseased. *How many years has this country been at war to have its skin so devastated?* In about fifteen minutes the pitch and speed of the rotors change and the grunts feel the chopper start its descent to the Landing Zone. Now the Marines start checking each other's gear. Mick crouched in the rear by the loading ramp. Looking out the helicopter's windows, the Marines could see their comrades below on the ground in a large circle defending the LZ.

The helicopter descended rapidly while the loading ramp at the rear opened. Squad Leader Holtzman leapt out as soon as the ground was visible and was off the Chinook before it touched down, his men following. They ran bent over and were directed toward the perimeter by the pathfinder. Mick quickly led his squad out to the perimeter where they fell down into a defensive line as the rest of the choppers came in one at a time to unload their cargo of combat Marines. Two hours later the Marines were on the move, traveling through saw grass, scrub and jungle. Tonight they will dig in as a battalion. Tomorrow, they would split up with each company making its own sweep, searching for the enemy.

It was hot, arid…the monsoonal mud long since traded in for the red dust of the dry season. Saw grass is given that name because its edges are serrated, so that if it rakes your arm or an unprotected leg, it leaves a bloody trail where it has passed. In fact all the vegetation has thorns, are poisonous or have some vicious defense system. Elephant grass is found in the wetter regions. It grows twelve feet high and less than an inch apart. Stands of this grass are virtually impenetrable. If the infantrymen follows the paths through the tall grass, they are sure to be booby-trapped. To make a trail, one has to fall into the grass knocking it down, then walk forward two steps and fall again. This is exhausting work as not a breath of air stirs in the tall grass. Fire ants nest high in the grass and if one knocks down such a nest upon himself, it is akin to an attack by a swarm of hornets. The mosquitoes rule the night and carry malaria. The bamboo groves are the home of the bamboo viper that the men call "step and a half", because that is as far as you get if he bites you. Danger lays everywhere. Not just in the guns and mortars of the enemy and if there is any beauty in this land, the infantrymen doesn't see it.

After digging in for the evening, Mick and O'Meara were joined by Frenchy DeBeque.

"Well, how did you think everything went today?" the

Platoon Sergeant asked.

"Pretty good so far…hey, great move yellin' that S2 had cleared the LZ. The boys were gettin' nervous."

"You been here before, Mick?"

"Ya, this ain't my first barbecue. I guess this is our second go, eh Trace?"

"Yeah…but it don't get better by doin' it over and over," Commented O'Meara. "What do you think about these company sweeps, Sarge?"

"We tried 'em in 67 and they didn't work then. I guess they think the enemy has read the book since then and will react the way they say they're supposed to at West Point." The swarthy Sergeant stated.

Mick chuckled, "Yeah, my guess is they'll just drift in front of our sweeps till they get one company or unit just where they want 'em and then stomp on us."

"I'm not crazy about these tactics either, nor is Colonel Smith. They come from regimental or above." The men turned quickly to voice of Captain Weller.

"Howdy Captain. Grab a chair." Mick offered.

"Don't mind if I do, Holtzman. So, what do you think we should do to avoid this stompin' you're talking about?" asked the Company Commander as he squatted down next to the fighting hole.

"Don't move to fast or get to far removed from the protection of numbers," offered Frenchy.

"I would be real careful not to pursue what looked like a small number of enemy, as they could easily be bait to lead the outfit into a Custer and Sitting Bull type ambush," articulated Mick.

"Good observations gentlemen. Perhaps you could pass these thoughts to the other Platoon Sergeants, DeBeque. This can't come from me or even the Colonel. So, it'll have to come from the bottom up. I came over here to tell you I'll be replaced in a few days. I'll be going to regimental S-3 Operations and Plans. You'll be getting a new Commanding Officer, a Captain Blackwell," explained Weller.

"Where's he from, Sir," The Squad Leader asked.

"He's reporting in from stateside."

"Combat Experience?" Frenchy queried.

"Not that I'm aware of." Weller declared stiffly. "I wanted to tell you men how much I appreciated your support as both your Platoon Commander and Company Commander. I'd be grateful if you'd pass that along to the men."

With that Captain Weller took his leave. The three grunts just sat there for a few minutes absorbing what had just occurred.

"Now that's one hell of an officer!" Frenchy said.

"So, you wouldn't tell him to pin his Captain's bars up his ass, huh?" laughed O'Meara.

"No way! If he said to shit, I'd say how high and what color, Sir!" replied DeBeque with a wolfish grin.

"He came here to deliver a message." Mick said thoughtfully. "He's not happy about turning the company over to some stateside Captain with no combat experience. And then he filters the word to cover our ass up through the ranks, like he was a non-com or something…damn, are we gonna miss him!" went on the Squad Leader.

CHAPTER TWENTY-THREE
Prez Returns

The next morning the Marines moved out in company strength with Golf, Echo, and Hotel Companies heading off in single file. Hotel headed due north, Echo north-northeast, and Golf north-northwest in a fan shaped array. Fox Company and the Battalion Command group remained where they had camped and would act as a blocking force as each company made its sweep.

The grunts of Hotel Company moved out slowly. The temperature was intense, even at this early hour. In the distance, heat waves radiated, causing objects to appear to be wavering. The soldiers were carrying full gear, a rucksack or haversack, wearing a flak jacket, steel helmet, canteen belt with four canteens attached, bandoleers of magazines, claymore mines, fragmentation grenades, LAAWs, and of course their weapon and its accouterments. Along with their own gear, each man also carried ammunition for crew served weapons such as cans of machine gun ammo and rocket rounds. The infantrymen had been able to leave the mortar rounds they normally carried behind, as both 60 and 80 mm mortars were stationed with the battalion CP for the moment.

The idea was to go north about two thousand meters. Here, the three infantry companies would come on line, joining with the company on their flank, then sweep back toward the blocking force. After traveling about five hundred meters a halt was called. A Marine in Third Platoon was down with heat exhaustion. The Marines sat where they stopped, pulling out their canteens to drink the vile tasting, halazone purified water and take a salt pill so that they wouldn't become the next victim. The word came back that the man was one of the replacements just picked up while aboard ship and that the Corpsman thought he would be able to continue if his buddies carried his gear and he had a chance to cool down.

"His buddies will love that," Chuckled O'Meara.

"Yeah…we were all cherry once. Didn't you ever overheat when you were first in country?" asked Holtzman.

"No, I came in country during the monsoon so I didn't overheat. I damn near drowned!" joked Tracey.

"About my third Recon mission, along the Ho Chi Minh Trail, we were spotted by the enemy and had to didi ASAP. We ran about 3 clicks up this mountain and hid in the jungle. It was a good thing they didn't come after us cause I was seeing double. I had the dry heaves and doubt I coulda moved out to save my life," reminisced the Squad Leader.

The sun seared the men as they sat waiting. They couldn't be sure which was worse, walking in the heat and dust, or sitting with the sun beating down on you. Their senses were dulled by the inferno, making them more susceptible to a surprise attack or booby trap.

In half an hour the word was passed to saddle up and move out. The column proceeded northward progressing slowly through the never-ending saw grass and brush intermixed with small patches of elephant grass. The day stretched on as the grunts sweated and stumbled along through the heat.

In the early afternoon the companies stopped at the coordinates where they were to connect up with the companies to either flank, then go on line. The Marines turned, walking single file east and west. It took a little time and some confusion to link up with the other companies who were not exactly where they were supposed to be. Finally, the connections were made and the men turned back in the direction they had come. Now they were shoulder to shoulder in a skirmish line, prepared for the sweep.

Mick walked up and down the line in front of First Squad, warning the tired men to be alert for ambushes, booby traps, and antipersonnel mines.

"Pay attention you guys! This ain't gonna be no day at the beach. Keep your eyes and ears open! Move slow and careful. Watch for trip wires, bouncing betty's and toe poppers…this whole place may be wired. Don't go to sleep

~ 136 ~

on me!" the Corporal exhorted his men.

On command, the soldiers moved out walking abreast at the order, traveling slowly, fighting with the grass, brush, and other vegetation. The sweat poured from them now, stinging their eyes and the cuts and abrasions from the foliage. They had traveled back south about five hundred meters when there was a muffled thud followed by screams off to First Squad's right. A halt was called...First Platoon had a casualty. A Fire Team Leader had hit a trip wire and set off a grenade. The blast had blown part of his right foot off and serrated his lower body with a hundred pieces of shrapnel. The Corpsmen were controlling the bleeding and dosing him with morphine. Ten minutes later the company moved out again. The wounded man would be carried on a jury rigged litter, behind the sweeping company, to the CP from where he would be evacuated.

Mick's men were more attentive now, throwing off the shards of fatigue, forcing their consciousness to stay alert. They had seen the price paid for inattention. When the soldiers stumbled back into the battalion perimeter, they wandered back over to the positions that they had manned the night before and collapsed.

Frenchy DeBeque walked over and sat down next to Holtzman. "I told ya these fuckin' sweeps weren't any good in 67. And it's still the same old tune."

"Let's see...one good Marine crippled, one heat prostrated, should we radio in the body count." the Corporal added with sarcasm. "So how come we had to pack all our gear if we were coming back to the same old place?"

"Doesn't make any sense does it? We could of gone out in combat gear only, moved faster, beat the men up less and we might have avoided the casualties," commented the stocky Cajun. "I'll run it by Gunny Shaw tonight and maybe we can add some sanity to this stupid game."

DeBeque was leaving as Tracey walked over swearing, "Eat the apple...fuck the Corps! This is the dumbest buncha shit I ever saw!"

"Seems to be the opinion of the day, Trace. You go

down the lines to the right and I'll go left. Make sure everybody eats and get 'em drinkin' water. In this heat, with this level of frustration, these guys are gonna fall apart in a big hurry. We gotta keep 'em strong and alert. We have at least another week of this shit!" Mick explained. With this the Squad Leader set off. O'Meara dumped his rucksack disgustedly, took a deep breath, and headed down the lines the other way.

That night, Second Platoons Listening Post had activity. At 01:30 Tracey shook Mick, "LP's got gooks out in front of 'em," O'Meara said pointing to the radio he'd been monitoring.

Mick heard the company radio operator's voice coming rapidly across the static. "Lima Papa two this is hotel. If everything's all right and there ain't no gooks in sight, key your handset twice." There was no sound. "Lima Papa two, if you got the enemy in sight, key your handset three times." Click, Click, Click. "Lima Papa…two key your handset once for each enemy spotted." The radio operator kept asking questions as to the size, direction, and distance of the enemy force spotted.

"Trace…you monitor. I'm going down the lines, waking the guys…makin' sure they know where the LP is. Be ready…we may have to go out and bring 'em in." With that the Squad Leader was gone.

O'Meara continued monitoring the radio transmissions. The LP had spotted three or four NVA soldiers skulking around the outskirts of the perimeter. The listening post was well positioned and felt they could stay out. When Mick returned from alerting and updating the squad, O'Meara informed him of the gist of the transmissions.

"Well it's a cinch we won't be getting much sleep tonight." Holtzman pronounced, "You know they can do this every night…just sneak in probe, throw a frag, back off til we're totally frazzled."

Things quieted down for a while. Then at about 04:30 a Chicom grenade was thrown at Echo Company's LP. Sporadic firing began along the lines. All outgoing, no incoming. Mick sprang to his feet and charged up and down First Squad's positions making sure the men didn't fire as they might hit their own listening post.

Mick was standing the last watch. The lines had quieted down and he was wishing for that cigarette again. His body suddenly flushed and sweat began pouring from every orifice. Then the tremors shook him. It lasted only a few minutes.

"Just what I need." he thought *"I got alligators up to my elbows and I'm trying to get malaria!"*

The next day the tactics changed. The entire battalion would move out and relocate on high ground to the north, using this as a base to run the company sweeps from. First Squad was to walk point and Corporal Holtzman decided to be point man on this move. The weather was a repeat of the previous day. Blistering heat, with no let-up. Mick led off slowly. The pace must be slow or they would have more heat stroke casualties. He also didn't want a repeat of the booby trap casualty from yesterday because it would be himself or one of his men that would be wounded. Holtzman stayed off the beaten trails as they were sure to be booby-trapped. After covering about a thousand meters in two hours, he suddenly halted. Frozen motionless where he was, he let his eyes continue to rove over the terrain in front of him. His eyes had seen something that had signaled his brain to freeze him in place, but he wasn't sure what. *A trip wire, a toe popper, an ambush?* He crouched down, making himself small. His eyes coursed over the ground close to him…then the terrain a little further out… then the area even further away, then back, over and over, the eyes moving constantly.

Then he saw it! Six feet away in the knee-high grass something glistened. *Was it just a stalk of grass reflecting the sun?* Moving very cautiously, an inch at a time, carefully clearing each foot placement visually, Mick moved toward the reflective object. When within two feet of it the Squad Leader determined that it was in fact a trip wire. Freezing in place once again he tried to visually determine where the wire led. *Were there other wires? Was it attached to a grenade, or a larger device?* He visually followed the wire to a clump of brush and grass. Staring at the clump, he could just make out the shape of an unexploded, two hundred fifty pound bomb that the enemy had rigged to explode when the wire was tripped. Involuntarily he shuddered. If tripped, this booby trap could destroy the better half of the company. Holtzman turned and motioned Kuhl and the others back. Then he told Kuhl to call up the Combat Engineers and tell them that we have a booby trap that needs to be blown in place.

The battalion had to back up a good two hundred meters to gain enough space to protect them from the blast when the booby trapped bomb was exploded. Such devices are sometimes wired to other explosives and all hell might break lose when the Engineers fire the charges.

Mick waited, squatted, sweating, looking for the Engineers to come to him. They arrived in about five minutes. The Corporal let them approach, then held up his hand and stopped them. He pointed out the trip wire, then the shadowy silhouette of the two hundred fifty pounder in the brush. The combat engineers asked if Holtzman would help them make a clear safe path close enough to the bomb to lay C-4 plastic explosive next to it and blow it with a sympathetic detonation. The Squad Leader cleared a path to the brush pile. It took him ten minutes to cover the ten feet. Mick then happily departed as the two explosives experts began placing their charges.

Minutes later the Engineers returned on the run yelling "Fire in the Hole!" meaning that the time fuse was lit and the detonation imminent. A minute later there was a muted detonation followed immediately by a tremendous blast. The Marines lay flat on the ground, the air above them filled with shrapnel. They stayed down for several minutes to be sure there were no secondary explosions. The explosives men went back to check their work, returning minutes later to tell the Corporal that the booby trap was cleared.

Mick again moved out. He made his way past the huge

scar and crater where the booby trapped bomb had exploded. He mentally noted the destruction that the device had caused and redoubled his efforts at observation and care. Two hours later they came to the rise that was their objective and here, a battalion perimeter was set up.

They were not the first soldiers to dig in on this terrain. There were old fighting holes, long since over grown with vegetation. *Had these positions belonged to the Japanese in W.W.II? The French in the fifties? The Viet Minh?, ARVNs, or the NVA?* Many armies had been here, fighting and dying for a point of insignificant high ground.

"Don't use any of those old holes," Mick ordered the squad, "No tellin' what you might find if you dig down in 'em."

The tired Marines dug their holes again and as always dug them deep. A grunt's fighting hole is his protection in an attack, or mortar barrage. That hole is his safety.

The next morning, the Grunts headed back out on their company sweeps. This time Golf Company stayed back to support the Battalion Command Post and act as a blocking force. Today the soldiers carried only combat gear, the three infantry companies fanning out as before, then going on line and sweeping toward each other or the battalion perimeter.

Echo Company encountered a small group of enemy which ran in front of them, staying several hundred meters ahead. Captain Engleton, Echo's CO had been a Platoon Commander when that company was ambushed and decimated during Operation Meade River. The word that the NCO's had filtered back about possible ambushes had reached him and he was careful in his pursuit. The three or four enemy ran past a tree line and Captain Engleton decided that he had gone far enough. He wasn't leading his men in front of that tree line, so he had his marksmen fire at the retreating group of NVA. The first volley brought down two and the second a third. As the third one fell the tree line erupted in fire from about three hundred yards. The ambush had been set and baited. The Captain simply had not taken the bait. Then, when the Marine riflemen killed their comrades used as bait, the North Vietnamese had opened up from a distance. The ensuing firefight lasted about twenty minutes with the Marines having the advantage. Echo Company took one man killed in action and three WIA. In the tree line there were six NVA dead as well as the three that the Marines had shot at long distance.

Hotel Company had moved to assist Echo but had arrived too late to participate in the battle. That night, when the tired grunts returned to the perimeter, a helicopter re-supply was underway. Mick took four men to the LZ to bring back First Squad's share of the supplies. When he arrived the last of the Chinooks was unloading. It dropped the cargo net carrying supplies, then settled to the ground about ten feet to one side. To Mick's surprise the Prez came down the unloading ramp along with another Marine in shiny new issue, wearing Captain's bar's in plain sight!

"That must be the new CO. Somebody better tell him he's making a target of himself," judged the Squad Leader.

"Hey Prez, what the hell you doin' here?   You were supposed to skate for another two weeks."

"Yeah…I know but I couldn't stand that ship no more. I'll tell ya about it later. Here's the platoon's mail." drawled Lincoln as he handed over a large bundle of letters. "I'll catch ya'll later, I'm gonna go check my squad."

Mick took the proffered mail and clasped his buddies shoulder. Then the two parted, headed in different directions. The Corporal sorted First Squad's mail out of the larger bundle. Mick stopped about the fifth letter down as there, staring up at him, was a letter from Lori. Holtzman quickly pocketed the letter and finished sorting. He then directed the four men to grab their share of the re-supply and head back to the squad area. On his way back, the Squad Leader spotted the dusky Platoon Sergeant.

"Hey Frenchy…here's the platoon's mail. I pulled out mine and I think the Prez got Second Squad's as well."

"What's the Prez doin back?   He had more time to recoup!" said DeBeque as he accepted the letters.

"He said something about not bein' able to stand the ship no more. There might be a story here. Stop over to my pos a little later and we'll debrief the big man," Holtzman remarked with a grin.

Mick led the working party to First Squad's area, then began passing out mail. When he approached Ski's position, he noted the team leaders tension but there was a letter from his fiancée in the stack which should relieve him. Holtzman hurried back to his position where he found himself alone for a change and quickly opened his letter. He began reading. The Squad Leader was deep into his letter when O'Meara returned. He didn't even hear the Grenadier's approach, Tracey saw his friends concentration and decided to visit Tex and Wiley.

The letter was warmer…more personal than the last, although there was no mention of their past…or a future. Lori did tell about her present and there was no mention of a steady boyfriend. Mick thought about her long dark hair, the smell of her, the feel of her next to him. *Damn! Will I ever see her again!* He decided he would write another masterpiece back. Did he dare sign it "Love, Mick?" "*No, might scare her off.*" So he would proceed an inch at a time. *"After all, Rome wasn't built in a day."* The theme of the popular song played in his mind once again as he began formulating his letter.

"Words,
It's only Words,
And words are all I have,
To take your heart away"

Holtzman didn't get much time to plan his next masterpiece, as a few minutes later, George Washington Lincoln came moving along the lines looking for his friend. The Prez was followed by Vasquez, his First Team leader, guns Squad Leader Willie Parker, a new kid from third squad they called Hamburger, and Leroy Wright.

"What's Happening, Bro!" cried Lincoln as his long legs

carried him to Mick's position.

"Que Passo," joined Vasquez

The three signed, each man repeating the ritual in turn. The commotion alerted O'Meara who returned to the position followed by machine gunner Tex Schultz. Moments later Sergeant DeBeque appeared as if on cue.

"So, Prez, what's the deal? Whatcha doin' back in the bush? You've only been gone two weeks?" asked Mick.

"Well, after y'all left, things kinda went downhill. Ya know that old lifer First Sergeant that's always aboard ship but never in the bush? Well the son-of-a-bitch comes down to the compartment and starts tellin' me I got to go on this detail and that detail...got a shine my boots...all kinda chicken-shit stuff. So I got pissed yesterday and told him if he ever showed up in the bush, his life expectancy was about two seconds!" the Prez explained.

"So what did he say?" quizzed Holtzman.

"He said I was on report and that he would get my ass court-martialed. So I went up on the flight deck and waited for the next medevac chopper to come in. I helped unload it... grabbed some 782 gear and a weapon and jumped the next bird out," finished the Prez.

"Now the SOB will probably write ya up for being AWOL!" laughed Frenchy, "Can you imagine writing a Marine up for leaving the safety of the ship to go back to his combat unit in the bush?"

"Hey, Prez, ya know anything about the new Captain?" Mick inquired.

"Ya mean the one that was on the chopper with me? Who is he replacing?"

"Captain Weller," answered Holtzman.

"No way! Captain Weller's the best CO we ever had!"

The conversation began to drift around about good officers, bad ones, old times and bad times as more men joined the circle.

Lincoln was relating stories about LZ Margo and Operation Meade River. For the enjoyment of the telling, and to watch the eyes of the newer Marines.

"Ya know…on Margo, we lost the entire 60m mortar unit. Then at Meade River we lost Echo Company. Ol' Mick there went out on ten killer teams in 12 days! He be one bad dude!" the Prez waxed.

"If I remember correctly, there was one Lance Corporal Lincoln on all them night actions as well." responded Mick.

"No…I wasn't on the one with you and Lieutenant Baker for the prisoner snatch. I got some sleep that night." added Lincoln.

"You had a Lieutenant that did four man killer teams?" inquired Hamburger.

"You bet!" went on Lincoln, "Mr. Baker went out all the time."

"What was the prisoner snatch all about?" Frenchy asked.

"Well, intelligence wanted us to get a prisoner or two for interrogation to find out what the gooks were up to. The cordon was drawn tight and we were hittin' 'em with air and arty every day. They would try to fight their way out by day and sneak out in two or three man groups at night. We'd been havin' success with the Killer Teams, so they asked us to get a prisoner." Holtzman explained.

"Well, Mr. Baker and Mick brought back two!" declared the Prez.

"Yeah, but one didn't live very long and the other didn't give us the info to prevent the Echo Company ambush," Mick tried to downplay the action.

"Shiiit!!" responded Lincoln, "Mick just ain't gonna tell you how he took out the point man for that NVA squad that night," said the Prez.

"You mean to say a four man Killer Team took on a squad!" one of the newer guys asked, his eyes wide.

Lincoln continued, "You bet your ass! They went out that night… Mick on point… to where they was gonna set up an ambush. Mick, he heard somethin' and hunkered down in the bush when the point man for this gook squad comes up and stops inches from our man here. Mick, he takes the dude out with his bayonet…drags the body off the trail and then sets up the ambush on the spot. A couple of minutes later the bad guys come lolly-gaggin down the trail and Mick and the LT they blow the claymores and open up. When it's all over they check and there's two gooners alive so they grab 'em and drag 'em back to the lines."

"So did they give you a medal for that Corporal Holtzman?" asked Hamburger.

"I should smile." Said Mick, "The only person that said good work was Mr. Baker."

Changing the subject the Corporal asked, "How come they call you Hamburger man?"

The PFC shrugged self-consciously at the attention and responded, "My first Fire Team Leader, Lance Corporal Gomez couldn't pronounce my name, Hornslager, so he called me Hamburger."

"And Hamburger it stays!" called out O'Meara, getting a laugh from all present.

The conversation continued about other times, other actions.

CHAPTER TWENTY- FOUR
Dear John

The next morning was another blistering day. It was Hotel Company's turn to stay back, guard the CP and act as a blocking force. After checking his positions, Squad Leader Holtzman held a planning session with Lincoln and O'Meara. Then he began his letter.

He carefully re-read Lori's letter looking for places where he might be able to push the action just a little. Then he started his reply, not really telling her about what they were really doing, but relaying a funny story.

Dear Lori,

It was great to get your letter, and know that you are doing well in California. When times are tough over here I often think of that day we spent at Devil's Lake. We sure had a good time, at least I did.

Last Tuesday we camped by an abandoned Vietnamese village. In this part of the orient lives a small lizard that resides in the bamboo, particularly the bamboo of thatched huts. This creature makes a shrill call that sounds kinda like phueekyuu. Naturally the Marines call it the F__ You lizard.

In the elephant grass there lives a bird whose call sounds like reeeuhupp and of course Marines call it the RE-Up bird. As I am sure you know re-up means to re-enlist, an idea not popular with the Marines over here.

Well, the other day the two creatures sort of got together near evening. First we heard the bird call, "Reeehupp, Reeehupp!"

Then it seemed as though the lizard answered, "Phueekyuuu, Phueekyuu!" then the bird, "Reeeuhup, Reehupp!" the lizard, "Phueekuu!" You should have heard a hundred Marines cheering for that lizard.

Mick continued the letter responding to each paragraph

from Lori's, and trying to move the emotional tone up a notch at each opportunity. He contemplated his closing and settled for "Sincerely", but wished he'd been bolder after he'd sealed the letter, and wrote FREE VIETNAM on the envelope.

That afternoon the other companies swept back. There was some sniping and a few minor skirmishes where the enemy fired a few rounds then took off, but no major contact.

The pattern was set. The next day the battalion moved out en masse to a new central location where they dug in and began the fairly useless task at hand. The grunts were sweating and breathing hard in the one hundred plus degree heat. The infantrymen trudged along, carrying their heavy loads, the sweat streaking the pervasive red dust, their minds far away as they humped. Each seeking that place within their consciousness where they found solace.

Corporal Holtzman would mentally add up the weight of the gear that he carried. He started with his ruck sack in which he carried all his personal gear, a poncho, poncho liner, letter writing gear, spare socks, spare t-shirt, a spare jungle shirt, C-rations, two hundred rounds of M-16 ammo not loaded in magazines, two extra canteens full of water, battle dressings, a carton of Lucky Strikes, a pair of French field glasses taken from a dead NVA officer and 10 to 20 spare M-16 magazines to pass out to new men when they arrived in the field with the issued five magazines. The rucksack weighed in at 35-40 pounds. Attached to the pack was his entrenching tool, a folding shovel weighing three pounds, then his M-16 assault rifle at seven and a half pounds plus the 20 magazines he carried in bandoleers at seven-tenths of a pound each, adding another fourteen pounds. Then five M26 fragmentation grenades at one pound each, a LAAW or Light Anti-Armor Weapon at four and three quarter pounds, a claymore at three and a half pounds, perhaps a 3.5 rocket round weighing eight and a half pounds. Then there was his flak jacket and steel helmet. By the time he got this far, he'd lost track and had to start the addition over.

The hump ended on another anonymous piece of terrain that, as before, had been home to other soldiers in other times. The tired Marines were given their positions and they dumped their gear. They pulled out their entrenching tools and dug in. When the fighting holes were dug the men began to cook their C-rations and brew up the C-rat coffee and talk. Corporal Holtzman checked his lines making sure that each man understood his individual responsibilities. When Mick arrived at Boone's hole, the tall hillbilly had some disturbing news.

"Mick, ya better go check out Ski, something's wrong." Riley stated flatly.

"What do ya mean?" demanded the Corporal.

"He ain't talkin'. He's kinda pulled up inside hisself, ya know." added Boone.

"What do you think...you're his best friend?" grilled the Squad Leader.

"Did he get a letter from his fiancée last mail call?" The Tennessean asked.

"Yeah, he did...I know how important they are to him." replied Mick.

"Well, he's been actin' funny for a couple of weeks. The letters haven't picked him up, but he won't talk about it. I wonder if he didn't get a DJ." finished Riley.

"Shit!" responded the Squad Leader, "I'll go check him out."

Holtzman headed down the lines toward First Team with his thoughts in turmoil. He didn't feel good about dealing with other men's emotional problems. As he neared Ski's position, he slowed and watched carefully. The other three men in the team were busy brewing up and talking. Joe Sokouski's handsome face stared into the surrounding jungle oblivious to the others.

When Mick approached the position, the three riflemen looked up while Joe continued to stare into space.

"I need you three to go to the company CP and check in with the Platoon Sergeant to see if we have re-supply." the

Squad Leader said indicating the three riflemen. The three looked at each other, perplexed, as no helicopters had been heard. One of the men started to complain when another grabbed his sleeve nodding towards their team leader. Without a word the three headed off in the general direction of the Command Post.

"OK Joe, do you wanna tell me about it?" Mick asked.

Slowly Joe Sokouski tore his eyes off the jungle and looked up at his friend. He slowly shook his head, then he choked out, "Make Crawford team leader. I'll be a rifleman."

"No way! I need you, Joe...your team needs you, the squad needs you and we need you as Team Leader."

Ski turned and looked up into Mick's eyes. Ski's watery sky-blue eyes met the Corporal's steel blue eyes only for a second. He then looked down into his fighting hole saying nothing.

"Man, I know you're hurtin', but were in the shit, man...I need you. You're my best team leader...you'll probably get the squad when Tracey and I are gone. Get your shit together! It don't mean nothin' man!" the Squad Leader begged.

Mick put his hand on Joe's shoulder but he got no reaction. He could see the tears falling into the bottom of the fighting hole.

"It don't mean nothin! It'll all come out in the wash, Marine," Mick said again, not knowing which words were the magical ones which would release his friend from this evil trance. Having run out of words the Corporal walked away, at first aimlessly. Then he hurried back to his position.

When he arrived at his pos, he called out to O'Meara, "Hey Trace! We got a problem. I think Ski got a Dear John from his fiancée. Could you go down and cheer him up?"

"What do I look like, the Ski Pilot?"

"No, I know you're not the Chaplain, but Ski needs a friend just now and you've been through it. I thought maybe you could help." countered the Squad Leader.

Tracey looked over and said, "Sure, I'll give it a try buddy." and he was off in the direction of the First Fire Team's position.

Twenty minutes later O'Meara returned and shook his head. "He ain't havin' none of it, Mick. He just sits there and stares. He'll probably shake it off in a couple of days."

"Yeah…probably." said Holtzman, unconvinced.

That night there were more incidents of Chicom grenades thrown at the Marine's LPs and sporadic probing of the lines. The enemy was getting bolder. Squad Leader Holtzman wondered as he watched the sun come up, *"How long would it be till the Communists decide to engage us?*

That morning, Platoon Sergeant DeBeque stopped by Mick's position, "Holtzman, this new Captain Blackwell is wantin' to take over the company, but your man Weller is holdin' on for dear life."

"So, what's the skinny?" inquired the Corporal.

"Well, Blackwell wanted to take over today, but your Captain headed for the battalion CP and spoke with the Colonel." replied Frenchy, "Then he and the Colonel came up with a new strategy. They decided that the enemy was runnin' ahead of us as you guessed they would. So they moved Echo out before dawn to an old paddy dike about three clicks out. Echo will set up behind the dike and we'll head out with Fox Company as before, except, when we get two clicks out and go on line, we'll drive forward towards Echo. If they're runnin' in front of us, they'll get pinned."

"It just might work and it'll sure beat the Polish mine sweep we've been doin' the last week or so," the Squad Leader commented.

"Well, they're briefin' the Platoon Commanders now so the Bird Man will probably call you up shortly. Gunny Shaw briefed me earlier this mornin' and told me to pass the word to you," DeBeque finished.

"Well, thank you, and thank the Gunny," responded Holtzman.

"We're all in this together ya know," declared the Platoon Sergeant with a knowing smile.

Twenty minutes later the word was passed for Squad Leaders up. By then Mick had already explained the plan to the other Squad Leaders, Lincoln and Schneider. Lieutenant Byrd gave them a briefing however, the plan was not explained as well or in the detail that Frenchy had given Mick and that he had relayed on to the others. Byrd seemed surprised when there were no questions.

Within an hour of the briefing, the Marines were moving out in the same style as they had for the past week. The weather was still blazing hot. The men seemed more tuned in than before as Holtzman had informed them of the change in tactics. Mick had changed the order of march. Boone's Third Team lead off with Ski and First Team following. Leroy's Second Team brought up the rear. When he had announced the change, Ski, whose team was usually in the lead, heard the change. He didn't even look up. This order of march put Ski and his team in the vanguard just behind Mick and Kuhl.

Three and a half hours later the Marines stopped their march. They broke out of the columns and went on line but instead of turning and sweeping back to the blocking force as they had previously done, they swept in the direction of march, They moved forward to where Echo Company was waiting to see if this tact would flush the enemy.

When the company went on line, the infantrymen moved forward. After linking up with Fox Company, they stayed abreast of each other, about ten to fifteen feet apart. After they had covered fifty meters, Fox Company opened up. They had flushed about ten NVA troops who ran from them. Two enemy went down. The grunts pushed forward through the saw grass and brush another fifty meters. Suddenly, Corporal Holtzman noticed the grass moving about twenty-five meters in front of his squad. "Hey, watch the grass up there! I think it's full of gooks." he called, indicating the area.

Bloop, bloop, came the report of O'Meara's grenade launcher, followed milliseconds later by the blast of Tex Schultz's M-60. The machine gun rounds shredded the grass just as the grenades landed and exploded. This was followed by screams. The rest of the squad opened up. Mick called a cease fire seconds later as they were taking no return fire. The Marines continued to move forward. When they passed through the offending clump of grass, they found two dead Communist soldiers and blood trails through the grass indicating that they had wounded others. The Marines continued forward. When Hotel Company traveled five hundred meters they heard a tremendous burst of fire to their front. The tactic had worked. That was Echo Company "gettin' some". The grunts slowed their advance to avoid taking friendly fire from Echo. Five minutes after Echo opened up, there was silence. Squad Leader Holtzman slowed his men and told Kuhl, "Monitor that radio…call in for a Sit Rep. We better be signaling our position to Echo damn quick or were going to be on top of 'em."

Seconds later Kuhl responded, "I got your situation report and the six wants you to mark our pos with a green star cluster." The sweeping soldiers stopped. The Corporal prepared the pop up flare then looked to Kuhl who had his ear to the head set. Kuhl looked over and said, "Now!" Mick fired the pop up. It went straight up about 75 feet and burst open, releasing green colored pyrotechnics that floated slowly to the ground on its tiny parachute. At the instant Holtzman had fired his pop up, so had every other Squad Leader in Hotel and Fox Companies, making their lines visible to the Marines in Echo Company.

"We are about one hundred fifty meters from Echo's lines," reported Kuhl, "The Captain says move ahead, dead slow."

"OK, guys, slow and careful. Look sharp now. Don't go opening up on Echo. They're dug in and will blow our ass to hell. Watch the grass for dead and wounded gooks," admonished the Squad Leader.

The grunts inched forward. When they had traveled another fifty meters, Leroy Wright called over that he had a dead gook.

"Well, make damn sure he's dead!" Mick called back.

His order was followed by the report of Leroy's M-14. More single shots were heard as the sweeping Marines came upon apparently dead enemy soldiers in the tall grass.

"Start talkin' it up First Squad! We gotta be within 50 meters of Echo. I don't want those crazy bastards to light us up now!" commanded the Squad Leader. In seconds the Marines were hooting and hollering at each other. The tactic was picked up by the other squads and platoons. Seconds later they broke out of the saw grass and twenty meters in front of them was the paddy dike and Echo Company. The men of echo were standing and sitting on the six foot high mound of dirt waiting for their fellow Marines to appear, between the two groups of Marines were the bodies of thirty dead enemy soldiers.

"Good work, Echo!" Hollered Boone, holding up his hand with his fist closed. The salute was returned by the men of Echo. The sweeping Marines now began the slow, unpleasant task of checking the dead and collecting their weapons and personal papers for intelligence to peruse. Then, the long hot march back to the battalion perimeter.

CHAPTER TWENTY-FIVE
KIA

As the men arrived at the battalion perimeter, they dropped their combat gear next to the positions they had occupied the night before. Mick walked the lines making sure the men were eating and caring for their feet. Kuhl dropped off his radio at Holtzman and O'Meara's position, then he proceeded to join his fire team. The sound of choppers filled the air. A re-supply was soon in progress.

"Shit!" reflected Holtzman, *"I was hoping that this would satisfy the brass and we'd get helo-lifted out of here."* With a re-supply coming in, they were obviously going to be there a bit longer.

When Mick returned to his position. O'Meara informed him that he had sent Wright's team to the LZ as a working party. Mick nodded.

"Company CP radioed that we got the LP tonight," Tracey added.

"Which team had it last?" asked Mick.

"Boone had it night before last and Leroy night before that. So it's Ski's turn." the Irishman responded.

"Yeah...I guess it is," the Squad Leader replied.

"He's a big boy, he'll handle it. This'll give him something to keep his mind off his fiancée." O'Meara finished.

Mick nodded.

Holtzman walked down to First Fire Team's position. "Hey, Ski, you guys got listening post tonight," the Squad Leader announced. Ski looked up, nodded, then looked away.

"That mound out there thirty meters or so...with the tall grass to either side. That will give you cover and concealment. One man stays here. I'll have Leroy send over another Marine to man this position. Pick up the radio at the platoon CP," Mick ordered.

Ski nodded, looking at the indicated mound. He told Crawford to go pick up the radio.

Mick headed back down the lines telling each position where the LP was to be placed. Then he returned to his own position and sat down with a tired sigh.

"Have some coffee, Bro." said Tracey, handing the Corporal a can of hot Joe. Holtzman wearily sipped it and lit a Lucky.

"You better eat cause you look like ya lost ten pounds," observed O'Meara.

"I'll eat somethin' in a while."

"Ya got the malaria, don't ya?" claimed Trace, "I saw you with the sweats and shakes the other mornin'. Go see Doc VD and maybe he'll medevac you."

"Yeah…likely story! Tex Schultz has had malaria for a month and he's still here. I'll be all right," replied Mick.

"You won't be if you don't take care of yourself."

"Why should I worry about takin' care of myself when I got you to worry about my ass every five minutes?"

"Somebody's gotta take care of your ass! You spend all your time worryin' about everybody else's."

"Eat shit mother O'Meara!"

The two argued on in friendship as O'Meara cooked some C-ration meals and shared them with his friend.

O'Meara, as usual, took first watch, leaving Mick with the last watch at daybreak.

Holtzman was sound asleep during third watch when Tracey shook him awake.

"Mick, Mick, somebody's keying their handset like crazy," Tracey whispered.

Mick stared out in the direction of their LP. It was as black as tar with only a few stars showing. He could hear the company Radioman frantically trying to figure which of the three listening posts had activity. It quickly became obvious it was their own.

"Tracey, you monitor. I'm goin up the lines to alert the men that the LP's got movement." said the Corporal. As he started to move, three loud reports out of the dark came with muzzle flashes from the LP. First Platoons position to Mick's right returned fire.

"No! No! Cease fire!" screamed Mick.

"Call for illumination! I need illum now!" the Squad Leader yelled, "Hold your fire, I'm goin' out and bring the LP in!" he yelled as he headed past the lines in the direction of the listening post. He ran in a crouch. He heard the crack above him and went down on his belly, just a second before the illumination round lit up the area. Holtzman poked his head up. He could see the mound now only 15 meters away. He resumed his crouch and covered the distance to the mound. "Crack!" another illumination round detonated in the air above him. As it lit up the sky, he could make out the listening post.

"Hold your fire! Hold your fire! It's me...I'm comin' for you." Mick yelled.

Holtzman could see Crawford looking around confused. Brown looked at him with the whites of his eyes plainly visible in his black face. As Mick ran up he yelled, "Grab the radio and your weapons we're falling' back." He saw Ski on all fours looking for something on the ground.

"Come on, Ski, we'll find it in the morning," said the Squad Leader as he reached down and touched the Team Leader's shoulder.

At the touch Ski collapsed and fell forward. Mick's hand came away wet.

"Shit! Oh fuck! Ski's hit!" the Corporal moaned.

Leroy Wright had come out from his position and was now spraying any bush or clump of grass in the area with his M-14.

Holtzman rolled Ski over. There was blood all over his chest. Ski's eyes flickered open and he mumbled "Roseann...,"

"You'll be OK, Ski!" Mick said, as he reached down and grabbed his and Ski's M-16s. He took the collar of the wounded team leader's jungle shirt in his right and then started back to the lines.

"Cover us, Leroy! Fall back, you men!" Mick yelled as he took off, dragging the wounded man over the tall grass. In a few strides he had picked up enough speed and momentum that Ski's body wasn't touching the ground, just bouncing from one clump of grass to another.

"Hold your fire! Hold your fire! LP's comin' in!" the Squad Leader yelled.

It seemed like mere seconds before he saw the silhouettes of the men as he crossed the lines. The Corporal didn't slow down as he passed through the perimeter on toward the platoon CP where he knew the Corpsmen would be.

"Corpsman up!" he yelled as he sprinted into the Command Post. He spotted Doc VD and gasped, "Doc, Doc, Ski's hit hard in the chest!" He gently brought his friend to a halt in front of the Corpsman.

Doc ripped the jungle shirt off revealing a bullet wound through the right side of Ski's chest. The Corpsman then rolled Ski on his side and determined that the wound was through and through. Corporal Holtzman helped Dougherty to place plastic over the wounds and tape it. Then they tied battle dressings over the wounds. Doc VD got a bottle of plasma started.

Ski's eyes opened and he looked at Mick, mumbling something unintelligible, then plainly, "Rose!" was all that came out.

"Joe, you'll be all right. We got a medevac chopper on its way...should be here in five minutes, hang on buddy," the Squad Leader implored.

It was more than five minutes before the medevac chopper came on station. Mick had heard Boston, the company Radioman, call asking what was holding it up. Doc and Mick heard the chopper at the same time. They looked at each other and VD said, "He's got a chance...it's a ten minute ride to the battalion aid station. We've radioed in his blood type, and they're waitin' for him there. The Captain said I can go on the bird with him," Doc said,

Holtzman nodded.

The Helicopter circled. Men on the perimeter lit trip flares to mark the LZ inside the battalion perimeter but the chopper continued to circle.

"What's the fuckin' problem!" the Corporal swore.

"He doesn't think the LZ is secure." replied Boston Jones, the Radioman.

"Tell him it's inside the battalion perimeter! How much more secure could it be?" exclaimed the Squad Leader in desperation.

Doc and Mick continued to work on Ski, running plasma and fluids into the injured Marine while the helicopter continued to circle. Holtzman heard Captain Weller get on the radio and try to bring the pilot down, but the bird continued to circle. Forty-five minutes had passed since the helicopter started its circling. Now the pilot's voice came over the radio indicating that he was getting short of fuel.

"No, God damn you! Drop the fuckin' bird take Ski and Doc with you! Then get some fuckin' fuel!" the Corporal screamed in frustration at the circling helicopter.

Five minutes later the CH-46 broke its circle and flew back in the direction it had come. Boston Jones was already calling for another medevac .

"Shit! He's stopped breathing!" Doc yelled.

Immediately, the Corpsman began giving Ski mouth-to-mouth resuscitation but in a few minutes the medic was running out of air.

"I can take over for you Doc, I learned mouth to mouth, in Red Cross," Mick asserted.

The Squad Leader took over while Doc caught his breath and took Ski's pulse.

"He's got a strong pulse…if we can just keep him breathing!" VD exclaimed.

A few minutes later as Mick blew air into his friend's lungs, he rocked back choking and spitting blood. Doc jumped in and took over but in moments he was choking too. They switched off back and forth, spitting out their comrades blood that came up from his lungs with each breath they forced into him. Minutes later Joe Sokouski's heart stopped.

Corpsman Dougherty tried cardiac massage, while Mick continued mouth to mouth.

Ski's heart wouldn't restart. He had bled to death internally. Doc VD grabbed Holtzman's arm and said gently, "He's gone, Mick."

"No! No! No!" the Corporal cried, as he tried to blow life into his dead friend's lungs. "He'll make it, he's got to!"

"He's dead, Mick. He bled out."

The Squad Leader, with his shirt, face and lips covered with his dead friend's blood, threw his head back, stared at the sky and screamed, "God damn you! Damn you to hell!"

Holtzman grabbed Joe's arm looking for a pulse. The arm already felt cold and a little stiff. In the early morning light the once handsome face ringed with blond hair looked different…lifeless, a smear of blood across his mouth. The Corporal dropped the arm. His hands fell to the ground at which he stared for several minutes. Doc VD put a hand on the Squad Leader's shoulder. The sun was now up and its rays began to warm the men. In the distance came the sound of a transistor radio playing Percy Sledge:

When a man loves a woman,
She can do no wrong….

Mick Holtzman stood up and started to walk away but he turned back just as the sounds of a helicopter reached the CP. Holtzman's head snapped in the direction of the sound. He had a look on his face that would frighten any living soul.

"It's a different bird Mick!" yelled Boston Jones, "It's not the same one!"

The stony look on the Squad Leader's face dissolved as he leaned over and cut one of the dog tags from Sokouski's boots. He placed it with Clarence's and two others in his jungle shirt's chest pocket. He then picked up Ski's bloody jungle shirt to cover his friend's face. Holtzman felt something in the shirt's pocket. He reached in and found two letters, one opened the other unopened. Mick put the letters in his pocket with the four dog tags. Then he placed the shirt over his friends face. He saw the four Marines staring at him nervously, holding a poncho and he realized that they were there to load Joe's body onto the helicopter.

Mick turned and watched the helicopter approach from the east. It came straight in. Someone threw a green smoke grenade and the helicopter, without a moment's hesitation, set down next to the smoke.

Holtzman turned back toward his position. He didn't want to watch his friend's lifeless body thrown aboard the chopper like so much cordwood. Mick made about ten steps when suddenly the anger, frustration, guilt, and sorrow of the last few hours, weeks and months overtook him.

"Why?" he gasped to himself, "Why?" And then the tears came…trickling at first. The stream grew, flowing stronger. He walked on, blinded…stumbling…other Marines staring in awe that this hard man had broken.

"Come on, Mick!" called O'Meara, grabbing his friend's arm and leading him toward their position. "We're moving out in five minutes."

When Holtzman arrived at the position he collapsed into the fighting hole, just sitting there weeping.

"Mick! We're movin out. I got the men all saddled up. Here's your weapon. I brought it back from the CP." Tracey said. "Come on, Mick, we got to go!" he begged, looking at his friend with concern.

Corporal Holtzman pulled his head up, took a long shaky breath and mumbled, "You move 'em out, Trace, I'll catch up with you."

"Ya, OK." O'Meara said unsure what to do next. The company was moving. Wright's Second Team went by looking away as they passed their leader. Tracey remained standing by his friend, unsure, then Boone's Third Team passed, "Come on, Mick, we got to go."

"You go! I'll catch ya later," the Squad Leader mumbled.

O'Meara moved off uncertainly, looking back every few steps, then turning and speeding up to catch up with the disappearing First Squad.

Second Squad was now passing where Mick Holtzman

sat staring into the bottom of his fighting hole as if he could find the answers he was looking for there. Occasionally a grunt would look over at him then quickly away. Most averted their eyes as if he wasn't there.

"Mick! It's time to go," the Prez's rich bass voice said gently, as men continued to move past. Lincoln reached down and picked up his friend's rucksack and threw it effortlessly to his huge shoulders along with his own. He then reached down and gently grasped Mick's flak jacket and lifted him to his feet. "Come on, man…we gonna walk together for a while." The Prez put his arm around Holtzman's shoulder and then started walking slowly. Marines were passing the two without a second look.

An hour later, with his arm still around his friend's shoulder, the Prez and Mick had picked up the pace and were now between Second Squad and First.

"Thanks, Prez. I'm OK now." said Holtzman.

"Like hell you're OK! You ain't OK, I ain't OK, none of us'll ever be OK!" Lincoln insisted, angry now. A single tear making its way through the red dust on the shiny black skin. "We all be fucked up by this shit! We ain't never gonna be the same…we just got to go on, Bro. Your squad be needin' you, the platoon be needin' you. You got to go on! It don't mean nothin', Bro!"

Mick didn't answer.

"It don't mean nothin'!" the Prez repeated with feeling, shaking Holtzman a little.

Mick's tear stained blue eyes met the wet brown eyes of his comrade, "It don't mean nothin!" he repeated and embraced Lincoln. He pulled away, they touched closed fists and Holtzman turned and stretched his legs to catch up with his squad.

CHAPTER TWENTY-SIX
Ski's Letters

That evening when the battalion stopped and was digging in to form a defensive perimeter, Mick looked over at O'Meara and asked, "Who'd ya put in charge of First Team?"

"Crawford...but I told him it was temporary. He wasn't real excited about it anyway. He's only been in country a couple of months." answered the Irishman.

"Call up Leroy and Boone. We need to reorganize," the Squad Leader ordered.

The two arrived shortly and the four sat down on the ground for the conference.

"We have to reorganize our teams." Holtzman stated flatly, looking from man to man. "Boone, Third Team is now First Team. I'm taking Franklin from you Leroy, making him Third Team Leader and giving you Brown in his place. He's green and has an attitude so you got your work cut out for you."

"Franklin will make a good team leader," Leroy Wright said nodding sagely, "He moves good in the jungle and learns fast. As for Brown, he won't be able to scream prejudice when I send him on a workin' party." the Team Leader smirked.

"I'm gonna to be dependin' on you three." Mick said looking at the two team leaders and his grenadier. "I'm gonna need all the help I can get from you."

"You got it,"

Shortly after the team leaders left, Platoon Sergeant DeBeque approached. He stopped about fifteen feet away. He made eye contact, then hand signaled the Squad Leader to join him. When Mick was within earshot, Frenchy suggested, "Let's take us a little walk." The two walked away from the others then sat on their heels on a small knoll.

"I debriefed the two men who were with Ski on the LP last night while you and Doc were workin' on him."

Frenchy started, "I figured it would save you having to do it again tonight."

"Thanks, Sarge."

"They told me your man Ski was on watch and that he woke up the others. He signaled that he had seen three gooks skulking around in the grass in front of their position. He motioned Crawford to start keying the handset to get Company's attention. They told me they were doing that when Ski got up on his knees and opened up.

"Why the hell would Ski do that? He was experienced enough to know to throw a frag. It won't give your position away, nor attract friendly fire." Mick said, slowly shaking his head in puzzlement.

"Captain Weller is writing Ski's folks but that will be his last act as Company Commander. Blackwell takes over in the morning. Mr. Weller would like to see you ASAP, and if you could, take Ski's personal effects over when you go. I know this is tough…he was your friend." DeBeque finished.

Holtzman nodded, "I'll take care of it. Frenchy, why wouldn't that chopper land? Doc said Ski had a good chance but that chopper circled for an hour and then left!"

"I don't know, Mick…I just don't know." replied the Cajun.

O'Meara had already gathered Joe's personal effects into a ditty bag. He picked it up and headed for the Company Command Post.

When Mick arrived at the CP, he found the Captain sitting against a small mound of dirt writing with a board across both knees as a desk. Captain Weller looked up at his approach.

"These are Ski's things, sir," the Corporal said as he placed the ditty bag near the Captain's feet.

"Thanks Mick. I know you two were tight and that makes this tough. I've written his parents…anything that you want to add?" the Captain asked.

Mick shook his head.

"I'm also writing him up for a Silver Star for the action in

~ 164 ~

the valley, where you two swam the river and were involved in taking out that fifty caliber," Captain Weller said this as he handed Holtzman the sheet on which he was writing.

"That would be nice for his family, sir." The Squad Leader replied, staring blankly at the sheet of paper.

The top of the form listed all the information about Ski. His name, rank, serial number, date of birth. Mick was just starting to read the commendation the Captain was writing when something above caught his eye. Date of Birth 12/20/49, Mick read it again, that was his birth date. The hair on the back of Mick's head stood on end and a chill went down his back. They had been connected in a shared day of birth and now were connected in death.

"What's the matter, Corporal? You just turned white," Weller asked with a confused glance.

"I didn't know it till just now, but Joe and I were born on the same day, the same year." replied Holtzman, "It kinda took me by surprise. Thank you sir, I'm sure his family will appreciate it. He was a good Marine."

Corporal Holtzman headed back to his position. Tracey was out checking lines. *"Thank God for Trace,"* he thought. Then he fell dead asleep. Mick was so exhausted from the previous night's actions and the emotional breakdown of the day that he slept for five hours straight.

O'Meara found him out like a light when he came back so he simply spread a poncho liner over him and let him sleep, not waking him for watch. When Mick awoke, it was past midnight. He looked over and saw Tracey on watch.

"How long you been on watch?" Holtzman queried. "Why didn't ya wake me?"

"You were sleepin' like a baby, bud. I couldn't stand to disturb that innocent smile on your face," O'Meara said.

"Well, I better take the rest of the night to even things out then," the Squad Leader suggested.

"Bullshit! Just give me a couple of hours and wake me at two as usual. It'll all come out in the wash Marine." Tracey said, smiling as he used one of Mick's favorite phrases back at him. With that Tracey lay down rolled over and was asleep in three minutes.

His mind still in turmoil, Corporal Holtzman first thought of Lori, then, unbidden, came the vision of Ski smiling and alive. Then he saw him cold, bloody, and dead in the morning light. He thought of their shared birth date and how he had held Joe while he died.

There was a loud crack and an illumination round burst seconds later. It lit up the area as bright as day. Everything seemed OK. Mick reached for Lori's letter and felt the others. He had forgotten about them. He pulled the two letters out examining them in the light of the illum rounds. The top one he recognized as Joe's fiancée's handwriting. It was open. He read the return address and his skin crawled again. The address read:

Roseanne Antoni
131 Langdon St.
Madison, 5 Wisconsin

That was his home town! He knew where that address was! It was in the University district among the fraternity and sorority houses. He opened the letter and began reading:

Dear Joe,

As you know I am troubled that you have chosen to be a part of this criminal war that is being illegally waged against the innocent peasants of Vietnam, by this country's military industrial complex.

When I became engaged to you I was still in high school and naïve. I had no idea that your uniform was that of individuals who spend their time in Vietnam, killing babies and torturing innocent people who simply want to live in an agrarian socialistic society.

Since I have been at the University I have learned that what you do is criminal, disgusting, and

~ 166 ~

hateful. I have no idea what I ever saw in you, or
how I could have been attracted to a man who could
be so cruel to these innocent peasants.

I am therefore calling off our engagement, when
you return don't bother to look me up. I wouldn't
want to be seen with someone who could be in the
military, let alone the most perverse unit in the
military the Marines. From what I hear they are
about the same as the Gestapo.

I hope that someday you will realize what a cruel
and indecent thing you have done, and take steps
to rectify the injustices you have performed.

> *Sincerely,*
> *Roseanne*

Mick could not believe his eyes. He folded the letter and put it back into the blood stained envelope. *"No wonder Ski was all fucked up! He really loved this bitch, and she sends him this!"* he angrily thought to himself. It took the Corporal a while to absorb what he had just read and the impact that it must have had on his friend. He looked at the letter as if it were a serpent, something evil and sick. He contemplated destroying it, but finally put it back in his pocket. Then he changed his mind and placed it in his letter writing gear in his rucksack. He didn't want that letter close to Lori's. He still had the second letter in his hand, the return address read:

Audrey Ferguson
114 Pintail Ln.
Bessemer, Michigan

The letter was unopened although it had been postmarked the same as the other. Mick opened the letter with his bayonet and began to read.

Dear Joey,

Every night on the evening news we see pictures from Vietnam and the reporters tell how many American boys were killed that day. It is so frightening. I wish you were home safe, and that Curley, you and I, could go for a long walk in the woods.

Curley is fine, but he misses you, I take him walking in the woods and throw a stick for him, but I know he would rather be duck hunting with you.

I am so proud of you, as I am sure your parents are. I know you are doing the right thing in trying to help the people of Vietnam find freedom. I hear things on the news that reporters say about the war, and sometimes things people say about our soldiers that are negative, but I am sure that they are wrong.

I worry so much when I hear about the fighting in the area where your unit is.

I have never told you before that I fell in love with you when I was twelve. I was afraid that you would think me a fool, or a stupid little girl, but now I am so afraid that something will happen to you. I know you are engaged, but if you ever need a friend, or more than a friend, remember I have loved you longer than any woman other than your mother.

Please be careful, Curley and I will always be waiting for you.

Love,
Audrey

Mick Holtzman's mind was now truly in turmoil. A "Dear John" from the woman Ski loved that was damning and accusing, and a confession of love from a girl he'd known for a long time. *"Ski why didn't you open the second letter?"* Mick thought. He stared at the letter for awhile then folded it carefully and put it back in its envelope. Then he placed it in the plastic baggy where he kept Lori's letters.

He didn't mind having this one close to hers.

The Corporal knew that he should take the letters over and give them to the Captain in the morning but he hesitated. The "Dear John" would cause Ski's parents pain and anguish. The return of either would help nothing. He decided to keep them, although unsure for what purpose.

The Squad Leader spent the next hour wondering about Audrey, Roseanne, and Lori. He had never understood girls, partly because he had no sisters. Women were, and would always be, a mystery to Mick.

CHAPTER TWENTY-SEVEN
Mast

The next day brought more company sweeps. The Marines encountered no signs of the enemy and thankfully, no booby traps. Just long, hot days pushing through the thick vegetation and fighting the thorns of the "wait a minute bushes" while wishing they were somewhere else.

Corporal Holtzman was quiet...he had retreated into himself. He still did his job efficiently and with care but was obviously having an internal struggle. Several more days of non-productive company sweeps followed. The men didn't bitch as long as they weren't taking casualties. On the third day as the men came back to their positions, Frenchy DeBeque sought the Squad Leader out.

"Hey there, Corporal...you been keepin' a pretty low profile as of late," the Platoon Sergeant opened.

"Yeah...thinking....you know." Mick countered cryptically.

"No, I don't know! What are you thinkin' about?" came the Cajun's retort.

Mick looked up at DeBeque from where he sat and decided to go for it. "I'm thinkin' of requestin' mast. I want to see that chopper pilot in front of me and ask him why he wouldn't land."

The Platoon Sergeant was silent for a few moments, then said, "They won't like it, you know...the brass I mean. They don't like nothin rockin' the boat between them and the air wing. But I understand. There was no reason he shouldn't a landed and Ski would have had a fightin' chance if he had."

Request of Mast is an ancient Marine tradition that began in the British Royal Marines well before the Revolutionary War. The procedure allowed the lowest ranking Marine, or any Marine, to request an audience with the next in his chain of command and present his case or complaint. If not satisfied he could request mast to the next level. The request could conceivably go all the way to the

Commandant of the Marine Corps.

"Well, you're the next in the chain of command, so I've presented my case to you. I guess now it goes to the Platoon Commander." Holtzman asserted.

"I hear ya and I'm with ya but I think you're buyin' yourself a boatload of trouble," countered the dusky Sergeant. "It won't bring him back."

"I know it won't. I don't blame the fuckin' pilot for his death…just for not doin' his job. I'm responsible for his death! I sent him out there knowing he was screwed up." The Squad Leader said, the pain evident in his voice.

"Hold on a minute there Marine!" Frenchy said jumping into the fray. "You can't take responsibility for every fuckin' thing that happens! The orders came down to send out an LP…you sent the team whose turn it was. You ain't Super Marine, you can't see into the future and you can't be responsible every time somethin' bad happens."

Mick just looked at DeBeque. The Platoon Sergeant knew he wasn't going to convince this young NCO that he was not responsible for his friend's death, nor would anything, or anyone, get in the way of his request of mast.

The next morning the word came that they were being pulled out. The battalion would be helo-lifted back to the ship that afternoon. The Marines were thankful. They didn't like Dodge City and would be glad to be out of it.

When they arrived aboard ship, Mick went through the normal rituals of collecting the filthy jungle utilities, passing out clean replacements, distributing mail, sending the men to the showers and finally off to the chow line.

That evening the Squad Leader headed up on deck. It was already dark as he made his way to the quarterdeck and forward near the bow. He stood staring out to sea, letting the salt spray and ocean breeze flow over him. It felt good…clean, a sort of baptism. Perhaps it could purify him.

Finally the Corporal turned around at the sound of approaching footsteps. The footsteps came from Platoon Sergeant DeBeque who had been searching for him.

"I thought you might be up here," Frenchy began. "I

conveyed your request for mast to the Birdman. He asked what it was all about and I told him. He didn't give me a time or appointment or anything, just sorta nodded. When I left, he took off and ran over to Battalion. I saw him in a huddle with that Lieutenant Gregory that he's buddied up with."

"So when do I see him? I'll have to go a lot higher than a Platoon Commander to get an airwing pilot called on the carpet," countered the Squad Leader.

"I'll hit him up tomorrow, but I'm sure he was runnin' to tell the Colonels Aide what you're up to. So you can expect to start getting' some interference soon," the Sergeant explained.

"I suppose…what kind of flak do you think they'll try?"

"Oh, first they'll pass the word up through the NCOs, maybe to me, maybe to the Company Gunny. If you keep after it, they'll figure ways to slow you down,. This ain't no democracy you know," the stocky Cajun advised.

"Yeah, I knew this wouldn't be no day at the beach, Sarge…just want to have some idea as to what would be comin' at me."

"I'll help you and keep you as well informed as I can. When I have direct orders with regard to this, my attitude will be very formal so you'll know. I'm on your side on this Mick, but if I get orders, I'll have to carry them out, just so you know." Frenchy finished.

"I got it, Sarge. Don't get your ass in a sling for me. I'm bringin' this down on myself," the Corporal declared.

By the next day it was all over the ship that Corporal Holtzman had requested mast and wanted the helicopter pilot's wings. The enlisted men were a hundred percent behind him as were most, if not all, of the NCOs and Staff NCOs. Infantry Marines want to know that if they are wounded they will be transported quickly to the nearest medical treatment, which had not happened in Ski's case. The men were proud that this junior NCO was taking the bull by the horns and trying to right this wrong.

After breakfast, on the way back to the compartment,

every Marine Mick passed was high fiving or signing with him. Later that morning the Prez and Mick led Second Platoon in physical training on the flight deck. There weren't the usual catcalls and complaints. An hour after PT, while he was crossing the hanger deck, just below the flight deck, the Squad Leader ran into Platoon Sergeant DeBeque.

"Well, I checked with the Lieutenant this mornin' and he said he hasn't figured out where he can fit you into his busy schedule yet. So I guess the plan is to stall you." Frenchy told him.

"How long can they keep that up?"

"Long enough to see if it'll work, then they'll come up with some other way to back you off," the Sergeant responded.

The Corporal just shook his head and continued on his way to the laundry to see if the squad's jungle utilities had been washed yet.

When he arrived back at Second Platoon's compartment with the clean utility uniforms, he began passing them out. O'Meara, Leroy, and Tex were playing Back Alley Bridge as usual…bull-shitting as they played.

"Hey, Mick," O'Meara called, "You heard the latest? The Colonel turned down those Silver Stars that Birdman and Gregory wrote up."

"Oh, gee…that's too bad." Holtzman said sarcastically, "So what did they get? Bronze Stars, Navy Commendation, or what?"

"Naw, the Colonel didn't give 'em nothin'. But the scuttlebutt has it that Morrillo is going to get something." Tracey went on.

"Shit, I can't believe that…they're actually going to give a medal to a guy who deserves it?" added Tex Schultz.

"I'll bet them two Lieutenants put themselves in for the Medal of Honor next time," chimed in Leroy.

Mick watched the card game for a while, listening to the jibes and jousts of the conversation and adding a comment or two where he could.

The next day was Sunday. After morning chow Frenchy

DeBeque appeared in the platoon's compartment and announced that the Chaplin would be holding services on the flight deck in thirty minutes. He added that there would be a memorial service as well. When Mick arrived on the flight deck he was surprised to see the entire company there ahead of him. Many of the men weren't religious, but all were present to pay their last respects to their fallen comrades. The Corporal took his place at the front of First Squad and his wasn't the only tear to fall quietly on the deck during the memorial service. After the service, the usually boisterous compartment was uncharacteristically quiet. O'Meara, Leroy, and Willie were back at the card table. Most of the rest of the men were reading or writing letters home, or just crapped out catching some Z's.

Corporal Holtzman wasn't sure what to do. He had completed all his duties, written a letter home, re-read Lori's letters again, then re-read the letter from Audrey to Ski. Feeling jumpy and nervous, Mick lit another Lucky Strike and inhaled the smoke deeply, feeling it bite down into his lungs.

"Hey anybody got a shit-kicker they ain't readin'?" the Squad Leader called out to no one in particular.

"Yeah...I got one here that I just finished. It's called *Blood on the Chisholm Trail*. Do you want it?" replied Hamburger.

"Yeah, I'll give it a whirl. Thanks Burger."

The PFC tossed him the book. Mick fell back onto his rack and began reading the western.

Books are at a premium in Vietnam. In a way, they offer an escape to another time and place. Westerns seemed to be the most common novel found among the Marines. Perhaps that was all they could get or maybe they preferred them. Whatever the reason, the books are read until they literally fall apart. It is considered a sin to burn or damage the books. Every Marine has at some time or other been reading a book when he got to the last chapter and found it torn out. Probably used for shit paper by some jerk.

Holtzman read for about an hour but couldn't shake the

nervous, jumpy, feeling. Putting down the book, the he headed up on deck to get some air. The sea air was fresh and tasted good. Holtzman had always liked the sea and the mountains on family vacations as a boy. As he crossed the flight deck, he spotted Sergeant DeBeque on an interception course.

"Corporal, hold up there a minute!"

Mick stopped and waited for the Creole Sergeant.

"I've got your audience with the Lieutenant. His lordship will see you at 10:00 hrs. in his cabin." announced Frenchy.

"So...after I visit with him I will have to go to the Company Commander...this new guy Blackwell. Then to the Battalion Commander and then I'll be gettin' somewhere," responded the Corporal.

"Yeah, but it won't happen fast, you can bet your ass." said Frenchy.

"Thanks, Frenchy, I'll be there."

Holtzman continued on to the quarterdeck and his position near the bow. Mick sat looking at the South China Sea and the shoreline in the distance till the sun went down. An hour or so after sundown he started back towards the compartment. As the Squad Leader crossed the flight deck the smell of burning rope crossed his nostril. *"Well, someone's blowin' a jay,"* he thought.

As he neared the ladder way to below decks, a familiar voice called out from the fantail,

"Hey Bro, Y'all come on over and visit."

Mick approached the fantail and saw the burning embers of several marijuana cigarettes.

"What's happenin!" said the Prez in a very relaxed voice as he drew on the reefer.

"You know...same old shit," responded Holtzman.

"You want a hit, man?" asked A. J. Vasquez.

"He don't smoke grass," Lincoln interjected, "but he be cool."

"We're with you on the pilot deal, Mick." chimed in Willie Parker. "The brothers know you'd be doin' it if one of them got left like Ski."

"Thanks, we all gotta stick together," the Corporal said, then signed with each of the men in the group as he left to go below.

Holtzman awoke at 03:00 hours in a steamy sweat, the perspiration running out of every pore in his body. He felt like he was on fire. This lasted for approximately three minutes and was followed by chills and shakes. Now he felt like he was in a deep freeze. His body shivered and shook. The episode finally passed and he lay there exhausted, wondering how long before the malaria got bad enough to disable him.

O'Meara's head appeared next to Mick's berth, "You gotta see the Doc man, you can't go this way for long!"

"I talked to him the first day we came aboard. He told me to keep takin' my malaria pills...and he drew a blood sample. He told me last night they couldn't find no germs in the sample."

"So what does that mean?" questioned Tracey.

"I guess you don't officially have malaria till they find the bug," concluded Holtzman. "Catch some Z's, dude, you may be First Squad Leader before long."

"Kiss my ass! I was a Squad Leader before I joined up with you. I like things the way they are, so start takin' care of yourself," retorted O'Meara.

Mick woke again at 05:45, fifteen minutes before reveille. He felt tired...un-rested, but decided to beat the rush and have a leisurely shower before the masses arrived.

The water seemed to soothe him. He stood under the main stream of the shower head and let the water spray over him as he kept gradually turning up the hot water until the shower room was filled with steam.

When the Corporal heard reveille played over the loudspeakers, he turned the water off, grabbed his shaving kit and lathered up. In actuality Holtzman didn't need to shave. He grew no true beard at this early age, only peach fuzz that was bleached transparent by the sun. Mick shaved because he would be appearing before Lieutenant Byrd this morning. Although he saw the Lieutenant every day, this was going to be official business.

As the Squad Leader left the head, the Marines were trooping in yawning, walking half blind with the sleep barely out of their eyes. But boy, were they glad for the luxury of a morning shower! Holtzman found the platoons compartment half deserted. He dug under the mattress and recovered the carefully folded starched and pressed new utilities that Gunny Shaw had obtained for him. It seemed a long time ago that he had put the utilities on to visit First Sergeant Riker and find out about the Enlisted Candidates Program. Mick decided to wait till after chow and physical training to put on the crisp clothing. He settled for the Jungle Utilities he had worn the previous day.

It was Holtzman's turn to lead the men in physical training after chow. Mick went through the usual calisthenics but kept the repetitions to a minimum, thereby finishing PT by 09:15. This gave him time for a quick shower and to change into the starched uniform. As Mick left the platoon compartment for his meeting, Lincoln called out, "Right on, Mick… GET SOME!!!"

"Get some!" The cry went up from every man in the compartment. The rumor mill was running at maximum efficiency and everybody knew where the Corporal was going and what his mission was. The men held their closed fists up as a salute as he left the compartment.

When crossing the flight deck the Squad Leader spied Frenchy waiting for him at the hatchway into officer's country. Mick stopped. They shook hands. The Corporal nodded and they proceeded down the alleyway to Lieutenant Byrd's compartment. At the open hatch-cover DeBeque rapped his fist on the hatch three times, stepped inside, came to attention. "Sir, Corporal Holtzman is here as requested, Sir."

"Send him in Sergeant," responded the Lieutenant.

Frenchy turned, took a step back, and nodded to Mick. The Squad Leader stepped into the compartment, took one step past the Platoon Sergeant and came to the position of attention. "Sir, Corporal Holtzman requesting mast, Sir!"

"Very good, Corporal. That will be all Sergeant. You can close the door on your way out," Byrd instructed.

Frenchy winced as the officer referred to the hatch cover as a door, but turned smartly and exited the compartment, closing the hatch behind him. *"I guess the Lieutenant doesn't want any witness to hear what goes on,"* the Frenchman assessed.

"All right Holtzman, what's your beef?" asked the Platoon Commander in a not-too friendly tone.

"Sir, I demand an explanation from the pilot of the medevac chopper that circled us for an hour while we had a man seriously wounded...needing evacuation and medical treatment," stated the Squad Leader.

"You know, Holtzman, you are going to open up a can of worms here. I understand that you had everything going your way before you started rocking the boat. Sergeants list, Enlisted Candidates Program, a clean record...do you understand what I'm saying, Corporal?"

Mick could read between the lines, but he wasn't going to make it easy for Byrd.

"No Sir, the Corporal does not understand. Does that mean the Lieutenant is refusing my request for mast?"

Byrd's face flushed red, "You know damn well it would be illegal for me to refuse your request for mast. I'm trying to point out to your not-so-sharp mind that things might not go so nicely for you if you rock the boat."

"Sir, the Corporal doesn't have a college education as does the Lieutenant, so you'll have to make it plain to me. Does the Lieutenant mean that my name will be dropped off the Sergeants list if I proceed?"

The Platoon Commander looked even more frustrated, "Of course, that's not my meaning! That would be blackmail! I am just trying to advise you that this course of action could cause you problems, Corporal."

"I'm afraid you will have to be more specific, Sir. I believe it is every Marine's right to request mast without fear of reprisal...Sir."

Lieutenant Byrd was now totally hamstrung. His plan

had been to nip this request in the bud by implying that there would be consequences if Holtzman pursued his plan. Mick had blocked him at every attempt. If he had told him he would be off the Sergeant's list he could be court-martialed. Byrd wondered if DeBeque had his ear to the door. He was sure he did and he wasn't going to risk his career.

"All right, Corporal, your request has been duly noted. You may leave."

"Thank you, sir. I guess then I must move my request to the Company Commander."

"I wouldn't do that if I were you."

"Sir, a Marine is dead! If that helicopter had landed when it came on station, that man would have had a fighting chance to live, Sir! Good day," Mick finished.

The Lieutenant sputtered as the tall lean Marine did a smart about face, took two steps to the hatch, turned the handle hesitating a second, then proceeded out of the compartment. Byrd almost screamed, "Where the hell are you going?" until he realized that he had dismissed him.

After the hatch closed, Lieutenant Byrd let out a sigh of frustration and anger. The door to the head that had been slightly ajar opened and Lieutenant Gregory stepped into the room. "Well, that didn't go as planned. Why didn't you just tell him that if he pursued this that he would be off the Sergeant's list and his recommendations for the Naval Academy would not be forth coming."

"I'll bet that Sergeant DeBeque had his ear to that door and listened to the conversation. If he heard me use those threats to derail this request for mast, it could cost my career," Byrd replied.

"We both know that it has come down from regiment that they don't want this request for mast to screw up relations with the air wing. If we can stop it, it will be a feather in our caps and might bring a meritorious promotion or commendation," Gregory asserted.

"I wasn't willing to face a potential court martial for a feather in my cap," said Byrd.

"Well, we better find some other way to stop this cocky bastard. How about have the NCO's tell him of the consequences?" suggested Gregory.

"I don't think that will stop the stupid son-of-a-bitch! I don't think he's smart enough to realize he's screwing up his career." uttered the still frustrated and out maneuvered Platoon Commander.

"Well, I have another idea," said Gregory with a smile. "We will have to get Captain Blackwell on our side, but I don't think that will be a problem."

CHAPTER TWENTY-EIGHT
Hill 55

When the hatch covers handle turned, Frenchy DeBeque leapt back from it and stood unconcernedly to one side. The slight hesitation that the Corporal had made was just enough time to be out of the danger of being caught spying. Holtzman marched through the hatch and closed it firmly behind him. Glancing at the Platoon Sergeant, Mick nodded and the two headed for the flight deck side by side without speaking a word. When on the flight deck and away from curious ears Mick said, "Well, did you hear any of that?"

"Yeah," replied Frenchy. "The whole nine yards. You tried to force his hand with the threat and he didn't have the balls to go for it."

"I think he knew you were listenin' at the door," said Mick with a thin smile. "He sure was sweatin'."

The two continued on, side by side and walked to the fantail near the stern of the ship. They hung over the rail and stared out to sea.

"You know they'll pull you off the Sergeant's list and might mess with the Officers Candidate program if you continue...maybe more," declared Frenchy.

"Yeah, what's a stripe compared to a life? We need to know that if a grunt is hit he'll get a medevac damn quick. These guys are a lot less likely to lay it on the line if they think they'll be left to bleed out while some wing wiper flies in circles around them," replied Holtzman, "Hell, you lost all your stripes! Not just one that nobody had given you yet!"

"Mick...I lost my stripes cause I did somethin' stupid, not because it was the right thing to do. I respect what you're doin', especially because you know you are gonna pay a price. I think your career in the Corps is more important to you than you let on. I hope this don't screw up the Naval Academy deal, but if it does, don't give up. Apply for OCS when you turn twenty. We need good officers in the Corps and you'd do just fine."

"Thanks Frenchy," the Corporal responded.

The next day Mick went to see Gunny Shaw. Here, he formally forwarded his request of mast to the Gunny for an appointment with his new CO, Captain Blackwell. Gunny Shaw nodded as the Squad Leader made the request. "Let's take a little stroll, Corporal."

The two headed out onto the quarter deck and walked toward the bow. "I know what you're doin' and why," the Gunnery Sergeant began, "You know they'll make you pay, don't you?"

"Yeah, I know, the Sergeants list, the Enlisted Candidate Program, what else?"

"Who knows, Mick, they may trump up some charges and court martial you. I just want you to know I'm proud of you for stickin' up for your men. I'll do anything I can to help you, but the new CO is a book officer and from stateside, with no combat experience. I won't have the pull I did with Mr. Weller."

"Thanks, Gunny, I'll survive," the Squad Leader said, his tight smile returning for the first time in a week.

The routine aboard ship continued. After PT the next morning, Holtzman was told to report to the Platoon Commanders cabin.

When he reported, he was surprised because he had thought that the LT might have another go at trying to stop the request for mast...but that wasn't the case. The Platoon Commander informed him that the 9th Marines over on Hill 55 were having a rough time of it and could use a little reinforcement. The Company Commander had decided to send First Squad and a machine gun team over there for a week. Mick was to have his men geared up and ready to go at 09:00 the next morning.

Holtzman had heard about Hill 55. It was located on the main infiltration route towards Danang. The Ninth Marines had fortified bunkers on the hill, but they were routinely shelled, mortared, and rocketed. The hill was often attacked by both NVA and VC. Combat patrols and ambushes saw regular activity. *"Looks like the boy's vacation is over! Guess I won't get any boxing in this go-around."* Mick calculated.

The next morning First Squad and Tex's gun team were on the flight deck in full battle gear at 08:45. The helicopter was brought up from the hanger deck by the huge elevators with the accompaniment of those resounding Klaxon horns. The squad loaded aboard and off they went. Twenty minutes later they landed at the permanent LZ near Hill 55.

The night before, Holtzman had a meeting with the squad, telling them what little he knew of their mission, and the dangers of Hill 55. The dangers included the availability of drugs and alcohol due to the proximity to Danang.

"When we get there, play by the rules," the Squad Leader ordered. "We don't know these guys…stay out of trouble. If you have any at all, tell me. I won't let them split us up."

On arrival at the LZ, The Squad Leader disembarked the chopper first as always and led the men at a jog away from the rotors. After all the men had moved safely away from the chopper, it lifted off and began its return trip to the ship. The squad watched as the bird began its return to their home. Mick looked around to find a welcoming committee, or someone to get direction from. There was no one there.

The terrain was typical of I Corps. Red dirt, saw grass and other mangled vegetation here and there. The hill was obvious to the north one hundred meters away. A road ran next to the LZ. To the south, there was a village and beyond that, a river twisted its way to the hill and then back around the ville to the rice paddies beyond. A group of Vietnamese children came on the run from the direction of the ville. The first ones began begging for food or cigarettes, followed by a second wave of older kids carrying fiber bags used as sandbags. These now contained ice, sodas, and beer which they were offering for sale to the recently landed grunts.

"Hey Mick! This is a civilized fuckin' area," commented O'Meara.

"Yeah…wait till them kids are leading their papa-san into your hooch with a satchel charge some night," responded Holtzman.

He ignored the children and the beer. He started up the road toward the gate to the compound on the hill. The squad followed but not without doing some commerce.

Fifty meters up the road the Corporal stopped at the gate and checked in with an uncaring sentry who just pointed them on up the hill. The squad wandered on, passing work details of Marines fixing or stringing barbwire and other menial tasks.

Soon the Marines started seeing bunkers and tent hooches that housed the Ninth Marines and their offices.

The Squad Leader stopped in one that said CP on the sign and walked in. A "Sleepy" looking enlisted clerk was at a desk shuffling papers. Mick approached and introduced himself.

"Howdy, I'm Squad Leader, First Squad, Second Platoon, Hotel Company, Second Battalion, 26th Marines. We've arrived to reinforce the Ninth Marines," the Squad Leader stated.

The clerk typist looked at Mick as if he were an alien from Mars, then finally asked, "Do you have orders?"

"Well, I was given orders to come here," retorted the Corporal.

"Let me see them," the clerk demanded.

"See what!"

"The orders!"

"They gave me the orders verbally, told me to load the helicopter with my men at 09:00 and here the fuck I am, so where do I go?" Holtzman responded starting to lose his patience.

The enlisted clerk looked at Mick but his eyes only held those of the infantryman for a second. "Well, I don't know anything about this. You better see the Company Gunny."

"No shit!" responded the disgusted Squad Leader.

The clerk walked toward the back of the tent and opened a canvas door. He conversed with someone and a few minutes later a Gunnery Sergeant in jungle utilities stepped out. He glanced at Holtzman and motioned him back into the private office.

Mick entered the tent office and stated his business. "Corporal Holtzman, First Squad, Second Platoon, Hotel Company, Second Battalion, 26th Marines, reporting as ordered."

"You must be the Corporal that Gunny Shaw called me about this morning. The son-of-a-bitch woke me up at 05:00 and thought it was funny! My name's MacDonald I knew Shaw back in Korea," MacDonald explained.

"Gunny Shaw is a good man. I've been proud to work with him, Sir," the Squad Leader answered.

"Well Shaw says you're the best. So, I'm glad to have you but not sure why you're here. We put out a request for reinforcements a month ago, then about a week later got replacements and we are damn near totally operational. But the shit hits the fan here regularly. If you're as good as Shaw says, we'll be using you and your men for night ambushes."

Gunnery Sergeant MacDonald then went about the process of billeting the reinforced squad. Showing Mick the Chow Hall and other accommodations. He told him he would be attached to First Platoon, Able Company 1/9 and would be primarily responsible for night ambushes and actions.

Holtzman's squad was billeted in a bunker occupied by one of Able Company's squads. When he entered, there was only one Marine in the bunker. The Corporal inquired into which racks were not in use and lined the 14 cots up along one wall. He had his men dump their gear there. It was near noon so Mick headed for the mess hall to get some lunch with his men. The food was fair, the mess hall informal. About halfway through the meal a Sergeant stopped by the table and introduced himself as Able Company's Platoon Sergeant Gieger. Gieger sat down and chatted while Mick and his men finished lunch. Holtzman's squad was sharing quarters with Able Company's Second Squad, which was presently out on patrol and would have the ambush that evening. Mick's squad would take over those duties beginning tomorrow. Gieger told the Squad Leader to stop by the company office around 14:30 so he could be in on the debrief of the squad now out on patrol and thereby get the skinny on the area of operation. The Corporal assured him that he would be in attendance.

After they finished eating, the men went back to the bunker. Mick had an informal gear check and warned the troops about contraband. Then he went out to explore and poke around Hill 55.

By 14:00 Holtzman had been to every gun emplacement and defensive position on the hill. He had catalogued each position and the fields of fire from those positions. The next day he and his men would be out patrolling in front of these positions and at night they would have to move past and through these fields of fire to gain access to ambush sites. He would not place his ambush in front of these positions for fear of danger from friendly fire.

After his tour of the hill the Corporal looked back in on his men. O'Meara was reading a playboy and smoking.

"Where's everybody at, Trace?" The Corporal queried.

"Oh they're checkin' things out I s'pose. What're you up to?"

"I'm on my way to that debriefin' and try to learn the background about this AO. Wanta tag along?"

"Hell, can't dance, got nothin' else on my agenda...yeah, I'm comin' Mick."

"Something weird goin' on here Trace. These dudes really weren't expectin' us and don't really need us. They're gonna use us just 'cause we're here. So, why are we here?"

O'Meara looked at his friend and shrugged. "It's out of my pay grade dude."

The two walked down toward the company office as a squad of infantrymen headed up the hill past the two, with one of the grunts peeling off and into the office.

That must be the patrol, Holtzman thought. The two friends walked into the tent that served as company office. Sergeant Gieger was present as well as a First Lieutenant and a thick stocky Corporal. Gieger looked up and began introductions, "This is Corporal Holtzman of the 26th Marines, Lieutenant Cook, First Platoon Commander, and Corporal Gunderson, Squad Leader of Second Squad." Mick nodded and shook hands with each man in turn and then introduced O'Meara.

Then the debriefing began in earnest. Squad Leader Gunderson described his patrol route and findings in detail. He then pointed out where he was going to set up the night ambush. After the debrief Mick began asking questions about enemy activity in the area, likely routes for enemy soldiers, known hot spots or strongholds. The Platoon Sergeant and Lieutenant answered most of the questions. Corporal Gunderson headed back to his squad.

That night Holtzman and his squad would stand interior guard in fortified positions on the hill. This was easy duty compared to what they were used to. As usual, Mick and Tracey checked the men on a regular basis. At 03:00 some of the positions below on the hill opened up toward the river. The positions to either side of Holtzman's did as well. The Squad Leader moved throughout his men warning them not to fire unless they saw muzzle flashes or movement. After the commotion died down one of the Ninth Marines in an adjoining position asked why the new guys hadn't fired.

"We don't fire till we have targets!" replied Mick. His comment was greeted with silence.

Chapter Twenty-Nine
26th vs 9th Marines

The next morning after chow, First Squad prepared to go out on patrol. Gunderson's squad had just returned from a non-productive ambush.

"Hey Mick," one of the men called out, "soft covers and jungle shirts or flak jackets and helmets?"

Before the Squad Leader could answer, Gunderson yelled, "You'll wear flak jackets and steel pots here!"

Some of Holtzman's men began to grumble.

"Is that Ninth Marine's protocol?" asked Mick.

"That's the way you'll do it while you're here!" replied Gunderson.

"If that's the regulation that's the way we'll do it, but get one thing straight. First Squad is mine! You ain't givin' any orders to my men." clarified Holtzman.

"This is my bunker and I'll do any damn thing I please!" replied the stocky Corporal.

"You won't be doin' shit with my troops, Gunderson!"

"First Squad saddle up...flak jackets and soft covers. On the road." Mick ordered.

Gunderson glared at Holtzman from under thick eyebrows.

Mick led the men down to the main gate where they proceeded through and down the hill. They followed the road toward the ville for a few hundred yards then off the road onto a paddy dike running parallel. This was going to be a long patrol. The men traveled with a ten to fifteen foot interval between them. The Squad Leader walked point, stopping often to observe and evaluate.

As the patrol approached the Village a ragged group of children approached cautiously, some begging, others with beer and soda's for sale.

"Didi, Didi-mau!" The Corporal shouted, stopping the approach. "Didi!" he yelled again and pointed back toward the ville and the kids wandered back in that direction.

Holtzman had learned from Gieger that the NVA were

mostly in the hills to the west. However, they would regularly come to the village and extract taxes of rice or money from the local peasants, with the help of some VC sympathizers in the village. The patrol skirted the village, observing the obvious ingress and egress routes. When they came to the river, Mick spotted a likely ford then led the men across. They continued along the far side of the river across from the village, now heading back in the general direction of the hill.

They moved slowly, observing the village and shores for evidence of activity. When the Marines had passed the village, the river made a ninety degree bend near Hill 55. Here, near the bend in the river, on the opposite shore, was a spit of sand. It looked like a natural ford. Mick could see tracks leaving the sandy bank heading into the river in a westerly direction where most enemy activity had been reported.

Corporal Holtzman stopped. He tapped the stock of his weapon three times with his signet ring and stared at the sandy spit. The men alerted at the sound of the tap. They knew this meant pay attention and that they would probably be returning here. The men saw where he was looking and after a few inconspicuous seconds, the Squad Leader moved on. He continued far upstream passing under, but across from, the heavily defended hill and re-entered the perimeter from a little used gate through the wire and mines on the opposite side of the compound.

It was still early only 12:50 hours so the Corporal sent the men to secure their gear, eat, and catch some Z's as they would be out all night. Holtzman headed to the company office and gave Gieger a synopsis of the patrol and pointed out the sandy spit on the map where he planned to set up his ambush.

Platoon Sergeant Gieger liked the plan, commenting that it was further out than most of their squads went.

"This way we won't be shootin' mama-san in the ass when she goes out of her hooch to take a shit. Nobody with any legitimate business should be walkin' down that spit at night." Mick stated.

Gieger told the Squad Leader that he'd tell the Platoon Commander the plan when he returned from a meeting. If any changes were to be made, he would send a runner. Otherwise, Mick was to stop by the office just before they left the compound for their ambush.

Corporal Holtzman led his squad with the machine gun team down the hill just at dusk. He stopped by the company office and informed the Platoon Sergeant of his route to the ambush site. It would be very different from the route of the patrol. *"Rule number one, never go the same way twice."* he thought.

At the bottom of the hill he set the men in single file till the light was completely gone. Each man was clad in jungle utilities with soft cover. Each had his twenty loaded magazines in bandoliers. They each carried five fragmentation grenades. The squad had three claymore mines, O'Meara had the grenade launcher and 100 rounds of ammo, Tex carried the M-60 machinegun with three hundred rounds in an assault pouch. His B gunner carried the tripod, an M-16 and more gun ammo.

Mick moved them out one at a time, listening to each man as they walked past. He didn't want a pocketful of change giving away their position. As the last man passed him in silence, he stretched his long legs and moved back to the front of the column leading them past the LZ, then off the road to a grove of bamboo. Here they stopped for five minutes while Mick surveyed the ground between their present position and the ambush site.

When he had satisfied himself, he moved off slow and low. He walked in a duck walk that shortened his six foot two height to about three foot five. The others followed suit. Mick stopped about every ten feet and looked and listened because eyes and ears were the secret to night actions. They reached the grassy sand spit without incident. There was a well concealed small mound in the center, where they positioned the M-60. He spread the men out in line facing the river with one behind facing the rear.

Holtzman and O'Meara then set up the Claymores. They put two in front, crisscrossing the kill zone, the area directly in front of the ambush, and one behind to blow if they were surprised or needed an escape route. The electronic detonating cords were reeled out and back to the center of the ambush where the Squad Leader and Grenadier attached them to their hellboxes.

The men then settled in for the night. Every other man could catch some sleep, but snoring was not allowed. The men were well rested this night and few slept. Everything remained quiet till 02:00. Tracey nudged Mick who had momentarily drifted off. O'Meara pointed to his ear then jerked his head toward the Ville. He had heard something from that direction. Then the Squad Leader heard a crunch of sand, the rustle of fabric and a raspy breath. There were men in front of them, walking into the kill zone between them and the river. Mick held the two hellboxes and waited till the enemy soldiers were in the middle between the two claymores. He counted to three and punched the handles to the hellboxes. There were two loud detonations as the shape charges exploded. Ball bearings filled the air through the kill zone. At the same instant the machine gun chimed in with Tex ripping off 20 round bursts. O'Meara's grenades were landing about one every two seconds and with the sound of eleven M-16s and one M-14 firing fully automatic, the noise was ear-splitting.

After about thirty seconds Mick yelled, "Cease Fire! Cease Fire!"

The fire slowed but didn't stop entirely. "Cease Fire! Damn it!" The silence was truly deafening after the roar of explosions and small arms fire. "Kuhl! Call the Hill and tell them to send up some illume over us."

"They're already on the horn, Mick, wantin' to know what kind of contact we've made."

"Shit…give me that handset! One niner, this is two alpha. We have made contact. Request illumination so we can count enemy dead. Alpha two has no casualties…over."

"Roger Alpha two. Illume on its way. Give us a sit rep

ASAP...niner out."

Seconds later there was the tell-tale crack over head and the illumination round lit up the night sky. The Marines kept their heads down for a few seconds then began to peer through the saw grass and sand at the carnage that lay in front of them. There was what had been five armed men, the AK-47s and SKS assault rifles lay on the ground. The men, some still burdened with thirty pound sacks of rice they had probably just extorted from the peasants, lay in grotesque positions, their bodies ripped and mangled by the explosions and the deadly hail of gun fire.

Mick picked up the radio and motioned everybody to stay put. "One Niner, this is two alpha...over."

"Go ahead two alpha" came the reply.

"We have five KIA, November Victor Alpha here, over."

"OK two alpha. Take their weapons and come on in." replied the hill.

"Negatory on your last. They have a shipment of rice as well as weapons. We have a good position and not long till dawn. We will stay here and see if anyone comes by to see what happened. Two alpha out." The Squad Leader finished and let out a sigh. He was thinking that he didn't want to try to get back inside the hill's lines after dark after witnessing the performance of the previous night.

First Squad hunkered down and waited for dawn and all remained quiet after the ambush. First light arrived in about two hours and forty-five minutes. Mick got back on the radio to call for a squad to help his men carry the weapons, rice, and bury the enemy dead. While they waited, Mick's men took a closer look at their work. Holtzman had noted that some reveled in the death of the enemy while others were sickened, some just curious. He knew they had done their job well last night, but now he would just like to get away from the aftermath.

After the squad from the Hill arrived, they buried the dead and First Squad was back on the road and up the hill in an hour. The Corporal sent his men to shit, shower and shave, while he went to the company office for debriefing.

The debriefing went well. The Ninth Marines hadn't been having many hits on their ambushes and the five enemy, several hundred pounds of rice and weapons were a big haul. When the debrief was over Mick went to the head and stuck his head under the tap. That was about all the shower he was going to manage until later. The mess hall would close in five minutes and he needed food more than being clean.

Holtzman could feel his body wasting away. He was losing weight, probably down to a hundred fifty from one seventy-five. The fevers and chills were just sucking it off of him.

The Corporal hurried to the mess hall and managed to get down a decent breakfast, which he ate alone in contemplation. He thought about his request for mast. *"How long was it going to take to get to a level where he might actually get the helicopter pilot in front of him? Was it going to cost him his career? Sergeant? the Naval Academy? Well the request wasn't progressing very fast here. "Hmmmm, I wonder if that's why we were sent here?"* He knew he wouldn't quit but he also knew that his stubbornness was a fault and a virtue at the same time. It was something he could learn to control and use as an asset in the future.

The Squad Leader finished his meal then headed back up the road toward the bunker where his squad was billeted. As he approached, Boone Riley came out of the bunker on the run.

"Mick, we got problems. That asshole Corporal is fixin' to whip O'Meara!"

"What…what the fuck happened?" Holtzman yelled as he broke into a run.

"They had words. That Gunderson guy threatened to whip Tracey's ass so he told him to start the dance."

Mick broke through the hatchway into the bunker and there was Gunderson, about two hundred pounds of him, on top of one hundred forty pound O'Meara, pounding away.

Holtzman crossed the barracks in two strides and laid a jungle boot to the side of Gunderson's head. The impact knocked him off of Tracey. The stocky Corporal rose to his knees, shaking his head like an angry bull.

"I'll kill you, you fucker!" he growled.

"Better get started dick-head!" Mick retorted.

Gunderson charged, Holtzman stepped to the side leaving his right leg in place, tripping the larger man as his momentum drove him past. When the stocky Corporal crashed onto the floor, Mick landed on his back with both knees, taking the bigger mans breath completely. Realizing his temporary advantage he quickly applied the judo choke hold Hadaka Jima or the "naked strangle".

As Gunderson tried to get his breath back, Mick would choke it off again. The heavier man cursed and swore but Holtzman had him and was not turning him loose. Mick had learned long before that if you fight a man and hurt him, he won't want to fight you again. If you beat a man, beat him severely…completely…leave him with nothing. Holtzman didn't want to fight Gunderson again.

Finally the stocky Corporal quit cursing. Holtzman released him and stepped across the room. O'Meara was sitting on his rack rubbing the cuts and abrasions on his face, fingering his bayonet. The men of Gunderson's squad were sitting against one wall staring nervously at the men of the 26th Marines. Slowly Gunderson got to his feet. He turned and looked at Holtzman with hatred radiating out of his eyes. Gunderson took two steps to his rack and reached for his M-16 then froze. As his hand touched the weapons stock, Tex Schultz chambered a round in his M-60 machine gun. The sound froze the action. Every man in First Squad had a weapon in his hand, some were aimed, others just pointed in the direction of the men of the ninth.

"That's about enough of that!" Mick yelled, noting that none of his men put their weapons down. "We're here to kill gooks not Marines!"

Somebody took a deep breath and the tension seemed to dissipate with that.

"All right men…you start cleaning this place up. We want to thank the ninth for their hospitality." the Squad Leader said with a look to Tex and O'Meara to hold their positions.

About half of First Squad began cleaning the place up, righting the cots that had been turned over. Someone found a broom and started sweeping. Mick, Tex, Tracey, Boone and Leroy all maintained tactical positions in the room. Gunderson stood up and walked out of the bunker.

As the overturned cots were realigned, the floor swept, and gear straightened up, several members of Gunderson's squad left the bunker. Leroy Wright pulled the magazine out of his M-14, popped the round out of the chamber and began field stripping the weapon for cleaning. Seconds later the sound of Tex opening the receiver on the M-60 and removing the belted machine gun ammo followed.

"We goin' out again tonight?" questioned Wright.

"Yeah…I think it's safer out there than in here," replied Mick, which generated a chuckle or two.

The Squad Leader stood up and motioned O'Meara to follow. They headed out of the bunker.

"You OK, Trace?" Mick asked as they walked down the road. O'Meara's left eye was black and swelling and there were other abrasions on his face.

"Yeah, but I'm glad you got there when you did. He was thumpin' me good. You sure ain't lost it, Mick!"

"I had to use every trick in the book, Trace. I'm not as strong as I was a month ago."

"The malaria?"

"I suppose." The two walked on in friendship chatting about everything and nothing.

That afternoon Holtzman reported to the company office and found Sergeant Gieger in charge as usual. He gave Gieger his plan for tonight's ambush, which involved crossing the river upstream from last night's position.

"We consider that side of the river their territory, Corporal." the Platoon Sergeant said with raised eyebrows.

"Well again, if anybody shows up over there, we can bet

they ain't friendlies." the Squad Leader responded. "Just one thing, you got a fifty caliber site that overlooks our ambush position. I don't want them openin' up on us if we hit the shit."

"I'll spend the night at that position Corporal. Satisfied?" Gieger said.

"That'll do."

Chapter Thirty
Rock Apes

That night, First Squad left the hill just as they had the night before, following the same route for about fifty yards. Mick then led them off the road and around the other side of the LZ. They went to the river where they sat quietly for twenty minutes. When satisfied, Mick started out into the river. This wasn't a ford so it would be a deep crossing. The water was mid-chest halfway across. They waded out quietly onto the other bank where they sat another twenty minutes until they had drip dried.

Mick moved off to the west, past where the river made its turn around the hill. Here, there was a foot trail leading to the mountains toward the west. That was his ambush site. Holtzman set the men on line along the high side of the path with the two end fire teams slightly back, giving him some flank protection. O'Meara and the Squad Leader set out the three claymores as before, two in front, one to the rear. Then they settled in. This night they slept in watches. All was quiet until just before dawn. It was just beginning to gray up and at 04:30 Boone signaled movement to the west. The grunts tensed up.

Mick was able to make out four...no, five silhouettes moving towards them. The first two he was sure were female and well in front of the other three, something about the last two said male. *"What the hell?"* he thought.

As the two girls came into the kill zone, he could not detect any weapons on them. He could make out weapons on the last two. The one in the middle he guessed was an adult mama-san. The girls and women could have been conscripted to work for the enemy as they often were. Holtzman made his decision, he let the two girls pass, then the mama-san. When the two men entered the kill zone he fired his hellboxes a little late, allowing the old lady to live. The ambush once again turned the dawn into a raucous tumult of noise that lasted only one minute. The claymores had done their work and the two enemy soldiers were down.

Mick raised up to look down the trail to see what happened to the three women. He could see the girls running for the ville then an AK-47 round whistled past his ear. Mama-san had produced the weapon from under her kimono and was now firing at him. Before he could bring his weapon up, Leroy Wrights M-14 spoke and mama-san did a slow back flip in the air.

"Thanks, man!" Holtzman said. Leroy got to his knees and took a bead on the fleeing girls now 300 yards away. "Hold your fire, Leroy. Let 'em go!"

Wright lowered the rifle and looked at Mick.

"I don't know Leroy, they weren't armed. I screwed up lettin' mama-san go, maybe I'm gettin' soft."

Leroy shrugged.

Mick radioed in the Sit Rep and again asked for help to bury the dead. The squad was back on the hill before 08:00, plenty of time for chow. Holtzman stopped by the company office to debrief. Gieger was there as always, but also present was Lieutenant Cook and Gunnery Sergeant MacDonald.

"You must get lucky every time you go out!" MacDonald commented as Mick walked in. "Shaw said you were good...guess he wasn't lyin'."

Mick gave a concise descriptive account of the operation then lapsed into silence.

"Well, you've done us some good here. We'll be sorry to see you go." said MacDonald. "I got the word this morning that your unit is helo-lifting out to reopen Hai Vahn Pass north of Danang. Gunny Shaw is having a chopper sent to get you and your men at 13:00 hours.

"No rest for the wicked!" Holtzman commented. "We'll be ready at the LZ at 12:30."

True to his word, Holtzman had his squad fed, resupplied and in position at the end of the LZ at 12:30. The Chinook arrived at 12:50 and they were airborne by 13:00. Forty-five minutes later the helicopter was landing near the top of Hai Vahn Pass north of Danang on highway one, the road to Hue City and Cua Viet. It is the main thoroughfare in South Vietnam.

Most of the rest of the Battalion Landing Team had already arrived. Mick debarked the big bird first and spotted Lurch, the air/infantry liaison. The Squad Leader asked where Hotel Company was located. The six foot five LZ boss gave an arm signal over the rotor wash and Holtzman headed the squad in that direction.

In a few minutes he spotted the company and they saw him coming.

"Hey, it's Mick and First Squad!" Hamburger shouted.

"All right, that's our man! He know this AO!" Lincoln rhymed in.

Gunny Shaw smiled but noticed that the new CO, Blackwell, seemed surprised by the joy the men showed to see one of their own back.

Shaw quickly briefed the Corporal. It seems that a company sized unit of NVA had been ambushing the truck convoys along the pass for the last three days, slowing down the resupply to units north. The Battalion Landing Team was to hunt them down and eliminate them. They would be sweeping into the mountainous jungle from the top of the pass, driving downwards, pushing the enemy in front of them.

Holtzman nodded and moved his men up with Second Platoon. The Marines proceeded into the high jungle. Once under the double canopy, movement slowed quickly. The terrain was steep, the vegetation thick and the light was low.

By the time darkness arrived, the infantrymen had only covered about a thousand meters of descent without any contact with the enemy. The grunt companies were having a hard time keeping in contact with each other due to the difficult terrain. A halt was called and the men attempted to regain contact. They dug in on the steep hillside for the night.

The night passed without much trouble until 01:00 when a man from Third Platoon threw a frag at some movement.

"Pass the word, don't throw any frags!" Mick called. "There's rock apes all over this mountain and if you throw a frag at 'em, they think it's a game and throw it back and those bastards are damned accurate!"

Holtzman got on the radio and gave a similar warning. Seconds later his radio sputtered,

"Hotel two alpha. This is Hotel six. Where did you get that information you just passed on?" came Blackwell's voice.

"Been here before six. Lost a man to a rock ape last go-around."

"Information is supposed to go through channels, two alpha, not be chattered away on the open frequencies," the Captain sputtered.

Mick didn't answer, then in a few minutes, "Did you read me, two alpha?"

"Negatory Hotel six, you are coming in poorly, only read you one by four. Much static," replied the Corporal. O'Meara, smiling, came over with a plastic foil C-ration bag and during Mick's transmission crumpled it near the mouth piece, creating tremendous sounding static. The two were holding in their laughter so hard that tears were running down their faces. "Crashck, shewee, Radio Check." Mick said into the hand set. He broke down laughing as he released the key.

Holtzman looked up to see Frenchy DeBeque standing a few feet away with a smile on his mustached face. The Sergeant wiped the grin off and walked over, "I passed the word about the apes. We had 'em up in Dong Ha on my last tour. They can be damn dangerous."

"Guess the Captain didn't believe me," said the Corporal.

"Oh, he don't know nothin' yet." DeBeque replied, "Better get that radio checked out in the mornin'." he finished swallowing a grin as he left.

The rest of the night passed in silence. In the morning the men cooked up coffee on their heat tabs and then proceeded down the mountain in the early morning dusk

Holtzman took the point, moving slowly and carefully. After about an hour he heard the sound of water up ahead, and he proceeded forward with care. In front, and a hundred feet below, was a braided waterfall with four to six streams beginning here, ending there, then beginning again. It was breathtaking. Mick heard something that made him freeze. It was a human voice in the sing-song Vietnamese language. He crawled to the edge of the falls and peered through the vegetation. There, a hundred feet below were three Vietnamese males showering under the streams of water. Their weapons were laying on the shore and they were being guarded by a clothed and armed sentry. The four enemy soldiers had no idea they were under observation. The Squad Leader signaled Leroy to move his team down hill to the base of the falls and Boone to move his uphill. When the team leaders had accomplished their task, Mick raised his M-16 to his shoulder and drilled the sentry through the chest. Yelling "Dong Lai! Dong Lai!, don't move!"

The three naked soldiers froze. They weren't even sure where the shot had come from and their weapons were on the shore, fifteen feet away. When no other enemy appeared, Holtzman stood up and signaled Leroy to move down and take the men prisoner while Boone and First Team covered from above. Leroy collected up the men's clothing and weapons, produced some parachute cord and bound their hands. Under Mick's direction, they hobbled their feet as well.

"Check the one I shot." said Mick.

"Hell…you put it dead center boss!" Wright declared.

"Check him anyway…take his papers and weapons. Give these three their sandals back but no clothes."

"What's going on over here?" came Captain Blackwell's voice, "I thought I heard a shot."

The Corporal turned to see the new CO pushing through the jungle into the now crowded clearing. He seemed kind of confused by the scene in front of him.

"We just took three enemy prisoners and one KIA sir." explained Mick.

"Why didn't you take the other prisoner as well?"

"He was armed sir…easier to shoot him," responded the Squad Leader.

Blackwell shook his head in consternation, "Why are they naked?"

"They were bathing and if we leave them that way they are less likely to try to run."

"Well Well! What do we have here? I should have guessed that wherever there's action we we'll find Corporal Holtzman!" came Colonel Smith's voice as he and his Radioman Webb pushed into the clearing. "I bet that your old Platoon Commander, Lieutenant Baker will be glad to get these three."

"I am sure he will, sir," chimed in Lieutenant Byrd who was now joining the group. "But we'll have to haul them all the way down the mountain. It'll take a whole squad to guard them."

The Colonel grinned, "I doubt it, not the way he's got 'em trussed up."

"Sir, if I may?" interrupted Mick, "The road switches back and is over that way about five hundred meters." as he pointed in an easterly direction.

Blackwell consulted his map. "Wrong, Corporal, we are here," he pointed to the map, "and the road is at least two thousand meters away."

"The map's incorrect Captain. There is a switch back up there five hundred meters. We'll have to climb a couple hundred feet elevation to get there though," Holtzman stated.

Angered, the Captain said, "What makes you think your smarter than the map?"

"He's been here before Captain," broke in the Colonel, "The Corporal and his Recon Team kept this pass open to Hue City at a very important time. Also I've been following his point lead for six months and he hasn't got us lost or ambushed yet. He has my confidence. Corporal, what do think the enemy is up to?"

"Sir, it's likely they broke up into small groups like this and dispersed. In a week, two weeks or a month, they'll get together again and ambush another convoy. They've had their fun for now," replied Mick.

The Colonel nodded his head, "Likely…very likely. OK, you lead us to the road. When we get there, we'll call motor transport and take this company and the prisoners down the pass to the Esso Plant. I'll have Fox, Golf and Echo continue down the hill till they get to the road about two thousand meters down. I'll travel with you, Corporal."

"That would be my pleasure, Sir! Just one request Sir, could you have Webb remove that whip antennae and replace it with a tape? I don't want every gook sniper in the jungle shootin' at me," Holtzman replied, turning quickly to hide his smile and setting off in the direction he had indicated.

The Colonel frowned as he followed the Squad Leader. *"I think I just got told off by a nineteen year old Corporal!"* he thought to himself.

After a short climb and about five hundred meters the troops stepped out onto the road where it switched back up the steep part of the pass. Holtzman sent a fire team to the high curve and another to the low curve of the switchback, effectively securing the area.

The Colonel got Motor T on the horn and within an hour the grunts were loading onto trucks for transport to the fortified area below.

Lincoln came by and high fived, then signed with Mick, "My man! You saved us a damn long walk, Bro!"

Holtzman smiled and jumped into the waiting truck, "No sense chasing rock apes around that mountain all day"

The big four-deuce trucks moved the company of Marines and their three prisoners down the pass toward the north side of Danang Harbor. Here, on the isolated north shore, is the Esso Plant, probably left over from French colonial days. It may have been a refinery once but was now a fuel storage facility, with a number of huge storage tanks. The area around the facility is fortified and defended by Marines. There are rocket and mortar attacks generally every week or two. Infantry and sappers are always on the try to blow the fuel.

The trucks gears whined as they descended the steep pass. As they came out onto the flatter coastal highway, they picked up speed, heading for the compound. Pulling through the barb wire gates into an enclosed parking area, the Marines debarked their transport and found Lieutenant Baker happily waiting for the three prisoners.

The infantrymen of Hotel Company unloaded quickly and were shown where they could billet. "*This was going to be sweet...no interior guard...no damn fighting hole to dig...a mess hall and even an Enlisted/NCO club. Too good to be true*"*!* thought Mick.

"Hey Mick!" called Frenchy DeBeque, "After you get your men settled and fed, meet me at the club. I feel a few brews comin' on!"

"You bet Frenchy, you can be sure that after chow that club is gonna get full."

Chapter Thirty-One
Pinning on Stripes

Later that night, Mick pushed his way into the Enlisted/NCO Club which actually consisted of a large thirty by forty foot tent on a wooden platform. Even with the sides of the tent open, the noise inside was startling. Marines who were stationed at the Esso Plant and were off duty were present as were many of the infantrymen from 2/26. The Squad Leader was making his way toward the bar to buy a beer when he heard his name and looked up. In the far corner at a table, Frenchy DeBeque was yelling to him over the crowd, motioning to come over. At the table with DeBeque was Gunny Shaw and the Platoon Sergeants from First and Third Platoon whom Mick new vaguely. The table was piled high with full beer cans.

"Hey, Corporal grab a beer and a seat." the stocky Cajun called out as Mick neared the table.

Holtzman got to the table and perfunctory introductions were made. The Squad Leader picked up a Pabst Blue Ribbon and opened it with a church key someone had supplied. He held it to the light for inspection the other NCOs watching, waiting for his comment.

"Well, this sure beats the hell out of Carling Black Label or Tiger Piss!" the Corporal said, grinning.

"There it is!! There it is!" DeBeque seconded.

The Non-coms sat in their corner and got serious about the beer drinking, talking, jibing with each other, recounting tales and wolf stories. Keeping everything in perspective with one PBR after another.

"Say Mick, where's O'Meara tonight?" inquired Gunny Shaw.

"Oh, I think he'll be down later. He and the Prez are checking things out," the Corporal responded. He knew that they were down at the mortar shack smoking Jays.

"Well, don't let him get too fucked up," commented Shaw reading between the lines. "We got a little ceremony for him tonight."

Holtzman glanced at the senior Sergeant and Shaw smiled and rolled a Corporals chevron from his fist. "We got his overdue stripes straightened out and now all we got to do is catch him and pin 'em on."

The ceremony known as pinning on stripes is in fact illegal, but is practiced by all enlisted and NCO ranks. The way it works is any man who holds rank above you could come and strike you in the biceps for each stripe you earned. And when you made Corporal, all Corporals and Sergeants holding rank longer, also pin the stripes of the new non-com on the legs with a knee buck. This also has been made illegal as some men have been crippled by the practice. It is, however, a ceremony of honor and O'Meara wouldn't want the rank without the ceremony.

"He'll be here, Gunny and he'll be damned surprised," the Squad Leader responded.

The conversation continued along with the demise of the large quantity of beer that Shaw and DeBeque had stocked the table with. The two Platoon Sergeants from First and Third went to the bar for resupply, leaving Shaw, DeBeque, and Holtzman alone.

"Before we get too loaded Mick, I got some word to pass. Remember, you didn't hear this from me, but ya need to know," the aging Gunnery Sergeant said. "That little trip to Hill 55 wasn't an accident, nor was it necessary. Captain Blackwell, Lieutenants Byrd and Gregory cooked that up. They know regiment doesn't want you to proceed with your request for mast and they think they can delay it if they send you all over hell's half acre on missions. The three think they'll look good to regiment if they do this."

The Corporal sat quietly absorbing the news, the two Sergeants watching his response. Holtzman turned the Pabst up, drinking the entire can in two swallows. He put empty can on the table, pulled out a Lucky and flicked his Zippo to light it. He took a deep draw on the cigarette.

"I'll resign as Squad Leader!" Mick said.

"No! Damn it, we need you!" responded Shaw.

"I can't have my men endangered on missions they get

sent out on 'cause I'm rockin' the boat!" stated the Corporal. "They can't force me to be a Squad Leader."

"Don't bet on it," responded DeBeque.

The Squad Leader quietly pondered this exchange for a moment.

"Gunny, if I put in for a transfer to a CAP Unit how long would it take to process?" Holtzman asked in a rhetorical tone.

"About ten seconds, Mick. You know they can't get or keep people, let alone combat veterans in the Combined Action Program," Shaw answered looking nervous.

"So...I could still request mast while I was in a CAP right."

"Right, it would probably go up faster. They would be playing to you, but you might not live long enough to get it done," the Gunny stated.

The Combined Action Program is set up to help the peasants of Vietnam. When they have finally had their fill of the Communists stealing their rice and conscripting their children, they apply for CAP. The Marines send a small group of combat soldiers and Corpsmen to the village where they train the locals to fight and defend themselves as militia. The CAP unit lives in the village and works with and fights beside the peasants. The program is so effective that the enemy targets all CAP villages and when they attacked them and were able to over run them, the Marines and defenders were usually tortured to death as a message to other villages.

"Gunny, are we goin' aboard ship tomorrow?" Mick asked, and Shaw nodded.

"Then I need to get the request to Blackwell tomorrow. If I'm delayed, I'll put in for CAP and go that route. I'm not trying to shit in your hole, Gunny, but I gotta protect my men."

"I hear you, Mick," Gunny Shaw said, taking a deep pull at his brew. "If you show up at the company office, say, at 10:00 hours the Captain will be there. I would of course be required to forward your request to him at that time."

"I'll be there, Gunny."

The two Platoon Sergeants reappeared with their arms loaded with more Pabst Blue Ribbon cans and the conversation drifted elsewhere. Ten minutes later O'Meara and Lincoln appeared with their eyes red from the reefer smoke, but still ready for more.

"Hey, Trace!" Holtzman yelled with a grin. "Over here."

As the two sauntered through the crowded bar, Frenchy got up and escorted them the last few feet. He then made sure that both men had a beer. The conversation was friendly and flip for a few minutes.

"Gentlemen! Gunny Shaw has an announcement to make." DeBeque said this in a formal tone and put his arm around O'Meara's shoulder as if in friendship. Tracey sensed something, but that arm would stop any movement.

"We have a new Non Commissioned Officer to add to our ranks this evening. Tracey O'Meara has been meritoriously promoted to the rank of Corporal." Shaw rolled the Corporals chevron across the table to Tracey. The other Sergeants and Corporals Lincoln and Holtzman began the cheers that turned into a chant.

O'Meara stood shaking his head, a wan smile under his dapper mustache. DeBeque picked up the chevron and pinned it to Tracey's pocket. Then he grinned and said, "Now we really need to pin them on."

First Platoons Sergeant Stevens stood on one shoulder, Frenchy on the other. The men gave a count of three and simultaneously hit O'Meara in the shoulder. Then another three-count and the second stripe was on. On the third three-count, the knees bucked into Tracey's thighs almost taking him down. A cheer went up, then the next two took their places. O'Meara was offered pain killer in the form of Pabst Blue Ribbon which he used with reckless abandon.

Tracey survived the ceremony but seemed to be having trouble walking. *Was it the beer or the thigh bucks that made him stumble?* He had a bemused, half smile on his face as the Sergeants sat drinking and telling stories. He was now one of them.

The next morning they were awakened at 06:00. There were a lot of big heads and when the choppers came for them, the sound of the rotor blade was enough to make several men ill. The hung-over Marines loaded aboard the choppers and were flown back to the ships they called home in the South China Sea.

Corporal Holtzman had not been immune to the hangover and had wondered for a moment on waking what camel caravan had wandered through his mouth the night before. O'Meara was barely mobile, so the Squad Leader had others carry his M-79 rounds for him.

Now aboard ship, he delegated some of his usual duties. He was going to be in the company office at 10:00 hours no matter what. Quickly the youthful Corporal changed into the starched utilities he kept for official business. He had already run through the shower and given himself an unneeded shave. He quickly climbed the ladderways to the hanger deck, which he crossed and then up to the flight deck where, on the other side, stood Frenchy. When Mick crossed to him the Cajun said, "Good luck, I can't go with ya but we're all behind ya."

The lean infantryman continued on to the hatch of the company office where he stopped and did a time check. Zero nine fifty nine hours. He took a breath and stepped inside. An enlisted clerk looked up and asked his business.

"I'm here to see the First Sergeant."

With that, acting First Sergeant Shaw stepped out of his office looking surprised and motioned the Squad Leader in. When inside Shaw said in a loud voice, "What can I do for you, Corporal." Mick understood that the CO was inches away across a metal bulkhead.

"Sir, Corporal Holtzman requesting mast to the Company Commander, Sir."

"Have you followed the chain of command, Corporal?" Shaw asked.

"Yes Sir, I first requested to my Platoon Sergeant then my Platoon Commander, and the Company Commander is the next in line, sir."

"Take a seat in the office Corporal." the Gunny said winking at Mick.

Holtzman stepped back into the company office and sat in a straight backed metal chair that was painted battleship gray.

Sergeant Shaw took a step to one side of his desk and opened up the door to the adjoining office where Captain Blackwell was sitting behind a desk.

"Corporal Holtzman is here requesting mast, Sir."

"Tell him I'm not in." Blackwell said, his face reddening.

"He knows you're in Sir. Standard operations say that I must give him an appointment," Shaw explained, further angering the officer.

"He's a god-damned trouble maker!" cursed the Captain.

"Sir, he's the best Squad Leader in this battalion." the acting First Sergeant said, focusing on a point six inches above the Commanding Officers head.

"Regimental wants this request quashed! We'll see how far he gets if he's busy fighting gooks in the bush."

"I have it from good sources Sir, that he is onto that tactic and if his request does not move forward he will request a transfer to a CAP Unit which, of course, would be immediately granted. The CAPs would be so happy to see him they'd push his agenda for him. In the end, you'd irritate regimental because your actions would move the request forward. You would also make Colonel Smith of Battalion really mad as he would lose his favorite point man. That wasn't the result you had in mind was it Captain?" the old soldier finished, still focused above his CO's head.

Blackwell fumed. How could he be outflanked by a nineteen year old Corporal with no formal education. He thought and thought but seemed boxed in by any action he took.

"Of course you are just following orders if you audience his request, and although you won't get a feather in your cap, you also won't get a bloody nose. The request would go to the Colonel and it would be up to him to put it to rest, Sir." Shaw pointed out.

"OK, OK. He can make his request at fourteen hundred hours," the Captain said slamming his fist on the desk.

"Yes,Sir!" responded the acting First Sergeant, who then stepped back into his own compartment.

Blackwell was furious. He felt he had been out maneuvered by a kid Corporal. Then that big old doltish Gunnery Sergeant had read chapter and verse to him from Marine Corps Regulations Manual. This was just supposed to be a stop on his way up the corporate ladder. Blackwell hadn't really any desire to be a Marine. He wanted to be an oil executive. In college he had interned at a large oil firm and found that all of their executive staff had been Marine officers. When he went back to school he entered the reserve officer training program. Blackwell had managed to keep himself out of combat till this assignment and now, if he could just get through this, it wouldn't be long before he was sitting in the boardroom and could be done with the Marine Corps and those uneducated boobs that populated it.

Shaw stepped through his office, out into the company office and announced in a theatrical tone. "Corporal, come with me!"

When they had exited the compartment and were safely alone in the passageway, the Gunny stopped, smiled, and said, "Fourteen hundred hours today. I don't think he'll even try to hard-ass you because you've boxed him up good. After him, it's the Colonel. He likes you Mick, but he's got the word to stop you. Things could get really ugly then."

"I know Sir, but it's somethin' I got to do. Thanks for your help," Mick said as he left.

That afternoon, the meeting with the Captain was perfunctory. He didn't really have a lot to say except that he hadn't sufficient rank to call a flying officer on the carpet for a Corporal.

Holtzman could taste the contempt that Blackwell had for the enlisted and non-commissioned ranks. *"He's not gonna last very long, or be able to command with that attitude,"* Mick reckoned.

Corporal Mick Holtzman had decided to pull out all the stops. The next day, after performing his duties aboard ship, he hung out on the flight deck, chatting with the sailors and air crewmen who worked there. Eventually a UH-34 was brought up from the hanger deck and made ready for flight. The Squad Leader inquired as to its destination and was told it was going over to the carrier. The Corporal finagled a ride and ten minutes later was walking the decks of the USS Valley Forge, headed for the battalion offices.

Mick stepped into the battalion office and a clerk typist asked his business. He stated he was present to see First Sergeant Riker. Moments later Riker stepped from his office and motioned the young Corporal inside.

"What can I do for you, Corporal. I thought that we had completed all your paperwork for the Enlisted Candidates Program?"

"I'm not here about that, Sir. I'm here with a request for mast to the Battalion Commander."

"What! What's this about?"

Holtzman quickly summarized his request with regard to the helicopter pilot who refused to land and medevac Ski when he was wounded.

"Corporal, you know we don't want to start a pissing match with the air wing." Riker started off in a kindly tone.

"Sir, it's my right to request…"

"Don't tell me about your rights, Marine!" Riker bellowed, "I've served this Marine corps for twenty-two years! I know what rights you got."

The Squad Leader stood at attention and stared straight ahead unmoved.

"Your gonna fuck up a promising career soldier." Riker growled.

"Joe Sokouski's career got fucked up permanent that day, Sir."

"Suit yourself, Corporal. The Colonel is over at regiment today. I'll present your request and he will listen to your grievance. I'll contact Shaw as to when. That will be all!"

Mick did an about face, left the office, and headed in the direction of the flight deck.

"Stubborn, young, dumb son-of-a-bitch, Riker mumbled as the door to the adjoining office opened and Colonel Smith appeared.

"Well, it looks like no one has slowed him down." the Colonel offered.

"Yeah, he's stubborn as hell and twice as smart. I knew he was coming…just didn't know it would be today. Gunny Shaw called me yesterday and told me how the kid boxed his Company Commander. Says he'll put in for a CAP unit and forward the request from there," explained Shaw.

"So we'd lose a good Marine and this thing will still piss off the air wing and regiment," the Colonel said, pondering the options.

"Don't lean on him…it won't help now. Stall for a couple of days then give him an appointment. Seems to me he's got a legitimate beef." said Smith.

"Sir, yes Sir!" answered the First Sergeant.

Chapter Thirty-Two
Saving Captain Blackwell

Before trying to hitch a helicopter ride back to his ship, Mick went to the Commissary where he bought a carton of Lucky Strikes for himself, a carton of Kools for Lincoln and various other luxury items for O'Meara and the others.

On arriving back aboard the Duluth, the Corporal passed out the goodies he had purchased to the men in the compartment. When he handed Lincoln the smokes his friend smiled and said. "Thanks Bro, did ya see the Colonel today?"

The rumor mill was hard at work and damned accurate. Mick shook his head.

"No...he wasn't in. But I should get to see him soon. How'd y'all know?"

"Well we knew ya saw the Captain yesterday. We know you. Mick, you don't waste no time man." the Prez explained.

That evening Frenchy DeBeque appeared at the platoon's compartment hatch, got Holtzman's attention and the two went for another walk.

"We're movin' out in the morning, the American Divisions taking a licking down by Chu Lai and the Battalion Landing Team was being sent to help them out. It's a different deal down there, more VC, more booby traps, harder to tell the good guys from the bad." the Platoon Sergeant informed him.

"So, when are we leavin'?" the Corporal asked.

"We'll get briefed and maps in the mornin', they figure first bird leaves around 10:30. Thought you'd like a heads up."

"Thanks Sarge."

Mick went to the platoon compartment's hatch and caught Lincoln and Schneider's attention. The two joined him in the passageway where he explained the news. The three Squad Leaders walked back into the compartment together where Holtzman announced, "There will be weapons and gear inspection in one hour."

This was greeted with moans and cat calls.

"You heard the man!" Lincoln exclaimed, "We goin' out tomorrow, down south by Chu Lai and y'all need to be ready."

The men grumbled, but an hour later each Squad Leader inspected each of his men's weapons and combat gear, ensuring that they would be ready for action in the morning.

Reveille came early. The Marines were in the chow line by 06:00 hours. While the Squad Leaders were briefed, the men of Second Platoon had an hour and a half to themselves as they had made ready the night before. Most of the grunts took the time to write letters home. Many traded for books they had not yet read and the radio playing in the background was a constant companion.

> *Hey there little red riding hood,*
> *You sure are looking good.*
> *Your everything that a big bad wolf could want.*
> *Owoooo!*

At 09:30 the men trooped out onto the catwalks to either side of the flight decks as they waited their turn to load into the helicopters. The same fear of the unknown lurked just below the surface of each infantryman's consciousness. Each dealt with these butterflies in their own way. Corporal Holtzman gazed out toward the open sea, his mind on a dark haired girl ten thousand miles away.

The noise inside the Chinook made conversation impossible as the helicopter flew southward over the open sea. Mick always wondered if any of them would survive if a chopper went down over the water. He doubted that any of the Marines would. As heavily laden with weapons and combat gear as they were, they would sink like lead bricks. Soon the grays and blues of the ocean were replaced by the greens and browns of rice paddies and jungle. Mick noted a change to the sound of the rotors as the helicopters began losing altitude. The Squad Leader saw the clearing ahead and the red smoke drifting in the wind. He tensed as the rear cargo ramp began lowering. He leapt out, landing on the ground five feet below before the chopper set down. He ran toward the smoke until he saw six foot six Lurch, the LZ boss, pointing him toward where Second Platoon was supposed to go. The Marines ran to the perimeter of the landing zone where they took up defensive positions until the wave of helicopters had finished unloading and departed. After that, they pushed the perimeter out another one hundred meters and took up new positions from which they could defend the landing zone for the next wave of helicopters. With each wave of Chinooks, the Marines increased the size of the defended perimeter until the entire battalion had landed.

When the last of the choppers departed, the grunts wasted no time and began the march to the southwest where elements of the Army's American Division had encountered a large concentration of enemy soldiers.

The terrain in this area differed from that in the Marines normal area of operation. It was flatter, more agricultural. Here, there were rice paddies separated by tree lines and hedgerows, then areas of jungle, and a large number of civilians as well. All of the rice paddies were being worked. There were women, children, old men, and water buffalo in most of the paddies. They stopped their work and watched as the Marines went past, gazing with seeming neutrality at the infantrymen. *How many armies had passed through this land that these people, seeing a battalion of heavily armed Marines, show no surprise or fear?* They acted as if it was an everyday occurrence.

As the Marines continued their southwest march they could hear artillery and small arms fire in that direction. After an hour's march, along with the sound of weapons, they could hear the motors of armored personnel carriers in the distance.

"Well…it won't be hard to figure out where we're supposed to go." Mick said to O'Meara as he passed the grenadier.

Seconds later a burst of automatic fire came from a tree line one hundred and fifty yards to the Marines front. The infantrymen hit the dirt, or rather dove into the muddy rice paddy. Return fire from the Marines raked the tree line. Holtzman moved his men forward, toward the tree line one fire team at a time with the rest of the company giving them covering fire. When they reached the tree line and searched it, they found nothing, just as Mick had suspected.

This was an old VC game. The Viet Cong were not known for their marksmanship, so they sniped on fully automatic hoping for a hit, firing a burst and then running away. One gook sniper could really slow down their progress.

"What did you find?" Captain Blackwell wanted to know as he came up with the rest of the company. The Corporal held out his cupped hand which held five empty AK-47 shell casings.

"He fired a burst and then didi mau'd" the Squad Leader replied.

Blackwell stared not comprehending the reply.

"Di Di, same-same as "skied out"...run off, it's Vietnamese Sir." Holtzman explained. "He's probably two or three hedgerows up by now...then he'll fire another burst and stop us again."

Blackwell's face darkened. Here was this damned Corporal speaking to him in Vietnamese and explaining enemy tactics to him like he was a school boy. "Well, what are you going to do about it?" the Captain asked in frustration, "We can't have one enemy soldier stopping us every five minutes."

"Oh, I'll think of something sir." Mick said with the tight thin smile reappearing on his face as he turned away from the Company Commander.

As the men moved out, Holtzman dropped back to Boone Riley, "Hey Boone, you gettin tired of carryin' that LAAW."

"Are you sayin what I think your sayin? Take out a sniper with the LAAW."

"Hell yes…why not? There's plenty more where that one came from. You'll have to be ready though. There won't be time to assemble it after he fires the burst and we'll have to guess where he's liable to fire from."

Boone pulled the collapsible rocket launcher off his pack and assembled it with a grin. He then sighted in on the next tree line.

"Naw, he won't be there. It'll be two, three or four hedgerows up. Look for the kind of spot you'd want to fire from." advised the Squad Leader.

The grunts continued their march but moving a little slower, worried about the sniper in the hedgerows and tree lines. The infantrymen had covered another five hundred yards when Mick saw the place. A hedgerow about three hundred yards away that had a large earthen bank. Just the kind of cover and concealment to fire a burst, get down and get away.

"Hey Boone, you see what I see? I'm bettin' that's where our man is gonna loose his next barrage from."

"Yeah…I got it scoped Mick. I'll keep my eye on it."

The march continued, Boone and Mick both watching the hedgerow in question intently. When they were about a hundred fifty meters away, Mick saw something move near a large palm tree in the hedgerow.

"Boone…to the left of the palm tree…I got movement!"

The tall hillbilly knelt on one knee with the rocket launcher on his shoulder. He looked behind him to make sure the back blast wouldn't hit anybody and said casually, "Fire in the Hole." He took careful aim to the left of the palm and squeezed the firing mechanism of the LAAW. There was a whoosh, then the palm tree exploded and dirt flew everywhere in the tree line.

"Let's hope you got him or that Captain is going to be climbin' my ass." the Squad Leader said as he maneuvered his men toward the tree line to assess damage. The large palm tree was down on the ground and next to it was the remains of the VC sniper, his AK-47 smashed to pieces by the LAAW's blast.

"Who fired that LAAW?" Blackwell shouted, rushing toward where the men of First Squad had gathered.

"I told Riley to fire the LAAW sir." Holtzman responded.

"What the hell were you shooting at?" Blackwell still couldn't see the dead sniper from where he was.

"Shooting at the sniper sir."

"I didn't hear any sniper fire." responded the Captain.

"He didn't get a chance to fire sir, I was afraid he might get lucky and hit someone."

Blackwell now red in the face climbed to where Mick and Boone were standing and saw the dead VC and his bent and twisted weapon on the ground before him. The Captain took several deep breaths, trying to get his temper under control.

"Don't you think that's a little overkill, a light anti-tank weapon for a VC sniper?" the Captain spit out.

"Well Sir, the VC ain't got no tanks and I figured you didn't want to stop the march for this jerk every five minutes and the price of a LAAW is a hell of a lot cheaper than a dead Marine sir." Holtzman responded, as he moved his men off.

Blackwell stood there angry, feeling he had been bested again by this boyish Corporal, but unsure what to say or do to appear to be on top.

The Marines continued moving towards the sounds of battle ahead, there were no more sniping incidents. About 14:00 hours the column stopped as the battalion deployed in the new order of march. The men of Hotel relaxed and smoked or ate C-rations.

Mick sat smoking, looking forward in the direction of travel. Movement attracted his attention to his left. Captain Blackwell, company Radioman Boston Jones and a squad from Third Platoon were moving out in front of the company toward a couple of abandoned hooches several hundred yards away, but off the line of march. *"I wonder what he's up to?"* Holtzman thought. The Corporal pulled the French Field glasses he'd souvenired off a dead NVA officer and watched the patrol through the glasses. He then glassed the village and swept the binoculars back toward the patrol. The glasses stopped their sweep suddenly and jerked back to a tree line between the patrol and their objective. Movement…he could make out three or four human forms crouched in the brush.

"Shit! Their gonna get their asses ambushed!" he cried out. "First Squad, Follow me!" He took off at a dead run toward the hedgerow.

The men of First Squad were surprised but jumped up following there Squad Leader who was sprinting and by now a hundred feet ahead of the others. Mick new the only chance for the Captain and his group would be if he could engage the ambushing VC from their flank before they opened up on the patrol. The VC had guessed that the Marines would send someone to look at the abandoned village and had set their ambush site accordingly.

When Holtzman was within two hundred yards of the tree line he stopped and took three deep breaths. The patrol with the Captain was coming into range of the ambush. Mick dropped to one knee and moved the selector on his M-16 to semi-auto. He put the weapon to his shoulder and began firing well aimed shots into the hedgerow. Those in the patrol hit the ground. The VC in the tree line opened up, tearing up the turf around the patrol. Mick was taking fire as well.

"There must be a platoon of 'em in there." said O'Meara as he joined his friend firing the M-79 as he spoke. It was a long shot and missed the target by twenty feet. The rest of the squad had joined the two Corporals and Holtzman could see Lincoln coming on the run with his men following.

"First Fire Team…prepare to go!" a second's pause, "Go!" the Corporal yelled.

Boone's team charged forward and as they ran, Holtzman ordered, "Second Fire Team prepare to go! Go!" Leroy and his men charged. The Squad Leader continued to leap frog his men forward, moving up fifty yards with each rush. The others would set a base of fire while the next team rushed. Tex was hammering away with his M-60 and the VC had turned their machine gun away from the patrol and onto the attacking squad. Mick and his men were now one hundred fifty yards from the ambush site. More team rushes brought them within a hundred yards. The hail of fire coming from the tree line was increasing. The VC had nowhere to run and were fighting in desperation.

O'Meara now had the range with his grenade launcher. The Marines rushed again and were now within fifty meters of the enemy, pouring deadly fire into the hedgerow. Mick, Tracey and the gun team made the last rush as he was nearing the others. The Squad Leader felt something grab his right leg and he went down in a heap. He continued forward in a crawl until he was even with the others and began firing his weapon into the VC, just fifty meters away. As he changed magazines he looked back and saw his right leg bent at a grotesque angle between his ankle and knee.

Mick had been firing full automatic during the rushes, spraying the tree line. He switched back to semi-automatic and waited for a muzzle flash in the trees. He put a round dead center on the flash, then waited for another and another. The volume of fire from the Communists began to diminish. Blackwell's patrol had begun firing back and effectively put the VC in a crossfire. Tex's machine gun was ripping up the vegetation of the hedgerow like a lawnmower, O'Meara was launching the Grenades into the trees above the VC, getting deadly air bursts that showered the enemy below with shrapnel.

Suddenly there was no more fire coming from the enemy. The Marines kept firing for a few minutes then the Squad Leader yelled, "Cease Fire!" and the firing slowed. "Cease Fire!" it finally stopped. Silence!

Then from the hedgerow, "Chieu Hoi, Chieu Hoi," two VC stood up with their hands over their heads and took a step toward the Marines. Leroy Wright drilled one of the VC just before the M-60 cut down the other.

"Chieu Hoi my ass!" Tex Schulze said.

Holtzman looked around and saw that Lincoln and his

men were on line to the left of his squad. He waved at the Prez and he nodded back understanding the unspoken communication that combat soldiers developed.

"OK men, First Squad will sweep the tree line, Second will cover us. Put a round into everybody you see that ain't a Marine…move slow and careful!" the Squad Leader ordered. The men began getting up. "Their all yours now Trace, take 'em through there and make sure no one gets hurt."

"What!" O'Meara looked sharply at his friend who was still down on the ground.

"The squad's yours now, my leg's broke! Take over damn it!"

"Shit! Corpsman Up!" Tracey yelled.

"Whose hit!" someone called.

"Mick's hit in the leg" responded O'Meara. The men began to come towards their Squad Leader.

"God damn it! Sweep that fuckin' tree line! And be careful! O'Meara's in charge! Now do your job!" Holtzman bellowed.

Tracey led the men to the hedgerow looking back every few paces.

Mick turned himself around and sat up. As he did so, a groan escaped him.

"Stay still Bro, the Doc's on his way. The patrol took casualties too. I think Boston's hit hard." the Prez said from a few feet away.

"Shit! Boston's a good man, we went on liberty together a couple of times back in the states." Mick mumbled while lighting up a cigarette.

Lincoln pulled out a battle dressing and cut the leg of Holtzman's trousers open with his bayonet. He bound the battle dressing in place and sat down next to his friend.

"You be skyin' back to the world Mick."

"Yeah, but I didn't plan on goin home peg legged."

"Shit! Doc be along quick, he'll fix you right up."

"Don't bullshit me Prez, that son-of-a-bitch is broke bad."

"Hey Bro, these Doc's these days…they fix anything! You be as good as new in a few months."

Doc Kruger jogged up and began examining Mick. "I got here as quick as I could," he explained, "The other corpsmen are over with Boston, he's hit hard. Only reason he's alive is that the round hit his radio. It still went through his chest. They're pullin' radio tubes out of him now."

The Corpsman gave Holtzman a shot of morphine. He removed the battle dressing that Lincoln had put on, examined the wound, cleaned it and redressed it. He then splinted the leg.

First Squad had finished their sweep and were now coming back wanting to talk to and see their Squad Leader. Mick chatted with them, trying to say something to each member.

"Hey, will somebody get my letter writing gear in the top pocket of my rucksack?" the wounded Squad Leader asked.

"I will." called out Hamburger, already on the run to carry out the errand.

A poncho was produced and a litter improvised. Lincoln carried one corner, O'Meara, Tex, and Leroy the other corners. The morphine was kicking in as they lifted the Corporal and carried him to the LZ. The four litter bearers tried to joke on the way. When they arrived they put the Squad Leader down next to Jones who had two Corpsmen working on him. The four looked at Mick for a few seconds uncomfortably then Lincoln broke the silence.

"Will see ya Bro."

Through the morphine haze he answered. "Yeah, will see ya."

The four shuffled away.

CHAPTER THIRTY-THREE
On the Ward

Mick lay staring up into the blue sky, letting the morphine carry him away. He remembered looking at clouds as a boy, seeing sailing ships and horses in their shapes. Today's clouds could be the same ones he had looked at back then.

"Who's over there?" a weak voice with a Massachusetts accent croaked.

Mick jerked himself out of his trance and back to reality.

"It's me...Mick. How ya doin' Boston?"

"I'm hit in the chest. Where are you hit?" the Radioman asked.

"Oh, they got me in the leg Jonesy. We'll be OK Bro the Corpsmen will fix us."

"Do you remember that time we went to Diego together Mick?"

"Hell yes! We had a good time, got our pictures took and everything."

"I'm scared Mick."

The Corporal reached across and grabbed the radio man's hand, holding it gently.

"You'll be OK Boston, Heaven ain't ready for no black dude that talks like a Kennedy."

Holtzman continued to make small talk till the medevac chopper arrived.

The two wounded Marines were placed on stretchers in the medevac helicopter. One of the two Corpsmen caring for Jones boarded and continued to treat the Radioman during the flight to the carrier where the battalion aid station was located. The chopper was too noisy for conversation but when they arrived on the flight deck and were taking Jones' stretcher off, Mick waved at him. Minutes later his stretcher was taken off and he was carried into a passageway below decks. This was outside of the main operating room. Here he was placed on a gurney that was in line with a number of others, each with a wounded Marine on it.

Holtzman knew the drill, he'd been here before. A Corpsman arrived to examine the new casualties. The Corpsman examined Mick and put a tag on the gurney. His job was to triage the casualties. That is to determine which wounded could wait for treatment, which probably wouldn't make it and which were seriously wounded and needed immediate treatment. The triage duty was rotated daily as making life and death decisions about the wounded lay heavy on the minds of these medics. Those Marines whom they determined couldn't make it were given morphine and pushed to the side, where they were left to die.

Boston wasn't in the gurney line so they must have taken him straight in. In general, when casualties arrived they came in a bunch, not one at a time…overwhelming the medical services with sheer numbers. Hence the triage system was developed to save the largest number of wounded possible.

The Corpsman moved up and down the line of gurneys, checking the wounded Marines vital signs and treating where it was appropriate. In about fifteen minutes Mick was wheeled into the operating room where once again the dressings were removed, the wound examined, irrigated, disinfected, then redressed. A portable X-ray machine was brought over and several X-rays were taken of the leg. Then the doctors and corpsmen re-splinted his leg and he was wheeled into one of the hospital wards aboard the Valley Forge.

The Corpsmen moved the Corporal into a rack. It was a metal bunk bed with a real mattress. This was high class compared with the rack in the platoon's compartment. The bunk beds in the hospital ward were only two high and sported springs and wire mesh under the mattresses. Mick was given an upper bed at one end of the ward near the entrance, within minutes the Marine was sleeping like a baby.

Two hours later the Squad Leader was awakened by a Corpsman with a syringe. He informed the Squad Leader that he would be getting penicillin shots every two hours for the next few days. Mick was back asleep as soon as the injection was given. The night passed slowly, broken into two hour intervals of sleep interrupted by an injection. Holtzman's dreams were varied. During the first two hour stretch the dream was sweet. He and Lori were back together in the world. Just as things were really getting interesting, the Corpsman was shaking him, rolling him on his side and sticking him. He tried to concentrate on Lori as he fell back to sleep so he could return to his dream, but instead he returned to the night Ski was killed.

As Mick ran to Ski, his feet were leaden. As he got closer, he could see his friends handsome smiling face, but Mick was moving so slowly. As Mick got within arm's reach of his friend he heard the bullet strike Sokouski knocking him backwards, his chest covered with blood, gushing from a huge hole. Holtzman screamed and woke himself up. A few minutes later the Corpsman appeared and asked if he wanted a hypo of morphine. Mick told him, "No, I just had a bad dream." Instead of the painkiller the medic gave him his penicillin. *"Damn, "*the Corporal thought, *"My skinny butt is going to get awful sore."*

Finally the wounded soldier fell into a fitful sleep till morning. Mick awoke to a Corpsman with a syringe for another injection but who also wanted to know what he wanted for breakfast. To the sailors amazement Holtzman laughed and finally sputtered out, "You mean I got a choice?"

"Sure," the medic replied, "we got a menu."

Which brought on more laughter from the injured grunt. "A menu?!"

"Hey Mick! Is that you?" came a voice from the far end of the ward, "The food here is really good. Get Some!"

"McCabe! What the hell are you doin' here?" the infantryman responded, "You're the Colonel's jeep driver! Did ya get the clap on R & R or what?"

"Naw! Colonel made me his runner. I stepped on a toe popper and here I am. But the food is really good."

"Sorry McCabe, how ya doin?"

"No big deal Mick. This one only took off a couple toes, but it'll send me back to the world."

Toe poppers were a Communist antipersonnel mine, circular and a little larger than a silver dollar, and a half inch thick. They often took a lot more than a toe when a Marine stepped on one.

Holtzman made his choices on the hospital's breakfast menu. He had a giddy grin on his face as he did so.

After the Corpsman had left with his breakfast choices, Mick called out into the ward to see if there was anybody else he knew.

"Yeah Holtzman, I remember you, this is Cramer." a voice answered.

Cramer had been a Radio Operator with Second Platoon but had moved over with First Platoon months before.

"Hey Cramer! Long time no see. What are you in here for?" the Corporal called to the unseen voice.

"I got the Malaria Mick," Cramer called his voice sounding shaky. "The fevers and chills come on me and then I go into like a coma." the fear in the voice was obvious.

"You'll be OK Cramer. The doctors just got to get the medicine adjusted right and you'll be OK. I think I got it too. But they can't find the bug in me so they ain't givin' me anything for it. You hang on Cramer. They'll have you fixed up most riki-tic." the Squad Leader said with a confidence that he didn't feel.

"Holtzman?" a weak voice called. "This is Harris. What you gonna tell me?" Harris was Weapons Platoon Sergeant.

"What do ya mean Sarge?"

"How ya gonna cheer me up?" the weak voice sounded bitter.

"What happened?" Holtzman asked, feeling a bit more than apprehensive.

"It's gone!" the weak angry voice intoned. "It's gone!" the black Platoon Sergeant wailed.

Mick knew better than to ask what was gone, or how

much was gone. He was sure the Sergeant was referring to his genitals and details weren't going to make the man feel more optimistic. Mick thought quickly, looking for some magic words that could buoy this man's spirits. None came to mind. Holtzman had known Harris for six months or so, and although they hadn't grown close they had interacted as non-coms.

"How old are your kids now Sarge?" the Corporal finally managed after the uncomfortable silence.

"I said it's gone, damn it!" the Sergeants voice came back still bitter. "Don't ya understand it's fuckin' gone!"

"How old are your two boys Sarge?" Mick asked again, trying to keep his voice calm and even.

Silence followed, no one in the ward spoke.

"Those boys must be five and seven by now, right Sarge?" the Corporal asked once more, keeping a calmness in his voice he didn't feel.

"Yeah, they're five and seven." Harris' voice was weak, barely audible. "You remember their pictures Mick?"

"Yeah Sarge, I remember 'em well."

"The seven year old, Franky...he's playin ball already this summer." a hint of pride in the weak voice replacing the hollow bitterness.

"Did he play for little league, school or what?"

Harris talked on about his sons, then talked about his wife, then a thought must have crossed his mind and he stopped in mid-sentence. The silence was deafening, Holtzman knew what thoughts had occurred to Harris. Now, how to get him back onto safe mental territory?

"Hey Sarge do you remember when O'Meara came back from R&R?"

No response.

"He brought that bottle of 151 Ron Ricco rum with him, remember?

"Yeah, I remember." the disembodied voice trailed across the hospital ward weakly.

"O'Meara and I took the rum and went up to that coke machine between decks and started making rum and cokes.

At first we watched out for anybody coming up or going down and acted like we were just getting a coke and bull shittin'. But after a couple of those high octane rum and cokes we didn't give a shit."

"Yeah, I remember you two drunks." Harris said warming to the story.

"We just kept drinkin' the rum and cokes. After a while, we didn't care who saw us pourin' it down. Somebody must have reported us cause the prick squid Executive Officer started searching the ship, looking for us."

"Yeah, I come up to that coke machine and grabbed you two drunks and hauled ya down to Third Platoon's compartment while the Navy was searchin' Second Platoon's berth." Harris recollected.

"You just kept movin' us from one compartment to another, stayin' one step ahead of the shore patrol." Mick added chuckling.

"Yeah…and it wasn't too damn easy as drunk as you two assholes were. O'Meara got too drunk to walk so I carried his ass, then he puked on me. You were so drunk I had to lead ya and when I stopped you'd sit down, stare at your hands and say "My hands are laughin' and gigglin' like an idiot! What a pair!" The Sergeant was back on safe ground.

Mick took a deep breath and let it out slow, he managed to keep the Sergeant in safe territory till breakfast arrived.

Breakfast was really good. He had orange juice, coffee, eggs over easy, toast on the side with marmalade and a bowl of fruit cocktail. This beat the hell out of swamp water, C-rat coffee, and jam on a cracker.

CHAPTER THIRTY FOUR
Dreams and Sweats

Corporal Holtzman dozed off after breakfast. He slept fitfully for an hour then awoke with a start. Standing ten feet from his berth was Captain Weller, watching him. As Mick tried to sit up Weller spoke.

"Don't sit up on my account, Holtzman."

"Sir, if you could put a pillow behind my back it would make talking a lot easier."

As the Captain complied with the request he commented, "I wasn't planning on waking you. So when I saw you were asleep, I just looked at you for maybe a minute. Then your eyes popped open and you were looking all around."

"It's the Nam Captain. After you hunt and are hunted a while you get like an animal that way. If you stay out there long enough, you get to think you can communicate with your buddies without talking. You know, just a look and a nod."

"I noticed that about you in the bush, Mick. When I wanted you all I needed to do was start looking for you and you'd appear."

"Yes sir," the Corporal said with a smile. "Sir, I want you to know that you were the best Company Commander I served under. I guess my tour is over now."

"Thanks. That's high praise coming from you. I guess you saved Blackwell's life by busting up that ambush. The men will be coming back in this afternoon. When they got up to the Americal Division the enemy decided to take off into the hills."

"So the platoon will be on the Duluth tonight? I'm not sure how long I'll be staying here aboard the Valley Forge, but it would sure be nice to see some of the guys one last time."

"I talked with your Doctors Mick. They're planning to send you to Japan as soon as transport can be arranged, probably tomorrow or the next day."

"I guess I won't get to see the men then…won't be time for them to find flights over from the Duluth for a visit."

The Captain and the Corporal talked on about times past, remembering others they had served with. After about fifteen minutes or so Captain Weller took his leave.

The Corpsman came by every two hours and gave Mick his penicillin injection. About an hour before lunch, Sergeant Harris's voice called out.

"Mick, the Captain came by to see you this morning. He must think a lot of you. Hey! Did he know anything about the Company."

"Ya Sarge, they're coming in this evening."

"Mick, do you remember those pictures of my kids I showed ya?" asked Harris the desperation showing through.

"Sure do Sarge. Good looking boys…good looking boys." Mick replied not knowing where to go next.

"Yeah…they're good boys," Harris went on. He kept up the talk about his sons with Holtzman only having to add a word here and there. It was obviously the only thing that kept his mind off his medical condition. As the Corpsmen began serving lunch Harris said, "Thanks Mick."

Lunch was as good as breakfast. Holtzman had filled out the menu card that came with the breakfast as to his choices. *"Hell,"* he thought, *"this is one tough way to get decent food."*

After lunch the Corporal slept again, this time more soundly. He awakened in the afternoon to the sounds of the Klaxon horns bellowing indicating the elevators that moved the helicopters were operating. *"The battalion must be coming back."* he thought. Fox and Golf Companies billeted aboard the carrier, while Echo, and his Company were billeted aboard the Duluth.

It was getting close to dinnertime when Mick had another visitor. He saw him coming when he heard the far compartment hatch open. Holtzman watched him as he walked down the ward looking at each occupied rack. When he was about ten feet away their eyes met. He stopped there, then spoke.

"How are you doing Corporal?"

"Oh, my leg's busted up pretty bad, Sir."

There was an uncomfortable silence for a few moments as the visitor searched for words.

"I guess you saved my life the other day." Captain Blackwell stammered.

"You weren't the only one that was about to get ambushed sir." the Squad Leader said evenly.

"I've made some mistakes Holtzman." the Captain took a deep breath, "I guess I've got a lot to learn."

"Yes Sir…And you could learn a lot from Sergeant DeBeque, Corporals Lincoln, O'Meara, and Schneider. They have a wealth of experience in this war, as well as the confidence of the men."

Blackwell attempted small talk but that didn't go to well. He and the Corporal didn't have any shared times or acquaintances to discuss. The Captain left in a few minutes, following several pregnant pauses that left both men feeling uncomfortable.

"Hey Mick!" McCabe's voice came floating down the ward after Blackwell's hasty departure, "Do you suppose he'll ever get squared away? Sounded like he might be tryin' to eat a little humble pie."

"Don't know if he'll make a good officer or not…but he's on the right track today."

The two grunts continued to chat with a comment or two from Harris till dinner came.

Dinner was as excellent as breakfast and lunch. Mick hungrily devoured the portions. When he was finished the Corpsman came, removed his tray and gave him his penicillin shot.

The sounds of the elevators moving men and machines between decks continued but Corporal Holtzman was oblivious as he was sound asleep. He slept the sleep of the exhausted, dreamless. He woke with a start…hands flying out reaching for the enemy, he missed, grabbed again, then saw the Corpsman jump back with fear.

"Sorry…thought the gooks had got me. You better try

talkin' to me to wake me up."

"Shit man! All I did was touch you and you were fixin' to kill me!" The frightened sailor said. "I got to give you your penicillin shot."

With the injection finished the Squad Leader fell back to sleep. This time he did dream. Not the pleasant dreams of a girl back in the world but those haunting dreams of Ski. This dream had Ski on LP again, with Mick running to the listening post, calling Joe's name. Joe turns and smiles then his chest explodes in a fountain of blood. The night turns red. "Roseanne? Roseanne? Rose!" Ski calls out in the dream…until his words are drowned by the blood bubbling out of his mouth.

The Corporal awoke in time to stifle his scream. Lying in the darkened hospital ward the nineteen year old Marine tried to control his thoughts and put himself back to sleep. Predictably his thoughts wandered to home, to Lori. *"I wonder if she's got a boyfriend in California?"* he thought. *"Why wouldn't she?"* he answered himself, there had always been guys after her. *"Why would it be different in California?"* Finally sleep returned, this time allowing the young man some peace.

The Corpsman came to wake him for his 04:00 injection. This time he brought a flashlight and pointed it at the Marine till his eyes opened.

"You awake?" The sailor asked.

"Yeah."

"How come your soakin' wet?" the medic went on.

"Must be havin' another attack. I think I got the malaria." The Marine answered. "Doc VD, out in the bush told me to get a blood sample drawn when I'm havin' an attack. So far they can't seem to find the bug in my blood."

The Corpsman gave Mick the antibiotics, then returned with a fresh syringe and drew a blood sample.

CHAPTER THIRTY-FIVE
Postmark Vietnam

Holtzman awoke before the Corpsman arrived for his six o'clock shot. He wondered if he'd be leaving the carrier for Japan today. The medic arrived promptly with the antibiotic and breakfast. Mick ate slowly, his mind not on the food despite its quality. When the sailor returned for the tray he informed Mick that transportation had been arraigned and that he would be choppered off the carrier to Danang where he would be transferred to a medical flight to Japan.

"Guess I won't get to see the guys...there's no way that they could arrange flights from their ship to the carrier that fast. Besides they got plenty to do over there." the Corporal thought.

With breakfast over, the former Squad Leader was left alone with his thoughts. The noise of the huge elevators and Klaxon horns had subsided sometime during the night.

"Guess they're shippin' you out today Mick." called out McCabe.

"Yeah, the Doc said they had transportation into Danang connecting to Japan."

"They must think you're semi-critical or somethin' to get ya out so quick." Commented Cramer.

"I think they just don't know what to do with this leg." Mick replied.

"Mick! When they comin' for you?" Harris asked, worry evident in his voice.

"I don't know Sarge. Everything will be OK though. Right McCabe, Cramer!" The Corporal called down the ward, hoping the two got his drift.

"Yeah Mick, we'll take care of things here." McCabe's voice trailed down the ward but lacked confidence.

The youthful Corporal searched his mind, he needed someone to keep Harris's mind off his wounds. The only thing he had found that worked was his kids. But who? He doubted if Cramer and McCabe could do it, they'd try but neither knew the black Sergeant well.

Forty minutes later four Seamen appeared with a stretcher. The Ward Corpsman gave Mick his antibiotic injection along with a morphine shot. He grabbed his property which consisted of his writing gear, his wallet and his bush cover. The medics covered him with a sheet and transferred him to the stretcher. At that point Holtzman saw Captain Weller standing in the shadows. He stepped forward quickly and reached for the Corporal's hand, smiled and bid him good luck.

"Good luck Mick!" called out McCabe and Cramer.

"Mick! Good luck." Came Harris's voice.

"Take care, you guys." The Corporal said to the ward. "Sir" he said to the Captain with a little salute.

Weller clicked his heels and gave a formal salute as his former Squad Leader was carried past. The Corpsmen carried him to one of the smaller elevators and put the stretcher down. They pushed the controls and the horn sounded. The elevator made its way up to the hanger deck. They then picked up the stretcher and started off the elevator when a commotion started. Mick heard his name called. He looked up to see Lincoln and O'Meara coming towards him across the flight deck. Behind them were others, Boone, Leroy, Tex, Crawford, DeBeque, Hamburger, all of First Squad and many more from the platoon. Lincoln and O'Meara had foolish grins on their faces as they came forward.

"Hey Bro! Thought we'd come say adios." Lincoln said.

"Yeah…you get some over there in Japan!" Tracey added.

"Get Some Mick!" Tex yelled.

"Get some!" The others shouted in unison.

Lincoln and O'Meara took his hands, their eye's held, he nodded.

"One favor from you two. Sergeant Harris is down in the ward all fucked up…I think he got his nuts blown off. He needs people to keep his mind off his wounds. The only thing that worked for me was talkin' about his boys."

"I'll take care of him." Lincoln said, "Besides he's a

brother."

"I'll talk to him too." Tracey promised. "Me and the Prez can take shifts…come over every other day while we're aboard ship. So someone will see him every day."

"Thanks guys." The Corporals voice then cracked. "Trace, take care of the squad buddy." Mick squeezed Tracey's hand, then looked at Lincoln, "Prez, see ya in the world." The big hand encircling his squeezed. Mick was having a hard time seeing for some reason, but he nodded in the direction of the Corpsmen and they started carrying him to the flight deck amongst shouts and comments from the infantrymen on the deck.

Somewhere on the hanger deck the ubiquitous transistor radio wailed out Simon and Garfunkel's popular song "Homeward Bound".

> *Homeward bound, I wish I was,*
> *Homeward bound,*
> *Home, where my thoughts escaping,*
> *Home, where my music's playing,*
> *Home, where my love lies waiting,*
> *Silently for me.*

Holtzman tried to clear his eyes. He raised his head and looked at the men who had probably missed breakfast to catch flights from one ship to another. He gave another little salute as the elevator to the flight deck moved him up and away from these men who had become family. Now the tears flowed freely. *Would I ever see any of them again? Would they survive the war? What of those already dead?* Perhaps it was the morphine but he cried like a child as they loaded him on the UH-34 that would take him to Danang.

The helicopter flight and the transfer to a staging ward in Danang were a blur of hazy, morphine clouded remembrances. The drugs were starting to wear off when Corpsmen came for him again. One of the medics offered him another morphine injection which the Corporal declined. Once again he was shifted to a stretcher and carried to the airstrip and a waiting jet transport that was almost fully loaded with wounded soldiers. Mick lay on the rack, covered with a sheet and a blanket. His bush hat, writing gear and possessions were under the sheet between his legs. It was hot and sultry. He pushed the blanket down to his waist and looked around. The other Marines within view were all unconscious. A Corpsman was patrolling the aisle checking intravenous drips running to the more seriously wounded.

It seemed only minutes until the plane's hatch was closed and the big jet taxied out onto the runway. There were no windows in the transport but Holtzman felt the plane come to a stop. The brakes were applied, then the jet engines revved up till the plane began trembling. He wondered how the others could sleep. The brakes were released and the plane moved quickly down the runway. The Corporal could feel the plane gaining speed and momentum. Finally, he felt the plane lift off the ground and become airborne. The plane climbed for some time then leveled off and shortly after reached cruising altitude. The wounded Marine fell asleep.

Mick woke several times during the flight. He looked around but the others remained in their drug-induced sleep. The steady rumble of the jet engines soon put him back to sleep. Holtzman awoke again as the engines note changed, indicating that the plane was descending. The descent continued, leveled off, then began again. Five minutes later the engines reversed and he felt the plane's wheels touch the tarmac. The plane taxied for a while and finally came to rest. Within minutes the doors were opened and a ramp affixed. Corpsmen began removing the wounded onto stretchers that were placed in buses, one on top of the other, five high.

"Where we at?" Mick asked a medic as he was carried to the waiting bus.

"Yokohama, the Corpsman replied. "You're on your way to Yokosuka Naval Hospital."

The hospitalmen started to put him in one of the lower

berths but the Corporal asked to be placed at window level and they complied. Holtzman craned his neck about but could see only airplanes and buildings. Nothing to identify this as Japan. The bus moved off as soon as it was filled and soon came to a gate where there was an American Military Policeman on one side and a Japanese MP on the other. Once through the gate they were in the hustle and bustle of Yokohama traffic. The bus moved through streets crowded with automobiles and throngs of black headed, dark eyed Japanese. Mick decided it looked about like Okinawa except bigger and more modern.

In about fifteen minutes the bus wheeled into a complex of buildings, some old and some new. Here they stopped to be met by another team of Corpsmen who began removing the wounded from the busses, putting them on gurneys and taking them to the proper ward.

As he was wheeled into the building the Corpsmen passed up a bank of elevators and went down a hall to another group of elevators onto which they rolled the young Marine. After they started up, Holtzman asked why they didn't use the first set of elevators. The medic chuckled and explained that the first group of elevators were put in before World War Two, when this was a Japanese Military Hospital. Six foot two Marines didn't fit on those elevators in a prone position.

The Corporal was delivered to the Orthopedic Ward, where he was placed in a real bed. Mick quickly pulled the sheets over his nakedness as he had seen women in the ward and the hallways. The Corpsman chuckled and told Holtzman that he would bring him some pajamas.

"All you Marines act goofy as a pet coon when you see women in the hospital! What's with that?"

"Hell...I ain't seen a round eyed woman for damn near a year!" Responded the injured Marine.

The sailor walked away, shaking his head and chuckling.

Holtzman surveyed his surroundings. The ward was large with about a hundred beds. Against the walls were the beds with traction devices, looking like spider webs woven of aluminum and stainless steel. He looked at the beds closest to him then farther out but saw no familiar looking faces.

Suddenly Mick felt very alone, almost a little scared. Always before, there had been the others, the squad to think of, his comrades, the other injured Marines to occupy his attention. Here, there was no company, no platoon, no squad, or buddy. He was on his own now. He had no one to care for or vice-versa. The Corporal also realized a very real fear that he might lose his leg. He knew the wound was serious and they hadn't known quite what to do with it so he had been sent here.

"Wonder what Lori would think of a peg legged ex-Marine." He thought. Then the reality of the thought hit home. *"What would she would think?"* But not just Lori. If he lost his leg it was the end of his career. He could forget about the Enlisted Candidates Program. He could forget about Bainbridge and the Naval Academy. Becoming an officer would just be a dream. He would just be another nineteen year old cripple limping around on crutches or a prosthesis. *"Hell, I've lost the Sergeant's stripes, the chance to be an officer, now my leg?"*

Mick then became angry…angry with himself and the situation he couldn't control.

"Get hold of yourself asshole!" he thought. *"Ski or Clarence would be glad to trade their place with you, for a prosthesis!"* He reached into the ditty bag of personal possessions and clutched the four dog tags. He held them tight a few moments with thoughts racing through his consciousness.

Minutes later the young Marine pulled the plastic envelope that held his letter writing gear from the ditty bag. He opened it and pulled out Lori's last letter and began re-reading it. When he had finished he put it back and was pulling out his writing paper for a reply when his eyes fell upon the two letters he had found on Joe Sokouski's body. *"What the hell you gonna do with those?"* He wondered.

Mick began the reply to his former girlfriend's last letter. He explained where he was and how he'd arrived, but gave few details as to his wounds. Compared to the other letters he'd written her, this one was drab and lackluster. When he finished he wrote a letter to his Mom and Dad.

The Corpsman returned with the promised PJ's about the same time Holtzman had finished his letters. The medic helped him with the pajama bottoms and the Corporal pulled on the tops quickly.

"Hey, could you mail these for me?" Holtzman asked as the sailor started to leave.

"Sure." Came the reply. Mick didn't notice the frown on the Corpsman's face as he walked away. The Marine had addressed the envelopes as he had for the last year, simply drawing a picture of a stamp in the upper right corner and writing "FREE VIETNAM" within the box, it was their postmark.

CHAPTER THIRTY-SIX
Nurse MacGregor

Corporal Holtzman awoke the next morning and again, it took a few minutes to realize just where he was. The Orthopedic Ward at Yokosuka Naval Hospital was still dark. His eyes searched the darkness for something familiar. Within a minute his memory brought him back to the reality of the events of the last few days. He had been in this hospital since yesterday afternoon and as of yet, no doctor had examined him.

Mick lay quietly in the dark with unwelcome thoughts weaving through his brain. He reached down and clutched the ditty bag, feeling the shape of the dog tags, banishing the unbidden images from his mind.

At 06:00 hours the lights came on. Shortly after that the hum of activity began. Navy Nurses and Corpsmen began their rounds. Mick was staring at the ceiling trying to count the holes in the acoustical tile up there. He would get to around fifty then lose track of which line he was on and have to start over.

"You must be our new Marine." a soft, feminine, almost girlish voice said.

Holtzman looked over, startled. At the foot of his bed was a red headed nurse, in a white uniform wearing Ensign insignia on her collar.

"Yes ma'am, I suppose so." the Corporal stammered.

The freckle faced nurse blushed at the ma'am, but continued on.

"I am Nurse Sally MacGregor and I will be in charge of you and your recovery while you're here."

"Yes Ma'am." The young Corporal replied. The girl couldn't be much older than he was.

"You don't have to call me Ma'am. We're pretty informal here."

"All right, I will try to remember that Ensign MacGregor." Mick replied, with the right corner of his mouth tightening and curling ever so slightly in his characteristic grin.

"Ohhh! You Marines!" she exclaimed.

Frustrated, she pulled herself together and read a long list of questions from a form. When she got to the questions about previous wounds, her eyes opened wide at the description of his first wound and her mouth fell open when he said that his second wound had been a bayonet in the abdomen.

Finally, the questions over, the nurse informed him that breakfast would be served at 08:00 hours. Then she turned scarlet and asked, "Would you like a sponge bath Corporal."

"Whaa-What! No, No!" Holtzman gasped with a blush equal to the girls.

"Would you prefer that I bring some soap and hot water so that you could bathe yourself." MacGregor said still blushing.

"Yes. That would do fine, Ensign." Mick answered, regaining his composure.

"Alright," she blushed again, "would you like a back rub and massage."

"No, Ma'am, I'm OK."

The young nurse then breezed away, returning in a few moments with wash cloths, towels, hot water and soap which she placed next to the soldiers bed.

After Nurse MacGregor left, Holtzman carefully cleaned himself up using the supplies that the cute, young nurse had brought him.

Breakfast arrived at 08:00 as the nurse had promised and the food was excellent. At approximately 09:30 hours the Corporal noticed Nurse MacGregor and the other nurses taking their places by the beds of their patients. The red haired Ensign stood two beds up from his. Moments later Holtzman noted a group of white-coated naval officers enter the Ward and begin with the first Nurse's Station at the front of the ward. Medical rounds had begun.

"Perhaps now I'll get some answers." The infantry Marine thought.

Several times, while waiting for the procession to arrive in his area, Mick caught Ensign MacGregor glancing back at him. The last time it was so obvious that the freckle faced nurse blushed.

"Hmmm, I think she likes me." thought the young Marine.

Finally the entourage arrived at the infantryman's bedside.

"This is Corporal Holtzman," Ensign MacGregor announced. "He has received a bullet wound to the leg. It is his third wound."

An older nurse, wearing Lieutenant Senior Grade insignia on her white uniform, shuffled through cart full of charts, records and X-rays until she found Mick's.

The doctors glanced at the records, then examined the X-rays, they talked amongst themselves as if Mick wasn't there.

"Compound complex fracture of the tibia." one doctor said with a frown.

"Probable simple fracture of the fibula." another said, pointing to a spot on the radiograph.

"There is some bone loss on this open fracture." another stated.

"I think we should have a consultation on this one, gentlemen." The most senior officer stated, with that the officers and their assistants moved on.

Mick sat up looking confused. Nurse MacGregor reached over and squeezed his hand.

"They'll be back with some answers, Corporal." She assured him and quickly moved on to introduce her next patient.

Holtzman watched as they moved on, patient by patient down the ward.

"Jeez, they act like we are a side of beef or something!" he thought.

Finally the young grunt quit watching. He noticed with some surprise that several magazines were on the table at his bedside. Ensign MacGregor must have placed them there during the rounds. There was a Leatherneck Magazine published by the Marines, a Life Magazine and a Playboy. Mick began perusing the Playboy.

Several hours later as the Corporal was reading an article in Leatherneck, he became aware of someone standing at the foot of his bed. He looked up and straight into the eyes of Ensign MacGregor who blushed involuntarily.

"This is Captain Krieger, our senior physician on the Orthopedic Ward. He's here to discuss your case with you." The red haired nurse announced, with her blush fading.

"Good morning again Corporal. It looks like you've had a tough tour and this is your third wound." The Captain began. A Captain in the Navy is the equivalent of a Colonel in the Marine Corps, so this man had been a Navy Medical Officer for some time.

"Thank you Sir, the tour's been OK…what's going to happen to me now?" Holtzman asked bluntly.

"I guess that has been the question of the day." The Captain paused, "The bullet that passed through your leg took a quarter to a half inch of bone from the tibia, the large bone in your lower leg. Your body weight probably fractured your fibula. Were you running at the time?"

"Yes sir, I was assaulting an enemy position that was about to ambush some of our men."

"All alone!" The Captain asked astounded.

"No Sir, my squad was with me."

The Navy doctor absorbed this then went on.

"The fibula, the small bone in the lower leg, should heal fine. Because of the bone loss we may have trouble getting the tibia to heal."

"So what's the straight skinny, Sir?" Mick asked, pinning the Captain with his gaze.

"Well, there are a variety of techniques we've been trying without much success. If the tibia doesn't heal and fairly quickly, amputation becomes an option. However Corporal, there is a new technique that I have only read about. It is called dynamic compression. A metal plate is surgically applied across the fracture site. The ends of the bones are brought into apposition and the plate is screwed into place. The screw holes are angled such that they compress or push together the ends of the fractured bone. I think it is your best bet. I have signed orders transferring you to Great Lakes Navel Hospital as a referral for this procedure." The Captain finished.

"Thank you Sir, I can't say I understood everything you described, but anything is better than losing the leg."

"You're welcome Marine. And thank you for all that you have done for us. You should be on a flight back to the states in a couple of days. I leave you in the capable hands of Nurse MacGregor." With that Captain Krieger left, leaving the Ensign and Corporal both blushing.

Breaking the silence the nurse said, "My first patient when I came here had a serious fracture of the femur and Captain Krieger referred him stateside for this procedure. He was a Marine too, but he talked all the time, a Sergeant Morrillo"

"Hector Morrillo?" Mick exclaimed, sitting up quickly which caused a grimace.

"Why yes, did you know him?"

"I should smile, he was my Platoon Sergeant. I was with him when he was wounded. How did his leg do? Did he go to Great Lakes?"

"Why I don't know how his leg did…and I'm not sure if he went to Great Lakes or Balboa Naval Hospital." Replied the Ensign. "But he talked about a friend of his, a Squad Leader." She stopped as realization crossed her face. "You…It was you he talked about," MacGregor blushed again, "He thought a great deal of you Corporal."

"Wouldn't it be a kick in the ass if I ran into Morrillo at Great Lakes!" Mick mused. Then he quickly realized what he'd said. "Excuse me ma'am…kinda forgot where I was."

MacGregor smiled sweetly, "You're not the first Marine I've had as a patient. In fact Sergeant Morrillo had a little trouble keeping a civil tongue in his mouth also."

Corporal Holtzman lay back in his bed after the nurse

left. He stared at the ceiling, his mind swirling. In a few days he'd be on a plane back to the world, to Great Lakes Naval Hospital just outside of Chicago and about a hundred miles from home. He might not become a peg legged "former Marine" after all. Perhaps he could pursue a career as an officer. Lori was all the way out in L.A. so unless she came back for some reason he wouldn't see her. Mick pulled out his writing gear and started a letter to her.

Lunch came a few minutes later, so the youthful Marine finished the letter and gave it to the Japanese orderly that pushed a cart with magazines and books through the ward. On the side of the cart was a pouch that read "MAIL". Mick dropped his letter into the pouch without noticing that the other letters had U.S. postage on them.

CHAPTER THIRTY-SEVEN
Back to the World

Corporal Holtzman awoke around 02:00 hours with sweat pouring out of every pore in his body. A few moments later the chills began and the uncontrollable spasmodic shaking. The Marine thought to himself, *"Lost the stripe, no Annapolis, got malaria, likely to lose my leg if they don't ship me home, I'm in great shape!"*

In a few moments the Ward Corpsman came past and noticed.

"What's the matter?" the medic asked.

"I got the fever and chills, probably Malaria." The Marine responded.

"I'll be right back!" The Corpsman said. He sped off to the Nurse's Station.

The sailor was back in less than a minute followed by Nurse MacGregor.

"What's going on Corporal?" The Ensign asked.

"Oh, I got the fever and chills." Mick responded through clenched teeth, "Probably malaria."

"How long has this been going on?" Queried the nurse.

"I guess a couple of months. They couldn't find the bug in my blood in Nam." The Marine said with his teeth chattering from the spasms.

The Corpsman handed Ensign MacGregor a syringe and a blood tube.

"I'm going to draw a blood sample from you, Corporal." The redheaded nurse informed him. She swabbed his arm in the area of his elbow with alcohol and proceeded to draw the blood sample. When she finished she handed the syringe and blood tube to the waiting medic who headed for the Nurse's Station.

Sally MacGregor stayed where she sat, holding the hand of the young Marine as the fevers and chills coursed through his body. She occasionally reached up and wiped the sweat from his brow. She wasn't embarrassed now, this was what she trained for.

Holtzman seemed oblivious to her presence and her hand in his. The spasms were getting stronger with each attack. He withdrew into himself to find the strength to withstand the episode. The attack ended as quickly as it began and the Corporal fell into a deep sleep.

Ensign MacGregor stayed where she was. This Marine Non-com, who seemed so tough when awake, looked so boyish when asleep

She continued holding his hand, afraid that if she moved it would wake him. She wondered how one so young could have endured so much. A nineteen year old and a Marine NCO with three Purple Hearts! Sally continued to sit with her patient until at 05:15. When his eyes opened, he looked at her and their gaze locked for a few moments. Then, Holtzman closed his eyes, reopened them and spoke.

"This malaria, will it stop me from goin' back to the States?"

"I don't know." The girl answered.

"I can't afford not to go. It doesn't sound good for my leg if I stay here." The Corporal said not sounding very tough.

"Perhaps you could just write a report and put it in my medical records, then I could be treated when I get to Great Lakes." The Marine pleaded.

"Hmmm, that's not standard procedure." Said the freckle faced nurse. "But I don't see why you couldn't be treated there as well as here."

At about the same time both nurse and Marine became aware that they were holding hands. Again they blushed in unison.

"Well...I better go write my reports." Said MacGregor as she got up and started for the Nurse's Station.

"Thanks Sally." Mick said.

Ensign MacGregor stopped in her tracks, turned and looked at Holtzman. Then she nodded and walked away to the Nurse's Station, feeling like she was floating on air.

Mick lay in the bed staring at the ceiling, no longer counting the holes in the acoustical tile. His mind was overwhelmed with thoughts. His leg, his home, Lori, the squad and Nurse MacGregor.

The lights came on at 06:00, breaking him out of his trance. His thoughts turned toward food. The fever attacks were taking their toll and despite the good food he continued to lose weight.

When breakfast appeared the Mick scarfed it down in minutes. When the Japanese kitchen orderly went by with a tray for another patient her eyes widened at the site of the empty breakfast tray.

"You want more?" she asked in broken English.

Holtzman nodded in the affirmative, with a smile, and a few minutes later the Japanese lady returned with a second tray which he began on and ate in a more leisurely manner.

After breakfast the nurses lined up with their patients as rounds were held. The doctors stopped at Mick's bed for moments only, inspecting his chart to make sure his condition had not changed. After they departed he read the magazines that Ensign MacGregor had left. Reading even the advertisements in detail, he was trying to get a feel for what life was like back in the world.

Lunch came at 12:00 hours and the Marine bolted it down with the same vigor displayed at breakfast. However, there were no seconds this time. Holtzman was reading his magazines when he noted a commotion near the Nurse's Station. Several Corpsmen that had arrived and produced paperwork. A few minutes later they headed down the ward under the supervision of Nurse MacGregor. They stopped at the Corporal's bed.

"They're here for you Mick." Sally said. "There's a flight leaving for the states in a few hours and they have your name on the manifest."

The Marine looked at the girl and nodded.

"It will be good to be home, won't it?" She asked.

Mick nodded.

"Say something!" MacGregor said.

"Thanks Sally." Holtzman said lamely, as the Corpsmen shifted him from bed to gurney. His eyes were on hers as they wheeled him down the ward. He gave her a little salute and wondered why her eyes seemed so shiny.

He was wheeled out of the hospital into the parking area where he was loaded into a bus that was exactly the same as the one he arrived on. The bus was half full of other wounded soldiers. Soon the doors closed and the bus reversed the route they had followed to the hospital a week earlier. At the airport he was off loaded from the bus to a waiting jet aircraft and placed aboard on a stretcher.

After the plane was loaded and the hatch closed, the Corporal could feel the plane taxiing to take off position. Soon he was airborne, heading for the world. *"What is in store for me there?"* he wondered. It sounded like his best chance to keep his leg. Soon the rumble of the jet engines put him to sleep.

Mick awoke when the jet touched down. He looked at his watch and could not believe he had slept so soundly, so long. *"Where am I now?"* he wondered. The plane slowed its taxi and came to a halt. Moments later the hatch opened and a Crew Chief entered and began going about his business.

A few minutes later a middle aged woman wearing a smock with USO emblems entered and looked around the plane. At first the USO lady seemed disappointed as all the soldiers appeared to be asleep. Then she saw Holtzman watching her.

"Good morning Marine. Welcome back to America." The lady said, in a gentle tone.

"Where am I...or we?" Mick asked.

"You're in Anchorage, Alaska." The lady replied, "The medevac jets fly out of Japan and land here before continuing on to the continental forty-eight. Can I get you a donut and some coffee?" The USO Lady continued.

"Sure!" Mick answered. *"No wonder they call them donut dolly's,"* he thought after the woman disappeared.

In a few minutes the USO volunteer was back, with a cup of coffee in a cardboard cup, several donuts and a copy of the Anchorage newspaper. Mick thanked her and she wandered off looking for more soldiers who were awake.

Mick stopped the Crew Chief and questioned him as to their destination. He discovered that the plane was being refueled here in Alaska and would then travel to a medical facility outside of St. Louis. From there, each soldier would be sent to the appropriate hospital.

Several hours later the jet landed in St. Louis. After another bus and stretcher ride he was shifted onto a bed in a large ward. He lay looking at his surroundings, wondering how long he would be here. After a half hour or so a black female Corpswave appeared, holding a telephone. In a deep southern drawl she asked if he would like to make a phone call.

"What?" Mick asked, not quite understanding.

"Does ya wanna call home?" the girl queried.

"Well yes."

"What's the phone number?" The girl asked, as she plugged the phone into a jack by the bed.

It took the Marine a minute to search his memory for his parents phone number. The Corpswave dialed as he gave it to her then handed him the reciever.

At first Mick looked at the phone strangely, then put it to his ear, *"What should he say? Was anyone home?"*

Then the ringing stopped and he heard his mother's musical voice say "Hello."

"Hello, this is Corporal Mick Holtzman United States Marine Corps." He said hoping to be funny.

"Wh..what, Who is this?" His mother replied then called his father's name.

"It's me Mom…Mick!" he replied.

"Where are you?" Mrs. Holtzman gasped, "We've been so worried." He heard the phone click as the upstairs receiver was lifted and his father's voice was next.

"Mick, is that you?"

"Yes Dad."

"Where are you?"

"I'm at a medical facility outside St. Louis. They're supposed to transport me to Great Lakes Naval Hospital, but I don't know when."

The Corpswave smiled and informed him he would be leaving in about two hours and arriving in Chicago in about three. The former Squad Leader relayed the information to his parents.

"We were so worried! We got a telegram that you'd been wounded but no details…then, no word all this time." His mother almost sobbed.

"I wrote you a letter when I got to Japan, explaining everything. Mom, Dad, I got to go now…they need to let another Marine call home." Mick explained as the Corpswave motioned to speed it up.

"I'll see you at Great Lakes. I'm OK." He finished.

More bus rides, planes, Corpsmen and Corpswaves. Then he was deposited in the Orthopedic Ward at Great Lakes Naval Hospital just outside of Chicago. They pushed the gurney down the ward past bed after bed of shot-up servicemen. Holtzman glanced at each as he passed, looking for a familiar face, but there was none. Four beds from the end, next to the windows, he saw the vacant bed that was to be his. The Corpsmen installed him on the bed efficiently and disappeared. A few minutes later the Ward Nurse appeared and introduced herself.

"Good afternoon Corporal, I am Lieutenant Commander Stark, in charge of the Orthopedic Ward." The stern, salt and pepper haired nurse stated. This was no Ensign MacGregor.

The Head Nurse went over the rules and introduced him to the Nurse, Corpswaves and Corpsmen that would give him his medical care. She also informed him that medical rounds would be tomorrow. After the tough old nurse was gone, Holtzman's mind once again was flooded with thoughts. Some pleasant and some not.

Something caught his attention and he saw his Mother and Father standing at the front of the ward talking to the personnel at the Nurse's Station. In a few seconds he saw his mother start down the ward with his dad in tow. His mother, an attractive women, looked at each injured patient as she passed. When she came to his bed she looked at him and started to pass on.

"Margaret!" His dad's voice stopped her. She looked at her husband questioningly and Mr. Holtzman nodded to Mick's bed.

Margaret Holtzman looked back to the bed she had just passed. She stared for a second then gasped.

"Mick? Mickey?"

"Hi Mom." The Marine responded.

She went to the bed and grabbed his hand, trying to keep a poker face. He didn't look like her son! His eyes...they looked so old! He was painfully thin. He didn't look the same as the boy who had gotten on the bus for Milwaukee a year and a half ago.

His father, on the other side of the bed, asked, "What's your condition? Has a doctor seen you since you arrived?"

The infantryman answered the questions as best he could, trying to calm his dad who was quite capable of making a scene if he felt his son wasn't receiving adequate treatment. Young Holtzman explained what he'd been told in Japan and what was likely in store for him here. Both parents blanched when he mentioned the possibility of amputation.

Soon he changed the subject to more pleasant topics, such as his brother David and the community. Again Mick looked up to the front of the ward and saw Jamie Johansen, his old high school buddy accompanied by his girlfriend Sarah. Jamie had enlisted in the Corps six months ahead of him and had already mustered out and was back in civilian life.

The old friends greeted each other and the conversation lightened up. Mick was glad for the reprieve and was troubled every time his parents studied him with worried looks. The four stayed until five o'clock when visiting hours ended. Holtzman ate dinner at six and was asleep by seven. He was exhausted by the events of the day.

CHAPTER THIRTY-EIGHT
Morrillo Comes Callin'

Corporal Holtzman awoke before the lights came on the next morning. Again he had to think hard to remember where he was.

"Well today at 09:00. I should find out what happens next." He thought. *"God! I'm back in the world."*

His parents were coming back in the afternoon to find out what had transpired during the rounds with the doctors. Mick's father worked for a federal agency and his mother was a school teacher. His dad had been a Commander in the Navy during World War II and had never quite forgotten it.

The lights came on at 06:00 hours and breakfast followed. Mick ate well and managed a second cup of java which he savored after the tray was carried off.

He began studying his surroundings. If he craned around a bit he could see out the windows behind him and to either side. The patient on his right was in a plaster cast covering his whole body, except there were no legs coming out and only one arm. He had received his breakfast through a straw. On his left, the patient was whole but had a tent over his left leg. Across the aisle the patients were all in traction devices, with aluminum and stainless steel everywhere supporting shattered limbs.

"I guess I'm lucky no matter how this comes out." The Corporal thought.

"Hey buddy, who were you with down south?" asked the patient on his left with the tent.

"Hotel 2/26 and First Recon." He replied.

"I was with 1/5 near An Hoa." The fellow said, "Did ya ever get over that way?"

"Sure did…went through there several times on the way in and out of Dodge City and Arizona Territory." Holtzman stated.

Then a voice from the right said, "I was with the muddy water fleet down in the delta till they blew my boat out of the water."

Holtzman looked over at the man in the body cast, amazed that someone in his condition could talk, their eyes met.

"That was tough duty Sailor, I wouldn't have traded you for it." Mick told him.

The wounded warriors talked on, finding out things they had in common, and how things worked here at the hospital.

The Marine on his left, Richardson, had an open fracture of the femur. He had lost four inches of bone and they were trying to re-grow the bones back together. Davis, on the right in the body cast, was from Michigan and didn't talk much about his condition or prognosis. But he was happy to talk about his tour and even the ambush of his boat which had left him crippled.

He saw the doctors and nurses assembling at the Nurse's Station at the front of the ward and knew that medical rounds were about to begin.

Slowly the group progressed down the ward towards him, spending a few minutes at each bedside. Most of the patients had been here for a while and unless there was a change in their condition, not a lot to discuss. When they got to his bed Nurse Stark introduced him, but without the warm fuzziness he'd felt from Ensign MacGregor.

The doctors looked at the X-rays, pointing and talking with each other as if Holtzman wasn't there. They read the referral from Dr. Krieger in Japan suggesting the dynamic compression plate technique.

"Well I guess this will be your case then Hamilton." One of the more senior Navy Doctors said. A young Lieutenant Commander stepped up and took the X-Rays. He studied them and the records a few moments then addressed the group and Holtzman.

"Yes…Yes, I think that DNC will be applicable to this case. There is some bone loss but youth is on his side. With a little luck this should heal with no negative effects."

Nurse Stark then handed the doctor a page from the medical records. He read it and said, "Corporal, this indicates that you have been having fevers and chills, symptoms of malaria. Is that correct?"

Mick answered in the affirmative.

The officer looked at Nurse Stark and said, "Draw blood for a malarial profile, a CBC and a chemistry panel. Start him on anti-malarial meds. We are going to surgery on the day after tomorrow and I don't want him to die of malaria in the mean time. I want to put a dynamic compression plate on this fracture."

The doctor handed the charts back to the Nurse and moved on to the next patient.

"Well," Mick thought, *"He's decisive!"*

After the doctors and nurses had moved on, Richardson, on Mick's left, spoke up.

"Hey that's pretty positive news! That Doc seemed to think everything would come out OK. Hell…they told me I might be here for a year…and still no guarantee that I'll ever walk again."

"Yeah, that's good news Mick these doctors aren't ones to lead you on…sugar coating everything." Said Davis from his right.

"Well, at least I don't have to sit and wait. The waiting and not knowing has been drivin' me up the wall. In two days I'll have the operation. Then I'll find out what goes on from there."

The Marines and Sailors continued to talk with Mick asking questions about the hospital and the world outside. The others asking about his tour, then telling about theirs.

Just before lunch Holtzman was perusing a Life Magazine and didn't notice the Marine in a wheelchair enter the ward, make inquiries and head in his direction. The wheelchair and its occupant stopped at the foot of the Corporal's bed before he noticed it. Mick looked up from the magazine into the eyes of Sergeant Hector Morrillo.

"Hey there Corporal Holtzman, ya could have been ambushed sleepin' on the job like that!" Said the Hispanic Sergeant with a big smile.

"Morrillo! You son-of-a-bitch, where the hell did you come from?"

"I used to live in this ward, Mick. I got the word that a Marine from my old unit had been installed here so I came to see who it was. I got connections ya know."

"Yeah, Yeah, you were always connected Sarge. Damn! It's good to see your ugly face!"

"Hey, you ain't so damn pretty neither Corporal! You're skinnier and uglier than ever…why, I got a good notion to whip your ass. As scrawny as you are I could probably get the job done."

"So how's the leg?" Holtzman asked, glancing at the wheelchair and the plaster cast running from hip to toe.

"It's probably better than yours, Marine. They put a couple of plates in it about a month ago and the cast comes off on Wednesday. They say I can start walking with crutches a little then."

"Wednesday is when they're operating on my leg. They're going to put some kind of a compressing plate in it."

"Well then, we'll both have something to celebrate on Wednesday afternoon." The Sergeant said, with a conspiratorial wink. "I'll provide the refreshments."

"Hey, you guys wouldn't rat on us if we had a little celebration?" The Sergeant said looking at Davis and Richardson.

"Not if were included." came back Richardson.

"Just bring a straw!" Said Davis. Morrillo's eyebrows arched at the cockiness of the horribly wounded sailor.

The two talked on, remembering times past until Morrillo mentioned Ski. The color drained out of Holtzman's face and the grin faded. Silence replaced the boisterous chatter of minutes earlier.

"Ski got it, huh?" The husky Sergeant asked.

"Yeah…it was a bad deal." Mick said, his voice empty. The Corporal then gave the account of Ski's death and the events that occurred before and after.

"So those chicken-shit Lieutenants, Byrd and Gregory tried to fuck with you when you requested mast."

"Yeah, but Gunny Shaw and Frenchy tried to help."

"Frenchy? Not Frenchy DeBeque?"

"Yeah, he was your replacement, Sarge."

"No shit! Hell, I served with him stateside when they busted him down to private for tellin' some non-combat butter bar to stick it where the sun don't shine."

"He told me he served with you stateside…he's a good man."

"The best!" Morrillo invoked.

"How far did ya get requestin' mast?"

"I got through the Platoon Commander, Company Commander and had an appointment with Colonel Smith the Battalion CO. Then I got wounded and here I am. So I guess it won't go any further. I'll probably lose that third stripe and perhaps my orders to the Enlisted Candidates School will be changed or lost. I pissed off a lot of brass."

"So where ya gonna go with this thing now?" The Sergeant asked.

"Don't know where to go. I can't request mast here and the chicken-shit chopper pilot is God knows where. But something needs to be done."

"Has your Chickie been to visit yet?" The Sergeant asked with a sly leer.

"What Chickie?" The Corporal said trying to be poker faced.

"The one that sent you the letters that made you sweat and turn white when you saw 'em." Hector snickered.

About that time lunch came and Morrillo left so he could eat. But he promised to come back later.

After lunch the nurse and a Corpsman changed his bandages and irrigated the leg wound as they did each day. The jostling of the broken leg was painful but necessary. Mick got out his writing gear and wrote a letter to Lori, trying to fill her in on what had happened since he'd written in Japan. He finished before his buddy returned and put it in his drawer till he could purchase postage.

Hector Morrillo reappeared in the early afternoon. The two comrades continued their conversations. They included Davis and Richardson in them. The conversations brightened up this corner of the Orthopedic Ward and the fellow in the traction device across the aisle began joining in from time to time.

That afternoon Holtzman's parents returned to find out the news from the doctors. Morrillo tried to leave but Mick's mother kept him there, asking him questions.

Morrillo was having a hard time answering. As like most Marines, he had difficulty stringing together more than six words without using a curse word.

When Mr. Holtzman heard that the surgery was scheduled for Wednesday, he said that they would come down to check in on Mick in the afternoon. Keeping a straight face but watching Morrillo the whole time the Corporal said.

"It might be better to come down Thursday as I might be kind of "out of it" from the anesthetic. Why don't you call Wednesday night."

Morrillo had to turn away and look up the ward to the Nurse's Station.

Mick heard Richardson choking but managed to keep his face straight.

Five o'clock came and visiting hours were over. Morrillo took his leave and told Mick he wouldn't be up tomorrow as he had an appointment.

Time flew by and Wednesday morning was suddenly here. The Corporal received no breakfast because of his impending surgery. The Corpsmen came for him at 08:30 while the others were eating. As they rolled him down the aisle Richardson called out, "Get some buddy!"

"Damn right!" Davis chimed in.

The gurney carrying the infantryman was wheeled down the halls and into the elevators to the floor where the operating theaters were located.

Hours later the Marine awoke, his brain fuzzy from the anesthesia. He looked up at the acoustical tile, "*I'm in Japan!*" he thought. Then he realized he was wrong. Slowly it came back to him. They'd operated on him this morning. "*What time is it?*"

Minutes later a Corpsman came in checking on him.

"What time is it?" Mick asked.

"It's noon" the sailor replied. "That Surgeon is fast. He had you in and out of there in an hour."

Mick tried to look down at his leg but could see nothing except the sheets covering him.

"There's not much to see." The Corpsman said. "They sutured up the wound and installed a Penrose drain. You'll get a look at it when we take you back to the ward."

As promised, the Marine saw the wound was closed with about eight black nylon stitches. A pale yellowish rubber tube extended an inch or so out of the bottom end. Holtzman was surprised when the orderlies moved him from recovery back to the ward. He was prepared for pain in the fracture site when moved but there was none.

The former Squad Leader was back in the ward by one o' clock. He managed to get the Corpsman to bring him a late lunch. He was told he could use a wheelchair but it would be best to take it easy, and that the surgeon would tell him what he could and couldn't do during rounds tomorrow.

At three o'clock Hector Morrillo rolled into the ward. He was still in the wheelchair but the cast was gone.

"Hey Mick! Looks like we both made it."

"Yeah, but what's the deal? I figured you'd be walkin'!" Holtzman exclaimed.

"I go to physical therapy, I walk there using crutches. I managed about ten feet today, but I'll keep at it. What about you?"

"Oh, they told me I could use a wheelchair, but to lay chilly for a while. The Doc will give me the straight scoop tomorrow."

"Then tomorrow I'll come down after rounds and we can go out on patrol. I brought some soft drinks for a little celebration." The Sergeant said. He produced four cans of coke which he opened with a church key. He passed one to Richardson and Mick, telling then to drink a couple of swallows. He poured coke from the fourth can into a dixie cup. Then reaching under his tunic he pulled out a bottle and poured some Jim Beam whiskey into the can. He put a straw in it and wheeled over to Davis holding the can so the Sailor could drink."

"I can hold the can Sarge, I got one good arm." Davis said. "The good thing is I don't have to worry about falling down when I get drunk."

"Were going to hold you to that Petty Officer Davis." Morrillo said, using the man's rank for the first time. The Sergeant then poured whiskey into the other three cans giving Mick and himself the biggest slugs.

Holtzman had noted how Davis had puffed up at the reference to his rank. A Petty Officer First Class was the equivalent to a Staff Sergeant in the Marines and the next step up was Chief Petty Officer, the equivalent to a Gunnery Sergeant.

"So Davis, when they gonna promote you to Chief?" The Corporal asked with a smile.

"Shit, they ain't gonna make a no-legged, one-armed sailor a Chief!" Davis replied sarcastically.

"Hell, they ought to promote you just for survivin'!" responded the Texican Sergeant.

"Hey Sarge, did you ever get your medal?" Mick asked.

"What medal?"

"Seriously…we heard you were gonna be decorated for takin' out that fifty caliber gun when ya got hit." The Corporal said.

"Well no one's been chasin' me down to pin it on me." Morrillo commented while pouring more whiskey into his coke.

The four soldiers kept up with stories and jokes and soon none of them were feeling any pain.

At four thirty a Corpsman walked down the ward. They quieted down and tried to conceal their drinks. The Corpsman was carrying a telephone and plugged it into a nearby jack and said, "Telephone call for you Holtzman, it's your dad, the Commander. And if Nurse Stark catches you guys boozin' it up back here, you'll wish you'd never been born and I'll be a Seaman again." The medic handed the receiver to Mick.

The former Squad Leader took the phone and spoke with his father, trying hard not to slur his words. The infantryman explained that the operation had gone well and that he would know more after rounds in the morning. Then his mother got on the phone and he assured her that he was fine. By now the others were clowning and making faces at him. Holtzman had to stare out the window so he couldn't see Morrillo's face as he would have broke down laughing. His mother ended the phone conversation saying, "You'd better get some sleep, your voice sounds odd."

"Yes mom, I will, that's the anesthesia wearin' off. See ya tomorrow." Holtzman finished putting down the phone as all four started laughing.

Morrillo left just before dinnertime, wheeling himself out of the ward, somehow managing to keep a straight line.

CHAPTER THIRTY-NINE
Sergeant Carnady

The next morning Holtzman woke up when the lights came on. His head was splitting. He rolled over and tried to go back to sleep but found no relief. He opened his eyes. They felt gritty and the light hurt them. His mouth felt like a platoon had marched through it all night.

The hung-over Marine reached for the water glass on his side table and took a sip. He swilled the water around in his mouth, clearing the crud away. He then looked for a place to spit, finally settling on the bed pan. Moments later the same Corpsman that had brought the phone last night came down the ward and set breakfast on the tables with a sneer. He heard Richardson, who had been dozing, grunt, then retch as the smell of the food hit him. Davis yelled at the Corpsman to get the food away from him.

The Corpsman came back smiling, "Not hungry today fellows? I wonder why."

"Hey squid, payback is a motherfucker!" The former Squad Leader snarled as the smiling sailor removed the three trays. Mick remembered the crutches and wheelchair that had been left by his bed yesterday and he carefully sat up. He was surprised that the movement caused no pain in his leg. Carefully, he swung himself into a sitting position. When the injured leg was lowered from the bed the pain seared threw it. Holtzman grimaced and waited as the pain decreased in intensity. He reached for the crutches and stood up on them, keeping the injured leg off the ground. He tried a couple of experimental steps. Each time the good leg touched the ground, the wounded leg throbbed. He then moved out for the head where he was able to perform his toilet for the first time without the use of the hated bedpan. Using the crutches he made it back to the bed and noted that the leg was less painful on the return trip.

After getting back in bed Mick inquired, "You two gonna make it?"

"I don't think so." Richardson groaned.

"Put me out of my misery, Marine." Davis begged.

The three spent the next half hour describing their condition in the most colorful terms they could think of.

At about 09:00 rounds began. Finally, the group of white coated doctors and nurses made their way to the Corporal's bed.

"We operated on Corporal Holtzman yesterday, installing the dynamic compression plate across the open fracture of the tibia. The operation went well and we noted that the fibula was healing nicely on its own. How are you feeling today Corporal?" asked Lieutenant Commander Hamilton.

"Fine Sir." the young Marine lied.

"Good! Here's the program. The dynamic compression plate internally fixes your fracture so there is no need for a cast. Post operative X-rays showed that the ends of the bone were in apposition, so healing should begin." The naval officer said this primarily for the benefit of the other doctors.

"Now, what I want from you is a little cooperation. I want you to take it easy for a couple of days, then report to physical therapy and we will begin weight bearing exercises. This will help the healing process." Hamilton went on to describe what Mick could and couldn't do.

"With a little luck you could be walking with a cane in two or three weeks." The navy doctor finished.

After the doctors had moved on, Richardson commented, "That sounds like great news Mick."

"Sure does." chimed in Davis.

"Yeah." Holtzman replied, thinking that neither of these poor bastards ever get any good news.

A half hour later Morrillo wheeled into the ward. He stopped his chair at the foot of Mick's bed and asked, "How's the Squad Leader this morning?"

"Fine just fine…and you Sarge?"

"Fine." Morrillo said, although his blood shot eyes told a different story.

After carrying on with Mick's neighbors for a while the

Sergeant suggested that Mick get in his wheelchair and they'd go on patrol.

Moments later the two Marines wheeled out of the ward in single file. Morrillo led the way to an elevator. He pushed the button and wheeled in, followed by Mick as the door opened.

"Did ya have any breakfast?" The Sergeant asked.

"Hell no, I thought I was gonna puke." Answered the Corporal.

"Me too." Chuckled Morrillo. "Let's have an early lunch."

When they arrived on the ground floor, the former Platoon Sergeant led the way to a café. They wheeled up to a table and set the brakes on their chairs. Morrillo had a funny little smirk on his face.

In a few moments a cute blonde waitress appeared.

"Hello Hector!" the girl exclaimed with a very friendly smile, "Who's your friend?"

"Hi Susie." The Sergeant answered. "This is Corporal Mick Holtzman, the best damn Squad Leader in the Marine Corps."

Mick, shaking his head at his friends pronouncement, greeted the waitress politely but her attention was on Hector. Morillo was rattling on about nothing while the girl hung onto every word. Finally she took their orders and disappeared into the kitchen.

"I think she likes ya Sarge."

"Yeah? Do ya think she's a natural blonde or a bottle blonde?" the Texan said with a smile. "I intend to find out."

The girl was back in a few minutes with their drinks and stayed to talk with Hector for several more minutes while ignoring other customers.

The two Marines ate their sandwiches and paid the bill, leaving a nice tip for Susie.

As they left, Morrillo hung back and had a brief conversation with the girl, then he wheeled out to meet his friend.

"You're grinnin' like the cat that swallowed the

canary." Holtzman said.

"Yeah? Well, I got me a date with Susie for Friday night."

"Get some Sarge!"

The two then rolled back to the elevator.

"Anybody else here from the unit?" Mick asked as the elevator headed up.

"Not anybody I know of." Morrillo answered, "but after you check in at your ward we'll head down to Casual Company where I live. We'll have to pass the main office where you can check for mail, records, new orders or whatever."

The two buddies wheeled down the hall to his ward. Holtzman checked in at the front desk and was informed that nothing of any importance involving him was going on. He was told that lunch was being served in forty five minutes.

The Marines wheeled back out of the ward and down the hall to a sitting room where patients and guests could go for more privacy. It was unoccupied and had a good view of Lake Michigan. Here the infantrymen stopped, lit up and enjoyed a smoke.

"Well, I better get back to the ward for lunch." The Corporal said as he crushed out the Lucky Strike.

"Yeah, we'll continue the tour after lunch. I'll be up to get you about 13:30 hours." the Sergeant suggested.

Mick wheeled back to the ward and heaved himself up onto the bed as the Corpsmen started serving lunch.

Holtzman wasn't very hungry as he had just had a sandwich, but he managed to eat what was brought. Richardson and Davis were eating now as well. After lunch was finished Mick chatted with his neighbors when a Sergeant in greens walked down the ward.

The Sergeant stopped by the foot of Mick's bed and said. "Corporal Holtzman?"

"That's me Sarge." The youthful Marine answered.

"I am Sergeant Carnady from Marine Corps Operations here at Great Lakes. Are you ambulatory?"

"What's that mean." Holtzman asked.

"Can you walk?" The Sergeant asked.

"I can get around with crutches or a wheelchair. I'm supposed to start physical therapy and do some weight bearing exercises tomorrow." The Corporal explained.

"What's going on here?" Morrillo asked as he wheeled up.

"Holtzman, you need to get down to supply and draw a set of greens. Then go to the Commissary and get your ribbons for them. There's going to be an awards ceremony right here on Friday and you need to be here with your uniform on and standing tall at 10:00 hours."

Carnady continued ignoring Hector.

"What is this all about Sergeant!" Morrillo repeated, the voice of authority coming through, he wore nothing but pajamas with no rank insignia.

"Who are you?" Sergeant Carnady asked.

"Sergeant Hector Morrillo, you must not have a very good memory Carnady. I've been down to your operations office several times."

Carnady looked down at the paper he was holding. "Hector Morrillo…you need to be in a set of Greens standing tall at 10:00 hours as well. The Colonel's planning to decorate you two and some others in the ward."

With that Sergeant Carnady walked away, stopping at the Head Nurse's Station on the way out.

"You two jarheads gonna get decorated?" Richardson asked from the adjoining bed.

"Oh. They're probably gonna pin purple hearts on us, take a picture and send it to the home town newspaper." Holtzman commented. "Hey maybe your gonna get your medal Sarge."

"I don't like that stateside non-combat son-of-a-bitch!" Morrillo said, his eyes following Carnady out of the ward. "He's prejudiced!"

"Maybe he's embarrassed 'cause he was never in combat Sarge."

"I still don't like him…let's hit the road. We can go to

supply and pick up the greens then we'll go to the Commissary and get our ribbons and insignia."

Moments later the two friends rolled out of the ward in single file. They picked up a complete issue of greens which included: The green jacket with belt and buckle, two pair of trousers, four khaki shirts called tropicals, a pair of low quarter shoes with 3 pair of socks and of course the khaki necktie.

The two grunts then headed for the Commissary with Sergeant Morrillo in the lead. Upon arrival they went to the counter where the ribbons corresponding to your decorations were located, along with uniform insignia. The counter was clerked by a grandmotherly looking civilian lady.

"Good afternoon ma'am." Morrillo began, "We've got a tall order for you. We were just issued these Marine Greens and are supposed to wear them at an awards ceremony on Friday. We need our chevrons sewed on, all of our ribbons, the uniforms pressed and if possible, tailored."

"Oh my! That is a tall order. The ribbons and insignia are no problem but the sewing and tailoring could be. Wait just a moment, one of the tailors is married to a Marine and she might just do it for you on a rush basis." The lady picked up a phone and began dialing as Holtzman and Morrillo exchanged glances.

"She said yes. She can get your uniforms done by Friday." The lady said as she put down the phone. "She'll be over to take your measurements in about ten minutes." A look of concern crossed the woman's face. "Can you stand?" she said, looking at the two Marines in wheelchairs.

"Yes ma'am, we can stand for the measurements." Mick answered reading the ladies mind.

"Oh good. Let's get on with the insignia and ribbons before she gets here." The lady said, "Then I can have your ribbons in the proper order in a block for you to pin on when you get the finished uniforms.

Morrillo started off, listing his decorations, ordering Sergeants chevrons for his Jacket and each shirt. The lady jotted them down as he rattled them off.

"And you young man?"

Mick ordered the Corporal's chevrons for his jacket and shirts, then began to rattle off his ribbons finishing with a set of gold parachutist wings worn by jump qualified Recon Marines.

The elderly lady, who had obviously been doing this for some time, looked at the boyish Marine before her questioningly.

"He doesn't look that tough does he ma'am? But I'll guarantee that he is." Said Morrillo, chuckling.

Minutes later the tailor lady came. She quickly took the measurements of the two Marines and assured them the uniforms would be ready by noon on Thursday.

The afternoon was still young so the two Marines rolled out of the Commissary and down to Morrillo's room. The room was small, about ten feet by ten feet with a bed and a small dresser. There was a door to a bathroom that he shared with the room next door.

"Hey, maybe next week they'll move you down here." The Sergeant suggested.

"That would work for me." Mick responded.

The next few days consisted of physical therapy. Mick was able to support more and more weight on his injured leg each day.

On Thursday after lunch, the two Marines rolled back into the Commissary where they were greeted by the grandmotherly clerk and the lady tailor.

"I wanted to make sure the alterations were OK." the tailor explained.

Morrillo and Holtzman rolled up to changing room, got up from their chairs and limped in, pulling the curtains closed behind them. The clerk had attached the ribbons, marksmanship medals and parachute wings to Mick's uniform. The two Marines clumsily managed to get the uniforms on. In a few minutes both stepped out and stood for inspection before the two ladies. The uniforms fit perfectly.

"You both look very handsome." the clerk said.

The tailor, satisfied with her work. But Mick noticed a tear in her eye.

"What's wrong ma'am?"

"Nothing. It's just that you look too young to be wearing all those purple hearts. You see my husband is a Marine. He's over in Vietnam and my son is seventeen and he wants to enlist. You don't look too much older than he is."

Holtzman nodded, not knowing what to say.

The two Marines thanked the ladies, paid their bill and headed out. At four o'clock Morrillo took his leave and Mick rolled back to the Orthopedic Ward.

"Hey, look at all the decorations!" Richardson said as Mick arrived at his bed.

"Yeah, now you even look like a Marine." Said Davis.

The Corporal carefully hung the jacket up along with a fresh pair of trousers and shirt in the locker between his and Richardson's bed.

CHAPTER FORTY
The Awards Ceremony

Friday morning, after eating breakfast and chatting with his ward mates, Corporal Holtzman changed out of pajamas into the new pressed uniform. He was getting stronger from physical therapy. He could stand if he didn't bear full weight on his injured leg. After tying the neck tie he pulled on the jacket which Marines referred to as a blouse. He fastened the belt with the brass buckle. Mick then picked up his crutches and went to the head to make sure all was correct and inspect his uniform.

At 09:15 Sergeant Morrillo wheeled onto the ward wearing his new uniform. The two Marines checked each other over, making sure that all the creases lined up, while taking a good natured ribbing from the other patients in the ward. Sergeant Carnady arrived at 09:40 wearing his uniform with his single National Defense Ribbon. He informed Holtzman and Morrillo that they were to stand in the central aisle of the ward near the end, just past Richardson's bed. Mick went to the spot on crutches then leaned them against the wall. Hector rolled over in his wheelchair, stood up then pushed the chair between two beds but still within reach.

"I'll call you to attention when the Colonel is ten feet away." Carnady said.

"I hope I don't fall over." said Morrillo.

"I don't think I can click my heels." The Corporal said.

"Try to make it as snappy as you can." Carnady finished.

Moments later at the head of the ward, a Marine Colonel and Navy Captain appeared, followed by a Master Sergeant and a Senior Chief Petty Officer.

The officers and their attendants continued down the aisle. As planned, Sergeant Carnady called "Attention!" and the two Marines brought their injured leg to the good one and assumed the position.

The Colonel turned to the Master Sergeant and took a

paper. He began reading from it:

"Sergeant Hector Morrillo, the Commanding General of the Ninth Marine Amphibious Brigade takes pride in presenting you the Purple Heart Medal for wounds received in combat in the Republic of Vietnam. The Master Sergeant handed the Colonel a case from which he took the medal and stepping forward pinned it on Hectors Chest. The Colonel stepped back and was handed a second paper.

"The Commanding General of the Ninth Marine Amphibious Brigade and a grateful country take pride in presenting you the Silver Star Medal for courage above and beyond the call of duty during combat actions in Quang Tri Province, the Republic of Vietnam."

The Colonel then stepped forward and pinned the Silver Star Medal on Morrillo's uniform next to the Purple Heart Medal. He shook the Sergeant's hand and congratulated him. The Master Sergeant then handed the Colonel a third sheet.

The Colonel then read off the same message to Corporal James M. Holtzman with regard to the Purple Heart Medal. He stepped forward and pinned it to his uniform.

"Is this your third Purple Heart Corporal?" The Colonel said as he eyed the young Marines ribbons.

"Yes Sir!" the Corporal replied.

The Colonel stepped back and was handed another sheet from which he read:

"The Commanding General of the Ninth Amphibious Brigade and the Congress of the United States take pride in presenting the Bronze Star Medal for courage above and beyond the call of duty during combat actions in Quang Tri Province, the Republic of Vietnam."

The Colonel stepped forward and pinned the Bronze Star next to the Purple Heart Medal.

"Apparently you like to be in thick of things Corporal." The Colonel said as he pinned the medal on.

"Yes Sir." the Corporal replied.

The Colonel stepped back and was handed another sheet from which he read.

The Commanding General takes pride in presenting you with the Naval Commendation Medal, for valor above and beyond the call of duty. Your actions resulted in saving the lives of several comrades including your Company Commander, during combat actions in Chui Lai Province, The Republic of Vietnam."

The Colonel stepped forward and pinned the medal next to the other two. He then shook Mick's hand and congratulated him.

The Navy Captain was now handed a sheet from which he read.

"The Admiral Commanding the Seventh Fleet of the United States Navy takes pride in awarding the Navy Cross to Petty Officer First Class Roy C. Davis for courage above and beyond the call of duty during combat operations in Vietnam.

The Navy Cross is the second highest award that can be awarded to those in the Naval Service, second only to the Medal of honor." The Captain said as he pinned the medal to Davis's pillow. This was followed by the Purple Heart Medal which was also pinned to the legless sailors pillow. The Captain then congratulated Davis and stepped back.

The Navy Senior Chief then stepped to Davis bed and read.

"By these presents, let it be known, that Roy C. Davis was meritoriously promoted to the rank of Chief Petty Officer by the Office of United States Navy." The Senior Chief then placed the rank insignia on the pillow next to the two medals and shook the sailor's one good hand as he congratulated him.

Holtzman and Morrillo were beaming as they decorated and promoted the sailor. As the Senior Chief stepped back, Mick noted a single tear fall from Davis's eye.

Then the Master Sergeant stepped forward and spoke.

From the Commanding Officer, Second Battalion Twenty Sixth Marine Regiment, I do hereby meritoriously promote James M. Holtzman to the rank of Sergeant in the United States Marine Corps." The Master Sergeant stepped forward and handed Holtzman two Sergeant's chevrons and a folder. He said, "Get those Chevrons sewn on today. There is a note from First Sergeant Shaw in the folder along with your Sergeant's warrant."

The two officers and senior NCO's then did an about face and proceeded back up the wards aisle to the exit.

"Detail…dismissed!" Sergeant Carnady barked.

Holtzman reached for his crutches while Hector got back into his chair.

"Congratulations Chief! The Navy Cross! They don't give those away." Mick said to Davis, who was beaming with pride.

"Well hell Mick, you got three medals and a promotion." Davis retorted.

"Where the hell did the James come from?" Morrillo asked.

"Mick's a nick name…my middle name is MacLaughlin and somebody called me Mick when I was little and it stuck."

"Well now Jimmy, this is important news." Morrillo said with a smirk. "Come on Sergeant Jimmy, let's go get your chevrons sewn on. The nice lady at the Commissary is going to shit when you have to get a new ribbon block to hold all your medals."

"Oh go stuff it Morrillo! You got the flippin' Silver Star!" Holtzman exclaimed as he took the medals off put them in their cases. They stayed and talked to Davis and Richardson for a while then got into their wheelchairs and headed for the Commissary. They managed to get the chevrons sewn on his jacket and ordered the new ribbon blocks for both Sergeants.

While in the store Mick caught Morrillo buying some "Brut"…a men's cologne.

"Hey! You planning to be Sergeant "smell good"." The new Sergeant ribbed.

"I gotta smell good on my date with Susie tonight."

"Oh yeah…that's right…tonight's the big date. Where ya goin'? The base theatre?"

"Naw, we're goin' off base, I got liberty startin' at five…she gets off at five thirty. Haven't you got a liberty chit yet? You could go home this weekend." Morrillo explained.

"No, I don't really want to go home on crutches. I'll wait till next week. I should be on a cane by then."

CHAPTER FORTY-ONE
Liberty

Sergeant Holtzman didn't see his fellow Marine all weekend. Morrillo disappeared early on Friday and wasn't back in his room at all on Saturday or Sunday morning when Mick checked.

"Morrillo must be doing some good. Get some Sarge!" Holtzman thought.

Mick thought about his men every day since leaving the battlefield. He knew very little about what had happened since his departure. He had considered writing Lincoln, O'Meara or the others but feared the letter would come back marked KIA or give him bad news.

The former Squad Leader went to physical therapy each day, even on the weekends. He was getting stronger and stronger by doing laps and walking between the two rails that he used to take some of the weight off his bad leg. The therapist indicated that he was going to recommend that they re-X-ray his leg next week and start him on a cane. This was good news to the junior Sergeant.

On Sunday afternoon, as Mick was heading to check Hector's room, a clerk called out to him as he passed the Marine Operations Office.

"Hey Sergeant Holtzman, congratulations! Your getting new quarters down at the Casual Company dorm. The room right next to your buddy Morrillo is vacant. Do you want it?"

"Sure…you bet! Thanks." Mick called out as he rolled past.

As Holtzman neared his buddy's room, he saw the door ajar. He pulled to a stop in front of the open door.

"That must have been one hell of a date!" Mick said.

Morrillo turned around looked at his friend and just smiled.

"I thought they might have thrown you in jail or somethin' when you never came back." Holtzman continued.

"She's a natural blonde Mick." Hector said as they both laughed.

Morrillo confided then that Susie and he had planned to go to dinner and a movie Friday night. When they finished dinner and got into Susie's car they started necking and decided to can the movie and adjourn to Susie's apartment. They had stayed there until he had to return Sunday afternoon.

"Sarge, Sarge, Sarge! When's the wedding?" joked Holtzman.

"And she can cook!" Added the Texan.

"Hey they're movin' me down here to the room next door." Mick explained.

"Great!"

When Monday came the new Sergeant had his leg X-rayed. The Penrose drain had been removed three days following the surgery and the wound was healing well. After physical therapy Mick collected his possessions from the Orthopedic Ward and said his goodbyes to Richardson and Davis, promising to visit as often as possible. The Marine then moved to the room next to his buddy in Casual Company.

That afternoon, the two Marines decided to do their last wheelchair patrol. Both of the Sergeants were using crutches more and more. As they passed through the hall to the elevators they noticed a patient sitting in a wheelchair in front of the doors. It would have been hard not to notice him as he had been horribly burned. The left side of his body was covered with burn scars, including his face. An IV bottle hung from a pole on the chair. Where his left ear should have been there was a grotesque hole.

As the two Marines headed into the elevator Mick made eye contact with the burned Marine.

"Howdy." said Holtzman

The burned man smiled with the right side of his face and gave a little salute as the doors closed.

"I'd bet he got it with willy peter." Hector commented.

"Yeah, that white phosphorus burns and you can't get it

off. It burns down through clothes, skin, whatever, till it's all gone." Mick said.

The two Sergeants continued on to the deli where both had a snack and Morrillo visited with Susie.

On their return to the ward, when the elevator doors opened the same burn patient was still in the wheelchair facing the elevators.

Mick wheeled over to the patient.

"Howdy again! What outfit were you with." the Sergeant began.

"I was with Charlie Company 1/9." the burn victim explained.

"Jesus, 1/9! Weren't they the battalion called the "Walking Dead"?" Mick asked.

"Yeah, but I fooled 'em...I lived."

The four Marines sat in the hall talking and sharing stories. The burn patients name was Hutchinson. He had been burned as Morrillo guessed by white phosphorus during a mortar barrage. He explained that he had a Corpsman push him out into the hall so he could watch people come and go.

"I get kinda bored in the ward all day. It'll be a while till I can use my bad arm to push the wheelchair." He said.

"Well, where do ya want to go?"

"Nowhere right at the moment." Hutchinson said as he looked at the clock above the elevators. In a few minutes the Candy Stripers from Lake Forest High will come through. I like to watch them. They take one look at me and down the hall they go!" The burned man said with a smile, on the good half of his face. "Hey, why don't we have some fun? When the door opens push my chair in. Then push the up button. They'll have to ride to the ninth floor with me."

The semi-ambulatory Marines thought this was a great idea. They further modified the plan by sending Morrillo down to the main floor where he waited until a group of six giggling, teenage girls got onto the elevator. Then he wheeled in and pushed Hutchinson's floor. When the elevator stopped and the doors opened, Mick pushed

Hutchinson into the elevator. Hutchinson made gurgling noises as he rolled into the compartment with the girls. The look on the faces of the teenagers was priceless and as the doors closed, the Marines were rolling with laughter.

Three minutes later they pushed the elevators call button and when the doors opened there was Hutchinson sitting in his wheelchair laughing. Hector and Mick helped the burned Marine into the sunroom where they could watch people enter and leave the hospital. They stayed there telling and retelling the story for an hour. They then wheeled Hutchinson back to his ward promising to stop by and take him for a ride now and then.

On Tuesday, Mick was told by the therapist that the X-rays had shown that the bone was healing well. Now he could start walking with a cane for short periods.

The Sergeant was delighted with this news. He took the cane they issued him and went back to his quarters.

Morrillo had been issued a cane the week before and had used it when on his date with the waitress. When Hector returned to his room that afternoon Mick suggested they go to the deli where Susie worked and have dinner. This deli was really for employees and guests and the Marines would have to pay for their dinner, but going there occasionally made them feel independent and offered a change from hospital food. After checking each other's uniform the two limped down the hall towards the cafeteria.

When they returned they were so proud of their journey that they discussed going to the NCO Club the next evening for a beer. The club was outside the hospital about two blocks away.

When Mick woke up Wednesday morning he knew something was wrong. He swung his legs out of the rack and to the floor. A searing pain ran through his foot. The pain wasn't emanating from the wound, it was the foot which was cramping up. He swore and howled in pain, Hector Morrillo pushed his head through the door to the bathroom that the two shared.

"What's up?" the Texan asked.

"My foot's cramping up like crazy!"

"Yeah, it happened to me last weekend after I walked on the cane."

"What'd ya do for it."

"Oh, Susie massaged the cramps out, then I took a warm shower." Morrillo said.

"You probably needed a cold shower!" Holtzman said as he began massaging his foot. "I guess we won't be going to the NCO Club tonight."

"Speak for yourself, white man." Hector said grinning.

The massage and shower helped, but Holtzman stayed on the crutches most of the day and took his dinner in his room. True to his word, Morrillo went to the Club and had dinner and drinks. On his return he came to Holtzman's room and the two sat, talked, and drank the two beers he had smuggled in.

"Tomorrow, I'll try the club. If I can walk that far I can make it home this weekend." Mick said.

"Get some, Marine!" Morrillo said, as he saluted with his beer bottle and disappeared thru the bathroom door to his room.

Thursday Mick's foot was back to normal. The muscles in the foot, which hadn't born full weight for months, were getting used to the work. He used his crutches to get around that day but bore more weight on the foot. After physical therapy he visited his old ward mates and Hutchinson. In the afternoon he got his cane and with his buddy, limped to the Marine Operations Office. Here, he checked on his service record book which would contain his orders. The SRB still had not arrived. He then asked for a liberty chit for the weekend. The clerk gave him the paper then informed him that he would have to stand inspection at 16:30 Friday and that he had to return by 06:00 Monday.

The two Sergeants then limped off for the NCO Club. They sat down at a table. Morrillo leaned over and whispered, "I'll buy the drinks. You're supposed to be twenty one, but I don't think anybody will check you with Sergeant's stripes and all those ribbons."

Sergeant Holtzman shook his head in disgust. He had three Purple Hearts, a boat load of medals, and he still couldn't legally buy a beer for a year and three months.

Hector was quickly back with two ice cold bottles of Schlitz. The two infantrymen sat back in the darkness enjoying the taste of the beer, the darkness of the club, and the feelings of freedom.

"I wonder what Second Platoon is doin' right now?" Mick mused.

"You can bet your ass they ain't sittin' in a club drinkin' cold beer." the older Sergeant said.

"Yeah, that's for sure, You know sometimes I feel guilty sittin' here in the world, pretty much in one piece and them guys still over there gettin' shot at." The younger man responded.

"I feel that way too at times Mick. I just think we got to have as many good times as we can, do our jobs well, keep up the good fight for our buddies there and go on ya know. We gotta get some!"

Holtzman pondered his buddies philosophical statement over several swallows of beer and a drag off the Lucky Strike in the ash tray. Morrillo then changed the subject.

"So...You goin' home to visit the Commander this weekend?"

"Yeah. Still some unfinished business to take care of." Mick said mysteriously.

"The Chickie?"

"Naw, she lives in California now."

"What?"

Hector raised his eyebrows questioningly. Holtzman reached inside his tunic and produced a letter which he flipped in front of his friend. Morrillo picked it up looking at the address and postmark with surprise, noting the brown stains on the envelope. He pulled out the 'Dear John' that Ski had received and began reading it. As he got further into it he started pushing it away, finally throwing it to the table in revulsion.

"So that's why Ski went nuts and got hisself killed.

What are you gonna do?"

"Don't know…it's just unfinished business…don't know. I'll tell ya Monday."

The older Sergeant decided to leave it lay where it was and went for two more beers. The two sat comfortably in the shadows and finished their second Schlitz, making small talk. Then they ordered dinner.

After dinner the two returned to their quarters and turned in for the night.

Friday sped by with the Marines doing their usual course of events with physical therapy in the morning, lunch and visiting. Their ever growing list of injured friends, included associates or just Marines who didn't seem to have anybody.

In the afternoon Mick asked Hector if he wanted to go on liberty to Madison with him.

"Naw. Thanks, but your Mom would want me to have dinner and I'd be nervous as a whore in church. Besides," the catbird grin reappeared. "I got another date with Susie."

At 16:00 hours the two went to their quarters, changed into fresh uniforms then double checked each other. Mick packed a few extra clothes in an AWOL bag and went to Marine Operations for inspection.

At 16:30 Sergeant Carnady appeared and called the small group of fifteen Marines to attention. A Second Lieutenant with no ribbons came out and started the inspection. The non-combat butter bar stopped in front of Sergeant Holtzman looked at the ribbons and Jump Wings on his chest and said.

"You know there are regulations and severe penalties for wearing decorations or insignia you don't rate."

"He earned everything there Sir! I served with him!" Morrillo snarled.

The Lieutenant looked surprised and surveyed the older Sergeant. He decided not to get into a pissing match. He moved on down the line looking to see if each soldier was in appropriate uniform. He then returned to the office. Carnady dismissed the group and the men took off in all directions.

"See you Monday, bud!" Mick yelled at Hector.

"Yeah, if I'm still alive." The Senior Sergeant said with his catbird smirk.

CHAPTER FORTY-TWO
Return of the DJ

Mick limped out of the hospital and turned left toward the main gate. He stopped and showed his papers to the Shore Patrol Officer. He went out the gate and put his foot down on civilian U.S. ground for the first time in over a year. He walked to the highway a couple of blocks away and limped north until there was a good wide gravel shoulder. Here he stopped and faced the oncoming traffic, putting his thumb out in the classic hitch-hike.

Holtzman had decided to surprise his folks and hadn't told them of the liberty. One reason was that his father would have insisted on coming to pick him up, which would have meant taking time off work. Hitching a ride, he'd get to see the country...maybe get a feel for the "World" he'd left. It seemed so long ago.

After a few minutes a blue Ford Fairlane pulled over. Mick limped up and opened the passenger door.

"Where you headed Marine?" The driver, a man of about 50 asked.

"Wisconsin." Mick answered.

"Jump in...I'm going as far as Janesville."

The Sergeant jumped in and thanked the driver politely. The driver informed the Marine that he was a vet and had served in the Navy during World War II. The two kept up the conversation as they traveled. When Mick got off in Janesville, he was only on the side of the road a few minutes. This time it was a Korean War vet. He was going to work at the Oscar Meyer plant on the east side of Madison. They chatted and Holtzman looked at the miles and miles of corn fields interspersed with red dairy barns. This was the homeland he remembered.

The driver left him off on Gorham Street, near the university section of town. This was familiar territory for the Marine and only about a mile and a half to home. Holtzman continued down the street hitchhiking when he heard a car coming. He noted the students walking along the streets on this pleasant fall afternoon. They sure looked different from the clean cut type that were around when he had lived here. Most of them had long hair, many scruffy beards and some looked just plain dirty. Sandals seemed to be the most common footwear. The girls wore tee shirts and cut offs, many without bras. *"Very interesting,"* he thought with an inward smile. When he had graduated from high school in 67, there had been a small number of long-haired bearded types that hung out near the student union called Beatniks. From what he'd read, there were a lot more now and they were referred to as Hippies.

He had gone several blocks now without a ride. He noticed that the cars went through here at a good rate of speed, the drivers with eyes focused forward. A group of students were walking along about twenty paces behind him, one of them talking with agitation. Soon the group had grown to eight and were closing up on the Sergeant's position.

"Hey soldier! How many babies did you have to kill for those medals?" The loudest of the group shouted.

"Yeah…You baby killin' pig!" Another long hair joined in, pushing forward to about ten paces from the Marine.

Holtzman just stared at them. Why should they be mad at him, he'd been serving his country and helping to keep these guys from having to go over.

The verbal harassment grew in tone, volume, and vulgarity. The group was becoming threatening and had moved to within five paces. They were starting to circle the crippled soldier.

"Oh look-it! He's got a bum leg!" said a loud mouth, "He probably shot himself in the foot." he finished, laughing.

Another bounded in toward Mick cursing and spit at the Marine.

Holtzman dodged the spittle. A second tried it, coming closer and spit a goober that the Sergeant ducked. Mick flipped the cane in his hand and tripped the jumping hippie in mid-air with the canes hook. The longhair landed hard in a heap near the Sergeant's feet. The cane flipped again and the end of it was pressed against the spitter's throat.

"You motherfuckers want a piece of my ass? It's gonna cost! And you spit at me again, you may be talkin' with a squeaky voice the rest of your fuckin' life."

He removed the cane and the startled hippie scrambled to his feet and headed back into the crowd. Mick cracked him across the behind with the cane.

The crowd of longhairs moved back ten paces and continued their verbiage.

"Come on girls! I ain't got all fuckin' day to deal with trash like you. You want some? Come and get it." Holtzman challenged.

The hippies outnumbered him eight to one, but the Marines lack of fear or even worry held them stymied. Several stepped away from the group saying,

"He's just a military pig! Fuck him!" And they walked off.

Then individually and in small groups the other six dispersed calling out insults as they left.

The Sergeant turned and began walking west.

"Still a mile and a half to go and the whole damn university to go through to get home!" he thought. As he crossed State Street he heard tires stopping behind him. He turned and it was a police car which pulled up next to him.

"Where you going Marine? Get in." The officer ordered.

"Did I do something wrong? I'm headed home over by West High."

"You could cause a riot around here dressed in that uniform." The officer said, as he took off from the curb. "What's the address I'll give ya a ride. Son, you got every right to come home and in uniform but these rich-prick students hate the military and everything about it. They would probably gang up on you and try to mess you up."

"Yeah, I'm kinda getting' that impression. I just had a little discussion with six or eight of 'em." Mick responded.

It was just six in the evening when the policeman let Mick off at his folk's front door. He thanked the officer and proceeded up the steps to the front door of the three story brick house. He stopped at the door put down his AWOL bag. He took a deep breath and rang the bell.

In a few seconds his dad came to the door looking out to see who was there.

"Sergeant Holtzman reporting as ordered, Sir!" He spoke up with smile.

"How did you get here? Margaret! Mick's here!" Mr. Holtzman said as he opened the door and clasped his son's hand.

Mrs. Holtzman came from the kitchen wearing an apron and hugged him.

"How did you get here?"

"Oh, I found out this morning I could get liberty and just decided to hitch home." Mick fibbed.

"You should have called me Mick." Mr. Holtzman admonished. "Things aren't the same around here as they were when you left. You didn't have any trouble did you?"

"No Dad. Lots of nice veterans gave me rides, but I did notice what a dirty and disorderly looking lot you have on campus these days. Did I get here in time for dinner?"

"Yes, come on in son. Your mother is just serving up." They proceeded into the kitchen where his mother quickly put on another plate and silverware.

"If I'd known you were coming, I'd have had dinner in the dining room on the good china." Mrs. Holtzman exclaimed.

"Oh Mom, this is great. I don't need the good china and this will be the best meal I've had in a year."

Mick took off his jacket and hung it over a spare chair where it wouldn't get messed up. The three sat down, said grace, and began their meal.

"Where's David?" Mick asked. David was his older brother who was attending the university.

"Oh, he's living in a dorm on campus this semester." Mrs. Holtzman responded.

"I see you've been promoted and decorated since we last saw you." The senior Holtzman said, glancing at his sons uniform jacket.

"Yeah, they had a little ceremony last week."

"What are your orders? Do you know?"

"Well, if my service record book ever gets here, I'll find out.

After dinner Mick made a quick call to his high school friend Jamie and arranged to meet him at an old hangout later. He then sat around, watched TV and chatted with his folks for an hour.

"You going out tonight son?"

"Yeah Dad."

"Take the car." His dad ordered.

"I'll take the old car. I'm just going to meet Jamie and chew the fat."

"Be careful. The keys are in the dining room."

Mick headed upstairs to change. He walked into the room that had been his when in high school and nothing was changed. The room was freshly dusted but all his mementos were in the same place. He opened the closet and all his clothes were neatly hung as he had left them. He stared for a while. What would it have been like for his mom and dad if he hadn't made it home? What was it like for Ski's mom and dad when they had to go into his room and pack away and clean up his things? He shook himself and selected some clothes. He had to try on several pairs of levis to find ones which would fit, as he'd grown taller. He settled for a pair of black levis, a madras plaid shirt with a button down collar, his penny loafers and a pair of black socks.

He went back downstairs and took the keys to the 1958 Pontiac Chieftain from the dining room. He said goodbye to his folks and limped to the car.

He drove the four blocks to the "Grid". It had been a pool hall when he was in high school but had since got its beer license. In Wisconsin you could legally drink beer at eighteen but had to be twenty-one to buy anything stronger. Holtzman went inside to find his buddy Jamie, his girlfriend Sarah and her friend Marsha.

The four were all old friends and the conversation came

easily, helped along by numerous pitchers of beer. They talked of their high school days, laughing at their stupidity and foolishness. They discussed other friends, where they were, what they were doing. Jamie and Mick told some funny stories about their experiences in Nam.

As the conversations continued, Mick had been watching the comings and goings at the bar. Most of the young folks coming in were cleaner cut than those he had encountered earlier that day. He commented on that, then told the story of the spitting hippies.

"Oh! What a bunch of creeps!" Sarah exclaimed with real anger.

"Every place is different." Marsha said in a serious vein, "You just have to know which places the radicals hang out, but uniforms aren't popular anywhere."

"I don't quite understand that. We're doin' their fightin' for them while their butts are back here safe and sound. Why should they hate us? We're the ones bein' killed and crippled while they drink beer and smoke dope." Mick said, while lighting a Lucky Strike.

The four young people continued their conversations till about midnight. The party broke up, Jamie leaving with Sarah and Marsha and Mick leaving alone.

Holtzman wasn't quite ready to head home so he drove down to another little bar named Jingle's where he and Lori had gone when they were dating. He ordered a Schlitz and sat back in the darkness with his thoughts. Remembering the excitement of coming in here with a date. Both had been underage and had fake ID's. His thoughts wandered and settled on Ski. Had he gone places like this with his girl? The one that sent him the DJ? Holtzman knew he had. Ski had confided in the Squad Leader early on about his fiancée and his feelings for her. As time passed during the tour, he spoke of her less. Suddenly the cold beer tasted bitter and the cigarette foul. He stubbed the smoke out, left the beer on the table and walked quietly out of the bar.

The next morning Mick woke up at 07:00. That was the latest he'd slept since the Jim Beam party on the Orthopedic

Ward. He could hear his mother singing in the kitchen downstairs. He dressed quickly and joined his parents for breakfast.

"Can I make you some bacon and eggs Mick?" His mother asked.

"Sure Mom."

"So what's on your agenda today son?" Mr. Holtzman asked.

"Oh, I don't know, I guess I'll just cruise around a little…look things over."

It was Saturday so school wasn't in session. His dad offered him the use of the car and his mother told him that his brother David would be over for dinner at six and for him to try to be home by then.

The Marine went back to his room and shuffled through his civilian clothes. He found a pair of white levis that weren't too short and a tan tatersal check shirt with a button down collar. He made a mental note to shop for some new trousers and a couple of shirts. He searched through his drawers and his desk. In the desk he found copies of Leatherneck, the official Marine Corps Magazine neatly stacked. He had the address changed to home when he went overseas. In another drawer he found every letter he'd written home tied in bundles with a yellow ribbon. The discovery caused him to take pause and a tear trickled down his cheek as he realized how much his parents had endured while he was in harm's way.

By the time he was underway on his explorations it was 11:30. At first he drove around aimlessly, passing by places he'd played as a child. Places he'd had fist fights with the guys that later became his buddies. The memories were all running together.

He drove down toward campus and found a parking spot. It was lunch time and his favorite lunch place was the Brat House on lower State Street. With his cane in hand he limped into the tavern, ordered a draft beer and a bratwurst basket. He watched the patrons come and go as he enjoyed the German sausage, french fries and beer. He saw several young people take note of him due to his short hair, and his civilian clothing. The clothing, though only a year or two old, were no longer the fashion. *"Guess it'll be kinda hard to camouflage myself around here."* he thought.

Lunch finished, the Sergeant ordered another beer and lit up a Lucky. He thought about what he was going to do. Inside his shirt was the Dear John letter that Ski had received. The address on it was 131 Langdon Street, about two blocks away.

Holtzman sipped his beer and finished the smoke, then he got up and limped out into the sunlight. He crossed the street, turned left at the corner and walked the block to Langdon Street. He turned right and in two minutes was in front of the sorority house.

He stopped there for a minute. A girl with brown hair down to her waist walked out wearing cutoffs and a painted tee shirt.

"Maybe she's not here." He thought. Then he shrugged his shoulders and walked up and through the door.

Inside, there was a large hallway with a couch and some comfortable chairs for visitors. A desk was at the far end of the room and behind that a wide staircase leading to the second floor where the Mick assumed the girls' rooms were. Behind the desk, reading a paperback, was a chubby girl with long black frizzy hair. She was looking at Holtzman in an unpleasant, curious fashion.

"Is there something I can do for you?" she asked with authority.

The former infantryman approached and tried a pleasant smile without any luck.

"Yes. Thank you, I'm looking for Roseanne Antoni."

"What is your business with Roseanne?"

"I am returning something of hers."

The unpleasant clerk picked up a telephone, pushed a button at the base and then dialed two numbers,

"Roseanne, you have a male visitor. No, I don't know who it is." The frizzy haired girl said shortly into the phone. She put the phone down and said, "She'll be down in a minute." Then she went back to reading her paperback.

Sergeant Holtzman turned around, reached inside his shirt and retrieved the letter. He stood in the middle of the hallway at the position of "at ease" but was not at ease at all...not even sure what he was doing here. He just knew this was unfinished business. He felt a bead of perspiration begin to descend his forehead. His armpits were damp.

"Scared! Are you scared Sergeant?" he thought to himself.

About three minutes later a girl appeared and began walking down the stairs. He recognized her from pictures that Sokouski had shown him months before. She looked different. The blonde hair that she wore Jackie Kennedy style in the pictures, was now straight and halfway down her back. She looked slimmer, almost gaunt. The eyes hollowed, the words "strung out" clicked and stuck in the Marine's mind. As she reached the bottom of the stairs her eyes met his. She crossed the hallway slowly, examining the tall, short-haired man before her...curiosity showing.

"You asked for me?" Roseanne said looking up into the blue eyes.

"You are Roseanne Antoni?" Holtzman asked, knowing the answer.

"Yes."

"I have something for you." He produced the letter from behind his back and thrust it into her hand. Instinctively she took it. She stared at it for a second. Suddenly recognition flooded her eyes, then fear. Her eyes were glued to the envelope. They took in the brown blood stains on it. Her hands shook. She could not take her eyes off the letter.

"I took it from Joe's body after he was killed. He must have gotten it the day before." Mick's voice was cold and flat.

Her eyes were still on the envelope. With her voice shaking she asked, "Did you read it?"

"Yes." His voice cut like ice.

She raised her eyes, her foggy looking green eyes, into the steel blue of the Marine's, "I didn't want to hurt him."

She said pleadingly.

Holtzman said nothing. The cold blue eyes just stared at her. He wanted to scream. His emotions were turbulent, but he just stood there staring at the girl. She could not stand it and turned and ran up the stairs, disappearing at the top. He stood there a full minute then turned and walked out.

When he reached the street he took a deep breath and walked north a block to Lake Mendota. Here, he put his cane down and sat on the rocks at the edge of the large lake. Sergeant Mick Holtzman sat there staring out into the water for the next thirty minutes, as he had often stared into the South China Sea from the flight deck of his Air Amphibious Assault Ship. Finally he stood up and walked back to the parked car. He got in and drove away.

The rest of the day was spent driving around outside of town, mostly places where he had hunted, fished or played as a boy. He stopped in a woodlot where he had often hunted squirrels. He climbed to the top of the ridge to examine the fields that often held pheasant and quail. As he reached the ridge he saw out in the field, a pair of boys and a dog hunting. He sat down on a log remembering the innocence of those days, hoping that these boys could retain that innocence as long as possible. The Sergeant realized, with a sense of loss and regret, that he could never again feel that innocence of youth. It had vanished during his first firefight.

He drove up the driveway and parked the car at the side of his parents house. It was five thirty. He went up the steps and into the house. His father was sitting in the living room reading the paper. He put it down and looked at his son.

"Did you have a good day?"

"Yeah." The words sounded dead in the air.

The senior Holtzman dropped the paper, realizing something was wrong. He was about to inquire when the front door opened and in walked his older son.

Mick turned around and examined his older brother. He was an inch shorter than him, but stockier, outweighing the Marine by a good twenty pounds. His hair was dark brown, wavey and shoulder length. He was unshaven which gave his face the appearance of being dirty. He was wearing blue jeans and a tee shirt.

"Hi David." The younger Holtzman said as he stuck out his hand in greeting.

"Hi Mick...good to see you home, safe and...sort of sound."

The two exchanged pleasantries for a few minutes then their mother called from the kitchen that dinner would be ready in three minutes and to get cleaned up. Dinner would be served in the dining room. It was pot roast with potatoes, cooked carrots and onions. Mick's mouth was watering.

During dinner, the conversation remained polite for a while, then Mick commented, "Seems like things are very different here on campus in a year and a half."

"They are." replied David. "The war has changed everything."

"The war has been going on for six or seven years." The Marine commented with a questioning look.

"Yes, but now it's become obvious that we are losing it, that the government is just throwing away the lives of soldiers like you, to protect the government of the south." replied the older brother.

"I know that the government of the Republic of Vietnam doesn't give the people of the south the same freedoms that we enjoy here, however, they certainly allow them more than the Communists do to the north. I have seen the methods the Communists use to extract a rice tax from the peasants of the south. They'll torture an old man or a child until the community gives up half of the rice they need to survive. Those rice farmers don't give a damn about Communism or Capitalism. All they want to do is eat. As for losin' the war, where the heck are you gettin' that? When I landed in Danang, the city was a fortress. We had to run off the plane into slit trenches as the airfield was being rocketed. Before I left you could drive in any direction around Danang for twenty miles and find U.S. civilian aide workers on public improvement projects without armed escort. I find it so interesting that people who have never been to Vietnam or heard a round fired in anger are experts. None the less, those of us who just returned from there six weeks ago are dumb SOBs." He said, voice rising.

"That's enough!" The senior Holtzman thundered. He had been afraid the meeting would get out of control.

"How is your Italian class going David?" Mrs. Holtzman said trying to bring peace and change the subject.

Dinner was finished with a stilted conversation carefully avoiding any discussion of current events. After dinner Mrs. Holtzman served coffee. David took his into the living room and turned on the TV. Mr. Holtzman said, "I think I'll have a cigar out on the porch. Do you want to have a smoke, Mick?"

"Sure." The Marine realized there was more to the invitation than a smoke. He and his dad had never seen eye to eye and talk came with difficulty between the two.

The retired Naval Officer and Marine Sergeant took their coffee, sat on the steps and lit their respective smokes.

"Give your brother a little slack Mick. He's backed way off on his attitude since the first time you got hurt. He's impressionable and these opinions are popular with his friends."

"Yeah, well they aren't very popular with my friends."

"Mick, something happened to you today. I could tell when you got home." The senior Holtzman said. "Would you tell me about it?"

The younger man took a deep drag on the cigarette then told his father the story of Joe Sokouski, his death, the letters, and his visit to the sorority today.

"I don't know if what I did was right Dad, I just had to do somethin'!"

His father was quiet a long time.

"I can't imagine what a letter like that would do to a young soldier. I know it would have devastated me. I don't even remember hearing of anyone getting such a letter in World War II, although I'm sure it happened. She must have been totally self-absorbed not to realize the consequences of such action."

The two men sat quietly together drinking their coffee and finishing their smokes. A feeling of togetherness rather than conflict pervaded into their relationship for the first time in years.

"Oh Mick, there's a letter for you." The elder Holtzman said. "With all the excitement I'd forgotten. It's from Lori."

Mr. Holtzman smiled as his son immediately stubbed out the cigarette and went inside to find his mail.

CHAPTER FORTY-THREE
Guard Duty

Mick read the letter and then started reading it again. Lori hadn't gotten his letter from Japan. She knew he was wounded but had no details. This letter had probably crossed the one he sent from Great Lakes. He read it again. She really sounded worried.

The next afternoon Mr. Holtzman drove Mick back to the Naval base and hospital. The young Marine limped into his quarters at five in the afternoon and was surprised to find Morrillo there.

"Hey! What's the deal Hector I thought you'd stay with your girl till tomorrow mornin'?"

"Oh, we got along alright. I just wanted some time to myself. So what happened on your trip?"

Mick gave his friend an abbreviated picture of the spitting hippies and returning the Dear John to Ski's former fiancé.

"Get some Mick!" Morrillo said. "You did some good Bro."

The two Sergeants turned in early so they'd be sharp at formation in the morning.

After formation the next morning Sergeant Carnady informed the friends that they were to report to the Marine Operations Office. When they arrived they were ushered into Carnady's office where they were told that the Lieutenant had decided that the Marines that were ambulatory and housed in the Casual Company dorms needed to have something to do. Therefore, Morrillo and Holtzman were to set up a Marine Guard, utilizing those men. Carnady told the pair of Sergeants that a small room down the hall would be their guard office. They headed off to inspect it.

The room was about ten by ten, with a large, battered metal desk in one corner and a straight backed office chair nearby. A layer of dust covered everything.

"It ain't much but it's all ours." Morrillo said shaking his head.

"I'll go draw some cleanin' gear and get to work field-dayin' the place. Why don't you go see what you can scrounge. As I remember, you got connections." Mick said.

"If I see any of them ambulatory Marines, I'll send 'em down to help."

Holtzman headed for supply to draw cleaning gear and whatever else he could manage. When he introduced himself and told his mission, the enlisted supply clerk looked at him questioningly and called Sergeant Carnady, who couldn't be reached for half an hour. Finally his request was cleared. The supply clerk gave him the cleaning supplies and then said, "We got a couple old chairs back there collecting dust. You want 'em?"

Holtzman checked the chairs out and said he'd be back for them.

When Mick arrived back at the Guard Office it was empty. However, in a vacant corner was a large stainless steel coffee machine and in front of the desk was a metal pivoting office chair. *"Hector at his best!"* he thought.

As Mick began swabbing the deck, two ambulatory Marines arrived, Wilson and Meyers. These two were buddies from the same small town in the hills of Tennessee. Wilson had lost his arm just above the wrist and the same day Meyers had lost some toes to a grenade.

"Hey Mick, what's the deal? Morrillo sent us down here." Wilson queried.

"Were back in the Corps fellows. Carnady says we have to mount a Marine Guard. This is HQ." Holtzman continued to mop despite the presence of the two enlisted men.

"Where'd the coffee mess come from?" Meyers asked.

"It appeared while I was getting cleaning supplies. I think the Sarge is hard at it."

Meyers grinned, "We'll need a table to put it on, Coffee, cups, sugar, cream, maybe some towels and napkins." The smile broadened, "I'll be right back."

As Meyers disappeared, Wilson, looking around, found

a rag and supplies. He began dusting everything in sight. Fifteen minutes later Meyers returned carrying a folding metal table under his arm. He set the legs down and moved it into the corner and placed the coffee machine on top of the table. Ten minutes later, four more enlisted Marines showed up grinning ear to ear. From their pajamas or uniforms, they produced six coffee mugs with Navy insignia on them and as many spoons.

"Hey, you four follow me. There are some chairs down at supply they said we could have." Holtzman ordered.

When they arrived at supply Mick told the clerk he was back for the chairs and the clerk motioned them through. The Sergeant and four enlisted went into the rear and picked up the four chairs. He noted another folding table gathering dust against the wall and nodded at one of the PFCs who grabbed it with a smirk. They headed out with Holtzman blocking the view while thanking the Seaman clerk. His men headed down the hall with their booty. When he got back to the office, the chairs were cleaned up, the second table set up next to the first and sitting on top of the old desk was a portable typewriter.

"Where the hell did that come from?" The Sergeant gasped.

One of the PFCs giggled, "I thought you might need it for Guard Rosters and such, so I liberated it on the way down the hall."

The smell of fresh brew was coming from the machine and the six enlisted men were sitting on the chairs in a semi circle facing the desk. Meyer's pointed at the desk and said, "Sit down Sarge, you're in charge here."

Mick Holtzman walked over, half closed the door, then sat down in the swivel chair smiling.

"If this stuff stays here long, people will get used to it and think it belongs to us, so just act like it's been ours forever. I know you guys aren't probably excited about playing toy soldier out there, but try to have fun with it. And now we got a home!"

"Yeah, damn right and it's gonna get nicer and nicer."

replied Wilson.

"I don't mind openin' the doors for the officers and civilians." One of the enlisted men commented. "Besides we'll get to check out the skirts!"

"You'll all need to go and draw a uniform issue if you don't have one. I'll get it OK'd at supply. We'll meet here tomorrow after formation. We'll brew some coffee and continue implementing these orders." Holtzman schemed.

The men left, chattering away with plans to liberate this or that for the guard office. They were just like little boys, planning to fix up their clubhouse.

There was a telephone on the floor next to the desk. Mick picked it up and lifted the receiver. *"Hot damn there's a dial tone!"*

Hector Morrillo walked into the office five minutes later to find his buddy swiveled back in the liberated office chair with his feet up on the desk, talking with supply on the telephone.

Sergeant Morrillo directed the two enlisted Marines to put down the armloads of gear they were carrying and told them they were dismissed. The two smiled, looked the room over with approval and walked out. As Mick was finishing his conversation with the supply clerk, Hector placed clean, white folded towels under the coffee machine. He folded another and put the cups on it. Then he produced a stainless steel sugar tub and cream vase. Seconds later he revealed a framed photo of the Commandant of the Marine Corps. He found a nail on the wall and hung it. With him were two other framed pictures by combat artists, but they'd have to wait as there were no more nails.

"Looks like the boys got busy!" Morrillo said grinning as Mick hung up the phone.

"Yeah, we may have to slow 'em down or they'll have everything that isn't nailed down in here." Mick chuckled.

The two sat together as in the old days, sharing a cup of Joe, making plans, and smoking.

The next morning after formation the Sergeants headed for the Guard Office. Upon entry the place was abuzz with noise and activity. There were about fifteen ambulatory Marines in the room, all talking, most smoking and everyone with a cup of fresh, hot coffee in their hand. More goodies had appeared. There was a tray of sweet rolls, very similar to those served at breakfast, and a fruit basket with apples, oranges, bananas, and grapes.

A private jumped out of the swivel chair and motioned for Mick to sit.

"No, Sergeant Morrillo is the senior NCO here! Carry on Sarge."

Morrillo took center stage. "They told us we had to set up this little guard unit here. Well, we will, but by damn were a gonna have fun doin' it." The men let out a muffled cheer.

"We'll need two men on the front doors, two more at the elevator banks inside and one on the side door. They need to be manned eight to five. That's 08:00 to 17:00 hours. We'll split into shifts. I need every man to sign in each morning and pick up his duty assignment. We will work with you as to your doctor's appointments, disabilities, leave, liberty, girlfriends…whatever. Every man must get his uniform issue drawn and get squared away. If we got to play soldier, we will look like Marines." Morrillo declared.

Holtzman then took over, "Report back here tomorrow morning after formation in the Uniform of the Day. We'll have details and duties arraigned. You men feel free to stop by any time because this is your place as well as ours." Mick then pulled himself to the position of attention. "Guard detail… Tenhut!... Dismissed!"

The men happily came to attention then fell at ease and began conversing in groups of twos and threes. Most left to get their uniforms. Others stayed to chat.

The next morning the twenty or so ambulatory Marines showed up in their greens, shoes and brass gleaming from polishing. After everyone enjoyed a cup of coffee from their new and ever enlarging cache of supplies, Holtzman called the detail to attention. Morrillo then took over and read off the guard shift and assignments. He made sure there were no conflicts and then called the room to attention. He dismissed all but the first watch. No one left the room. In the hall Morrillo lined up the five man detail with the help of Mick and the Corporal of the Guard. He then marched the detail of six to the front of the Hospital only fifty yards away. In the Guard Office the Marines watched through the windows. At the front door Hector called a halt, then gave a command. The first two men in the column turned to the outside, took two steps then halted. Then, on command, they turned facing out from their respective doors. The men in the office cheered softly. The two door guards then, in unison, opened the doors and the detail marched though, stopping in front of the elevators. Here the process was repeated, peeling off two more men to operate the elevators for the visitors. The Sergeant then took the remaining enlisted man along with the Corporal of the Guard and marched them to the side door where the enlisted man stayed while Morrillo and the Corporal marched back. Upon entering the office there was another small cheer and then happy chatter from the waiting Marines.

Holtzman hardly ever used the cane anymore. His leg became stronger each day. The guard duties kept the men busy during the week and gave them a central focus.

Several times Mick went to the Marine Operations Office to see if his Service Record Book with his orders had caught up with him. Just as before, after lots of delay, the answer was no. In October he checked again. Sergeant Carnady came out and informed him that there was still no sign of his SRB but that he was being granted a week's leave before he was to report to his new duty station.

"What new duty station?"

"I have orders for you to report to the Second Infantry Training Regiment, Reconnaissance School, Camp Pendleton, California. Perhaps you'll find your SRB there."

Exasperated, Holtzman took his copy of the orders along with the leave papers and headed back to the guard office. *"Guess it's a cinch I won't get to the Naval Academy."* Mick thought in frustration.

"What's up big guy?" Hector queried as his friend walked in, looking disappointed. "Hey, it's the Corps man! Somehow they screw up everything." Morrillo went on. "What you gonna do?"

"Well, I guess if things aren't straightened out when I come off leave, I'll report to Pendleton and start an inquiry as to the other orders from there."

At that moment the Corporal of the Guard returned with the last watch. After he dismissed them the five immediately began grousing.

"Sarge, there's a god-damned naval officer that's screwin' with us. Every day he jumps us about this or that or the other. Why today he jumped one of the guys at the elevators for not salutin'."

"I told him that by regulation we could not salute indoors unless under arms Sarge." Meyers explained.

"What did he say?" Holtzman asked.

"I don't think he knew what under arms meant! He just read me out and left."

"I got an idea!" Wilson spoke up excitedly. "Put me on the front door when he comes through tomorrow!"

"But you can't salute! You're right hand is gone."

"Exactly! I'll salute the arrogant SOB anyway." Wilson said.

Mick looked at Hector. There was a small grin starting at the corner of the stocky Sergeant's face.

"Why not? Maybe it'll brighten up that non-combat SOB!" Morrillo said.

A general buzz began and ideas were flung against the wall to see if they'd stick. Wilson was grinning ear to ear. He had unpinned his jacket sleeve and when it hung down the lack of his hand was not immediately apparent. Wilson started practicing snappy salutes with the amputated forearm. He had lost the arm about midway between wrist and elbow so when he saluted the maneuver looked OK as the stiff jacket fabric held the position correctly for a tenth of a second, then the fabric folded and collapsed down where his arm ended.

"I'm a gonna practice saluting all night!" Wilson said as he left.

The next morning every Marine in Casual Company was present and others from the wards were rolling in. The word was out.

The watch was set with Wilson on the door that he could open with his good left hand, leaving the amputated right hand available for the salute. The men crowded the guard office watching through the windows. Some were loitering on the hospital grounds to be closer to the action.

"That's him! The squid officer coming out of the parking lot with the lady!" One of the enlisted men shouted. The officer was headed straight for Wilson.

Another officer was ten paces in front of the couple. Wilson came to attention opened the door and stood at attention as the first officer passed by without a glance. The officer who had caused the problems approached and Wilson repeated the performance. The officer stopped. He eyed Wilson who was standing at the perfect position of attention.

"Don't you know enough to salute a superior officer soldier?" the man asked.

"Sir, Yes Sir!" Wilson answered and snapped his salute. The empty sleeve came up to the correct position and then the fabric folded and hung from where his arm was amputated, Wilson held the salute.

"Oh my God!" The lady with the officer said. She appeared ready to faint.

The Navy Officer stood there dumb struck, staring at the young Marine saluting him. The right arm made it even with his ear. From there the empty sleeve hung pointing to the ground.

Finally the naval officer got hold of himself and took the woman by the arm. He moved on, looking back several times. Wilson snapped the arm back down after the man passed and closed the door. He never cracked a smile or gave any indication that this was a set up.

The Guard Office was filled with giggles, laughter, and guffaws. Those men who had loitered outside had to turn away or fall down with mirth.

"OK, OK, we got some today. Now you guys get out of here and keep it quiet. There's liable to be repercussions." Morrillo announced.

 The crowd began moving out, laughing and chattering as they left.

Mick looked over at Hector. They saluted each other with their coffee mugs. Five minutes later the phone rang.

"Marine Guard, Sergeant Morrillo, Sergeant of the Guard speaking. How may I be of service. "Yes Sergeant Carnady, what can I do for you."

Hector was quiet for a moment, "I have the watch list right here. We have Meyers and Wilson on the front door." another silence. "Yes, Wilson is an amputee, but every man on the guard has something wrong with him. It was Wilson's turn at the door. I got other men with prosthetic arms, legs, etc. If you want healthy, whole guards, get them elsewhere." With that Morrillo hung up the receiver.

"I don't like that guy!" Morrillo said smiling with satisfaction.

CHAPTER FORTY-FOUR
Number One is the Loneliest Number

October days were cool and crisp in the morning, warming pleasantly by midday and cooling off again in the evening. Mick Holtzman had seven days of leave and he was bored. His friend Jamie was in college, pulling straight A's. They occasionally met for a beer, but he couldn't monopolize his time. He walked the fields he had hunted as a youth, often flushing pheasant, quail, or grouse. Mick thought about getting a hunting license and shooting some birds but was satisfied just to enjoy the scenery.

He sat on a hilltop watching the squirrels play in the hardwoods, his mind elsewhere, back in Nam with the squad. He wondered how O'Meara, Lincoln and the others were doing, but he was still afraid to write and receive bad news. As evening approached he drove home. After dinner his father asked if he'd like to share another smoke on the front porch.

They took their coffee and lit their smokes.

"You seem restless son."

"Yes sir. I guess it's the screw-up with the orders. The lack of action or somethin'."

"I can start an inquiry on your orders." The elder Holtzman suggested.

"No Dad. This is my career, let me handle it."

"Something else on your mind?"

Mick pulled out the other letter to Ski.

"He didn't get two Dear Johns did he?"

"No, this one is sweet, go ahead read it."

Mr. Holtzman read it quickly then said in a choked voice. "Why would he put himself in danger knowing someone cared so much for him."

"He never read it Dad. It was unopened when I found it. Morrillo, you and I are the only ones that have read it."

"Jesus. What are you thinking?"

I thought I'd return it. She doesn't need to know he didn't read it. It's so sweet, if I could make her think Ski appreciated it...I don't know."

The senior Holtzman puffed the White Owl cigar, "Take the car. It's a long drive."

The next day Mick was up early. He packed a few civvies in his AWOL bag and after breakfast he carefully put on his uniform, all but the jacket which he kept on a hanger and hung in the Chieftain. He said his goodbyes to his parents and drove out to I 90-94 heading north. He took the US 51 exit which would take him north through Wisconsin and deposit him to his destination in upper Michigan. He enjoyed the scenery. He had hunted deer, ducks and geese over much of this ground as a lad and these were good memories.

Despite trying to ignore the thought, the object of his mission kept coming back to him. *"Just what am I tryin' to prove or accomplish?"* He really wasn't sure, it just seemed like more unfinished business.

As he drove north, the surrounding forest changed. There were fewer hardwoods and more pines. It was noon when he passed through Hurley, on the border, and about one when he arrived in Bessemer. Mick found an A&W Root Beer Stand that had a pay phone outside. He looked in the phonebook and found the only Fergusen on Pintail Lane. He took a deep breath and dialed the number. *"She's probably not at home...perhaps away at college."* he thought, *"I've probably driven all this way for nothin."*

"Hello?" a melodic voice said.

"Hello, is Audrey Fergusen there?"

"This is she."

A moment of silence went by.

"My name is Mick Holtzman, I was Joe Sokouski's Squad Leader and I wondered if I could have a moment of your time?"

Another moment of silence passed.

"Yes, yes, I remember...He mentioned you in a letter. I'd like to see you...talk to you." Audrey said in a choked voice.

Quickly she gave him directions to the house and the

Sergeant told her he'd be there in five minutes. Mick took out his uniform jacket, put it on and slipped Audrey's letter inside. He drove the mile or so to a turn-off and found Pintail Lane. He drove slowly to the address. He parked the old Pontiac across the road and walked to the gate. As he went through the gate and it swung shut behind him, a huge brown, curly coated dog jumped off the porch and bounded towards him with his tail wagging in an excited circle. When the dog was six feet away it suddenly came to a halt, staring curiously and a little sadly at Mick.

"Hi Curley! Guess you thought I was someone else." Mick said offering his hand to the big dog. The dog sniffed his hand good naturedly and gave a little tail wag.

Mick heard a screen door slam and looked up to see a vision. On the porch stood a girl of medium height, with wavy auburn hair to her waist. She wore a man's white shirt with the tails tied at her midriff and blue, bell-bottom jeans. The boyish clothes did nothing to hide her womanly attributes. She possessed a figure and curves that the young Marine had never imagined. She jumped off the porch and stopped next to the big dog.

"I guess both Curley and I hoped you were Joey, when we saw the uniform." Audrey said sadly.

"I'm sorry, I didn't want to cause you more pain." The Sergeant said uncomfortably.

"It's not your fault…we just miss him. Shall we walk?" She started out the gate with Mick keeping stride.

They tried small talk, but nothing seemed to work. Finally the Marine said, "I wanted to give this back to you," and he handed her the letter.

She looked at it and clutched to her breast. Then the torrent was unleashed. She pushed her head into Mick's chest sobbing uncontrollably. He put his arms around her in a comforting way as she continued to sob and pull herself closer. Holtzman was uncomfortable. As she wept he was aware of her body pressed against him. His body responded. He tried to stiffen himself and step back but she held tighter. Finally she regained control, but didn't release the now thoroughly embarrassed Marine.

"I thought he'd never received it." She said, through tear stained eyes.

Mick's impulse was to bend down and kiss away her tears. Instead he reached down and gently brushed them away saying, "I'm sure it gave him great happiness to know that someone cared for him so deeply."

"I wasn't his girl you know…he was engaged."

"Yes I know."

"I did love him, ever since I was a little girl, It's silly I guess." Audrey said the tears starting again.

"I read the letter…I hope you'll forgive me. That was why I wanted to return it to you. Any Marine would have loved to receive such a letter. He was a good Marine and a good friend."

Now the tears were coming out of Mick's eyes. The girl threw her head into his chest again and both wept. Inevitably the Sergeants body once again responded to the feelings of a warm damp woman pressed against him. This time he didn't try to pull away. He just stood there till his tears stopped. As if on cue they both moved apart and began walking down the lane.

"I'm glad you came." Audrey said.

Mick tried to keep the conversation going. He told Audrey some of his and Ski's adventures, trying to keep things light. The lane ended in a cul-de-sac and they continued around it, heading back toward the house.

"He thought a great deal of you." Audrey confided while staring up into the Sergeant's blue eyes. "I think now I know why."

They had reached her gate and stopped.

"Thank you for coming all this way." Audrey said, staring up at him. Then she stood on her tip toes and pressed her lips against his for a second.

The Marine stood there unsure what to do.

"I know this isn't the time, but I'd really like it if you'd come back and visit again. Would you write me?" The girl asked.

"Yes, my orders are all screwed up. As soon as I get things straightened out, I'll write."

He looked at her as he prepared to leave. Their eyes met and she threw herself into his chest again.

"Thank you again for coming...please write me!"

"I will." Holtzman said in a husky voice as he turned for the car.

Mick opened the door of the Pontiac and then looked back. Audrey was standing on the porch. She raised her hand and waved and the Sergeant snapped off a salute. Then he got into the car and quickly drove off.

He drove back south with his mind in turmoil. Near the small town of Minoqua he stopped at a roadside table in the pines by a lake. Leaving the engine running and the door open, he got out and sat on the picnic table. He lit a Lucky Strike and stared into the lake's waters. His thoughts went from Lori, to Audrey, to Sally MacGregor. *"Would I ever have a girl I could call my own?"* Deep inside the Marine Sergeant, a lonely boy was trying to break through the tough facade.

As he stared over the water the radio in the Chieftain played Three Dog Night's latest hit.

One is the loneliest, number,
One is the loneliest number,
One is the loneliest number that you'll ever do
One is the loneliest, One is the loneliest,
One is the loneliest number that you'll ever do.

CHAPTER FORTY-FIVE
Lori

Sergeant Holtzman arrived back at Great Lakes a day before his leave was over. There hadn't been anything to do in Madison but drink beer and that wasn't much fun by yourself.

Mick felt lost. So many events that were out of his control, Annapolis, California, Recon School, Lori, Audrey. *"Where am I goin'?"*

Holtzman stopped by the Marine operations office and checked in. Sergeant Carnady came out of his cubicle and started across the room.

"Hey, any sign of my service record book yet?"

"Nope." Carnady responded. "But I got your travel orders and plane tickets here. You're back a day early."

"Yeah...you know how it is, I love this place, just can't stay away." Holtzman said taking the orders and tickets.

"Your flight leaves from O'Hare to San Diego in two days...you'll have to arrange transport from San Diego to Pendleton."

Mick nodded as he headed down the hall. He stopped by the guard office and found Hector there.

"Hey Bro, what're you doin' back? You're a day early?"

"Oh, just ran outta things to do. Hey, let's have dinner at the NCO Club, I'm shippin' out in two days."

"OK, dinner and a few brews. It's gonna be lonely around here without you." Morrillo said.

"You'll get by, now don't go gettin' teary eyed on me. If you get lonely there's always Susie." Holtzman said with a smirk.

"Yeah...there's always Susie!" Morrillo said with his catbird smile as Mick headed off to his room to begin packing.

Mick pulled out his sea bag and packed his uniforms, folding each neatly. During the process Mick pulled out the Leatherette folder containing his Bronze Star Citation. He started to put it in the sea bag when he remembered that the

Master Sergeant at the awards ceremony had said there was a note in it. Holtzman opened the folder and inside was the warrant for his promotion to Sergeant and an envelope with his name on it. He opened the envelope and read:

Sergeant Holtzman,

This letter is accompanying your promotion to Sergeant and the three medals you have been awarded as it is the quickest method I have to communicate to you.

When Colonel Smith heard you were wounded and the circumstances, he immediately ordered your promotion to Sergeant. The Colonel and Captain Weller wrote your Bronze Star commendation for the diversionary actions Sokouski and you performed on the Song Lai River. Ski was awarded the Silver Star. I thought you would like to know that. Captain Blackwell wrote the commendation for which you received the Navy Commendation Medal. He seems to be coming around.

The Colonel wanted me to inform you that your orders for Enlisted Candidates Program are still on, and I personally placed them in you service record book.

First Squad is doing fine under the leadership of O'Meara, although he bitches about one thing or another every day.

Colonel Smith has asked the air wing for an explanation of the actions of helicopter pilot that wouldn't land for Ski despite the flak from regiment.

It was a pleasure to serve with you and I hope we will serve together again.

Semper Fi,
First Sergeant David Shaw

Holtzman digested the news.

The two Sergeants had dinner at the club that night and Mick told Morrillo about the letter he had discovered.

"Well, First Sergeant Shaw covered a lot of ground in a short-short. He says the squads doin' OK with O'Meara runnin' it. Sokouski got a Silver Star posthumously. Captain Weller and the Colonel wrote me up for the Bronze Star. Blackwell, that no-combat SOB, wrote up the Navy Commendation and the Colonel is requestin' an explanation as to why the chopper pilot wouldn't land to medevac Ski."

"Well, things are workin' out. If Colonel Sparky Smith gets that helo pilot on the carpet in front of him, he'll wish he'd never been born. So are you satisfied?" Morrillo asked.

The two sergeants sat in the comfortable gloom of the NCO Club sipping their beers, deep in their own thoughts, as the jukebox crooned the hit song by the Box Tops.

> *Gimme a ticket for an aeroplane,*
> *Ain't got time to take a fast train.*
> *Lonely days are gone, I'm a-goin' home,*
> *My baby, she wrote me a letter.*

Thursday came and Mick was packed. He stopped by the guard office and said his goodbyes to the men after formation. He had done the same to his friends on the wards the day before.

"Well Sergeant, it's been a pleasure to work with you again." Holtzman said with that tight grin starting at the corner of his mouth. "Hell, I may be right behind you Bro! It's getting' a little cool for a Texican way up here." Morrillo said, as he shook Mick's hand. The younger Sergeant headed out the door and to the waiting bus.

At O'Hare he had a short wait for his flight. He noted several longhairs eyeing him and his uniform but he had no trouble.

After the flight took off the stewardess came down the aisle asking what the passengers wanted to drink.

"What can I get for you Marine?" She was an attractive woman around thirty.

"Scotch and water." Mick replied, wondering if she'd ask for his ID.

The stewardess eyed the young Sergeant, the four rows of ribbons and the gold jump wings and said.

"Do you want ice with that Sergeant?"

The flight to San Diego was pleasant. Holtzman enjoyed several more drinks and the stewardess kept him supplied with magazines and newspapers.

As Mick exited the plane the stewardess spoke to him. "Thank you Marine."

The Sergeant looked at her questioningly.

"Thank you for serving our country," she replied. "My little brother was a Marine...he was killed at the Battle of Hue City."

"I'm sorry Ma'am." The Marine said, before heading down the steps to the tarmac below.

The Sergeant walked out of the terminal and found a bus labeled Camp Pendleton and climbed aboard. An hour later he was stepping off the bus at Camp Horno on the Marine Base at Pendleton. He walked across the parking lot past a number of office buildings to Recon School where he headed to the office. He went in and stood at the counter for a few minutes until a Gunnery Sergeant noticed him. He saw the Gunny eyeballing his ribbons and jump wings as he approached.

"Can I help you Sergeant?" The Gunny asked.

"Yes Sir. Sergeant Holtzman checking in." He said handing the senior NCO his orders.

The Gunny perused the orders then said. "You know I have your SRB here." He walked back to his desk and retrieved the thick file of records.

"I've been looking for that." Mick said, then quickly explained his conflict in orders.

The Gunnery Sergeant leafed through the record book, reading the documents quickly.

"OK. Here's the deal Holtzman. There won't be an opening for you at the Naval Academy Preparatory School until next semester, so the Corps sent you to us as an instructor till then."

"Well, that's good news, I was afraid that I was gonna miss that trip." The young Sergeant said.

The Gunny was quickly reading through the records as the two talked.

"No, you're not missing that trip...looks like there are a lot of people interested in making you an officer. I'm Gunny

Jacobs by the way."

"It's a pleasure to meet you Gunny."

"I see you know Gunny Shaw."

"Yes Sir, but it's now First Sergeant Shaw." Holtzman responded.

"Yeah, Shaw and me go back to Korea." The senior Sergeant said with a faraway look. "We will be glad to have you here as an instructor Holtzman. I don't have anything for you to do until Monday. So you can stow your gear in the NCO barracks and then you might as well take liberty till 06:00 Monday. Think you can find something to do till then?"

"I imagine I'll think of somethin' Gunny." Mick said with his characteristic tight smile.

Jacobs filled out a liberty chit for Thursday thru Sunday and handed it to Mick who then headed to the recon NCO barracks. He found a bunk, hung his uniforms in the wall locker and put the rest of his gear into a foot locker. He packed his AWOL bag with some civilian clothes, shaving gear, and a few other necessities and headed back toward the gate.

As he crossed the parking lot a Corporal heading in the same direction called out to him.

"Hey Sarge! Where ya headed?"

"L.A." Holtzman responded, noting the jump wings on the Corporals chest.

"That's where I'm headed too, wanna share a cab? We'll get there twice as fast as a bus without all the hassles."

"Sure thing." Mick responded and changed direction to the line of ancient Cadillac limos in the parking lot. The two Marines went to the cab at the front of the line and told the driver where they were going. They dickered over the price a few seconds then jumped in.

The cab took off and the driver asked again where in Los Angeles the two were headed. The Corporal rattled off an address in Alhambra and Holtzman asked the driver if he could find 101 Citrus Street in Cyprus. The driver answered in the affirmative.

"So Corporal, I see your jump qualified. Are you with Recon School?" Mick asked.

"Yeah, I checked in earlier today and had just gone back for my liberty chit when Gunny Jacobs said you were headin' off for liberty too." the Corporal explained.

The two continued to talk as they rode towards Los Angles. Corporal Curtis had finished his tour in Vietnam and was being reassigned here. They compared notes on Vietnam, jump school, recon and just about anything that came up.

The cabby let Curtis off first. Now Mick started getting nervous. The driver made a few turns then pulled over.

"This is it Marine…101 Citrus Street."

It was five-twenty as Mick paid the cab driver. He turned and looked at the building behind him as the cab pulled away. It was a two story building that might have been a house once, but now converted to apartments. His palms were sweating as he picked up the AWOL bag and headed up the steps. As he approached the door he wanted to turn around and run.

"Scared, ain't you Sergeant?" he thought to himself. He reached his free hand into his trouser pocket and felt the four dog tags taped together as he walked up the steps into an alcove. There were four mail boxes here and a door on each side. The address he was looking for was" 2 A", the doors here were labeled "1A" and "1B". Holding the four dog tags tightly Mick climbed the stairs. Here there were two more doors. His heart was pounding as he set the bag down in front of "2A". He gripped the tags tightly before he brought his hand up to knock.

"What if she's livin' with some guy?" he thought, as his hand fell. He pulled the tags out of his pocket and read Ski's name on the top tag. He knocked on the door three times. A bead of sweat pushed its way past the brow band of his overseas cap and started its descent down the forehead.

Suddenly the door opened and there stood Lori with dark hair, framing her face and falling to her shoulders. Her hazel eyes curious, then surprised.

The Author

Vietnam 1968   **Afghanistan 2004**

James August is the authors pen name, a veteran of both the United States Marine Corps and U.S. Army Special Operations Command. James joined the Marine Corps shortly after graduating from high school in 1967. August trained and served as an Infantry and Reconnaissance Marine in Vietnam in 1968 and 1969.

After the terror attacks of 9/11 James August left his professional life as a Veterinarian and returned to the military, this time as an officer in Army Special Operations Command. James had two combat tours in Afghanistan while attached to 3rd Special Forces Group.

James August lives in the mountains of Colorado with his wife and dogs.